PENGUIN BOOKS

Remember This

Alexandra Campbell is an experienced journalist who has worked for many women's magazines and national newspapers. She is the author of several plays for Radio 4, as well as several non-fiction books on interiors. She is also the author of four previous novels, *The Office Party*, *The Ex-Girlfriend*, *The Daisy Chain* and most recently *That Dangerous Age*, all published by Penguin. She lives with her husband, David, and children, Freddie and Rosalind, in Faversham, Kent.

Remember This

ALEXANDRA CAMPBELL

PENGUIN BOOKS

PENGUIN BOOKS

Published by the Penguin Group
Penguin Books Ltd, 80 Strand, London WC2R 0RL, England
Penguin Group USA Inc., 375 Hudson Street, New York,
New York 10014, USA
Penguin Books Australia Ltd, 250 Camberwell Road, Camberwell,
Victoria 3124, Australia
Penguin Books Canada Ltd, 10 Alcorn Avenue,
Toronto, Ontario, Canada M4V 3B2
Penguin Books India (P) Ltd, 11 Community Centre,
Panchsheel Park, New Delhi – 110 017, India
Penguin Group (NZ), cnr Airborne and Rosedale Roads,
Albany, Auckland 1310, New Zealand
Penguin Books (South Africa) (Pty) Ltd, 24 Sturdee Avenue,
Rosebank 2196, 2094, South Africa

Penguin Books Ltd, Registered Offices: 80 Strand, England WC2R 0RL

First published 2005

1

Set in Monotype Garamond by
Palimpsest Book Production Limited,
Polmont, Stirlingshire
Printed in England by Clays Ltd, St Ives plc

To Freddie and Rosie,
in memory of P.C.

Prologue

The Boathouse is an old stone cottage, overlooking a secret cove, tucked into the mouth of the river as it opens to the sea. Twice a day the waves retreat, to reveal, miraculously, an acre of perfection, a generous golden expanse of sand between the water and the dark, speckled rocks. And then the sea returns, and the beach vanishes again. Behind the cottage there is a fringe of fir woods and wild flowers. They tumble down the steep hillsides that drop to the beach, concealing any presence of a house to the casual walker.

It is an enchanted cove, and, like all magic places, is difficult to find. The insignificant turning left, just beyond the village of Salt Creek at the mouth of the River Dart, is easy to miss, and the narrow, rutted track peters out to a bumpy path. On either side, honeysuckle, cow parsley, red campion and thrift jostle the side of the car like clamouring hands, and overhead the thicket of branches from the ancient trees is low and twisted.

When you have parked the car in the cool darkness of the trees, you will find a faint trace of a path, edged by wild basil and wood anemone. Follow it down to where the cove opens to the sea. Here the wind will blow your hair across your face, its touch like that of a new lover, or even, perhaps, a ghost. Pull up the collar of your coat, and scramble down a long flight of ancient steps to the jetty, and you will find the Boathouse seemingly carved out of the rock behind.

There has been a cottage there for hundreds of years, they say, but no one knows exactly how long. Perhaps it had boats once, or maybe the Victorians gave it the name out of some romantic notion now lost in the mists of time. It has seen, probably, the sails of Sir Walter Ralegh's ships, returning from the New World with their tobacco and potatoes, and it has watched the grey, armoured hulks of the Second World War patrol the coastline in defence of the nation. But they, like us, left no impression on the rocks and the tide.

Enchanted places have the power to change us, to germinate and nurture that tiny seed of happiness, avarice or desire that each of us have kept so carefully concealed. Faced with the wildness of the sea and the sound of the birds, you can be different. But when you leave, you leave nothing behind. The tide will swish over the sand and wipe away your footsteps.

*

In 1964, the Boathouse was owned by the Devereaux family. Bertie Devereaux's parents had bought it in the thirties. Bertie now motored down from London with his own young family every year so that they could experience the wild, idyllic summers that he had enjoyed as a child.

Bertie's sharp, clever face would soften, as he forgot that he was a famous writer, columnist, political adviser and party-goer. He left his mocking laugh and cigarette-holder in London, as he chopped logs for the fire, his shirtless back muscular and gleaming with the effort. The man who would never have thought to empty an ashtray in London took on a primeval role as hunter-gatherer. He selected and graded the fallen branches from the neglected woods, hacking and stacking, and, when the sharpening wind blew in off the sea, cleared and lit the fire.

Fragile, beautiful Maud always left her make-up on the dressing table in London, swapping her tight mini-skirts for a baggy pair of Girl Guide shorts. Stripped of her false eyelashes and pale frosted lips, her hair no longer a neat geometric chunk but a tangle of silk in the breeze, she looked, once again, like the shy debutante who had fallen in love with difficult, forbidden Bertie.

The children of people like Maud and Bertie were often easily forgotten, but here it was a child's world. Chris lost that dark watchfulness that made him look so much older than eleven, and ran, whooping and shouting, through the woods, careering down the steep stairway to the beach, leaping from one narrow, twisting step to the other, followed, as usual, by Tom. They raced along the creamy sand.

Tom could be plaintive and sullen in London. Out here, in the wildness of the flower-covered cliffs, engaged by the constant drama of the sea and feel of the sand between his toes, he was a sturdy little boy, contented to dig sandcastles and roam.

And watching them, as usual, was their friend, Dora Savage, Bertie's secretary and confidante to them all. As soon as she stepped from the car into the ferny chill of the woods and smelt the mixture of damp earth and pine, she felt the weight of expectation fall away from her. The rigid structure of 'you should' and 'you shouldn't' that had dominated her life ceased to exist, and, like the wild foxgloves and lupins that escaped from distant gardens to splash their purples and yellows across the cliffside, she was free to be herself.

'It's just the same,' shouted Chris, completing his lightning tour of the cliffs, woods and beach. 'Nothing has changed.'

'I don't want it to change,' said Tom, trailing behind. 'Ever.'

In London Bertie was often impatient with his sons. Here he made the effort to explain the world to them. 'Everything has to change, Tom,' he said, gently. 'Otherwise there would be no progress.'

And the grown-ups set about their annual game of playing house, as Maud laughingly called it, opening up the Boathouse's cobwebby cupboards and washing dusty spotted china, until everything was as airy and orderly as the inside of a yacht.

But it was Bertie who broke the spell of happiness, setting off a waterfall of consequences that trickled down over the years, beyond his death and touching the lives of people he never met. As the evening sun slanted towards them, low and dazzling across the sea, Maud and Bertie sat out on the jetty, on the old bench that Bertie's mother had placed there many years earlier.

Dora was about to join them from the kitchen until she caught a glimpse of Bertie's face. She shrank back into the doorway, knowing that this should be private.

'Maud.' He picked up his wife's hand as if it were something delicate he was afraid to break. 'I have something to tell you.'

I

'I suppose Chris is giving the address?' Lily Devereaux asked, as they drove through the rolling green swathes of Dorset, Somerset and Devon to Maud's funeral. The countryside hurtled by, too fast for her to see it properly. Tom's driving was tense and erratic, but whether this was caused by her presence, so many months after they had agreed to part, or by his mother's death, she wasn't quite sure. Her hands tightened into fists every time he accelerated too suddenly.

'Of course. We went through it together.' Tom and Chris were close, even for brothers. Tom liked to meet him in a pub at lunchtime every Saturday and they spoke on the telephone several times a week.

'You were wearing that jacket when I first met you.' Tom changed the subject. 'I'm amazed you still have it.'

'Leather lasts. It's OK, isn't it?' She was defensive, wary of the accusations they'd been hurling at each other for a couple of years. Tom had finally moved out six months ago and an unsettled calm had descended on the household. They had got on better.

And when he'd appeared at the door, in the

pouring rain, to tell her that Maud was dead, he asked her to come with him to the funeral.

'Of course,' she said. 'Of course.' She held him tight, shocked by the news. 'Do you want to come in?'

He shook his head, his face wet with rain or tears.

'Call me,' she'd said. 'Call me if you need to talk. I'm here.'

And he had.

They turned off the main highway into narrow, winding lanes, which forced Tom to slow down. High green banks and stone walls, studded with primroses and wild garlic, brushed past Lily's nose, and, every so often, she glimpsed a flash of green, orderly field, grazed by cotton-wool sheep.

'It's so pretty,' she offered.

'It's perfect,' he said. 'Now that Ma's dead, I expect we'll come back. Open the place up, have holidays here again.' He turned round in his seat. 'What about that, children? Holidays in Devon?'

But Billy was immersed in the chunka-chunka-chunka of his Walkman and Daisy was asleep, her corkscrew blonde curls spread out against the seat and her cheeks delicately flushed. How did we create something so beautiful and precious? thought Lily, for the umpteenth time, as she reached behind to adjust something: just an excuse to touch her daughter without waking her. She thought of Tom and the children, enjoying the perfect family holidays without her, and a tightness caught her throat. That was what happened when you divorced. You only belonged in half their lives.

'You really do have to drive slowly down these lanes,' said Tom. 'If you go any faster than fifteen miles an hour, and you meet someone coming the other way, you'll definitely have a crash.'

They parked by the church and got out of the car, stiff and overheated from the drive, Lily curious to see the village that Tom had talked about so often. Perhaps he should have brought them here before. It was a Norman church, she thought, or even older, with a low lych-gate under which even she had to stoop.

Tom stopped to talk to the vicar, and Lily pretended to study the gravestones a few feet away from him. It would feel awkward to be introduced either, erroneously, as a wife, or, embarrassingly, as an ex- or almost ex-wife.

A soft, sweet breeze ruffled the grass. Beyond the stone tower, the land fell away sharply, down to the estuary, where yachts were anchored on a sheet of glittering water. It was an elusive view, offering glimpses and promises. There were secrets and deceptions hidden in the landscape, she thought, like the tiny white or stone cottages that looked like humble labourers' homes but which, according to Tom, were now worth far more than most ordinary people could pay.

Every time she turned her head, she saw another bay or path hidden around the bend, drawing the eye deeper into the earth. She could only catch the edge of it all: the tip of a pink-washed cottage, the first rungs of some mossy stone steps or the start of a stone-flagged path as it twisted and snaked between old, thick walls. The village of Salt Creek, tucked into the protective fold of the curving Devon hills, looking out over the water as it had for almost a thousand years, guarded its mysteries well.

Like marriage. You started out with the exquisite freshness of newly ironed silk, the perfect matching shoes embroidered with rosebuds, the tumbling bouquet of artfully arranged flowers, and your future seen through the gauzy veil of love and optimism. And then. Well. Then was another matter. Then was now, a precariously balanced imitation of family life, a soon-to-be-ex-husband borrowed for the day to present a fictitious portrait of unity for a funeral.

The children tugged her hand. Views bored them.

'Look,' she said. 'This church has been here since the thirteenth century. That's eight hundred years.'

'Oh joy, oh joy.' Billy's voice was scornful and flat. At ten, he tried hard to be cool, but his cynicism sounded contrived. Lily couldn't help smiling.

There was a movement in the shadow of the porch.

'Good morning.' The man wore the deferential expression of the professional mourner. 'Friend or family?'

How could you answer that? Separated wives could hardly be called either. Maud had been gentle and wise, more than a mother-in-law and yet not quite a friend, not exactly. Sometimes Lily thought that she had fallen in love with Maud and the Devereaux family rather than with Tom himself.

Daisy smiled at the man, revealing two lost teeth. 'My granny died. That's why we're here.'

He bent slightly at the waist, with real sympathy this time. 'I'm very sorry to hear it. You deserve a special place to sit. Follow me.'

They followed his bandy-legged, dot-and-carry gait down the worn, undulating flagstones. Billy scuffed his ten-year-old feet, trailing behind them, refusing, as usual, to meet anyone's eyes.

Lily felt a firm, gentle pressure on her elbow as Tom caught up with her and steered her into the family pews, with the rest of them. Nothing has changed, said that touch on her arm.

And when she turned to look at him, what she saw was a nice, middle-aged man, open-faced, with slightly thinning brown hair blown in the salty breeze; a decent man, grieving for his mother. She moved her arm, fractionally, to create a space between them, but sat down where he had indicated. He needed her now, and that created its own rules.

Billy settled himself a few feet away on an empty pew, stabbing at a burbling Gameboy, engrossed.

'Billy,' she hissed. 'Not in church.'

He ignored her, and she decided to wait until more people arrived before enforcing her words. It didn't matter what he did when the church was empty. The fewer confrontations the better, or so she understood.

She watched him. His dark, glossy head reminded her of some wild water animal, like an otter, sleek and utterly involved in whatever he was doing. Except that his was an altogether more confrontational species, one that had been born to swim against the stream, whose first instinct when faced with anything new was to fight, kick and punch. Life would never come easily to him.

People began to shuffle in.

'Billy.' She spoke softly. 'No.'

He threw the Gameboy away angrily and it bounced on the stone floor, scattering tiny plastic pieces.

'Look what you've made me do,' he shouted. 'It's broken now.'

As she picked up the bits from the floor and fitted them together again, she bit back her retort. He would always be harder to love than her gentle, sweet little girl, and that made her feel guilty. Love was supposed to be so wonderful and selfless. In fact, she thought, it was so often treacherous and damaging.

In ones and twos, mourners tiptoed into the church, speaking in whispers, occasionally genuflecting, settling down to study the order of service and raising a hand to old friends. Idly, because she had studied the carved bosses on the wall, and the Royal Coat of Arms of Charles II, 'granted in gratitude for the villagers' loyalty to the Royalist cause' several times over, Lily tuned into the conversation behind her.

'Bet there'll be arguments over the will,' murmured a woman's voice. 'There always are.'

'No money to argue over.' It was an older man speaking. 'Anyway, they're very close, those boys.'

'Doesn't mean anything,' said the first voice. 'People can quarrel over anything after a death. Especially if they're close. And there's the Boathouse. They've still got that, even if they never use it. You wouldn't believe what went on there in the sixties. You know, they always said that . . .'

Lily could hear someone else coming into the pew, and the noise of shuffling, as everyone rearranged themselves.

When the organ music rallied, she stood up with the rest of the congregation and half turned to see Maud's coffin brought slowly in, but she couldn't tell who'd been speaking, and why they should know so much about the Devereauxs.

Lily wondered if Chris, Tom and Cameron would open up the Boathouse again. It had been closed for nearly thirty years – since Bertie Devereaux had died there in an accident that no one in the family liked to talk about.

When Lily had first met Tom, they'd talked about having children at the Boathouse for idyllic, seaside holidays, but, like so many of their dreams, it had slipped through their fingers. Lily thought it was a shame that it had stood empty for so many years, but when she mentioned it to Tom, he always murmured something about repairs and everyone being so busy. Her theory, which she'd hesitated to mention, was that sadness held them all back, that Maud associated the Boathouse so much with Bertie and their golden summers there that she'd locked the memories up behind its thick stone walls.

Now, though, the Devereauxs would have to do something about it.

Cameron leaned forward in his pew and winked at her. He was one of life's Tiggers, she always thought, someone who tried everything, with the greatest of enthusiasm, until he found he didn't like it. The baby of the three. The spoilt one, according to Tom, but Lily didn't think that was necessarily fair. 'Family life isn't fair,' had been Tom's reply when she said this.

Beside Cameron, tucked protectively into his arm, eyes rimmed with red and hair electrically charged with emotion, sat his wife, Vicky, in a flurry of scarves and jewellery.

While Chris had the most commanding personality, Cameron dominated the family physically. He strode around as if on springs, his hard body revealed through ripped jeans and a T-shirt. Vicky had shoehorned him into a suit today, but without a tie, and his blond, shaggy-dog hair trailed round his collar. Lily suspected that he always had to prove that he was stronger, wilder and more creative than the other, conventional Devereaux brothers. She smiled back at him.

The vicar cleared his voice to say that he had never

met Maud, but that he had spoken to her friends and family and that she had obviously been a very special person.

She'd have to have been very special indeed, thought Lily, to be buried in the village graveyard, as the local parish council took vigorous precautions to keep holidaymakers out. Cottages might be snapped up at outlandishly inflated prices and rented out to identikit middle-class families for their healthy, happy holidays, but money couldn't buy you a place in the graveyard. You go back to where you belong, said the council, you can't muscle in here, even if you did manage to get the Post Office shop to stock oak-smoked salmon and balsamic vinegar. But the Devereauxs had owned the Boathouse for over seventy years, and Bertie had been buried there. Even the most anti-tourist church-warden could scarcely deny her the right to have her ashes interred next to her husband.

As the vicar scraped up a good, kind, charitable, all-purpose talk about the Maud he didn't know, one that could easily have been dusted down from many other similar talks, Lily peered up and down the pews. There was Dora, the family's oldest friend, her eyes reddened and her cheeks blotched in grief.

Lily, too, wanted to grieve for Maud, but it was difficult when part of her brain was distracted by trying to stop Billy from ripping out pages from hymn books, and another part fretted at the closeness of her husband. Her ex-husband, she reminded herself.

'Above all, Maud was blessed in her marriage,' the

vicar's voice droned on. 'I understand that Bertie Devereaux, one of the sixties' leading writers and columnists, and who is buried here in this church-yard, was devoted to his wife, and she to him. It was, as I have gathered from talking to their sons, Chris, Tom and Cameron, a marriage of equal but very different minds. Together they were always much more than each one of them was as an individual, and this, perhaps, is one of the greatest achievements anyone can attain in their lifetime. As the Bible says, the greatest of all is love, and Maud . . .'

Lily drifted off, fingering the comforting leather of the old jacket. She'd grown up in it, discovering food in Italy, getting dysentery in the Balkans, nearly being raped in Turkey, falling in love in Greece . . . and had then turned back when it hadn't worked out, up through the rural neatness of France, to bump into Tom on the ferry back to Portsmouth. She'd swapped the motorbike for a car, her backpack for a tiny cottage in London, roadside meals for couply dinner parties, raucous evenings in wine bars for National Childbirth Trust ante-natal classes and the open road for a job.

What would someone say at her funeral? Lily was at Dotcombomb for nearly forty years and in that time became invaluable in finding cheaper and cheaper ways of getting widgets from A to B? People at parties always sounded surprised she was still in business: 'I thought all the dotcoms had gone bust?' And then, when she explained, their eyes glazed over at the words 'hosting Internet sites for small businesses'.

If you've got two children, you can't simply don a leather jacket and take off. On the other hand, she thought as the burly undertakers inched out of the church with Maud's coffin, each measured tread carefully following the next, you can't always choose the time to say goodbye.

'Lily, dearest.' Outside the church, stunned by the fresh April air, she was enveloped in Vicky's cashmere softness, and almost choked by a tuberose waft of Fracas. 'It's all too, too sad,' she shrieked. 'I can't bear it.'

She stepped back and studied Lily. 'You've got so slim! I'm always saying that I simply must divorce Cameron to improve my figure. Now, tell, what's the news from work?'

'I've got to decide whether to take redundancy or go with the new company.'

'What are they offering?'

'Three days a week. Pension, health care, company car, gym membership, decent salary for a change . . . family friendly policies.'

'Fab, darling. I'm so thrilled for you. After all those years wondering whether the office would even be open when you got there on Monday morning. Cam darling, Lily's got a great new job. And she's so thin! I'm leaving you tomorrow to find a slender new me.'

Cameron kissed her on both cheeks while patting Vicky's plump bottom. 'Don't listen to her. I'm the only thing that stands between her and the biscuit tin. We've missed you, Lily.'

'I'm so sorry.' Lily squeezed his hand. 'About Maud. How are you?'

'It's a bugger, isn't it? I never really believed she would go. It didn't seem possible.' There was pain in his eyes. 'I only saw her last Wednesday. She seemed perfectly all right.'

'Cam went down to do some jobs in the house.' There was a note of warning in Vicky's voice, as if Cameron were about to be accused of some misdemeanour. Chris was standing beside them, and had once alleged that Cameron neglected his mother. 'Wasn't that lovely, Chris?' she asked. 'That Cam saw her just before.'

Chris was looking across the churchyard, as if counting and marshalling the guests. 'What? Mm. Yes, of course.' He strode off, and soon appeared to be redirecting some cars, which weren't, apparently, parked in the right place.

Vicky's eyes followed him. 'The new girlfriend doesn't seem to be around.' There was a small note of victory in her voice.

'Who's he going out with now?' Lily always wondered if Chris was an incurable romantic, constantly seeking out perfect love and therefore failing to find it, or whether he was merely an incorrigible rogue who couldn't commit.

'Some Sloaney interior designer called Sarah.' Vicky's voice was dismissive. 'One of his polo blondes. Anyway, she isn't *here*, so she can't be too stuck in.'

'You look a complete mess as usual.' Tom disentangled himself from an elderly lady and went over to Cameron, slapping him on the back hard enough to make him wince.

'Better than being bow-fronted like you.' Cameron patted Tom's belly and Tom pulled it in.

'You do talk a load of balls sometimes.'

This exchange was delivered in affectionate tones and seemed to satisfy both brothers. Cameron drifted off to receive condolences from other people.

'Dreadful talk from the vicar, wasn't it?' hissed Vicky. 'These small-town clergy must live on some other planet.'

'Oh. Not too bad, I didn't think, quite . . .'

But Vicky had turned away, to wrap herself around Tom in noisy commiseration. 'Honeybunch. What a rotten, rotten, crap thing to happen. How *are* you, Tom? How are *you*?'

'Fine.' Tom freed himself carefully. 'Hello, Vicky. How are you?'

Chris and Tom, Lily thought, were both behaving as if this were a distant stranger's funeral. On the other hand, they obviously regarded Cameron, who had wept silently during the address, as emotionally incontinent.

She shifted from foot to foot, suddenly wishing she could ask Maud about whether she should take what she was offered – a pleasant part-time job with lots of security and time off – or turn her life upside down and risk almost everything in search of something she couldn't even define?

'Oh, Maud,' she murmured, suddenly feeling that her absence had changed the landscape and the world was no longer quite what it had been before.

As she turned away from the other mourners to hide her tears by pretending to look at the yachts, Maud's presence hovered over the churchyard, as tangibly as if her perfume had blown in from the sea. Over the low chatter behind, Lily could almost hear her voice, frail but steady, talking to her.

'Go on. Be somebody. The children will follow you.'

The voice in Lily's head seemed so real that Lily turned to look for her, but all she could see was the wide open sweep of the bay and the gulls soaring up across the skies, as if escorting Maud's soul beyond the clouds.

2

Dora Savage no longer slept well. She lay awake at the deepest dip of night, listening to the howls of the foxes in the bushes. Maud's death had ripped something out of life, deep inside, leaving only pain and loss. Twice, she heard cries and, convinced that it was the sound of young women being mugged on Turnham Green, she jumped up, trembling at the thought of calling the police, and parted the worn curtains only to see an utterly empty road, fluorescent in the yellow light. The crying had been her own, she thought, or was an echo in her head.

What shall I do? she thought, bone-weary and aching. Now that Maud is dead? She turned over again, wondering if she could allow herself another Nurofen, or whether she should wait another hour. She hoped she wouldn't be too tired to enjoy the lunch party on Sunday. It seemed as if Maud would not let her rest.

'We're going to talk about the Boathouse,' Chris had said when he kissed her goodbye at the funeral, and the words echoed through her mind as she tossed and turned. They conjured up so many memories.

The siren of a police car wailed on a distant street. What should she do now?

'Write the story of your life,' said a voice in her head, and she saw, as clearly as if he and she were still at the Boathouse, Bertie Devereaux in his panama hat, pointing an unlit cheroot in her direction as he sloshed whisky into a tumbler. 'You can write, Dora, you know. You're as good a writer as I am, if you'd only believe in yourself. Leave your story behind for the boys.'

'No.' She found the courage to speak out loud to his ghost, across the years, from her bed in her narrow room in Chiswick. 'That's not good enough, Bertie. And you know it.' Writing it down, then leaving it for everyone to find after her death, was the coward's way out. She wouldn't be there to comfort them, or laugh with them, or to help them make sense of the parts that she didn't fully understand yet herself. She wouldn't be there to say sorry.

Over and over again, she told herself that everything was fine. She remembered Bertie leaning back in his wicker chair on the Boathouse veranda, with the sunlight across his ravaged face, saying, 'If it's not broken, don't fix it,' his self-mocking intonation robbing the cliché of its ordinariness.

'Look after them all,' Maud had said on the telephone a few days before she died.

Dora had switched the TV remote control to 'mute'. 'Of course.' She'd never considered the possibility of Maud dying. She was only seventy-nine. Dora thought she'd been spooked by the wind howling round the eaves of her little cottage. 'Don't talk like that,' she'd murmured, one eye on the final instalment of that very good drama about spies – oh, she'd forgotten the name of it already – as she hurried the phone call along. 'It's the weather that makes us all feel old and gloomy. There's nothing to worry about. The boys are doing so well.'

What did a programme about spies matter now? She wished she'd switched it off, like she usually did.

'They've got good lives,' she'd added, to reassure her friend. 'And you have wonderful grandchildren.'

But if she looked at it another way, she wasn't sure that Chris, Tom and Cameron Devereaux were all doing so well.

There was Chris, with his fine mansion and stream of glossy, spoilt blondes, with their sports cars and smart shoes and high, cultured voices. None of them had really touched his heart, she thought, and she couldn't help wondering if that was because he kept it locked away where no one could ever find it and hurt him again. The blondes always hung around hopefully – sometimes for months, occasionally for years – but they inevitably drifted on in the end, without explanation, or, apparently, fuss. Perhaps the fact that he'd never actually married any of them was irrelevant. Perhaps, Dora told herself, this was modern man. Chris was what articles in magazines now called a 'serial monogamist'. It was, these articles told her, the pattern for future unions between men and women.

And Tom. The quiet one. Seen by too many people

as the boring one: a pale, indistinct, beige blur against the sharp silhouettes of Chris's dark, dramatic good looks and Cameron's blond ebullience. She'd been so delighted that he'd found his Lily, and had Billy and Daisy. Of course, Billy was very boisterous; she often had to bite back remarks like 'children need discipline' when she was with them. But Daisy was a poppet. Lily and Tom had been like a building society advertisement or a couple on the side of a cornflake packet. Young and happy and focused on their family. So what had gone wrong? Dora had been bewildered.

'Don't ask,' Maud had said, placing her hand firmly on Dora's. 'Please, Dora dearest, don't go wading in there. Divorce is always horrible. If Lily or Tom want to talk about it, they will.'

If only Maud had been as sympathetic to Vicky. Was it because Cameron was . . . No, she refused to think like that. Cameron was everyone's favourite, the baby of the family. It was natural, perhaps, for Maud to see Vicky as competition, and to realize that marriage would take him away from her. Maud had never said she disliked Vicky, but she'd often admitted that she thought Cam was simply too young to get married.

Vicky was lovely: exuberant and generous, hopelessly unpunctual, dramatic and emotional. A bit like Maud, in fact. Perhaps that's what she hadn't been able to deal with. And Cameron and Vicky were fine, still together, still happy, with the absurdly named but utterly adorable Harley. But how much did Vicky mind not only being the emotional centre of the home, but also its chief provider? While Cameron perfected the art of producing obscure photographs? Once again, Dora's friends always told her that 'it was the modern way' and that couples these days were flexible about that sort of thing. Perhaps that was true of all of them. That the Devereaux boys – one single, one divorcing and one not earning any money – weren't damaged, just beings of their time.

These thoughts tossed and turned in her head as she fidgeted to get comfortable. If she lay on one side, her hip hurt, while the other was fine for a bit until her knee started a piercing protest at the pressure. And if she lay on her back, she snored so loudly she woke herself up.

Now, with Maud gone, she felt simultaneously the weight of the Devereaux family as her responsibility and a sense of disconnection, as if the ties that bound her to them had been broken at the funeral. Ever since Bertie had died, Maud had lived in Somerset and Dora in London, but they had spoken to each other, usually about the family, every week, and if either of them had had anything special to say, they had called the other first.

Now who would want to ring up a useless old lady? Without Maud and, before her, Bertie, to look after, what was the point of Dora Savage?

*

As the sharp lines of the early morning sun began to frame the curtains, Dora was comforted by reminding herself that Chris had invited her to join them for lunch that Sunday. 'It wouldn't be a family party without you,' he'd said, and she'd coloured with pleasure.

But then she remembered: 'We're going to talk about the Boathouse,' over and over again, and her happiness was tinged with apprehension.

The Boathouse. She wasn't sure if it had brought her the very best times of her life, or if everything that had stemmed from it had turned out a complete disaster. And then she thought about Chris, Tom and Cameron filling the Boathouse with their young children, making it a place of innocent games and laughter again, instead of the lotus-eating adult playground it had been in her time, and she felt the weight ease off her chest a little.

As the sun stole under the curtains and illuminated the cluttered room, she had another thought. She was weighed down, literally weighed down, by possessions. No wonder she couldn't see straight.

'Damn you, Bertie,' she murmured. 'I'm going to make my own decisions from now on. I've done what you told me for far too long. I'm seventy-four now, and I'm going to clear out my life. Work out for myself what I should do. And then I'm going to do it.'

Because, even more uncomfortable than the worn sheets that rucked up beneath her, their patches of bobbled polyester rubbing against her skin, was the thought that she was seeking her own redemption. Because that would be selfish. Redemption was something you can live without, she told herself. Or die without. If it meant hurting people.

With this she slipped into the deepest and most refreshing sleep she'd enjoyed for years, and woke up a few hours later suffused with a sense of adventure, like a child at the beginning of the summer holidays.

3

When Lily told everyone at Dotcombomb that she wasn't going to go to Brentford with the rest of the company they all reacted differently.

'Is this about getting back with Tom? Or have you got another man?' Julia's voice was a dentist's drill, a high, intrusive whine, demanding that Lily open up. Julia was obsessed with marriage. Lily had tried to tell her that it didn't mean happy endings – it was just a different sort of journey.

'Absolutely not.' Lily had no intention of talking about it, although she knew she'd transgressed some unwritten law of friendship in Julia's eyes by not furnishing her with enough evidence to help her form the right conclusion about the split with Tom. Julia thought that you should stay together unless your other half had done something really terrible. She was deeply frustrated not to know whether Tom had crossed this invisible line or not.

'It'll be lovely to be with the children,' said Brenda, who had chosen to retire early and was going to spend more time in her garden. 'How is your little boy?'

'Awful as ever,' admitted Lily, who had never been fazed by anything in her life until Billy was born. She instantly regretted her words. What mother could really say that about her child?

'He'll cause some serious damage one day unless you do something about it,' said Julia spitefully. 'He's obviously missing Tom.' As if Julia knew what a ten-year-old boy should be like. She wanted children, she said, with an elusive man called Matt, and these children, of course, would be perfect.

Lily burnt with anger, then damped it down. She'd had a lot of practice at doing that, during the last years of her marriage.

'Tom must be terribly sad about his mother dying,' said Brenda, who worried about everybody. Lily would miss Brenda, and the way they all knew about each other's lives, even if they'd rarely, if ever, met the people they talked about every day.

'Fine.' Lily felt like a stuck record. 'He seems fine.'

Tom always said that everything was 'fine'. Sometimes she wondered if something very different lay deeper down: nameless, shapeless fears that lived like prehistoric animals in the dark and rarely emerged.

'Bet there'll be rows over the will, though,' observed Julia, unconsciously echoing the woman in the church.

'Ooh, yes,' said Brenda. 'I remember when my grandmother died. Everyone had an equal share of what she left, except for her jewels. My aunt said that she should have them, as the only daughter. My father and his brother didn't exactly agree, but everything seemed too terrible, and they didn't like to say anything.' Brenda's stories were so full of cousins, aunts and uncles that they were often difficult to follow. She settled in for a satisfyingly indignant conclusion. 'It used to make him ever so sad when he saw my aunt and cousins wearing his mother's rings, and realize that there was nothing for his own wife and daughter. Not that I'm a jewels person, myself.' She patted her hair happily. 'But do you know, he saved up enough money to buy my mother one of the necklaces, then my aunt told him she'd already sold it. Well, he said, if you didn't want them, why not offer your family first refusal? You said you wanted to keep them in the family. Never said you intended selling. She was ever so offended. Didn't come to Christmas for six years.'

While Lily was still trying to sort this account out, Julia's face turned sour. 'When my mother died, my father remarried six months later. Then he died, too, only a few years after that. And all my mother's furniture, all her things, everything that we should have had, went to the new wife. Her children have them now: my mother's rings, the little desk she wrote at, the family painting of my mother . . . all of it belongs to another family. The new wife wouldn't even give us back the family photo albums from our childhood.'

Poor Julia. No wonder she was so bitter. Lily tried to understand how people came to behave like that and failed. 'Well, there won't be anything like that with the Devereauxs.' With a massive effort, she pushed a packet of Kettle Chips, bought as a celebration by Brenda, away from her and towards Julia, who was pale and thin. 'They've always been very close. They wouldn't dream of arguing about money. Chris has masses anyway, and I don't think the others really care.'

'Hasn't he ever had a long-term relationship with anyone?' asked Brenda, cosily determined to surround everyone with the loving collection of grandchildren and in-laws that she herself enjoyed.

'There've been girlfriends. And he's got a teenage daughter called Tash. She lives with her mother in Sweden. They never married. I think it was a one-night stand.'

She could tell by the expression on Julia's face that she was thinking of Matt and wondering whether she should simply spring a baby on him. 'No, Julia. Really. That's not the way to go.'

'I know. I know. But if I had his child, surely he'd have to recognize how good we are together?' And she was off, listing the magical evenings they'd spent together.

Walk away now, Lily wanted to say. Don't fall into the trap of thinking you're different. That you can change them. She hadn't managed to change Tom. In marriage, what you see is what you get. Times ten. Plus a few surprises.

But Julia wouldn't, or couldn't, listen. When she'd wrung the widest possible range of emotions, interpretations and conclusions from the few precious hours she'd spent with Matt, she returned to the subject of Maud's will. 'There must be a house, at least,' she persisted. 'I thought Bertie Devereaux was famous once.'

'Bertie Devereaux?' asked Nigel, their all-purpose accounts and purchase manager, who was delighted to move to Brentford and buy a cottage with his much older gay lover, Colin. 'Darling, you never told me you were related to him. It's too exciting for words. He was to journalism in the sixties what Ken Tynan was to theatre. Deliciously naughty boys, both of them, and if we hadn't had people like that, I don't think people like me would be legal.'

'My ex-husband was . . .'

But Nigel's mind had flitted on to other things. 'Now, darling, although I absolutely approve of your chucking everything in and rushing off like a complete madwoman into the sunset with your children, you must be careful about your pension. Keep the payments up. Promise me, puppet?'

Lily promised, and Nigel minced off, murmuring, 'Bertie Devereaux! Well, well, well! Colin will be fascinated.'

Julia and Brenda looked at her reproachfully, as if she'd deliberately concealed some delicious titbit.

'I think I do remember who he was,' said Brenda.

'Was he gay?' asked Julia.

'No, absolutely not, very, very happily married,' Lily assured them. The weight of Maud and Bertie's loving marriage had been one of the factors in sinking her own union, carrying with it, as it did, all the expectations of what a happy family would be like. 'Anyway, Nigel would have disapproved of him terribly if he'd actually met him, because he didn't believe in things like pensions. I remember Tom telling me that his father thought we'd all be wiped out by the Bomb in the fifties, and then, in the sixties, it was unspeakably uncool to plan ahead. Anyway, they thought the State would look after you from cradle to grave in those days. So you see, Julia, there isn't anything for anyone to get excited about.'

Just the Boathouse. A derelict cottage near the sea. Nigel's words had conjured up Maud's stories of parties at the Boathouse at full moon. 'We had to give them at full moon, my dear,' Maud had said, 'because everyone got so drunk and stoned that they would have fallen off the cliffs in the dark. The summers were better in those days,' she'd added. 'We camped out in the woods, and played guitars in the open air.'

Julia filed her nails, furious that Lily was leaving. It was as if she was letting them down, not going to Brentford. However, never liking the conversation to stray far from herself for very long, she reverted to the subject of Matt. 'Do you think I ought to email him back, or play it cool?'

There were only so many interpretations, and only so much advice that you could give, and only so long you could talk about one three-line email, but Lily, knowing Julia's hunger, was prepared to start the Matt conversation again and retrace their already well-trodden steps. 'Jules, I think you should wait and see,' she told her gently, wishing there was something more she could say. 'If you need to come round this weekend, if you're missing Matt, you can always call. Anytime. When noise and mess start to look better than an empty flat, you know where to find it.'

Julia blew her nose. 'Thanks.' She tried to make a joke. 'I suppose I should count my blessings. At least I don't have the problem of Billy in my life.'

4

Dora's tiny terraced house was stuffed. She'd chosen the wallpaper in the early 1970s and it had faded to the yellowing cream of old cigarette smoke with, apparently, a pattern of spiders crawling down the walls. They must have been stylized flowers once, she supposed. Every surface was piled high with possessions, each held on to for some long-forgotten sentimental or practical reason, and now smelling of dust, damp and ancient perfume. Chris, when he dropped in for a drink, often laughed: 'Really, Dora.' He'd flick aside books, newspapers or piles of clutter. 'This is the sort of house where you have to pick something up in order to find a space to sit down.' He usually added: 'Why don't you sell up? Buy a little cottage out of London and pocket the difference? You'd actually have something to live on, apart from your state pension.'

He was right, of course. A two-bedroom cottage in Chiswick could be exchanged for one somewhere else with quite a lot left over, and Dora knew she needed it. But it was her home. She had friends nearby. She knew the shopkeepers. The neighbours kept an eye out for her. It was near Chris. And being near Chris, especially now that Maud was gone, meant that she would stay in touch with Cameron. And Tom, and all the children. Would they ever come to visit her if she buried herself in Little Snoring on the Pillow? Probably not. Why should they? And where would she go?

An old stag's head, bought by Bertie as a joke, and hung with necklaces, scarves and hats, eyed her with cynicism.

There's too much here, she thought, again. Too many possessions. I can't think straight with everything crowding me in.

'I can't *think*,' she repeated, shouting out loud.

The dust of the house settled around her, as if puffed into small clouds by the force of her words. Was shouting at yourself a sign of senile dementia? She checked herself, always terrified that she might be slipping into that murky, helpless world where well-meaning people could scurry around making decisions for her.

She must work out what to do, where to go, who to be.

But how? Perhaps the answer was here, somewhere amongst the old photographs, foxed watercolours, framed menus, posters of long-forgotten plays and dusty piles of books, cushions and ornaments. Every room was stuffed with far too much: a tigerskin rug fought with a Persian carpet; a clumsy bean bag with an Ottoman footstool; the sofa and chair 'suite' from her parents' overstuffed Victorian house nudged some rickety, broken-backed dining chairs she'd never had time to repair; and curtains with faded, sun-rotted linings swamped a pair of cracked china Staffordshire dogs. Almost every possession reminded her of someone; many of these people were now dead. She couldn't bear the thought of others carelessly packing it all up after her death, ordering a skip or marshalling a house clearance agent to get rid of it. It was hers, her past, and she wanted to decide where it would all go.

Everyone needs to make an inventory of their lives at some time, she told herself, and now it's my turn. Room by room, day by day, hour by hour: I'm going to go through it all, and only keep what is most important to me. She would sort out the valuable from the tat, send things to auction, do a car-boot sale, and give some things away, either to someone who would particularly like them, or to charity shops. A great deal was valueless and would have to be thrown away, but perhaps she could raise enough money to pay for a holiday, or even, if she was very lucky, a new hip. Then she'd be able to decide what to do next.

She would start with the books. So many of them reminded her of Bertie, especially the Dawlish imprints she'd worked on when she first met him. She rummaged in a downstairs cupboard, and brought out some empty boxes, hoarded like everything else, against a day when they might be useful, and several squashed carrier bags. Books had always been her most precious consolation, her substitute for a family, and the food of her vivid interior life. She took them out of the shelves in groups, barely stopping to check their flyleaves for inscriptions, forcing herself to ignore the tantalizing back covers and the enchantment of the stories inside. She created a small, separate pile of books that might fetch a few hundred pounds in the collectors' market, such as the first editions of Dawlish writers who had since become famous.

She filled three carrier bags and two boxes with old paperbacks, until she came to the St John Conroy series of five thrillers, written by Bertie Devereaux in as many years from the beginning of 1949.

Dora Savage was twenty, in her first job: secretary to the publisher David Dawlish, or Mr Dawlish, as everyone called him. She thought herself very smart in her brown suit, hat and gloves. The sleeves were a little too short, and so was the skirt, because she was too tall, and the material was cheap and shiny because although the war was over, clothes rationing had barely ended, and there was never enough of anything to go round. However, it was her first proper suit, and she felt very grown up in it.

But the rest of her life was dreary. Even at her age, having known very little else except the adrenalin-fuelled tension of the war years, she could recognize dreariness. She ate it every day, in the dull, meagre food, with its four ounces of butter and thirteen ounces of meat a week; and in the evening, with nothing better to do, she went on endless dreary walks, past closed pubs and shops, in quiet shuffling South London streets. Occasionally a car would rattle past, but otherwise the only sounds were the footfalls and soft murmurs of other people like herself who had nothing else to do. She often bumped into people she knew, and they stopped and talked on the street corner, but there didn't seem to be much to say, except to complain about rationing or pass on tips about shops that were expecting something special.

Buildings were cracked and grey with dust, and huge bomb holes gaped like pulled teeth in every other street. Occasionally she passed an open pub, and would peer in at the warmth and cheerfulness, but some pubs didn't allow women in, and all would certainly have disapproved of a girl on her own. That world of cheerful camaraderie was a man's world, like so much else.

At ten o'clock every evening, Dora went to bed, covering herself with layers of blankets against the cold, sacrificing a finger from each hand in turn to hold up a book so that she could read. The poor fingers froze, but if she turned out the light too early, she found it almost impossible to sleep and the nights turned into a prison: endless, cold, dark hours of solitary confinement. In the morning she often scraped ice off the inside of the window, breathing on it to see if the world outside had changed. It never had.

Once a week she went to the pictures with a school-friend, Molly, revelling in the palatial atmosphere of the cinema, but even here, fuel was still rationed, and, in the winter, the permafrost of a large, unheated building penetrated deeply into their bones and chipped away at the fantasy. She occasionally met other women for tea in the Lyons Corner House at the top of Oxford Street, but most of the girls she'd grown up with had married early. Dora had always been an oddball, anyway, wrapped up in books, while the other girls concentrated on 'home economics' and the other skills they'd need as wives and mothers. A few had wanted to be air hostesses, but nothing had come of it.

So Dora's life in 1949 was an endless cycle of walking, work, sleep and lumpy, stodgy meals. Its weekly high point was Sunday's roast joint, thinly sliced to transparency to make it go round. They ate the remainder cold on Monday, and minced on Tuesday. They had sausages on Wednesday. The rest of the time her mother served up a rigid cycle of sad, greyish protein from tins: Thursday was oily, slippery whalemeat; Friday sharp, fishy pilchards; and, finally, a bit of variety on Saturday – gritty corned beef the shade of deep, vengeful garnet.

Bertie Devereaux exploded into this uneventful, monochrome world like a firework. He flung open the door of the narrow shoebox that served as an ante-room to Mr Dawlish's office and bounded in like an enormous puppy. She stood up in defence of her employer's door. She had Mr Dawlish's diary, and he was not expecting anyone.

'Excuse me. You can't go in there. Mr Dawlish . . .' As her eyes met his, she experienced a shock of recognition. For the first time in her life, she found herself able to look a man in the eye like an equal. Her mother, Cynthia, would have been scandalized. Dora had been brought up to think of her height as a serious disfigurement, and, if she could have done, Cynthia would have pressed her head down every morning, because men 'didn't like tall girls'. Dora had developed various fruitless mechanisms for trying to seem smaller, like slouching, wearing flat shoes (pointless) and lowering her eyes. This man, whoever he was, looked straight at her, as if he liked what he saw.

'Hello. You're new. Who are you?'

Challenged by the direct, intelligent look in his eyes, she had to struggle to remember her role as custodian to the door of the important Mr Dawlish. 'I . . . I'm Miss Savage. Mr Dawlish's new secretary.'

'And what's your first name, Miss Savage-Mr-Dawlish's-new-secretary?'

She was so overcome she forgot to be surprised at the instant familiarity. 'Dora.'

'Dora Savage.' He assessed her. 'What a lovely, wild name. It suits you.'

Dora tried not to blush. She knew she wasn't lovely. Not only was there the embarrassment of her height, but nothing else about her face or figure was in any way fashionable or attractive. She was flat-chested, had no waist or hips and her legs might have belonged to a lanky schoolboy. She had a narrow, white face, invisible pale eyelashes, and sandy brown hair, once blonde, which she wore long and straight with a side parting. Her mother would sigh, 'You know what they say. Men don't make passes at girls who wear glasses.' So Dora also seemed both vague and clumsy, because she was short-sighted and, without disfiguring wire-rimmed spectacles, couldn't quite see where she was going. Her mother had suggested, once, that she might look more feminine if she curled her hair, but after a disastrous perm which had left her looking like a horse in a wig, they'd both agreed that perhaps it was better left to nature, after all.

'You're a Modigliani.'

'What?' Dora tried not to sound stupid.

'He's a painter. Of interesting women, not chocolate-boxy blondes, like Renoir, but elegant, modern girls like you.' He lounged against her desk, and began to pick out letters on her massive sit-up-and-beg typewriter. 'The quick brown fox jumped over the lazy dog', he typed, with one finger, over a letter.

'Excuse me!' She was furious. You couldn't waste paper, or send out letters with errors in them, and if she made a mistake she had to start again, right from the beginning, lining up the carbon copy and feeding the pieces of paper slowly in without crumpling them. Sometimes it took her hours to type something exactly right, and she was a good typist, having graduated top of her class. 'You can't do that. I'll have to start that letter again, and I'm behind as it is. Mr Dawlish will be furious. You'll get me into trouble.'

He looked at her again, as if she was suddenly human to him, and not a joke. 'I'm so sorry.' He stood up. 'I wasn't thinking. It was selfish of me. Please accept my apologies.' He held out his hand. 'My name's Bertie Devereaux, by the way.'

She shook it. 'Of course, I know who you are now. You're late delivering your manuscript. It was supposed to be here two months ago. I've been trying to get hold of you, but nobody ever answers the telephone. Or replies to my letters.' Too late she remembered another of her mother's favourite dictums, which was that men didn't like being criticized. Until you married them, of course, when, as far as she could see from her parents' marriage, you could be as vile as you liked. She despised it all, and had often snapped that if she couldn't be equal and honest before, after and during marriage, then she'd never be married at all. Her mother replied that silly, modern notions of equality would get her nowhere, and that she had better drop them before she got left on the shelf.

'I didn't answer your letters because I never received them. I wasn't there.' Bertie wasn't offended. 'I was down at the Boathouse, finishing the book. And here it is.'

'Mr Dawlish will be pleased.' She took the manuscript. 'Shall I see if he's available?'

'If you would.' He flung himself down on a spare chair in the office, emanating confidence and energy. He had large, beautiful hands, dark eyes and a raw-boned face, like a hurried charcoal drawing, with exaggerated lines along the nose, cheekbones and deep, cleft chin.

The door opened. 'My dear chap.' David Dawlish hurried out and they shook hands warmly. 'How's Maud? Married life suiting you?' He turned to Dora. 'Mr Devereaux has just married one of the most beautiful women in London.'

She'd heard a little bit about this author: talented and difficult, perhaps slightly too fond of himself, unreliable as far as deadlines were concerned and always spending his advances almost before he got them, but 'a dream with words. One of the most talented writers of this generation.' He was forgiven everything for this.

They ordered tea, and settled down in Mr Dawlish's office to talk about the manuscript. She poured for them – Earl Grey and beautiful porcelain cups, because Dawlish & Sons had standards – while Bertie discussed a problem he'd had with his heroine, Hermione. 'Maud read it last night and says that Hermione can't have a degree from Oxford University. She says it makes her seem eccentric.'

David Dawlish laughed. 'Well, married life is obviously doing you some good. This is the first time you've ever asked for anyone else's opinion. You never take any notice of mine, certainly.'

'Ah,' said Bertie. 'The thing is, I need some money. I hope that St John Conroy will be a potboiler to keep me going while I write a real book. So it's got to be popular. I want every typist on the Clapham omnibus to buy a copy.'

'Then perhaps we should ask Miss Savage,' suggested David Dawlish. 'She travels to work every day on the tram from Stockwell.'

Dora flushed. 'Oh, do make her go to university. I wanted to, so much, but my parents said everyone would think I was weird.' They couldn't have been more horrified if she'd announced an intention to join the French Foreign Legion, and had warned her that being perceived as a blue-stocking would finally destroy her last chance of marriage. Without a husband, her mother warned her, she would finish up without a home, on the scrapheap of life. The Victorians had used the phrase 'a Fate Worse than Death' as a euphemism for rape, but, in reality, it was spinsterhood that really frightened women of Dora's mother's generation.

'Weird?' The two men both looked pensive.

'In that case,' said Bertie, 'Maud is right. Hermione definitely can't be considered weird. Miss Savage is obviously a very unusual and intelligent young lady and would never read a St John Conroy book on her way to work. You will have to wait for my proper book, Miss Savage.' He made it sound like a compliment, but Dora turned the words over in her head later, and thought that her mother, once again, had probably been right. Nobody wanted clever women.

Over the next few years Bertie crashed unpredictably in and out of the office, never making appointments and causing Dora anguish by messing up Mr Dawlish's diary, wheedling his way in ahead of eminent professors of literature and dames of this and that, and always managing to make her laugh while never returning any of Mr Dawlish's calls on time. Occasionally Maud came too, and Dora watched her, fascinated by the woman who'd captured such an unpredictable heart.

Maud had the pale, protected look of a girl who'd spent all her life in an ornate drawing room, hands folded demurely, waiting for her prince to draw up in a Rolls-Royce and carry her away. However, she seemed to lack the arrogance of her class. When she spoke, her clear, cultured voice was soft and hesitant, and her pronouncements, though carefully thought out, were delivered gently. She'd married at twenty-five, but seemed younger than Dora, whose edges had been knocked off by a life-time in South London. Maud always looked at Bertie as if he were a god, and he looked back as if she were a precious jewel that he could hardly believe he'd captured. When they left the office, the lavender, amber and sandalwood scent of Jicky hovered in the air, like a ghost of happiness, before dissipating slowly in the draughts of the battered

Georgian house that served as an office for Dawlish & Sons.

Later Dora discovered that Maud did, indeed, come from a privileged aristocratic family, but that she'd defied them to marry Bertie, who'd gone to a grammar school in the West Country. Astonishingly for the twentieth century, Maud's family had actually cut her off. They never relented, and she never spoke of them. That such an apparently pliable and demure girl could be capable of such defiance alerted Dora to the fact that there was more to Maud than first appeared, and the union of Maud and Bertie Devereaux always shimmered in her mind as the triumph of fairy-tale love over the relentless ordinariness of real life.

5

Lily woke up on Sunday morning and pulled open the curtains on to a transparently clear day, looking forward to Sunday lunch at the Devereauxs'. She missed Maud, and she also missed the children having a grandmother. It was as if Maud had been the silken thread that kept the family together. Lily's own parents had died, a year apart from each other, when Lily was in her twenties, and that had, she thought, been part of the reason why Tom had represented sanctuary.

As she pulled clothes out of the wardrobe, discarded them, and opened drawers, she let a little of the Devereaux warmth creep into her soul. She liked knowing that she was still part of it all. It made her feel less alone. She and Tom would briefly be a family again, with the children, but without the shadows that had hovered over the last years of their marriage. It would be lovely to see Cameron and Vicky, too, and to find out what Chris's latest girlfriend was like. Vicky had sounded wary about her when they'd last talked. 'She's going to be at lunch. Obviously determined to winkle her way into the family.' Vicky sounded scornful. 'She purports to be an interior designer. But I asked her about her turnover and didn't get a very clear answer.'

Lily didn't think Chris would be worried about the size of Sarah's turnover. Perhaps, at last, this was true love for him. She hoped so. Even though she no longer believed in happy endings, she couldn't help hoping for them.

She had to ferret about in her top drawer to find a pair of socks that matched, or a clean pair of tights without a hole, which triggered a faint anxiety about life without a salary cheque. She closed the drawer firmly on this.

What would the Devereaux clan be like without Maud at its head? Would it fall apart, or would someone else take over as its focus? Would it be Chris, as the eldest son? Or Vicky and Cameron as the established couple? It would all be about the tension between Chris and Cameron, that was certain.

Lily had been enchanted when she was first invited to their Sunday lunches. Tom had driven her, twelve years ago, down to Somerset, where Maud had presided over a long, narrow table overlooking a chocolate-box garden. The others – Chris and Cameron – seemed almost too huge and alive for the setting, as they ribbed each other constantly with barbed affection. Vicky had been a pre-Raphaelite Madonna, looking far too young, hardly more than a teenager, her large cornflower-blue eyes glowing at whoever was talking, and occasionally flashing extraordinarily white teeth in a vibrant smile. Cameron had handled little Harley in such an easy, loving way that Lily had felt tears start behind her eyes. Together they looked like an advertisement for something: a brand of jeans, or a designer perfume, perhaps. In those days, Cameron seemed set to become a top photographer, with Vicky as his adoring muse.

Now Vicky was marketing manager for a firm of chutney importers, travelling all over the world and coming back late at night, while Cameron fiddled about in his darkroom producing photographs of people with their heads out of the picture to portray the futility of art. Nobody knew if Vicky minded being the chief breadwinner, or whether she'd blossomed under the pressure. Occasionally people wondered, but they didn't ask, if Cameron felt emasculated. Chris, who could be cruel, occasionally jokingly referred to him as 'a kept man'. Cameron always replied with a laugh.

'Tom is the only sane one of the Devereaux boys,' Vicky told Lily. 'Chris is the Boss. He's absolutely impossible . . .' She nodded, smiling affectionately, towards the corner of Maud's sitting room, where Chris, in an armchair behind the business news pages, emanated a force field of 'Do Not Disturb' signs. 'And as for Cameron . . . Oh, well.' She sighed with mock exasperation. 'I do love him. Everybody does. But . . . well, you'll soon find out if you survive today.'

This is what I want, Lily thought. She was an only child, and had always wanted a big, welcoming family full of interesting people.

Maud brought out the photograph album and showed her tiny khaki-and-cream snaps with fluted edges from the fifties and sixties. There were women in bikinis, men in floppy hats and beads, with side-burns and hair curling down to their shoulders, and two little boys squinting into the camera, with the sheen of the sun on their skin.

'Where's Cameron?'

'He wasn't born until later.' Maud smiled. 'We always spent the whole summer at the Boathouse. Bertie used to write on the veranda, in the mornings.'

'Isn't that . . . ?' Lily thought she spotted a well-known face in the album, but couldn't quite think of his name.

'Oh, all sorts of people used to come down.' Maud wasn't interested in the celebrities. 'This one, much earlier, look, was my husband, Bertie, with Dora Savage, his secretary, who's become part of the family. That must have been nineteen fifty-nine, I think.'

Lily studied the photograph closely, as if to extract every milligram of information about Tom and his past from it. Bertie and Dora were holding glasses of gin to the camera and looked like film stars from the glamorous era of black and white. Bertie reminded her of Chris, with his dark gypsy colour-ing and intense, strongly drawn face, although his hair was longer and he wore his open shirt with a Bohemian swagger. Dora was tall and slim, with long straight hair in a side parting, a vivid gash of strong lipstick and a frilled, spotted bikini. Later, when Lily met her, she found it impossible to believe that this thin woman, with skinny curtain-pole legs and chaotic, colourful patchwork clothes, could ever have been that elegant, laughing girl.

This is what I want, she thought, looking at them all again.

Maud turned the rough olive-green pages of the album, tracing her finger, with its slightly swollen joints, down each photograph, telling Lily the details with affection in her cracking voice. She spoke of Bertie as if he'd only just left the room, and was still alive to her. Lily thought of her own parents' happy, easy marriage and was reassured.

When Maud, wafting an aura of lavender and Jicky, kissed her cheek and said, 'I hope you'll come back soon,' Lily replied: 'Oh, I will.'

What do you wear to your former husband's family gathering to discuss your ex-mother-in-law's property? It sounded like one of those conundrums with a trick answer. Lily discarded anything that looked even vaguely as if she might be a wild, divorced woman having too good a time – a raspberry cashmere top, for example – and then, looking at herself in the mirror, realized she'd dressed entirely in black, as if she was still in mourning. That might look as if she was overdoing the grief. She pulled on a soft, biscuit-coloured sweater that echoed the pale honey of her hair, and looked again. Tom particularly liked that sweater and she didn't want him to think she was dressing for him. She couldn't bear to start all that again.

In the end she decided that the black, with a pretty scarf, would cover all eventualities.

'Chris says you look like a sexy librarian,' Tom had told her once.

The thought of Chris passing judgement on her had inflamed her temper. 'I'd rather you didn't talk about me to Chris. I'm your wife, not some tart you've picked up in a pub.'

He'd held his hands up in mock surrender. 'Fine. Anything you say.'

It had stuck in her mind. Was it a compliment? Or a put-down? In a way, she knew what he meant. She liked quiet, soft clothes in colours that didn't quite have a name, like taupe and caramel, and she liked to emphasize her credentials with boxy horn-rimmed glasses at work. People don't mess with those sorts of glasses.

But sexy?

She could hear Daisy screaming. Billy had probably kidnapped her teddy and was hanging it from some dangerous part of the house.

'Stop that,' she shouted down the stairs. 'Or there'll be no sweets.' Tom would have waded down and walloped him, but Lily believed that was wrong. And who knew – perhaps Tom had been hit when he was a child, although he always denied it. Perhaps that was why Tom snapped and sniped and had turned into the man she couldn't stay married to. She didn't know. It was hard to understand how they'd found themselves divorcing when there'd been so much love to start with.

'No sweets,' she called, louder this time. 'No sweets if you don't stop that.'

Daisy's screams reached a pitch that demanded urgent investigation. Sometimes she had visions of Billy causing real, lasting damage, but she banished these. Tom always said that that was what brothers and sisters were like. Lily left the scarf as she hurried down to sort it out. As she took Daisy into her arms to comfort her, she saw Billy turn away, as if rejected. But she couldn't just put out her arms and cuddle him too. That would be as good as telling him it was OK to behave like that. He'd done wrong, and he had to realize that.

'You always pick on me,' he shrieked, kicking the door of each cupboard as he left Daisy's room. 'It's favouritism. It's girlism.'

She tried to ignore this. Don't reward bad behaviour with attention. That's what the childcare gurus said.

Sometimes she did wonder if everyone was right about Billy missing his father, and a pang of guilt about ending the marriage sliced through her, but what could you do? All she could say was that she loved her children and did her best.

By the time Tom had arrived, and they'd all piled into his car, and she and Tom had had their customary spats about tidiness and punctuality – oh, how the habits of a marriage survive months of separation, she thought — the Sunday morning traffic in London had built up. Everybody was going out somewhere, it seemed. The late spring sunshine baked the streets, and a transparent haze of petrol fumes hovered over the cars.

They arrived in Chiswick just as Cameron and Vicky's battered saloon, bought with a loan from Chris, drew up outside Chris's imposing red-brick mansion. Lily always thought that it would make an ideal home for a family, and that Chris must, deep down, have bought it believing and hoping that he would fill it with a wife and children. He, however, claimed to have recognized it as an excellent investment, often proclaiming that he found it essential to have so much space to himself. But there was something forlorn and disconnected about it, as if it had never been properly finished, and the odd touches left by successive girlfriends competed uneasily with each other and with the bare bachelor atmosphere.

Everybody tried to get in the hall at once, bumping into each other, kissing, and handing over bottles of wine, knapsacks with toys and a football, along with a tangled bunch of yellow and pink roses from Vicky and Cameron's tiny, abundant garden in Peckham.

'I'm Sarah.' Lily found herself looking into a fine-boned, tanned face, framed by blonde streaks.

'I'm Lily,' she replied. 'How lovely to meet you.'

'How sweet,' cried Sarah at Vicky. 'Real roses. What

a treat.' She held them at a distance. 'You are amazing, Vicky, that busy, busy job *and* Harley *and* growing your own roses. I don't know how you do it.' She bore the roses off and they weren't seen again.

Vicky bustled off, organizing the children. The pre-Raphaelite Madonna had turned into a woman, her pretty face settling prematurely into pouches and tendrils of hair flying outwards. But her customary slash of geranium-red lipstick and distinctive, voluptuous gusts of Fracas said that Vicky, like Maud before her, knew who she was.

'Now that the children are in the garden, I can say hello properly.' Vicky had reappeared. 'How heavenly to see you again.' She hugged Lily. 'Have you had a filthy journey over? I can't stand London, can you?'

Chris stepped forward to kiss her. 'Lily.'

He never used two words where one would do. And he'd lost weight, she noted. In fact, he looked almost gaunt. Maud's death, thought Lily. He's not sleeping. She recognized the dryness of tired skin, and the blue tinge under his eyes because she'd seen them on her own features in the mirror during the worst of the split.

'It's lovely to see you all.' She wished she could think of something cleverer to say. There was something imposing about Chris that always made her feel squeaky and foolish when she spoke to him. He was, as always, the epitome of rumpled cool, his open-necked shirt and dark, unshaven face contradicting the quiet wealth of his beautifully polished hand-made shoes. Tall and spare, he always seemed to look down on everyone.

'Come in here.' He commanded Lily into the kitchen where a young girl stood by a massive state-of-the-art kitchen range. That was new, thought Lily, briefly distracted. There'd only been an ordinary cooker there before.

Lily was astonished. 'Natasha!' Chris's daughter by the Swedish Ingrid. She remembered her as a charming child with braces and a ponytail, who visited Chris intermittently. She held out her arms. 'My God! You're so grown-up. I expect you get bored of people telling you that.'

Natasha approached her cautiously and gave her a tentative kiss, blushing. 'I am seventeen, now.' She had a trace of a Swedish accent. 'I was very pleased when they said you would be here.'

'Well, I'm thrilled to see you.' Lily stood back, taking in the elfin legs and arms and the slender neck, topped with smooth shiny blonde hair tied tightly back, and a tiny white T-shirt showing a flash of brown tummy. Natasha was an inch or so taller than she was, and had Chris's long oval face and striking cheekbones, along with the deep cleft chin that Lily had seen in Bertie Devereaux's photographs and on the faces of both Chris and Cameron. It was strange, seeing that genetic distinction passed down so exactly to a distant girl who'd been brought up in Sweden. In her own family, Daisy had the Devereaux chin, although it had skipped Tom and Billy. 'I can't get over you,' she told Natasha. 'You're so beautiful.' Her face predicted how Daisy might look when she grew up, although Lily knew that the same combinations of features, thrown together in a fractionally different way, could often be strikingly less successful.

Natasha blushed again. 'And how is little Billy? And Daisy?'

'He's ten now, and an absolute fiend at the moment. And Daisy's eight and still a darling. They'll both be delighted to see you. They're all in the garden.'

When Natasha had left the room, she turned to Chris. 'I didn't know Tash would be here.'

'Ingrid sent her over to me because she'd fallen in with a bad crowd in Sweden. It's not exactly convenient.'

'Hello, everybody!' As they returned to the hall, a long shadow appeared in the doorway, and there, aided by a walking stick, was Dora Savage, in one of her well-worn Indian hippy skirts and a baggy jumper she'd probably found in a charity shop, beaming at the prospect of a family gathering. She lived only three streets away from Chris, and Lily knew that she was an invaluable source of spare keys and plant watering for Chris, who, in turn, often dropped by to 'see that she was all right' and take round a bottle for them to share.

Tom and Cameron rushed to kiss Dora. She ruffled Cameron's hair affectionately. 'How do you stay so blond? Been dyeing it, eh?'

This was quite possible, but only Dora would have

dared ask. Dora adored him. So, according to the family legend, did everybody else, except possibly Chris, but Chris was the sort of man who thought that sniping was a form of affection.

'Where's that ridiculously named child of yours?' asked Dora. 'He'll be teased at school, you know.'

'No, he won't.' Cameron explained this every time he saw her. 'There aren't any Marys and Elizabeths any longer. Everyone's called Paris or Atticus these days.'

'Naming him after a motorcycle,' muttered Dora. 'Lucky you didn't have any more. You'd have named them after a Teasmade.'

'I'm sorry to tell you this,' said Cameron, 'but personally I haven't spotted a Teasmade since nineteen seventy-nine.'

Sarah directed them all into the sitting room. Lily needed no urging. From the moment she'd stepped into the house, she'd sensed change, a new brightness and sense of direction, and she suspected Sarah. Decorative changes were usually a good clue as to how deeply Chris's girlfriends had ensconced themselves, although most never ventured further than adding a few cushions, or prettying up the mantelpiece with a vase of flowers. They'd all had great hopes of one who'd painted the room green once, but the green had lasted longer than she had.

The green had gone. So had all trace of any other woman. The room hadn't been so much painted as remodelled into a 'space' in shades of taupe, cream and grey with blocks of seating curving round a massive coffee table. On either side of the fireplace, like sentries, were two chairs draped in bronze pleated Fortuny silk, and huge abstract paintings picked out the tones of the room.

'Oh!' gasped Vicky.

'It's amazing,' murmured Lily.

Sarah blushed. 'I met Chris at a party, and when he brought me back here after our first dinner together I convinced him that he really needed a proper designer to make the most of this. It's such a lovely big room, with wonderful windows. So I got him to take me on.'

Chris looked down at her affectionately, and, for the first time, Lily saw a couple developing in the way they interacted.

'Anyway,' she smiled, 'I have to admit that I had to keep coming up with new ideas to keep the project going because our relationship seemed to be staying rather platonic. I'd got to the point of suggesting he had the garden landscaped as well so that I could go on seeing him when he finally made his move.' She squeezed his arm, and he smiled again, obviously familiar with the story.

Yet Chris's smile was uneasy. 'I decided it would be cheaper to take her out to dinner again than agree to the landscaping. Although only marginally.'

Sarah giggled.

'Well,' said Cameron. 'You've certainly got him sorted.'

They edged towards the immaculate seating rather gingerly.

'Hey!' Cameron let out a shout of recognition at five books, propped so casually on the mantelpiece that you knew they had been arranged there purposely. 'Dad's books. In pride of place, no less.'

Chris glowered at him. 'Sarah likes the covers.'

'They're so now,' said Sarah. 'Retro paperbacks. Wonderful mid-tones. Those were the days they understood design.'

'A TV company rang me the other day. They're doing a documentary on sixties people and they want to include Dad.'

'Let's talk about it.' Chris's voice was flat. 'Later.'

Dora moved across to the mantelpiece and picked up the books. She had copies of these, somewhere in her attic. They were covered in rough papery card from the war-deprived fifties, in dull but chic colours of red, green or blue, with a stylized sketch of a woman on the front. She had an impossibly tiny waist, a mysterious hat tipped over to one side and she wore gloves. Bertie's female detective, Hermione St John Conroy.

The five St John Conroy books were a minor commercial success — although the critics sniffed that Bertie Devereaux had prostituted his talent — and he bought a little house in Chelsea with the proceeds. Chelsea was still cheap, although seedy, and Bertie and Maud needed to get out of their rented room in a bed-and-breakfast on the Cromwell Road because they now had a baby on the way.

They invited Dora, and Mr and Mrs Dawlish, which was a bit embarrassing, to dinner to celebrate, and opened a bottle of wine. Dora had never met anyone who drank wine before.

Although there were only five of them, it was the most formal event Dora had ever been invited to. Maud and Bertie's little Chelsea house was a typical London terrace, narrow and pretty, with a light blue front door and full-length first-floor windows set with elaborate curlicue railings. Inside it had a fragile staircase up to the small but elegant drawing room and down to a dark basement kitchen. There were two rooms on every other floor culminating in a low-beamed, irregular-shaped nursery in the attic for the baby to come. Maud was transparently proud of her new home.

'It's all a bit empty, I'm afraid. We only had enough money to buy the bed and the dining table and then, do you know what Bertie did? He bought a television set instead of a kitchen table. So I have to roll the pastry on a board over the bath.'

Bertie's office took pride of place, in the big front room on the ground floor and behind it, in something the size of a box room, was their 'dining room', with a dumb-waiter on a pulley and a hatch, so that food could be rattled up from the dank kitchen below. This reduced Maud to fits of giggles, and the four courses – consommé, sole Véronique, boeuf bourguignon and crème caramel – kept getting stuck. Bertie and Mr Dawlish spent nearly three-quarters of an hour with their heads in the hatch, shouting instructions and wiggling the fraying ropes.

They finally sat down to cooling food.

'This is delicious, Maud.'

Maud glowed at the compliment and murmured something about Elizabeth David.

'I'm a Constance Spry woman myself,' said Christabel Dawlish. 'That chicken dish she did for the Coronation has become my stand-by. It's a bit difficult to get curry powder sometimes, but I've got a little man who usually stocks some if you ever need it.'

'We watched the Coronation on television,' said Bertie, unable to resist showing off.

'As the crown went on her head, the sunlight caught a diamond,' breathed Maud. 'I really felt as if life was going to be different now. Better. A new era.'

'You noodle,' muttered Bertie, affectionately.

'One of my father's neighbours made his own set,' ventured Dora, 'with bits of old air-force radar. And copper tubing on the roof for an aerial.'

They looked at her in amazement.

'Good Lord. Did it work?' David Dawlish wiped his mouth with a napkin.

'Sort of,' admitted Dora. 'We had to squeeze our eyes up, and it's in lots of shades of green, but we could just about make out what was going on.'

'I'm not sure about TV myself. I don't think

anything will quite manage to reproduce the excite-ment of the theatre. It's just not the same.'

'I don't want things to be the same,' declared Bertie. 'We're the New Elizabethans.'

Maud gazed at him with adoration. 'Darling. It is awfully common to have a TV, though, you must admit. Do you think we could perhaps cover it with a tablecloth or surround it with bookshelves?'

'The Countess of Carlisle had a cabinet built for hers. You'd never know it was there,' added Christabel.

Bertie looked at Maud indulgently. 'Darling Lady Maud, you've *married* a common man. If I hear any more about covering up television sets, I shall demand sauce bottles on the table. And go out for my pint after supper every night.'

Maud giggled. 'Oh, Bertie. You are appalling.'

They kissed.

Dora felt like an intruder eavesdropping on their happiness. David Dawlish cleared his throat. 'What do you think about these atom bomb tests, Bertie?'

Bertie tore his eyes away from Maud. 'Atom bomb tests? They're a disaster! Did you read my letter to *The Times* the other day?'

'Do you think so? Well . . .' The conversation got going on more general terms again. Dora looked from one to the other and listened. Her parents never discussed food, or the theatre, or books, and believed what the Government said about atom bomb tests. Bertie's letter to *The Times* had been published, and, Dora gathered from Maud, who was rather vague about it, another newspaper had rung up and asked him to write an article based on it. Bertie, she told Dora, was delighted to be paid to inflict his opinions on everyone ('So much more exciting than just having silly little me as an audience,' she'd added wickedly).

When Maud flashed a conspiratorial look at Dora and Mrs Dawlish at the end of the meal, and suggested that they go upstairs to 'powder their noses', Dora flushed at the suggestion. But Mrs Dawlish obviously thought it quite normal and they left the men pushing a decanter of port at each other. Dora, feeling gauche and uncertain, remembered that these were dinner-party manners, so far only experienced through the pages of a country-house detective story. Upstairs, Maud perched on the edge of a double bed in a tiny bedroom, chatting happily, while they took it in turns to use what Dora had just learnt to avoid calling 'the toilet'.

Dora was mortified, again. She had never seen a double bed before, and there was something unnervingly sensual about the thought of so much comfort, and what two people might do if they brushed up against each other every night. Married couples in films always had twin beds, as did her parents. Yet Bertie lay in this bed every night with Maud. This, more than the wedding photograph and Maud's now almost full-term pregnancy, brought home to her that although he seemed, when he was talking to you, to be uniquely yours, Bertie belonged to this quiet, confident, fragile woman tapping her delicate high-heeled foot on the bare boards of their bedroom floor. Dora shivered, like a cat shut out in the cold.

'Dora! You're cold. I'm so sorry,' said Maud. 'One of the beastly things about being preggers is that you're always boiling hot, and forget your poor guests. Here, have this.' And out of her drawer, she pulled a silky, soft cashmere stole, in a pearly beige, and wrapped it around Dora. 'Keep it. It suits you so much better than it does me. I look washed out in pale colours.'

It was the most luxurious object she'd ever handled, let alone owned. As Maud waved away her protests, Dora caught sight of a luminous new presence in the round swing mirror on the dressing table. A woman as elegant as the one Bertie had foretold the first time they met.

Maud squirted a jet of Jicky behind her ears and on her porcelain-white throat, and handed it to her. 'Dora?'

And Dora descended, with Maud and Mrs Dawlish, in a cloud of extravagance, to the miniature 'drawing room', an everlasting loyalty to Maud, as well as to Bertie, beating in her heart. This new, colourful world, with its strange, sensuous scents and flavours, was as exciting and stimulating as the foreign countries she longed to visit.

Back in Chiswick, in the twenty-first century, Dora

wrenched herself away from her memories, and searched the immaculate sitting room for a seat that would be both comfortable to sit in and easy to get out of.

Vicky perched on the edge of a block of pale cream, and Lily headed towards one of the bronze-draped chairs.

'Won't the fabric flatten out if I sit on it?' she asked anxiously.

Sarah smiled but there was a flinty look in her eyes. 'Sit on those chairs? I'd kill anyone who tried.' She wasn't entirely joking. 'Now, drinks, everybody. What would you like?' She took the orders and disappeared with Chris.

Lily squeezed up beside Vicky on the endless sofa, feeling as if they were waiting in a very luxurious airport lounge.

'I don't want to be wicked,' she whispered to her former sister-in-law, 'but I'd love to know how far she's got in the rest of the house.'

'I think wickedness is essential,' Vicky murmured back. 'Let's both go upstairs to the loo and have a poke around. I'll bet you a fiver that the master bedroom is draped in swathes of cream, with marble in the en suite.'

Lily narrowed her eyes as she checked the room again. 'Nope. Not drapes. Understated off-white Japanesey, very functional. And a prison-lavatory loo next to a vast limestone shower.'

'You're on.' They giggled.

'You'll never guess,' whispered Vicky as they scuttled upstairs, after begging permission from Chris and Sarah. 'Poor Chris isn't allowed to have any of Maud's things. When we went to clear her house out, Sarah came too, and put the kibosh on Chris taking almost anything. It's practically all gone to us and Tom.'

'Perhaps Chris thought that you two needed more . . .' Lily trailed off. Best not to get involved.

'It's as if Maud wasn't good enough for Sarah in some way, don't you think?'

'Well, not necessarily.' Lily tried to soothe her. 'It's just that Sarah specializes in interior design and probably doesn't feel emotionally about furniture the way most of us do. You know, magazines always advise not hanging on to things just because—'

'The only thing they kept,' said Vicky indignantly, 'is that wonderful portrait of Maud in a backless evening gown. I mean, it's the best painting in the house. Typical of them to pick that one.'

'Oh . . .' Lily tried to think of something emollient to say, but Vicky was in full taking-sides mode, and was likely to interpret any defence of Chris and Sarah as an attack on herself.

Fortunately, Vicky changed the subject. 'What's your news? I'm sorry to hear you didn't get the job in the end.'

'Don't be,' said Lily. 'It was my decision. I'm going to take the summer off. Rethink my life. Start applying for jobs again in the autumn. It's very exciting.'

In fact, she felt disorientated and insecure, as if nothing fitted her any more. It was an uneasy feeling, but occasionally, like an unexpected ray of sunshine on a drizzly day, she glimpsed a challenge. An adventure. A chance to start again.

'And what about men? Are you fighting them off? Are you a gay divorcee or lonely single mum?'

'Neither,' admitted Lily. 'Hectic during the day. A bit quiet in the evenings.' This was as far as she was prepared to go. Nobody wanted to know about unhappiness, and, besides, getting the divorce going had been her choice. Tom had tried quite hard to change her mind. 'I'm rather dreading the hols though,' she added. 'Billy really needs a bit more space. He's like a caged beast in our tiny little house and garden, much as I love it all. Still, there's a decent park not too far away.' Her heart sank at the thought of marshalling the children out to the park, and sitting there supervising them for hours while they played amongst the empty crisp packets and discarded syringes. There was no question of leaving them there alone, not these days, when ten-year-olds were being stabbed for their mobiles. 'He needs me to let him off the leash a bit now, but I really can't. Not in my part of town.'

'Not anywhere these days,' said Vicky. 'Those little girls who were killed last year, they were together in the most peaceful country village imaginable. That's what scares me. I've always thought that if there were two together, in a quiet place, they'd be safe.

Now I don't think there's such a thing any more.'

They gazed at each other, each momentarily terrified for their children.

'But you can't think like that,' said Lily.

'No. Of course not. Aha! I owe you five pounds, I think.'

The bedroom was, indeed, modern and simple, reminding them both of a glossy book about modern Japan. 'Suede walls, though,' murmured Vicky, touching them reverently. 'Chris must be doing well.'

'Or he's terribly in love and can't refuse her anything,' added Lily, wondering why, in that case, he had shadows under his eyes. 'Oh, look, we're quits. Marble in the en suite.'

'Phew,' said Vicky. 'Cos I haven't got a fiver.'

'Things not too good at the moment?'

Vicky sighed. 'Oh, the boiler burst this month, and the car needed a new gearbox – remember we bought it second-hand when I started working again? That was six years ago, so it's pretty clapped out – and all on one income . . .'

'Nothing's working out for Cameron?' Lily hardly liked to ask. Cameron had principles and refused to do anything he didn't 'believe in', like photography for catalogues or cheesy wedding shots.

'Well, as a matter of fact, he has got a chance of a new exhibition. Very avant garde. In the Barbican. But he's—' She broke off as Sarah came into the room. 'You've transformed this.'

Sarah seemed pleased. 'Look, home cinema.' She pressed a button and a screen slid down over the window opposite the bed.

'Crikey,' said Vicky. 'Fantastic.'

As the screen slid up again, Lily saw Billy and Harley kicking a ball around the garden. Billy worshipped his cousin and was sometimes much calmer when he was around. Harley had that effect on people. Even when Vicky said things like: 'We're not sure whether to try for the music scholarship or just to keep it simple and go for a straight academic one,' nobody seemed to be tempted to stick their fingers down their throats.

'How's Cameron? About Maud?' asked Lily.

Vicky shrugged. 'OK, I think. He says that when his father died, the most terrible thing was his mother's grief, and they all had to try to keep her going and make her happy again. But her death isn't the same. They can just mourn without any complications, and, also, she was nearly eighty, so there isn't the same sense of a life unfulfilled.'

'What exactly happened when Bertie Devereaux died?' asked Sarah. 'Chris won't talk about it.'

Vicky looked vague. 'Cameron was quite young at the time, only six. So I don't think he really knows much about it. But it was a fall at the Boathouse. Although he'd been ill beforehand, apparently.'

'Oh, well.' Sarah's breezy tone categorized sudden death at much the same level of inconvenience as builders who installed the wrong kind

70

of marble. 'I came up to say that lunch was ready.'

'We'll be right down,' promised Lily, disappearing into the bathroom.

Before they went downstairs, Vicky put a hand on her arm. 'Chris is obviously really serious about her. If she's been allowed to do all this to the house.'

'Mm. She seems nice, though, don't you think?' Lily tried to reassure Vicky.

'Oh, I'm sure she's wonderful.' Vicky looked doubtful. 'But everything's so glossy and unreal. She's obviously very superficial.'

'I'm sure she's less superficial when you get to know her better.' Lily tested the water with a sense of wickedness. 'As a sister-in-law, for instance?'

Vicky squeezed her arm. 'I'd rather have you.'

And Lily felt the warm, protective umbrella of the Devereauxs spread reassuringly over her.

'Don't you think it's quite significant, though?' Vicky spoke in a whisper. 'As soon as Maud dies, Chris is suddenly able to make a proper commitment?'

'Mm.' Lily wasn't sure how much she believed in unconscious motivation and psychological theory. 'He's had serious girlfriends before.'

'Not like this. Take my word for it. Not like this.' And Vicky sailed downstairs with the confidence of someone who knew Chris better than anyone else.

6

Chris's dining room was unchanged and still smelt of old books and polished wood. Lily was reassured. This room was, she thought, the essence of Chris: walls and walls of books, a nice old table that had been handed down from the family house in Chelsea, and a big battered armchair, squeezed in by the fire.

The family automatically settled into its usual pattern of seating at the table: Chris at the head, Cameron as far down the table as possible with Vicky beside him and Tom in the middle on the other side. Vicky usually sat herself between Cameron and Harley, as if to protect herself from the barbs of Devereaux jokes, but Sarah had sent the children into the television room with pizzas.

Sarah laid bowls of salads on the table. 'Just help yourselves.'

'Yummy, Chris,' said Vicky. 'Just like being in a restaurant.'

'Heaven to have food someone else has cooked,' added Lily.

Cameron looked at his plate in amusement. 'Bit different from your usual bags of takeaway curry.'

'So,' said Sarah, brightly, when everyone sat down. 'Are any of you going anywhere interesting on holiday this year?'

There was a silence around the table. Poor Sarah, thought Lily. Of all the polite conversational openers she could have chosen, this was one of the worst. Dora had always gone to Maud during the summer. Heaven knew what she would do now. With things so up in the air between herself and Tom, planning was impossible; anyway, since Tom had half moved out and was paying rent, she wasn't sure they could afford a holiday. And it didn't sound as if Vicky and Cameron had money to spare either.

'What about you, Sarah?' she asked.

'We thought perhaps St Barts.'

The entire family registered the 'we', silently communicating without so much as a detectable flicker of recognition between them.

'Of course, the Caribbean's got very tatty these days,' she prattled on, 'but St Barts is still smart, and there's a new hotel I'd rather like to see, which has been described as "Nantucket-meets-St Tropez". Or we might do an eco-lodge in Africa. Everybody's talking about them.'

'What about the Boathouse?' Dora seemed anxious. 'Now that Maud's dead, I'd have thought you'd be getting on with repairing it.'

'Well, that's what we're here today to decide,' said Chris.

Lily hid a smile. If past family decisions were anything to go by, they were here today to be told what Chris wanted to do, and rubber-stamp it.

Sarah laughed. 'When Chris first told me about it, I instantly thought I'd never ever, ever want to spend my holidays freezing in a ramshackle hut anywhere between Ramsgate and Land's End. But the English seaside has got quite fashionable recently, especially if it's difficult to get there. Motorways and airports are really rather for the hoi polloi these days, don't you think?'

Nobody knew how to respond to this statement. The thought that Sarah might be turning her ice-blue eyes on to the Boathouse was alarming, not to mention the prospect of it being converted in Nantucket-meets-Ramsgate style.

'Oh, I think we should sell,' replied Chris. 'With today's fashion – which will be very short-lived, I can assure you, and the downturn is just around the corner – for battered old beach huts, it'll fetch a premium and I know you all need the money. We could get up to about half a million, which is too good to pass up when you think of all the repairs it needs. I mean, its real value is nothing like that.'

Dora's powdery face collapsed like a spent balloon. 'The Devereauxs sell the Boathouse? My dears, surely not? Wherever your father is' – she turned her face up to the ceiling as if looking for heaven – 'it would break his heart.'

'My father didn't believe in life after death,' Chris

informed her crisply. 'And I have no intention of having any sensible decision dictated by the purported wishes of a pile of ash.'

Two spots of colour burnt on Dora's face.

Lily, Sarah and Tom looked at each other.

'Chris,' reproved Cameron.

'I know. I know. I apologize, Dora.' He filled his glass again and checked everyone else's. They were all still full, except for Cameron's, so he pushed the bottle down the table towards him. 'But, really, we can't allow sentiment to overrule common sense.'

Lily wished that Tom would say something. Well, if he wouldn't, she would.

'I know it's none of my business, but wouldn't it be better to have the Boathouse than the money?'

Chris turned a furious gaze on her, and Lily had to force herself to hold eye contact. She thought he might say that she should keep out of it.

He took a deep breath, as if with exaggerated patience. 'I don't think you quite understand what a responsibility it is. Not to mention a drain on expenses. We're all extremely busy, and some of you' – he looked at Cameron – 'are short of money.' He drained his glass. 'That is what the Boathouse needs. Time and money. Just what we haven't got.'

'Still,' said Tom. 'The Boathouse is part of our family. Part of our past.'

Chris looked exasperated. 'That's not a reason in itself for keeping it.'

'We should take a vote,' said Cameron. 'Majority decision. To sell or to keep. One for all, and all for one. Like families do.'

Chris stared at him. 'And what happens when the Boathouse costs more to maintain and repair than either of you have got? I get asked to step in. That's what always happens. And what I'm saying now is that I'm not prepared to do that for something that isn't essential.'

Tom's face darkened. 'I'm outraged by that statement, Chris. I've never asked you for money.'

Chris raised an eyebrow. 'Not since the deposit for your first flat, you mean?'

'That was fifteen years ago. And I paid that back!' Tom thumped his glass down.

'Can't you ever think about anything else except money?' asked Cameron. 'You're the most mercenary man I've ever met.'

'Mercenary or not, I'm a very useful source of cash for everybody round here, even if they do pay me back – eventually.' Chris shot a look at Cameron. 'At least most do. All I'm saying, which you would know if any of you read the newspapers occasionally, is that times are very tough in the building industry at the moment, and I don't want any new responsibilities. And while you lot may be thinking about idyllic sun-kissed barbecues and drinks on the jetty, I can see an open cheque book, pouring rain and endless responsibility. Places like the Boathouse can be a bottomless pit. Why do you think Mother closed it up in the first place?'

Sarah looked extremely worried, and the fine spider's web of lines round her pretty blue eyes deepened fractionally. 'Darling . . .'

'What?' Chris glared at her.

'Please try to be calm.'

'Calm?' shouted Chris. 'I'm perfectly calm. It's the rest of you that are getting your knickers in a twist. I'm just pointing out a few sensible facts. I'm sorry if some people find that disagreeable.'

'I think the Boathouse could be made to pay its way,' said Cameron. 'We could rent it out as a location for shoots and films. I could organize painting groups, or bird-watching holidays using it as a base. Vicky and I could sell up in Peckham and buy a cottage down there and manage it . . .'

'For fuck's sake,' said Chris, quite amiably. 'We need some practical, workable suggestions here. We haven't got time to waste on one of your mad schemes.'

Cameron flushed. 'What do you mean, mad schemes?'

'Come off it. The dotcom company that collapsed before it could be bought for millions. The buy-to-rent scheme that never worked and means you've now got a bigger mortgage than before. You just jump on whatever money-making bandwagon's currently being talked about without knowing the first thing about it.'

'You can hardly say I know nothing about locations for photography.' Cameron was, as usual, just about managing to keep his temper.

'No, but you know nothing about business.' Chris dismissed him.

'I've learnt from the dotcom company and the buy-to-rent. You'd be surprised at how much I know about business now—'

'I would.' Chris was crisp.

'I think, Cameron' – Tom spoke gently – 'that what we really want from the Boathouse is an ordinary family base for holidays. To give our children what we had.'

'Yes, well,' said Chris. 'It would be a darn sight cheaper to get a package holiday in Mallorca out of a brochure every year, and the weather would be better. Vicky, what do you think about all this?'

Chris was an expert in divide and rule.

Vicky coughed. 'Well—'

'You want to get away from smog and crime. You said so on the way here today,' interrupted Cameron. 'I've told you. If we sold Peckham we could buy the whole Boathouse off Chris and he wouldn't need to worry about it.'

Vicky shot him an agonized look. 'I do quite want to get away from Peckham but Harley has got a lot of friends there, and I'm not really sure about the schools near the Boathouse and I don't really want to live in—'

'A rickety shack on the edge of a windswept cabbage field,' Chris completed her sentence victoriously.

'Well, there is my job. I couldn't possibly commute.'

'They don't have cabbages in Devon. Or at least not near the Boathouse,' muttered Cameron. 'And you could get a job like that anywhere.'

Vicky was obviously terrified that he'd pack them all up in the middle of the night and drive their ancient, battered car down to the middle of nowhere. Cameron, his sunglasses rose-tinted with childhood memories, obviously regarded it as heaven on earth.

'I think we should all think about it,' said Tom.

'Yes,' said Vicky. 'There's no hurry, is there?'

'What about this TV programme *Voices of the Sixties*?' Cameron raised the next subject.

'Tell them to get stuffed.' Chris poured himself another glass of wine. Didn't he ever get drunk, wondered Lily? He never showed it.

'I'd like some publicity for my next exhibition,' Cameron pointed out. 'It can't do me any harm to be labelled the photographer son of the charismatic columnist and author Bertie Devereaux.'

Chris glared at him for a few seconds and shrugged. 'Oh, well. You're too young to know what really happened, which is something. You know what they say, if you can remember the sixties, you weren't there.'

'I wasn't,' said Cameron. 'Anyway, I don't need to remember it. Dad talked about it all enough.'

Chris looked at Tom, who raised his hands in agreement. 'I don't mind. I don't see how even Cameron can drop us in it. I mean, it's not as if there were any great secrets.'

Lily saw Chris and Dora exchange glances.

'Just don't talk about the Boathouse,' ordered Chris. 'He wouldn't have wanted that.'

For a moment she saw the light of mischief in Cameron's eyes and thought he might say that he had no intention of having anything dictated by the wishes of a pile of ashes, but, flashing a glance at Chris's face, he obviously didn't quite dare.

Sarah brought in the next course, and, after a polite, stilted exchange about who had enough cream, and whether anyone wanted the sugar, there was another silence.

'So what *are* you doing this summer, Vicky?' asked Sarah, obviously doing her best to start the conversation again.

'Well,' said Vicky. 'Our au pair has just announced that she has to go back to Croatia for two months for some complicated family reason. She says she'll come back, but what do I do? It's impossible to get a good temporary one, and I don't want to lose her. Now, normally, Cameron could take over, at least for the school holidays, but he's got this exhibition coming up . . .'

'It's very important,' said Cameron in a warning tone, as if they'd gone over this time and time again. 'I can't possibly turn it down.'

'No, of course not.' There was a note of exaggerated patience in Vicky's voice. 'But I've got meetings in Paris, Frankfurt, Tokyo and Mumbai. Just for starters. So what are we to do with Harley? Maud, obviously, is no longer around . . .'

Cameron shrugged. 'We'll manage.'

'Manage?' hissed Vicky. 'Have you rung the agencies and seen how much those temporary nannies cost? Well, have you? Or are you expecting me to wave my magic wand as usual?'

Cameron leant back in his chair. 'Our domestic arrangements are hardly a suitable topic for Sunday lunch. We must be boring the others.'

'I'll have him,' said Lily, her heart swelling with the prospect of being able to help. 'I've decided to take the summer off.'

They stared at her with amazement.

'The sell-off plus a bit of a redundancy payment gives me a six-month breathing space,' she added.

Sarah looked appalled. 'Redundant? I'm terribly sorry.'

'Having extra children is no problem. Billy and Daisy need someone to play with.'

'Are you sure?' asked Vicky. 'All three of them, all day, in your tiny house in the middle of London – it's gorgeous, of course, but it is small – it's absolutely sweet of you to offer, but—'

'I was thinking I might take a cottage in the country. Or France, perhaps. Get away from everything.'

'I know,' said Tom. 'Lily could have the Boathouse for the summer. While we all decide what to do with it.' His eyes met hers, and she realized, with a pang, that he knew her very, very well. 'Perhaps I could come down for the odd weekend and take over,' he added.

'And we could do a couple of the weeks – maybe at the end?' suggested Cameron. 'Free you up to get away for a bit?'

The support they were all willing to give, and the warmth with which it was offered, reassured Lily that she was doing exactly the right thing. The Boathouse had been at the heart of the Devereaux family for years. Now, she, Lily, would be the one to restore it to its former glory.

'I could pop down and see what it would cost to renovate,' offered Sarah. 'I can get fabric at cost.'

Only Dora and Chris were silent.

'Well?' Tom looked at his elder brother. 'OK by you?'

'Provided that it's structurally sound, I don't suppose I can say no. I seem to be outvoted.'

Cameron began to clear the plates with Sarah. 'I'll do the washing-up, Sarah.'

'Would you, Cameron? That's really sweet of you.' She took an armful of glasses into the next room, and, once she had gone out, Cameron muttered, 'I know my place.'

Vicky placed a sympathetic hand on Lily's. 'Now you've got time to tell me everything about this awful buy-out, love. It must have been a terrible shock . . .'

Chris picked up his glass and the bottle, and went into the other room.

7

Dora kissed them all goodbye and walked home. The day, and Lily's plan to spend the summer at the Boathouse, had stirred up memories that made her heart race in an uneven, jittery way. It was an uncomfortable feeling: a mixture of apprehension and excitement, a fizz distilled from a peculiarly personal cocktail of regret, reminiscence and happiness. Looking back was a bittersweet addiction, and Dora had tried not to indulge herself during the lonely days since Maud's death.

She couldn't rest; she wasn't tired. The house felt suffocating. She decided to walk down to the river. The sight of water had always soothed her – it was one of the things she missed about the Boathouse. At one point, she had wondered whether she could sell her house in Chiswick and buy it herself, and then she had thought about old legs trying to stumble through the neglected undergrowth or totter down the impossibly steep steps and what would happen if she became ill without neighbours, and realized that age had thrown its noose over her just as youth had when she first went to work. It was Bertie and Maud who had freed her.

*

One day, a few years after Maud and Bertie moved to Chelsea, Dora answered her telephone.

'Mr Dawlish's office.'

'It's Bertie Devereaux here.'

Dora looked up at the door. 'Mr Dawlish is in with Sir Cyril.' She braced herself for a battle. 'He really *can't* be disturbed. I'll give him a message, shall I?'

'No, it's you I wanted to talk to. Will you have lunch with me?'

Dora was silent. She had discovered that there was one category of man who didn't mind tall girls, or girls with glasses, opinions or straight gingery-brown hair. Married men. She had learnt this lesson painfully, never initially thinking that the nice young men who took her to tea at the Lyons Corner House, or fumbled with her stocking tops at the cinema, had anything in mind other than a conventional courtship. She had once been to a hotel with one of them. It had been sordid, and it hurt, and she had hated the floppy rubber thing. The sense of shame had stained the next few months. No, she'd thought. This isn't right. I won't ever do this again. Even if I'm never loved any other way.

'I want to offer you a job.' Bertie spoke into the silence. 'I want you to come and be my secretary. Now that I've got a proper office at home, I need proper help. My work is changing. The newspaper stuff is taking over. I really feel I can make a difference, but I can't do it on my own. We would call you my personal assistant.'

Dora hesitated again.

'I need you,' he repeated. 'To be fierce with me. Maud hasn't got time any longer. Not with Chris only three and Tom still a baby. She's expecting again.'

Dora was worried. 'Isn't that rather soon after Tom?'

'I think so. That's why we need you.'

Mr Dawlish – or David, as she later came to call him in the more relaxed sixties – cautioned her against it. 'Look, I don't want to lose you, but it's more than that. Here you've got other young girls of your age around you, and young men. It's more of a life for you. And if you stay here, I think you'll be an editor eventually,' he told her. 'I believe that there will be more women working in this profession as editors, not just as secretaries, and I intend to encourage that. You're more talented than most of the men who work here. You could go far.'

'Would there be more money if I stayed?'

He hesitated. 'No. Not at first. You see, we obviously can't pay women as much as we pay men, because the men are supporting, or will support, families. And heaven knows, we can't afford to pay them much. But, in the long run, I'm sure you'd earn more. And it would be more satisfying.'

But Bertie had offered her a pay rise, and Dora was tired of worrying about money. Her sister, Betty, had married a bank clerk, and lived in Morden, and her mother had rented out Betty's room. Things were tight in the Savage family, and the South London district that her mother had been brought up in, once so proudly middle class, with its grand town houses and neo-Gothic church spires, was deteriorating into a scruffy morass of bedsits, landladies and poverty. They had three lodgers now, and Dora had moved into the room that had once been the dining room.

And she'd been at work long enough for all her original friends to have got married. They always left Dawlish & Sons a week before their weddings, and then disappeared for ever into some protected world at the end of a railway line. Starting over again with younger girls was beginning to depress her, and she needed a new challenge.

'Oh, well,' said Mr Dawlish, when she finally handed him her letter of resignation. 'I don't suppose it matters. You'll get married soon, I expect.'

Dora hoped he was right. So she took the bus to Chelsea instead of the tram to the City, and, on sunny days, walked down along the railway line, past the Battersea Dogs Home, through the park, over the bridge and along the Embankment, breathing in the changing of the seasons: the pale green new leaves followed by the thick luxuriant midsummer growth and then the reds and bronzes of autumn drifting down around her feet. As the sun glinted on the brown water and picked out the fairground frills of Albert Bridge ahead of her, her heart would lift, because although Bertie was difficult, demanding and unreasonable, he was also stimulating, funny and, occasionally, gentle and thoughtful.

Maud's pregnancy ended after six months, with a frail baby girl who died after a few moments of life, and was disposed of, as was usual, with the hospital waste. Maud hovered between life and death for a few days, haemorrhaging badly, and the doctor told her that it would be dangerous for her to have another baby.

'She never had a name,' Maud said once, chopping onions. 'You want to do everything you can for your children, don't you, and I didn't even give her a name.' Another time, she looked up from her book and said, as if from a long way away: 'I saw her face, just for a moment, you know. She was like a little china doll, with a tiny rosebud mouth. But they wouldn't let me hold her. They said it was better that way. They said I shouldn't dwell on it. She was just a miscarriage, you know, not a proper baby. That's what they said, anyway. But they wouldn't look at me. Nobody ever looked at me in that hospital.'

Otherwise the episode was never discussed, as far as Dora could see. Bertie closed the door of his office because the newspaper articles had now turned into columns. He wrote, passionately, about the death of the class system, women's rights, and the importance of nuclear disarmament, and claimed that it was hard to concentrate above the noise of the boys. Maud seemed detached, and often read a book or sat in a chair, her head drooping on her long neck like a rose beaten down by a storm, gazing at her hands, while Christopher or Tom tugged at her sleeve. Christopher was never told that he'd briefly had a baby sister, because it was thought best to protect children from anything that they might not understand, and, anyway, would he care? Bertie and Maud thought not.

When Tom stretched out his chubby arms, dribbling his customary toothy, endearing smile, neither of his parents seemed to notice any more, and Christopher's dark eyes grew watchful and wary. There was a heaviness over the little house in Chelsea, and Dora detected a gap between Bertie and Maud that each chose to fill with her presence. She became, informally and without rancour, a kind of messenger between them.

8

For two months Lily's life was suspended between the past and the future as she turned her role in Dotcombomb over to the suits in Brentford, and went to a number of leaving parties, including her own.

But July came, in the end, the last week of school loomed up, and she prepared to say a final goodbye to the traffic, to the politics of the coffee machine, the noise and smells of the city, to being stacked like cattle next to virtual strangers in the tube so that she could smell their soap and what they'd eaten for supper the night before, and the endless round of taking children from A to B in gridlocked traffic because there was no space at home for them to amuse themselves. There was a permanent low-level aggression to the city, like the background hum of traffic, and she wondered if this, in itself, had infected Billy. If she could get him out, and away from it all, she might be able to find the real, lovable boy that she was sure lay underneath.

And after the nerve-stretching years of her marriage breaking down, she wanted peace, to recharge her batteries and renew her faith in life.

But on Monday evening the phone calls started.

*

The first was from Chris.

'Oh!' Lily was flustered. In more than a decade of marriage, Chris had never phoned her. She'd picked up the telephone twice or three times a week, with the feeling that she would be wasting his time if she tried polite conversation, and had passed the receiver straight over to Tom. Chris never bothered with niceties about weather, and merely looked disdainfully amused if she did, as if she were a pet performing some strange but unnecessary trick.

She rushed in to fill the silence he always left. 'We're all so excited about going down to the Boathouse.'

'That's what I wanted to talk about.'

Lily felt the cold grip of tension somewhere deep within her belly. She didn't think she had the strength to stand up to Chris on her own. 'I know you're not very keen, but it would be so wonderful to get the children out of town. I've been having awful problems with Billy, who really needs more space . . .' She ran out of breath, feeling foolish as usual.

'Yes,' he said. 'I can see that. But the Boathouse is no longer a suitable place to take children. Nobody has lived there, or even stayed overnight, for nearly thirty years.'

'I honestly don't mind camping.' She tried not to plead. Please, oh please, she begged fate, or the telephone line, as she twisted it over and over. 'After all, that's part of the fun of it.'

'I think you may find otherwise.'

'In that case' – Lily felt very brave – 'I shall come back. And you can say, "I told you so."'

There was another of his lengthy silences. 'All right, as you're obviously determined. But I have one condition.'

'Oh.' Lily found that her knees were slightly shaky. Lack of lunch, probably. Even Chris couldn't make her tremble.

'I insist that I go down there first, to check it out, and if I find that it's dangerous, or not suitable, that everyone respects my advice.'

Her heart sank. He would find something 'unsuitable' about it and her summer would be lost. She was determined to fight this in every way she could. 'Can I come with you?'

There was another pause. 'OK. If you have the time.'

'I can do any day this week,' she said, quickly, before he could take it back. 'I'm a free woman now.' She heard the sound of a big desk diary being flipped over.

'Thursday, then. I do have one meeting, but I can rearrange it. I'll pick you up at seven a.m.'

'Right. Good. The children can sleep over at . . .'

The silence reminded her that Chris was not in the slightest bit interested in what she would do with her children while checking out the Boathouse. 'See you then,' she concluded.

It was only when she found herself looking at a buzzing receiver that she realized he hadn't said goodbye – or had he?

She sighed. A long journey with Chris would be quite a challenge. Perhaps she could mug up about cricket in the meantime. Or the property market. They had to have something to talk about. There were family traditions to help her: Chris was supposed to be interested in cricket and current affairs, and conversation with him was like being on a programme on Radio 4. Cameron had sudden, violent, short-lived passions for new hobbies, but was generally more arty, much more of a commercial-radio-station person, or someone who lived in his own party-going bubble. 'I don't suppose Cameron has even noticed the war in the Middle East, too busy watching TV reality shows and staying up till four a.m.,' was the kind of thing that Chris would say, if the family conversation ranged on to politics. And Tom, well, there was Tom in the middle as usual, a sort of ten o'clock news man, she thought, with football and rugby highlights. The one to turn to for a solid, sensible opinion.

Just as she was flipping fish fingers on to the children's plates, Vicky called. Lily lodged the phone under her chin, hunching her body awkwardly to hold the receiver in place.

'Look, I'm still worried about you having three children on your hands for most of the summer.'

'Don't be. It'll be a doddle.'

'Well, if you're sure . . . it would make everything so much easier for me. Cameron's like a cat on a hot tin roof about this exhibition, and thinks he's finally going to make it, and my company are being simply horrible at the moment. My new boss hates working mothers, and is being utterly vile. I daren't take any extra time off, or even leave five minutes earlier.' Vicky, usually so calm and competent, sounded close to tears.

'Well, it would be wonderful if Cameron were successful.' Lily wasn't sure how people 'made it' taking photographs of fried eggs on mohair sweaters, tampons in glasses of wine or people's feet, all of which had featured in his last exhibition.

'Has Chris rung you?'

Lily admitted that he had, and told Vicky about Thursday.

'Rather you than me. Whatever will you talk about on the car journey?'

'I can't imagine. Let's hope that there aren't any roadworks, and that there's something good on Radio Four.'

'I have to say' – Vicky settled in for a good grumble – 'I do think he's being unreasonable about this Boathouse thing. When you think of all the money he has, you'd think he could just . . . Oh, well, I know I shouldn't say it, but it's what I think . . . He should just sign his share over to us if he doesn't want it. It's not as if he needs the money from selling it. He must have spent a fortune on installing home cinema and suede walls in his bedroom.'

'Well . . .' This thought had crossed Lily's mind,

too, but she'd rejected it as being both greedy and not her business. 'I suppose it is his money, and he has earned it, and just because he's got much more than the rest of us, that doesn't mean he should give it away.'

'Oh, I know. I never thought I'd be so grasping, but somehow, seeing that flash car, and Sarah queening it in that perfect room, it just seemed unfair. Don't listen to me, Lily, I realize I'm being horrid, but sometimes, at the end of a bad day, if you come home to debts and a husband who's spent the day photographing other people's rubbish bins to expose the rotten underbelly of suburban life, you can turn into a horrible person. At least I can. Quite hideously selfish.'

'I don't think you're selfish. Just frustrated. I don't suppose you could use the rest of the money you inherited from Maud to buy him out?'

'There wasn't anything. At least, only a tiny bit, and that's gone on the gearbox. Bertie Devereaux didn't believe in pensions, so Maud even had to mortgage the cottage. Could Tom buy Chris out of the Boathouse, do you suppose, so we could own it as one-third and two-thirds?'

'We're still talking about money. It's very difficult,' said Lily, feeling guilt, a familiar grey glutinous mass of unspecified unease, quiver and wobble deep down inside. If they weren't divorcing, perhaps Tom could buy Chris out, and secure the Boathouse for their own children, and for Cameron and Vicky. 'I don't think Tom can really make any decisions at the moment. It's just that splitting up cuts everything in half, however fair you both try to be. We're both a bit short at the moment.'

There was a silence, while Lily also tried to suppress the sharp spikes of anger that she had managed to bury even deeper down in her consciousness, where they couldn't harm anyone. Occasionally they jutted above the viscous, sticky guilt substance, but they were too painful to endure for any length of time. She preferred to suppress the images that filled her brain when they emerged, hating to remember what Tom, a loving father and husband, had done.

'You'd think,' said Vicky eventually, 'that even if Chris doesn't want anything to do with the Boathouse, he could just leave it all to us. Not give us his share or anything, but leave it there, forget about it and not take any responsibility, and let us do what we like. I mean, he really doesn't need the money, and he'd even profit from us maintaining it without involving him, if you see what I mean.'

'Funnily enough, I think he's more likely to give away his share than do that. He's so very much the responsible one in the family that I don't think he could begin to conceive of ignoring any part of that responsibility, let alone not paying his fair share of the costs.'

'Yes,' sighed Vicky. 'And very irritating it is, too. Cameron's beginning to get totally fed up with Chris treating him as the younger brother and bossing him around all the time. He doesn't respect anything Cameron does, although Cam has achieved things he hasn't, like having a wife and family.'

Lily was surprised at the depth of her resentment. Cameron had always seemed cheerfully agreeable to being the butt of Chris's jokes, and, after all, it was difficult to take what he did seriously. But she also knew that if Vicky had said anything to Chris, he would have replied: 'He may *have* a wife and family, but he doesn't *provide* for them, does he?'

The ensuing family row would have reverberated for months, with anxious phone calls from Maud, imploring everyone to apologize and be nice to each other again. Dora would have ferried Maud's messages to and from Chris and Cameron, too, and would have sat down with Vicky for tearful girlie chats. Even thinking about the complexity and energy of it made Lily feel quite exhausted. She had better damp this line of thought down before Vicky could get up a head of steam and start a campaign on Cameron's behalf.

'Well,' she said cautiously, 'Chris is what Chris is. I think he's carried a lot of family responsibility since Bertie died, and not being married has meant that he hasn't really transferred that to another family the way most people do. I don't think we can change that; we just have to accept him the way he is.'

'Well, I'm sick of it always being us who has to do the accepting. Why can't he do some accepting for a change?' Before Lily could reply, she added: 'God, I'm sorry to burden you with this. I love Chris, you know I do, and so does Cam. This is my hard day – even my hard year – talking, not me.'

'I know that. Look, you don't have to worry about the children this holidays, because I shall love having them, and I'm so excited about spending the summer at the Boathouse, so I get loads out of it, too. You can concentrate on sweetening your nasty boss – I can't think of anyone better at getting the good side out of people – and Cam can do a marvellous exhibition and become famous at last. It's going to be a good summer.'

'You're right.' She heard an exhale of relief in Vicky's voice. 'Thanks for letting me whinge.'

'Any time. It's so nice to know that you do whinge. Most of the time you seem like superwoman.'

'Ha! Chance'd be a fine thing.' But she put the phone down sounding closer to her usual cheerful self.

Phew, Lily thought. Thank God she'd managed to stamp on that one. A huge family row was the last thing they needed at the moment.

After she'd put down the phone she remembered an incident from childhood. She'd been squabbling with another girl over who should have the last toffee, and Lily had won. Later she'd heard the girl's mother tell her daughter, in a whisper, that only children were always selfish. 'They don't understand families. They don't know how to share.'

Ever since then she'd always been very careful to think about other people, and what they needed.

Dora phoned just as Lily had settled herself down on the big, baggy sofa to watch television.

'I wanted to say,' Dora said in her precise, old-fashioned way, 'that I believe you're doing exactly the right thing in taking the children down to the Boathouse. I know that Chris doesn't approve, but don't you worry, I'll sort him out. It's time the old place was opened up again.'

'Mm,' said Lily. 'Good.'

'But you must be careful. Now, if you need any help, or get a bit lonely, I'd be only too happy to come down for a day or two, so bear that in mind.'

Lily wondered if Dora was angling for an invitation, and, selfishly and guiltily, hoped not. She wanted solitude: not to be away from the children, who had simple needs, such as being fed, clothed, washed or comforted, but out of reach of the noisy complexity of adult emotion. She'd had too much of it recently, with the divorce and Maud's death, and there was something raw and suppurating inside her that needed to heal in silence.

'Thank you, Dora, that's very kind of you. Once I'm settled, I'll have a much clearer idea of what it's going to be like.'

'Now, you'll find it all a bit rough and ready—'

'Chris said it was uninhabitable.'

Dora chuckled. 'He's such an old woman. It'll be

fine. We always used to gather wood from the fields and the beach, and cook on a log fire. It makes food taste . . . oh, you've no idea how marvellously fresh. And I'm sure the septic tank still works.'

'Mm,' said Lily. Her only experience of a septic tank had been in a country farmhouse in France, where it hadn't worked, and the result had been decidedly whiffy. 'I expect Chris can explain all that.'

'Well, you could always take one of those portable thingies they have in caravans,' added Dora, brightly. 'I'm sure they're not very expensive. Really, when you think about it, it's a very simple life.'

'That's what I'm looking forward to.'

'Don't forget to get the tide tables from the Post Office.'

'Timetables?'

'No, tide,' explained Dora. 'You can only get there in a car at low tide. So you have to do your shopping by tide table. Otherwise you have to carry it all through the woods and down loads of steps.'

Lily vaguely remembered someone saying something about this, and suppressed the notion that she might miscalculate and get her car, complete with three children and a week's shopping, swept away by waves and drown everybody.

'And there are a few things you absolutely mustn't forget: mosquito repellent; perhaps some of those citrus candles would be nice, too; and matches, of course; and candles, because although there is electricity now, the wiring's very basic – positively lethal in fact; for goodness' sake, don't let the children switch on any lights — so you'll want to do most things by candlelight, although you might be best taking a fire extinguisher just in case. A fly swat for bigger insects, and some Anthisan for when you do get bitten . . . Suntan lotion, obviously, you can get very nasty burns on quite dull days . . . Now, do take the children some beach shoes because although they don't have jelly fish very often, well, not unless it's very hot, I do always worry about weaver fish, which really can be dangerous . . . mind you, I think that's the north coast isn't it, not the south-west?'

'Goodness, well, I—'

'And it was very peaceful when we went there in the sixties, but I do hope you don't find it overrun with asylum seekers. They've brought the drugs problem with them, you know, and some of those seaside towns have a worse time of it than London does.'

Lily wondered what Dora was really worried about. Chris, Tom and Cameron had survived there, hadn't they?

'You see,' said Dora. 'It's all so different there. You can't always tell how it will affect you. Being so alone.'

By the time she'd rung off, Lily felt under siege. Insects, poisonous fish that burrowed under the sand to conceal sharp spines and asylum seekers peddling drugs hadn't featured in her dreams of beach houses. Did mosquitoes breed in the sea, anyway? She didn't know much about it, but she was sure not. She had imagined long, hot days in her swimsuit, reading books, sometimes to or with the children, sometimes on her own while they played with sandcastles, not this life of constant alertness against the forces of nature. For a moment she wondered if she was doing the right thing.

Lily had just slipped into the hallucinogenic phase of sleep, where reality and dreams merge in a swirling maelstrom of images, when the phone rang again.

It was Tom, a slight slur in his voice, as if he was tired, or had been drinking.

'Hello?' Her voice, she knew, sounded sleepy and frightened.

'I'm sorry. I've woken you.' He knew how much she liked going to bed early.

She shook her head, and sat up, to wake herself up properly. 'No. It's fine. Is something wrong?'

'I just wanted to talk to you about the summer. Do you really want to go down alone with the children?'

'Yes,' she said, firmly, in case he was going to suggest coming with her.

'Can you manage all three of them?'

'Look, I don't know why everyone thinks three children are harder than two. Apart from eating more, they're built-in company for each other. Billy worships Harley, and heaven knows I could do with that kind of back-up with the way he is at the moment . . .' Too late she realized that she'd precipitated herself into a Billy conversation, which she didn't want to have late at night when she was half asleep. 'And Daisy loves him, too,' she added, hastily.

'What's wrong with Billy?'

'Nothing. He's just a bit highly strung at the moment. I think . . .' Damn. Now she'd manoeuvred herself into a position where she might have to say 'he misses you'. She tried to collect herself. 'I think he needs more exercise. More freedom. And he'll get that down at the Boathouse.'

'Should he see somebody, do you think?'

Lily couldn't explain why she found this suggestion so distasteful. 'No. I don't think so. Not yet. He's just growing up. It's difficult, being ten, and then eleven, and—'

'It'll be even more difficult when he's thirteen.'

'Well, let's worry about that then.' Lily knew she was sounding prickly and defensive, but she didn't want Tom in her life. Not in that way. She did not wish to sit in a psychiatrist's office with Tom, talking about what was wrong with Billy. You never knew where that kind of conversation would lead, and she couldn't cope with it all now. Maybe she'd be stronger after a peaceful summer, but until then she knew she was better off managing alone.

'OK. But I still don't think Vicky and Cameron ought to let you take responsibility for their child for most of the holidays. I think you'll find it too much.'

'I can cope. Vicky has been so kind to me. I feel I owe her, and everyone's going to help.'

She lay back on the pillows, knowing that the deep

sleep she'd been on the verge of embracing would escape her now, all night. At least the Boathouse didn't have a phone. She could hardly wait.

'Lily?'

'Yes?'

'I miss you.' There was a break in his voice. 'And I miss the children. Kissing them goodnight every night. Waking them up in the morning.'

Lily's heart twisted. Of course he would miss them. She could imagine his pain, and couldn't have borne it herself: to share only a fraction of their lives, having been everything to them since they were born.

'Tom.' There was a warning in her voice.

'I know. I know.' He sounded resigned, accepting. 'I'm sorry. I really am sorry. I want you to know that.'

Sorry for ringing her, or sorry for everything? Lily didn't reply. He knew that there were times when sorry would never be enough. She waited, and almost thought he'd rung off.

'Lily?' The words were hardly more than a whisper. 'Come back. Please come back. For better or worse, we all belong together.'

She replaced the receiver without answering, overwhelmed by sadness.

9

Dora replaced the telephone with the feeling that she had failed Lily.

Be careful, was what Dora had wanted to say. The Boathouse is very seductive, but it doesn't belong to you. It stands alone, facing the wind and the waves, and people can only borrow it.

She mounted the stairs heavily, her hip throbbing. She would clear out the cupboard in the spare room, and clear her head in the process. You fought so hard to acquire possessions – and wisdom, she thought – and then you got to the end of your life and discovered that you couldn't pass them on. Like these. She pulled a pair of old white PVC boots out of the back of the wardrobe, and sighed. They were too wrinkled, hardened and distorted to be of use to anyone. You couldn't display them or pass them on for recycling. You could only throw them out. She held them close to her for a moment, like a favourite cat.

Dora bought the boots in Bazaar, on the King's Road. While she was paying for them, two women banged their umbrellas on the window.

'You're destroying the fabric of society,' one shouted. 'Everything we fought for in the War.'

The sales assistant took no notice. 'It happens all the time,' she said to Dora. 'Not so much now, but when we first opened . . .' She rolled her eyes.

Dora had felt middle-aged all her adult life. When she'd looked in the mirror she'd seen a woman not so very different from her own mother, her shoes matching her bag, hat, gloves and coat. The carefully regimented accessories had defined her existence to the point of rigidity, as if the full uniform of life had had to be worn, complete with medals, at all times. Even Mr Dawlish at Dawlish & Sons had never taken his jacket off in the office, and he'd been the boss.

Now, suddenly, the boots spoke to her of freedom. They didn't have to match anything. They were cheap. They were fun, and fun, along with everything else, had been rationed for far too long. Those women with their umbrellas had been right, she thought. In these boots she could be different. Disobey rules. In her own mind, she called them her seven-league boots, because she felt she could make great, giant, life-changing strides in them. At the age of thirty-three, Dora Savage looked in the mirror, and, for the first time, saw a vibrant, irresponsible girl smiling back at her.

Bertie and Maud, of course, had introduced her to the art of enjoying herself. They drank. They smoked. They welcomed people they hardly knew into their house. Dora couldn't place the exact moment they'd put the quiet, sad, hard-working years behind them, but they now seemed to be at the heart of one big, everlasting party. Everyone was invited. All the time.

It was so unlike Dora's home in Stockwell. Her mother would have been mortified if anyone had dropped by without an invitation. She was permanently afraid that allowing someone through the door, except in the most carefully controlled conditions, would reveal that the Savage household wasn't good enough. And that then they would tell the neighbours, and so everybody would know. All her life, Cynthia Savage had prepared herself to be judged on the cleanliness of her floors and the dust on her mantelpiece. Shame – and its avoidance – had been the driving force behind her, and all the other women Dora had known since childhood. It was the guiding principle of their lives. Anything that deviated from the norm, whether it was untidy hair, a different length of skirt, debt or an illegitimate baby, could bring your entire world crashing down around you in a chorus of disapproval and condemnation. You could only stave it off by cleaning the house from top to bottom.

But Bertie and Maud weren't worried about what the neighbours might say. There was a house full of jazz musicians on one side, and an elderly but poverty-stricken (and fortunately deaf) old lady on the other. Sometimes the jazz musicians' friends accidentally turned up at Bertie and Maud's and were welcomed in, or the other way round. Occasionally the old lady, confused, was to be found at their front door, hand trembling, trying to insert a key that didn't fit. Bertie always gave her a whisky before helping her back. Nobody seemed to care very much. Certainly no one ever cleaned anything. Maud's privileged childhood had left her completely ignorant of domesticity.

Dora had once heard a story about the Queen Mother attending a funeral and being collared by a senile duchess who had asked her if her kitchen was 'upstairs or downstairs'. The Queen Mother had admitted that she had no idea.

Maud was like that. She was an intuitive and experimental cook, but didn't connect it with the washing-up in any way. And it would never have crossed anyone's mind to expect a man to get involved.

Bertie and Dora always stopped work for lunch, and Maud would experiment with recipes from the latest copy of *Vogue*. They'd open bottles of Mateus Rosé, and carry on drinking all afternoon.

Dora remembered them jumping into the Bentley en masse, along with anybody else who'd dropped in, to pick Christopher and Tom up from school.

'Look,' said Bertie, tightrope-walking along the edge of the pavement with his arms outstretched. 'I can walk in a straight line. That's all PC Plod needs to know.'

'That wasn't straight,' giggled Maud. 'You wobbled at the end. Twice.'

'I challenge any of you to do better. If you can, you can drive.'

'But I don't know how to drive,' said Maud and Dora, in unison.

'Never mind about that. I'll sit beside you.'

Dora pretended not to be able to walk in a straight line, and so, she suspected, did Maud. David Dawlish said he couldn't even try. 'Can't see shtraight, let alone walk. Must get back to the office.'

'Oh, no,' said Maud. 'Don't be so dull. We need you here.'

'Good afterble, consternoon,' said Bertie, with a mock bow at a passing policeman.

'Go carefully, sir.' They waved at him, as they piled in, and Bertie tooted a farewell.

Christopher was furious when they arrived at the school gates. 'For God's sake, Dad. Don't come and pick me up in the Bentley. I'll be torn apart.'

'Rubbish.' Bertie regarded himself, and his boys, as invulnerable.

The boys squeezed themselves into a car full of drunken grown-ups, sitting on laps. Chris's long legs were draped out of the window, as they accelerated along the King's Road, with Bertie driving erratically and muttering about the importance of 'research'. 'A good writer goes out into the streets for his material,' he'd say. 'Christ, she's pretty.'

'Brake, Bertie, brake!' screeched Maud. 'I don't want to be killed just because you've seen a girl you fancy.' When Bertie braked they were all thrown on top of each other, and they screamed with laughter again.

'Stop here,' said Maud. 'Wait for me. I've got to buy some avocados. You can do prawn cocktails with them. Without the prawns, that is.' She staggered off, doubled up with giggles, and emerged with her arms full of wonderful exotic ingredients. 'Dora can help.'

So Dora found herself tasting and trying all kinds of extraordinary dishes and experiences, and generating tremendous complaints about garlic and irregular hours from her parents, but consequently spending an inordinate amount of time at the sink instead of with Bertie and his manuscripts. But it was a small price to pay for having a life that was definitely very different from the measured, formal pace that had prevailed at Dawlish & Sons.

IO

Chris's car, a long, low ice-blue Mercedes, arrived at seven o'clock on Thursday morning. Lily slid sideways into the leather seats. It was like lying down. But at least there was the handbrake between them, and the dirty muddle of North London crowding in from outside the windows.

'How long will it take?' she asked, hearing herself, too late, sounding like a fractious child.

'Four hours, perhaps, if we're lucky. With the new roads. It used to take for ever when I was a child.'

'Although there are always roadworks.'

'There are, indeed, always roadworks.'

Well, he must be finding this conversation intellectually stimulating. She wondered whether to try him on politics, or the environment, or books, but she was tired. It was too early in the morning.

'So,' he said. 'Devon, eh? I'd imagined you taking off to Marrakesh. Or Beijing.'

Lily remembered, with a flush of pleasure, the girl she'd been, the one who believed in adventure, then suppressed her. 'I've been there.'

'I'd forgotten. You've been everywhere.'

'I didn't mean it like that. I just mean that I've been to most of the places I want to go. I don't want to travel any longer.' She hadn't realized that until the words were out of her mouth.

'Why not?' He sounded interested.

She tried to explain herself. 'I'm not sure that I can see the point. I don't think that I'll find what I'm looking for.'

'And what's that?' Chris interrogated, rather than asking questions.

'I don't know.' This was hopeless. She tried again. 'I don't think that it necessarily gets you anywhere. Or perhaps it did when I was younger, but now, now I wanted to go deep rather than far.' She slipped him a glance, and slid down her seat, pulling her collar up. 'Sorry. Sounds pretentious.'

'Go on.'

'Well, I've travelled a lot. Looking at places and meeting people is fine, interesting, all that, but I don't really know my own country. And if you don't know your own country I don't see how you can know yourself, which might be a cheesy way of putting it, and isn't exactly what I mean, but it's the closest I can get.

'Tom and I always took the children to France, or Spain or Greece, or even the States, and sometimes they had a great time and sometimes they didn't. I don't know what they'll remember of it all, or whether it adds up to anything more than mere fun. I certainly don't think they've become more international as a result, or that they know any more about French or Spanish culture. On the other hand, maybe fun is all you need. Maybe it helps if people in different nations feel good about each other because they've had two weeks of lying happily on each other's beaches. I don't know.

'But I wanted them to be somewhere different for long enough to get to know it properly. Sorry,' she repeated. 'This is a rambling collection of thoughts rather than a conversation.'

'It sounds to me as if you're on a mission to find yourself.'

'In Devon?' Lily smiled. 'The British Consul in Peru once told me that it infuriated her when she had to rescue British backpackers who'd had all their possessions stolen. They always told her they'd come to Peru to find themselves. "I don't know why they couldn't find themselves in the Lake District," she used to mutter. "It's a lovely place. There's no need to come all this way and cause everyone all this bother."'

Chris laughed. 'Perhaps you'll find yourself in a dusty cupboard in the Boathouse, but I wouldn't bet on it.'

'Oh, I'm not really after enlightenment. Just a break. Before I decide what to do next.' She regretted her flights of fancy. And what she hadn't wanted to say was that there was something at the Boathouse that she thought belonged to her, or at least to the children. Tom's past. Tom's glorious, wonderful, unbeatable past that she'd never managed to live up to. The perfect family life that she'd failed to create. It had been his highest accolade on holiday to say, 'Ah. This reminds me of the Boathouse.' And she'd look at a little boat puttering across the horizon of a Mediterranean bay or at the battered paint of an old French farmhouse and wonder what had triggered the thought.

She was going to see if she could find out, and then prove that she could do it better.

'What did you do exactly at that dotcom company?' asked Chris. 'I've never really understood.'

'I organized. I'm not trained for anything. I just organize. Which is fine, but makes it a bit difficult when you're looking for something else.'

'I should have thought most companies would love an organizer.'

'Not if they can't label you. They have to call you something, like production director, and, working for a small start-up, I never really had a title or a job definition as such. My boss, Mike, used to refer to me as "one of my fellow directors" to make us sound grander than we really were.'

'Mm.' Chris was a good listener. 'Don't do yourself down. I think you've got something you could sell anyone, if you just think about how you present it. You come across very well, you know.'

She was embarrassed. 'I feel I've worked very hard for a long time,' she replied, then tried to change the subject. 'The bust-up between me and Tom was hard on the children, and we could all do with some time away from it all. I think I'm just not brave enough to take off across the world any more. Too dangerous.'

'But you never used to worry about the danger?'

'I was probably too stupid to know it existed. Now, it seems to be everywhere. Has the world changed, do you think?'

'Not so very much,' said Chris. 'You probably have.'

She shot him a glance. 'What does that mean?'

'Women change when they have babies. They get scared. Or maybe I'll call it "risk averse". Makes it sound like a syndrome.' He dismissed her, along with the rest of her sex.

'What do you know about it?'

'I do have a daughter, you know. Even if I've never exactly been around when she was growing up.' He turned to look at her, and she was struck, as she always was, by the deep, strong dimple on his chin, and the way it was mirrored around the family: on Cameron, on Daisy and in the old photographs of Bertie Devereaux.

It was strange to think that her children, so terribly, thoroughly and absolutely hers in her own mind, were also one-quarter Bertie, and that they had chins and probably other things, such as gifts, talents and even problems or illnesses, passed down secretly from him to them, in an invisible genetic code. And yet she'd never met him.

'I wish I'd known your father,' she blurted. 'Your mother's death seems to have unstoppered his ghost. He's like a genie released from a bottle. I look at all the cousins – my children, and Cameron's, and even your half-Swedish Natasha – and I wonder how much

Bertie they've got in them, and how it's going to manifest itself.'

'I don't think you should worry too much. Even Bertie must be diluted to some extent through two generations. I think Tom, Cameron and I are all very much like him, though. For better or worse. Worse probably. Bad-tempered and driven. It must be very difficult to live with.'

Was that a question or a statement? She wondered if he was talking about his succession of glittery blondes or her separation from Tom.

'Not Cameron, surely.' Lily kept the conversation away from the two of them, not wanting to reveal anything. 'He does about one photographic exhibition every five years.'

'Cameron,' said Chris, 'has the attention span of a gnat. I don't think he's ever grown up.'

Lily ignored that. 'And I'd call Tom solid, rather than driven. He always used to get home at six-thirty every night so he could read a bedtime story to the children.'

She stopped. He had, indeed, been bad-tempered. The sudden shouts of rage at quite trivial problems had chipped away at their happiness, had caught her on the raw after a hard day and had often flashed into fights between them. But what hurt so much was that it hadn't been all bad.

There was that pain again, and the anger, at what she and Tom had lost, and what Daisy and Billy had so innocently been forced to lose, too. Sometimes

Lily thought she was fuelled by the slow-burning combustion of rage. It stripped the flesh from her bones, consuming everything, giving her the energy to work each day and look after her children at night, driving her to ring friends and make arrangements, impelling her to volunteer for things, urging her on till her heart thumped uncomfortably in her chest and woke her up too early in the morning. Tamped down, controlled and civilized, the anger had been distilled, like the propellant for a jet engine or the core of a nuclear reactor. It was the rage that had damaged her inside and turned her into the sort of person she'd sworn never to become.

She hoped that the simplicity and peace of a summer by the sea would finally extinguish it. She didn't want to be this angry person, because anger eventually burnt up your core, and left you bitter, vindictive and empty. Otherwise the only alternative to feeling angry was feeling nothing at all.

She wanted to find something neutral to talk about. 'I suppose that you've been going to the Boathouse as long as you can remember?'

'Not quite. My parents didn't have a car when I was little. They used to have a motorcycle and side-car, but my mother decided it was too dangerous for a baby and they sold it. So I was six before we took a family holiday there.'

'It must have been magical.'

'It was. There's something about being six. For me it was when I realized I was part of a wider world.

I remember headlines for the first time, and how other people felt. Everyone was very afraid of the Bomb: it hung over our futures like a great black cloud. Britain was the third country in the world, after the United States and Russia, to have it, and we were very aware of what it meant. I knew that my whole secure world, including my parents, Tom and me, could be wiped out by a mushroom cloud, if Evil were allowed to Triumph. And I remember my parents shouting at each other, and thinking that had something to do with the Bomb, too.' He laughed.

'Around about then, I also worked out that my father was different – famous, even, and all that meant – because he wrote in newspapers and spoke on the radio. Until then I'd assumed that all fathers were much the same. And I tried to understand the concept of money, partly because farthings were going to be abolished, which my teacher, an elderly spinster, mourned as the loss of a way of life. But I also understood a bit more about money because we suddenly didn't have very much, and this, I think, in retrospect, must have been the cause of the shouting between my parents. My mother, it seemed, thought my father should write another St John Conroy book. He, for reasons I've never understood, refused.

'Then we were left a car, an amazing Bentley. It was grey and beautiful, and belonged to Great-aunt Fanny, whose chauffeur used to drive her from the house of one relation to another, on a constantly revolving mission to stir up as much trouble as she could. She was the only one of my mother's family to have defied the fatwa against her, and they corresponded two or three times a year. Occasionally the Bentley drew up outside our door in Chelsea, and Great-aunt Fanny would emerge, declaring the house "too sweet for words" and asking Mother, rather loudly, how on earth she "managed".'

'I can't believe,' said Lily, 'that your mother's family cut her off completely for marrying your father. What was so awful about him?'

'He was lower middle-class.' Chris grinned. 'His father had several grocer's shops in the West Country. They were far from poor, but they were "trade", which mattered terribly then.

'Anyway, the car changed everything. I think Great-aunt Fanny left it to Mum out of sheer devilry. She knew that it would infuriate the family because they'd realize she'd stayed in touch, and the cousins would be livid, too, because it was worth a great deal of money, yet it wasn't quite valuable enough to bother contesting in court.'

'Or perhaps she hoped it would be a way of them all starting to talk to each other again.' Lily wondered at the vindictiveness of these relations, these stony-hearted northern aristocrats who could banish their daughter just because she married someone from the wrong class. 'Perhaps she hoped that your parents would have to go up to collect the car, and that then they'd start sending each other Christmas cards and then . . .'

Chris shook his head. 'Fat chance. All we got was

a dignified silence. Great-aunt Fanny's chauffeur drove the Bentley down to London. I remember it arriving, and realizing how pretty my mother was, as she raced out of the house, laughing. Her skirt swirled out like a ballerina's as she threw herself round my father's neck, and his smile was like the sun coming out after a long, hard winter. I suddenly remembered that once they'd always been like that and wondered if the Bomb had gone away.'

Lily smiled. 'Do you think children today worry about bombs?'

'Probably not.' Chris neatly overtook a car and slipped back into the middle lane. 'Too busy watching reality TV and game shows to have the faintest idea. We never had any of that. Television was the news and a cartoon series about a cat called *Snagglepuss*.'

'So when did they take you down to the Boathouse?'

'That day.' His smile flashed again, lighting up his gaunt features.

He had a nice smile, she realized, studying his face in profile.

'That was the exciting thing about my father. He'd make up his mind to do something and do it, just like that. My mother asked if we could possibly go to the Boathouse sometime that summer, and he said, "We'll go now." She stopped, for a minute, and I thought: Oh no, they're going to have a row, but then she said, "Why not?" and they kissed each other until I said they were being yucky.

'I remember Dora and Ma rushing around the house

packing, handing me baskets and boxes for the car: treats like tinned fruit salad and Del Monte peaches and Carnation Milk. Even though my mother insisted we were "upper class", we lived on tins. Everybody did. Since then the real taste of summer for me has been that slithery, velvet texture of tinned peaches. It reminds me of toffee apples and candy floss.

'"There won't be a fridge at the Boathouse," said Mum, suddenly worried.

'"Come on," said Fa. "Most women don't have a fridge. And we only bought one eighteen months ago. It can scarcely have turned into one of life's basic necessities overnight. Anyway, there's no electricity down there."'

Chris was a good storyteller, thought Lily, visualizing the young, happy Bertie and Maud, whirling round the house, preparing to go away. 'But why, if she was prepared to marry a grocer's son, did she worry about eating in an upper-class way?'

He thought for a moment. 'I think she unconsciously divided it in her own mind. If it had anything to do with people, like whom you loved, or whom you were friends with, she was resolutely egalitarian. Rebelliously so. But she was mustard-keen on things like the way you held your knife or whether you said "toilet" or not. She called it "having standards".'

The miles sped past and the hours slipped away as he conjured up a seaside adventure that belonged to the days when Janet and John each fulfilled their own tidy, safe, predictable roles.

'Fa left the packing to Mum and Dora, settling his typewriter in the boot carefully, and then sitting in the driving seat. "Get a move on. We haven't got all day, you know." But he said it with a smile, and the sense of adventure permeated through to Tom, who was at the toddler stage of echoing everything that was said to him. "Haven't got all day," he crowed, bouncing up and down on the leather seats. "Haven't got all day."

'But that's what it took. We wiggled through London, and all the other towns, then up and down and round the hilly parts of Dorset and Somerset, Fa grinding the gears and stalling the car at Stonehenge, where we all got out and raced around the stones, while Fa tried to explain who'd built them and why. Then back into the car, and on, until the hills began to swoop up and down like a fairground ride.

'"Who's going to be the first to see the sea?" my mother asked, and we pressed our faces to the windows only to see high hedges twisting through Van Gogh corn fields. It was all so green, and tidy and neat compared to London. Tom and I rolled about on the back seat, wrestling, which must have tested even Dora's good nature to its limits, until we fell asleep on her lap.

'She shook us awake to point out a thin strip of twinkling blue water spreading out over the horizon and beyond. We almost held our breaths, as the Bentley turned away from the road and bumped down this narrow, rutted lane. Eventually Fa stopped, opened some gates, wedged the car under a dark clump of fir trees and told us we were there.

'When I got out, crumpled with sleep and sick, I was dazzled by flashes of glitter beyond the woods. It was the sun on the water. A fishing boat bobbed up and down, and seagulls mewed and swooped, and I saw that they were actually below us.

'By the time we'd all been hung about with as many possessions as we could carry, and staggered down the overgrown trail that led down to the bay and the Boathouse, I was so dog-tired I no longer believed this journey would ever end.

'But, when I first caught sight of it, a long, low stone cottage carved out of the side of the rock, I was immediately enchanted. I could see that the normal rules about climbing, running and staying clean weren't going to apply here, and that now we had the Bentley, we'd be able to come often.'

Lily was silent, thinking about Chris's story. He obviously loved the place, so why sell it?

'But you don't feel like that now?' she ventured.

'No.' His voice was curt. 'I don't.'

'Why not let Tom and Cameron have it, if you don't want it?'

'You sound like my mother.' The anger, just below the surface, notched up a fraction. 'It was the refrain of my childhood: "Let Tom have that, darling, he's younger than you." I used to wonder why the eldest always had to be the one to be sensible, to share the toy, to look after the younger ones, why Tom always had to be allowed to play with my friends and not be left out.' He gave a short laugh. 'Quite funny, really.

'Anyway, things are different now. Tom and Cameron are grown up. I don't have to do what they want just because they're younger than me. We can all make our own decisions based on common sense. And common sense says that we should sell and split the money. If we can't even agree that, how are we going to run the place together? I mean, a simple decision like what colour to paint the walls would cause as much debate as a White Paper going through Parliament.'

'Mm.' Lily was taken aback. She thought of Billy. Was she expecting too much from him? Did she expect him to look after Daisy? 'Billy hits Daisy.'

Chris took the sudden change of topic as if it were completely logical. 'Well, I didn't hit Tom. Rather the reverse — he used to really pile into me when no one was looking with his fiendish little fists, and as soon as I retaliated one of the parents or Dora would come out, and say, "Now, you're the big boy, you mustn't hit children smaller than yourself."'

There was tension in Chris's outline that warned Lily to drop the subject.

'I wonder if there'll be a local girl to help me out occasionally with the children. You wouldn't know where to start, would you?' she asked.

His shoulders dropped fractionally. 'Ah. Yes. Look. What I'm about to ask you is more than I should. You must say no if you have any doubts at all.'

'I will,' promised Lily, hardly thinking.

'I wondered if Natasha could come and stay with you down at the Boathouse. I know it's something of a responsibility, but I'd give her strict instructions to be a help – in fact, I'd pay her an allowance to be a kind of au pair for you.'

Lily was delighted. 'I'd love to have her. Of course. But won't she find it terribly boring? Just three children and one middle-aged woman?'

'You're hardly middle-aged.' Chris's eyes flicked, quickly, towards her in acknowledgement of something – Lily wasn't sure quite what. She felt both a twinge of awkwardness and a flush of pleasure. She tamped this down quickly.

'And Tash looks sophisticated,' he added, 'but she's a very simple country girl at heart. I don't have the time to look after her in London. Sarah's doing her best, but she's got a big contract on.'

'Well, I'll feel so much better knowing that I've got another pair of hands around, so the arrangement couldn't be better for either of us,' Lily reassured him, and her heart lifted. This was the family life she had feared being excluded from by divorce, but here she was at the centre of it, with nieces and nephews of all ages who needed her. She was involved still. She could help. An added bonus occurred to her: if she could give Natasha a magical summer at the Boathouse, surely that would influence Chris to keep it. How could he resist the pleas of his own daughter? And so the family row would be resolved. She was still necessary, after all. She was still part of it all.

'Well, that's settled,' she said happily as they drove towards the small town and their destination beyond.

11

They turned off the main road and began to nego-
tiate the new roundabouts outside town. Great ugly
sheds crouched on the edge of huge car parks, goug-
ing holes in the green countryside. They seemed
temporary, as if they might be blown away at any
moment. Houses were equally randomly scattered,
clustered in culs-de-sac and along roads, so unlike
London's geometric rows of similar terraces, thought
Lily, almost pressing her nose to the car windows to
see. Each one seemed to have been lovingly –
although not always perhaps strictly tastefully – built
for a different set of dreams. The mock-Tudor
cottage sat next to the modernist bunker, and the
solid Victorian villa jostled the plain, unpretentious
bungalow. Most houses had been altered in some way
since they'd been built: Lily saw Tudor lattice windows
on modern fifties boxes, and ugly flat-roofed exten-
sions tacked on to thatched or gabled homes.

'Seaside architecture,' said Chris. 'Never one of
Britain's strongest points.'

He was very judgemental, thought Lily. Not everyone could live in a mansion, and all that mattered
was that the people who lived in these houses liked
them.

But as they drove through the town, he stopped the car outside a little row of shops. 'We used to think this place was so exciting. We'd ride for miles on our bikes to get here. It was kid heaven.'

Buckets and spades, shrimping nets, colourful lilos and snorkels swung beneath the striped awning of a shop that proclaimed itself to be called the Happy Plaice, with beach balls, piles of jelly shoes, racks of saucy postcards, kiss-me-quick sunhats and T-shirts tumbling over the tops of baskets in a riot of primary colours inside.

'I never thought this would still be here. And the Post Office is still working. Although the hairdresser next door seems to have changed its name from Renee of Paris to Quik Kuts.'

They both laughed.

Lily leant back with a sigh of satisfaction. For the first time in a long while, she felt something other than anger or numbness. The summer stretched ahead.

At the end of the village Chris turned off into a meandering, high-sided lane with purple, cream and pink flowers threaded thickly through hedgerows.

'They don't use many insecticides on the fields here,' said Chris. 'So the wild flowers still get a chance.'

As the car zig-zagged round blind corners and accelerated up and down steep rises and falls in the road, towering spikes of foxgloves leant over almost to touch them, and cow parsley foamed in champagne-and-cream abundance. There were little flowers too, tiny buttons of cream, yellow and pink studded along the hedges and banks.

'Meadow peas,' said Chris. 'And that purple-blue spike-thing that looks like lavender is vetch. It's a weed, but I like it.'

'You obviously know a lot about nature.'

'Not really. But I spent a lot of my childhood with my nose in the grass, watching it grow, I suppose. Or lying on my back looking at the sky. If you do that for long enough, it's like tuning into a new, low-key drama. You realize that there's always something going on, it's just that you're normally too busy to notice it.'

Lily craned her head, trying to see over the tops of the hedges to the countryside beyond, peering through the occasional tantalizing gap or catching sight of a brief panorama of patchwork fields as they mounted the crest of a hill. It was an artist's dream of the countryside: rolling hills crayoned in emerald green and dotted with disapproving black-faced sheep; little pink matchbox houses perched on the tops of hills; and smooth slices of sea, so still and blue that they merged with the sky like an exercise in graded shading.

'These lanes were made by horses and carts over hundreds of years.' Chris had noticed her curiosity. 'Everyone was always careful to skirt round each other's fields rather than go the direct route. And it's very muddy and rainy here. Before they were tarmacked, the roads often got very waterlogged, so they scraped the mud to the sides. It only takes about two hundred years' – he flashed a grin at her – 'and you get these tunnel roads as a result.'

'What happens if you meet a car coming the other way?'

He looked amused. 'You reverse till you find a space. How are you on reversing?'

'All right,' said Lily, who could still remember the sense of panic induced by her driving test twenty years earlier. 'How does anyone ever get anything big delivered? Like a washing machine?'

Chris shrugged. 'I've no idea. Perhaps they're still washing their clothes in the river.'

They arrived at Salt Creek. It would have met the approval of the most determined conservationist. Grey stone walls climbed higgledy-piggledy up and down, and, behind them, picture-postcard cottages in pink, green and blue clustered together, clinging to the side of the hill. The church tower was silhouetted against the bay beneath. It seemed longer than three months since Maud's funeral had taken place there. Then she had looked at the village as a visitor. Now she was mapping up a temporary life down here, and it looked very different. It seemed brighter and more open.

'Why is it called Salt Creek?' asked Lily.

'It's the last creek out of the estuary – about as far as you can go and almost on the open sea. Further up towards Totnes, the water is fresh, then nearer Dartmouth it's a mixture of river water and salt.

Here it's wholly salt.' He got out and breathed deeply. 'Ah. Get back in, and I'll show you where the pub is.'

They drove down a deep, narrow lane, banked with high stone walls. The pub, the Salt Wind, stood facing out to sea, with its own jetty. The road ended abruptly in the greenish-grey foaming water.

'Our nearest civilized outpost,' declared Chris. 'Be careful when you park in the pub car park, by the way. It's over there on the sea front, underwater at the moment. It looks perfectly normal at low tide, but is three feet deep in water at high tide. You could get your shoes wet.'

'Where's the Boathouse?'

'Round the corner of the bay. When the tide's out there's a great beach stretching right round the cliff. You can drive the car to the door of the Boathouse, so that you don't have to take shopping and suitcases through the woods. It's got a jetty with a slipway just outside. But the tide's up, so we'll go round by the woods now.'

'Mm.' It all seemed terrifying.

They got back into the car, and turned off the narrow, rambling lane on to an even narrower unmade track, bumping along it until it almost ran out into a mass of honeysuckle-covered bushes. Chris stopped by a pair of big iron gates. They were held together with a rusty chain and padlock.

He shook his head as he struggled with the lock. 'We'd better replace this and get you a new key. It's rusted.'

He pushed the gates open and drove the car in. 'The gates are a bit pretentious for a cottage, but it was originally part of a big estate. There's been some kind of a boathouse here ever since Sir Walter Ralegh's day. After that there were a couple of old cottages on the site, probably for fishermen or smugglers. Then the Victorian owners got grand ideas and rebuilt the main house, which is about a mile inland, and turned the Boathouse cottages into a kind of summerhouse for guests, where they could paint or take tea, or swim in the sea in privacy.'

He locked the car and stretched. Lily breathed deeply. The air was cold and fresh, as if sealed off from the outside world. It smelt of damp forest, earth and the faintest trace of honeysuckle sweetness.

Chris hoisted a knapsack over his shoulder and set off downhill. 'These woods were once gardens.' He waved around him. 'Long ago, in Edwardian times, when there were fifty gardeners, the banks were partly terraced and planted with exotic plants. That was when the house ran its own regular boat to Dartmouth to pick up guests, and King Edward the Seventh moored his yacht outside when the young princes were at Dartmouth Naval College.

'Then it all went in the Great War, like so much of that lifestyle. Both the sons of the house were killed, but one left a widow, who was pregnant with a daughter. That daughter is now an old lady of nearly ninety, and she still lives up at the big house, in a fading, ruined testimony to Edwardian greatness. Bits of the estate were sold off, which is when my grandfather acquired the Boathouse. My mother tried to maintain our couple of acres, and the old lady still has one gardener, but most of it has been allowed to ramble out of control. That's why you can see palm trees and rhododendrons amongst the pine woods.'

As they picked their way down, Lily felt as if the past was almost close enough to touch. She sensed the presence of the Edwardian gardeners, those invisible workers who had disappeared to the shadows of the Front, as she followed Chris over the ghost of a path. It was hardly more than an indentation in the ferns, twisting and turning in hairpin bends down the cliffside. Tiny, creamy spires of pennywort lined the way and pink thrift, as pretty and delicate as carnations, was sprinkled amongst the greenery. Deeper in the dense vegetation, the sharper, dramatic outlines of garden shrubs gone wild punctuated the dark green gloom.

Chris seemed to know the way by heart. As the breeze shifted and they got closer to the edge of the cliff and the path, the sharp, salty smell of the sea bit into the air. The only sounds were the cries of seabirds, circling and swooping in the bay, and the distant phut-phut-phut of a motorboat.

'These banks are covered in snowdrops in January.' He stopped, indicating the rough ground towards the edge of the cliff. 'Then there are drifts of bluebells at Easter, and wild flowers pretty much all summer. The Edwardian gardens have escaped and colonized the cliff, so there are often amazing splashes of yellow and red.'

The sky and sea glittered brilliantly ahead of them in the sunshine.

'How can you bear to sell?' Lily burst out. She'd meant to avoid the subject, wait until the right time to tackle him, but it seemed so mad. He clearly loved the place. It didn't make sense.

Chris's eyes were cold. 'I don't think "bear to" comes into it. I'm making a business decision. Not letting my heart rule my head the way the others do.'

Lily dropped her head. 'Sorry.'

'I apologize. I didn't mean to snap. What I mean is that holiday properties, particularly unique ones like these, are very much in demand now, but this place is very cut off and costs a fair amount to maintain, and if there's any kind of a downturn that could easily change. Quite drastically, even. It's not like a little bungalow in a seaside town that will always have a market because it appeals to retired people as well as holidaymakers. I think we can maximize our assets if we sell now, and both Tom and Cameron could do with the money, frankly.'

But why do you have to take the decision for them? She kept this question to herself. Everyone knew that the words 'control freak' came to mind when you thought about Chris. He couldn't make them sell, presumably, but she knew the power of his personality would gradually wear them away.

'Let's go down and open up the house.' But he remained standing, looking at the view, as if searching the horizon for something.

They had come to a clearing, where woodland gave way to open garden, with a steep flight of steps cut into the cliffside, leading down to the beach. They picked their way carefully.

She glanced back at the top of the hill. Huge, dark-green pom-poms sat like squat sentinels of the bay. Rhododendrons. They would be glorious blazes of colour in May.

'Careful,' said Chris. 'It would be easy to trip.' He looked at her shoes. 'Those aren't very suitable.'

She flushed at being judged a trite, city girl. 'I'll be fine.' At his doubtful look, she added impatiently: 'For goodness' sake. I have walked the Inca Trail, you know. And the Great Wall of China.'

He was amused. 'In high heels?'

'Devon,' she said, with all the dignity she could muster, 'is far more manicured than China.'

He laughed and put a hand on her arm, lightly, to make his point. She was very aware of the contact, of his fingers touching her bare skin. 'There's a rhyme about the River Dart,' he said. 'Every year it claims a human heart. Don't underestimate the power underneath the prettiness. Up that estuary is one of the most treacherous rivers in Britain. It is dangerous here, you know.'

'I know.'

This was where Bertie Devereaux had fallen to his death.

At the bottom of the steps, Chris opened the weathered front door with a big iron key. Dust danced in the sunlight, as if surprised by the intrusion. They stood looking at the one long room that made up the ground floor. It smelt of ancient wool and damp, and there was a big stone fireplace at one end, surrounded by battered leather sofas. The windows were misted up with dried salt from the sea.

'Nothing's changed,' said Chris as if to himself. 'It's all exactly the same.'

'I imagined it would be more run down than this,' said Lily.

Chris looked out of one of the deep-set windows. 'Oh?' His voice was casual. 'As a matter of fact, I have contacts with a small company down here, and I've always got one of their teams to come in once a year and do anything that needs doing.'

He turned round to see her look of surprise. 'It's just good business practice to look after one's assets,' he added. 'Letting water and weather get into a property is disastrous.'

Lily was sure that neither Tom nor Cameron knew this. The reason why they had never brought their children here was because it was supposed to be almost derelict.

She looked round at the low spacious room, at

the honeyed oak beams striping the ceiling and the big stone fireplace at the other end. She decided to risk a challenge. 'I believe this can be a happy place again. And if so, if this summer works out, and the Boathouse turns out to be the best thing for the family, not a source of arguments or trouble, even if it does cost a bit to maintain, will you think again? Perhaps give it another try?'

She thought he'd stopped listening, but he let out a laugh, a short, irritated bark. 'We'll see.'

She felt dismissed, like a child. She was determined that he should take notice of her. 'Will you come down? During the summer? And see what it's like?'

Too late, she realized what emanated from the stiff way he held himself and the angle at which he had turned away his face: reluctance. However beautiful it was, he did not want to be here.

'Very well,' he said finally. 'If you ring me and ask me to come, I shall.'

He took her round the Boathouse.

'The main room.' Three sofas clustered comfortably around the fireplace, a scrubbed wooden table across the middle indicated a dining area, and there was a strip of kitchen by the door. 'As you can see, everything happens in this room, except sleeping.'

He led her up a narrow staircase to the two bedrooms, one above the other, both as long and wide as the room downstairs, and each with views over the sea, framed by fading red check curtains. 'And there's one more bedroom to the side,' he added. 'It used to be Dora's. Unless guests came.'

'Where did guests sleep?' She'd heard about the parties, the well-known people, the nights spent over bonfires on the beach, the laughter and music that had drifted across the bay and the ideas that had been tossed to and fro on the jetty. Where had all those people come from, and where had they stayed?

'Oh, here and there.' Chris was vague. 'Sometimes we children camped outside and the guests had our room. The pub has rooms. Some of the cottages in Salt Creek do b & b. Some people crashed on sofas. Or brought sleeping bags.' He raised an eyebrow. 'Or shared beds with people they didn't really know. All that sort of thing.

'Now then. The practicalities.' There was a water heater, installed in the seventies. It still worked.

'Mm,' said Chris. 'Lethal.' He grinned.

'I've seen worse,' Lily said firmly as they went downstairs again. 'What about lunch?'

She'd brought a plastic supermarket carrier bag with a loaf of fresh, crusty bread, a chunk of best mature cheddar, some butter and a knife. 'Oh, and some lager. Not very cold, I'm afraid.'

Chris ripped away the tab on the can, broke off some bread and hacked at the cheese. 'Everything tastes good by the sea. Let's sit outside and watch the waves. This was always my favourite place to eat.'

They ate hungrily, in silence, on a couple of

wooden chairs they'd taken from inside and wiped down. Lily felt the sun penetrate deep down into her bones, suffusing her with tranquillity.

Chris leant back with satisfaction. 'Thank you. That was great. But, still, I should have taken you out to lunch somewhere.'

'I don't expect men to take me out to lunch.' She was surprised that Chris should feel under such an obligation.

He smiled. 'You should. It's better than dinner. My father always said that girls thought that lunch didn't count.'

'Didn't count as what?'

'He used to say: "Oh, you can get away with anything at lunchtime, women think affairs are something that happen after sundown."'

Lily felt something shift inside her. 'Surely Bertie didn't have affairs? Tom always told me that they were everything to each other.'

'They were.' Chris stretched out in the sunlight, easy with his casual admission. 'But Dad liked "lunching"' – he waved his fingers in the air to indicate quotation marks – 'with pretty women.'

'So everything wasn't enough? To stay faithful?'

'They were very, very happy together.'

'But not happy enough,' she repeated, the rage stirring again, curdling the food inside her. Was infidelity expected in this family? Just part of the deal?

'Was that what happened between you and Tom?'

Lily flushed. 'I've always promised myself never

to talk about Tom to his family. To criticize him.'

Chris nodded but didn't say anything.

'And anyway,' she added, trying to justify her reticence, 'I'm afraid our story was a very commonplace one. Very ordinary. Nothing you haven't heard from a thousand other divorced couples. But I still didn't want everyone talking about it. I don't really want people knowing. Any more than they have to.'

It had mattered, that. The humiliation of people judging her. The thought of their friends and family dissecting what had gone wrong, apportioning blame and adding their own views. Their story being fodder for gossip, passed on to mere acquaintances at parties and railway stations and over telephones as a delicious conversational titbit. Just thinking about it had made her cringe.

Too late, she realized that she had virtually answered Chris's question. He used silences as an interrogatory technique. Lesser beings scurried to fill them. She sighed.

'He's a fool, in that case,' said Chris. 'If that makes you feel any better.'

She smiled weakly. It did. A bit. 'Your parents,' she said to divert the conversation away from her relationship with Tom. 'I thought they had the perfect marriage.' It had always been, according to family legend, the standard which everyone had to live up to. The one she and Tom had failed to achieve.

'Bertie loved Maud as much as anyone could love anyone. But infidelity wasn't so important then.

People didn't divorce. Hardly ever, anyway. It was too serious. A woman on her own literally had nothing, and little chance of anything. Now it's the man who's the one who loses out if he strays.'

'So it's nothing to do with love, then?' She couldn't keep the sharpness out of her voice. So he thought Tom was the one who had lost out. 'Fidelity's some kind of fashion statement, something that reflects your time, like a hat or a hemline, rather than a principle you can believe in?'

'Love,' he said, 'is a sociological phenomenon. It's the way we dress up our desires to make them acceptable. Of course, it's different in different societies or different times.'

'Well.' She was unwilling to engage him further, not when they had hours ahead of them. 'That's wonderful. Isn't it?'

'It's low tide now,' he said. 'Shall I show you how to pump up the pontoon in case anyone needs to come here with a larger car?'

Game, set and match to Chris. She suspected he knew exactly how she felt about pumping up pontoons.

It was only later that she thought he might have been deliberately changing the subject.

As they walked across the firm, damp sand, picking their way carefully over rocks and seaweed, his mobile sounded. She thought it was a bird at first. She didn't expect technology to intrude here.

Chris drew it out of his pocket and unfolded it. 'Yes?' Pause. 'Yes. No. Yes. We'll sell it then. No. Tell him to get on with it. I don't want any delays. No. That's my final offer. Yes. No.'

The second time it rang, he sounded less impatient. 'Yes. Fine. OK. Good.' He folded it up and returned it to his pocket with the words: 'Sarah's working on a house nearby. She's coming round in about half an hour.'

Lily was surprised to feel disappointed. Being alone with Chris hadn't been as tricky as she'd expected it to be. Still, it would be even easier with Sarah around.

Half an hour later, perfectly timed with the low tide, Sarah drove up without apparently worrying about pontoons, twisty, winding roads, directions or reversing. Lily wouldn't have been surprised if the sea had rearranged itself to fit in with her plans.

'Darling!' She kissed him. 'And Lily. What a treat!' She felt the satin softness of Sarah's cheek brush against hers like a breath of gossamer. 'Isn't this a marvellous coincidence?'

Lily wondered whether it was.

'I'm working for a middle-European prince who's trying to buy up the estuary. Actually, I think he's a drug-dealer; they always like waterways. So useful for getting packages in and out of the country.'

Lily blinked.

'And look what I've brought! Provisions!' Sarah opened her boot and brought out a freezer bag. 'Just a little portable barbecue and some ready-made kebabs from the butcher. A bag of salad. A bit of French bread. I thought we might barbecue something this evening.' She took another carrier bag out of the car. 'And a bottle of champagne. And mineral water, of course, because Chris is driving back. I don't know why you do it, Chris. Anyone else would spend the night. Four and a half hours each way. You must be mad.'

'The beds will be damp,' said Chris. He sounded irritated.

Sarah stopped to look at the Boathouse, etched into the side of the cliff as if it had been carved by the wind and waves. 'Fabulous. Completely wonderful. God, I know my fake prince would just love to get his hands on this. He's looking for a discreet place to park the getaway yacht.'

Lily failed to disguise her look of alarm.

'Oh, don't worry,' she added. 'I wouldn't dream of telling him. After all' – she seized Lily's arm in a conspiratorial manner – 'it's up to us girls to persuade Chris that we need to keep it all in the family, isn't it?'

Sarah continued to enthuse over the inside of the cottage, running her hands lovingly over the thick, white walls as if they were the legs of a horse she intended to buy. 'Peasant workmanship,' she murmured. 'You can't beat authenticity. Or fake it. Look at the depth of the brick on those windows.'

She peered into the inglenook fireplace and up the

chimney. 'Do you think we could light it? Or will we be kippered?'

'Kippered.' Lily was pleased to know something that Sarah didn't. 'Chris is going to have it swept. He knows a man, apparently.'

'I must say, he's very efficient. Looks after everything. I suppose it's having been single for so long.' She began to lay the fire, piling the logs on in a neat geometric stack. 'Logs are so much more stylish than coal, don't you think?' She sat back on her heels. 'Was he really single? All this time? It's hard to believe.'

Lily went over to the window. 'I always think that boats look so serene. I could watch them all day.' She was trying to think of something that could be defined as both truthful and tactful about Chris's former girlfriends. 'Well, everyone has a bit of a past, don't they?' she said eventually. 'I mean, they wouldn't be normal if they didn't. But I don't think you need worry about it. You should ask him. I think he's always been perfectly honest.' To his women, was how she'd nearly concluded the sentence, but stopped herself in time.

Sarah moved on to the kitchen: a strip of a sink, stove, fridge and a few cupboards. 'Definite potential,' she murmured. 'Definitely.'

Lily wondered if she was talking about interior decoration or Chris. Both, probably.

Sarah began to scrub the big white china sink and its battered teak draining board.

Lily opened a cupboard and fought her way

through the cobwebs to find a brush for the floor. 'Ugh. Not a place for arachnophobes, I don't think.'

Sarah laughed. 'Are you sure you can manage here on your own? You won't be spooked?'

Lily began to sweep the floor, soothed by the domesticity of it. 'I don't think so. It feels quite safe.' The wide oak boards were knotted and bleached with age, and by the time she'd mopped them down, they gleamed with the pale, incandescent lightness of old weathered wood. Women had washed this floor for generations. It was a comforting thought.

'Chris says you have to be careful,' warned Sarah. 'That it's not as chocolate-boxy as it seems.'

'No, I expect it isn't. But I think I can look after myself. And the children.'

'I'm sure you can. What's this?' It was Lily's carrier bag of bread and cheese, which was beginning to smell.

'I . . . er . . .'

'Big black dustbin bags,' chirruped Sarah. 'I knew they'd come in useful. Shall I chuck?'

Lily nodded, and Sarah consigned the now revolting carrier bag to the bin. Then she wrung out her cloth. 'Shall we air the upstairs bedrooms for a bit? I do love the way Chris is so close to his family. Especially Tom. Do you know, we had him round last night?'

Lily's heart quickened. 'Did you?'

'He's an absolute darling, isn't he? Oh, sorry; of course, you probably know better, and I'm speaking out of turn, but he does seem so terribly nice.' Sarah looked directly at Lily. 'He's still in love with you, obviously.'

'Did he say so?' Lily could feel her temper rising.

'Not in so many words, but . . .' Sarah opened the cupboard to see what was inside. 'Oh, my God. Polka Dot. The real thing.' She took out some blue-and-white spotted mugs and plates. 'Dartmouth Pottery. The original nineteen fifties stuff. What a find. I simply adore those spots. They look so modern and fresh even after all these years. Do you think you'll ever get back together?'

Lily almost missed the question as Sarah took three sets of dusty cups and saucers out of the cupboard to wash them.

'No. Really. No. It's left a hole in his life, but love . . . What he feels for me isn't love. Not as I recognize it.'

'Are you sure? I mean, do any of us recognize love when we see it?' Sarah stopped rinsing the cups and turned to face her. 'I'm sorry. I'm being tactless. I'm afraid I ramble on and ask people the most filthy personal questions. Please forgive me.'

'Honestly, it's fine. It's just that we won't be getting back together. It does take a time to get divorced so I've been able to think about it.'

'Yes, he said he moved out nearly nine months ago now. You've had a rough time,' reflected Sarah. 'Separation and then redundancy. It could hardly be a worse combination. And I don't suppose Maud dying helped. Even if she was only your mother-in-law and not your mother. I think it's very tough on you.'

'I'm quite a tough person.' Lily swallowed. Sarah's sympathy was so unexpected that tears stung the back of her eyelids.

Sarah turned back to the sink. 'I think you're marvellous. And you've done a wonderful job with the children. It can't be easy protecting them from divorce.'

'It isn't. And I think Billy's suffered.'

'Maybe he's a bit . . . boisterous. But it's nothing. That's what boys are like. I'm sure he'll grow out of it.' She looked out of the window, her eyes searching for Chris. 'Do you think being here makes Chris sad? He was here when his father . . . died, wasn't he? I wish I could get him to talk about it. He seems to have such a lot of emotional baggage.'

Lily reflected that Sarah was a great deal nicer than Vicky gave her credit for.

Dora, in 1963, would never have heard the term 'emotional baggage'. Children were seen and not heard in well-run households.

But Maud and Bertie's was not a well-run household and she still wondered about them occasionally. They had been devoted parents when little Christopher was born. He'd been the sun at the centre of their own tiny universe. Now they lived in a different world, where children didn't exist. Either they hadn't been born yet, or they were safely looked after by nannies. Or those who bore them disappeared entirely. Maud and Bertie couldn't afford to disappear – his newspaper work demanded his presence at the centre of London life – and they couldn't afford nannies. Newspapers didn't pay that well, and drinking wine every lunchtime and opening a bottle of Scotch in the evening wasn't cheap.

And Maud was the last woman to be left on her own with two children. She had no idea of mothering. She'd been brought up in the nursery of an aristocratic stately home, with a nanny and an under-nanny, and had only seen her own mother once a day, formally dressed, at teatime.

Dora was acutely aware that her position, as a spinster, scarcely qualified her to comment on what was, or wasn't, an ideal upbringing for children, and this one, with its conspicuous lack of plain nursery food and regimented bedtimes, might well be the best and most brilliant start in life. The dreary South London existence she was running away from, where everybody knew everything about everybody else, and the entire street seemed to have a collective responsibility, which included discipline, for the children who lived in it, wasn't one she would have necessarily wished on them. But she couldn't help feeling uneasy when she saw Christopher give Tom his breakfast and get him ready for school, or when she saw them coming home again, the smaller boy, his face filthy and his shirt-tails out, trailing tiredly behind the leggy, pre-adolescent Chris, as he'd suddenly declared himself to be called. Still, the boys were always together, so they had each other.

Dora also saw that Maud's lax mothering was, in some ways, merely that Maud and Bertie came first with each other. It seemed as if they saw each other in colour and everyone else in black and white.

Passing the open drawing-room door, she'd once heard Bertie ask Maud where the children were.

'I've no idea, darling, I haven't seen them for days. You know what a perfectly frightful mother I am.'

Bertie had walked slowly up to her and kissed her on the lips. Once. Twice, and then, lingering, a third time. 'You are the most bloody wonderful mother. In the entire universe.'

Maud's laugh was low and throaty. 'Darling, you're just saying that. And I'm terrible, really terrible. I gave Chris a jam sandwich today instead of lunch. And Tom had . . .' Whatever she intended to say next was muffled by another kiss. 'Bertie, we've been married for a whole fourteen years, you know. You ought to be bored stiff of me by now.' Dora closed the door, gently, on another laugh from Maud, but she needn't have worried. Neither of them would have noticed if the Life Guards had trooped through the room complete with horses and band.

While the boys didn't have anything that resembled a formal bedtime – Maud waved them out of the way when people appeared and Dora had often gone upstairs to find little Tom asleep in Chris's bed – they seemed perfectly happy, and everything about

Maud and Bertie's household was so much nicer and more fun than anything she had ever experienced in her own childhood. Chris and Tom, she supposed, were lucky to be growing up in the thick of life, opening their front door to anybody from the First Sea Lord to a leading film director and being expected to talk equally sensibly to either, rather than protected and cut off from real life like most children of their age.

And Dora had her own belated growing-up to do. She woke up to food first, then clothes, then, finally, sex. The sixties was her decade and she couldn't believe she'd actually been lucky enough to find herself alive in it. Instead of having to have her stockings darned and redarned by the old woman at the dry-cleaner's, and endlessly unpicking old sweaters and reknitting them to make new ones – something she had been hopelessly hamfisted at – she could go down to the High Street and buy a cheap copy of the latest fashions or stockings in packs of five. Even though she was equally useless at sewing, Mary Quant patterns were so simple that she could run up a shift in an afternoon, and, as they used so little fabric, she could afford a new dress every Saturday afternoon if she felt like it. Maud and Bertie egged her on, because they loved fashion: Bertie outraged everyone by wearing black or white polo neck sweaters instead of a collar and tie, adding a velvet smoking jacket on top *during the day*, and Maud had been one of the first women to swap her sleek, sculpted curls for a bouncy geometric Vidal Sassoon bob. So Dora found herself in an environment where clothes were no longer a method of classifying and controlling people, but the first step in enjoying yourself. And for the first time in her life, she was able to acquire lots and lots of them. It made her feel good about her body for the first time, and she learnt to walk down the street as part of a proud elite.

She also found that the characteristics that had marked her out as so shamefully different in the fifties – the long, mousy hair, the skinny frame and the thin, boyish legs – were perfect for the time, too. Pretty faces mattered less than style; highlights transformed the hair; and false eyelashes, like great dark spiders, gave her colourless, horsy features definition. She even managed to ditch her glasses – now terrible dark horn-rims – for the new contact lenses, although they felt like dinner plates in her eyes. It took her a long time to save up for them, though, and they were her personal hostages to fortune, constantly threatening her with bankruptcy by falling out. Bertie frequently came upstairs to find both Maud and Dora on their knees with their noses in the carpet in search of a lost contact lens, and would enquire as to whether they'd joined a new religion.

'Pretty much,' said Dora with feeling, as she found the tiny piece of glass, licked it, and fiddled around in front of the mirror until she had manoeuvred it in again. 'These things are worth about a month's wages.'

Money, it was true, occasionally emerged as an irksome reminder of reality in an otherwise permanent party. Bertie Devereaux was one of those names that everybody had heard of, and he seemed to be everywhere, but he wasn't rich. He regarded the newspaper columns as a necessary evil while he wrote the Great British Novel, and he spent several days a week in front of a blank piece of paper, crossing out and rewriting endless short scenes. His fame meant nothing to the bank manager, who wrote cross letters about overdrafts and budgeting, all of which Bertie threw away without reading. The higher salary she had earned for the first year had never been raised in line with inflation, and Dora could see advertisements in the paper that promised much more than she was getting. Everybody suddenly seemed to have so much money, even girls younger than she was. But that didn't matter. Maud had a splendidly aristocratic disregard of money and what other people thought, and was perfectly happy to serve sausages to a Cabinet Minister, and then call him a horrid little jumped-up man behind his back when he'd gone. Inevitably, a few months later, there would be an article in *Vogue* or *Harpers Bazaar* declaring sausages to be the '*dernier cri*', as some bemused magazine editor, expecting royal hospitality at one of 'London's leading political and artistic salons', had been first scandalized and then entranced by such cavalier treatment.

Anyway, Bertie and Maud were so generous and

such fun that Dora didn't need a higher salary, and, as Bertie said, only boring people planned for the future. 'If we have one,' he'd add. 'With the Bomb we probably won't.'

She frequently spent the night with the Devereauxs in Chelsea, partly because the night buses were few and far between and partly because she was unable to tolerate the constant carping from her parents. They were appalled at everything she did. When her mother found *Lady Chatterley's Lover* in her bedroom, she ranted at her for weeks on end. 'What will the neighbours say?' she screeched, over and over again.

'Why do the neighbours have to know?' Dora asked wearily. 'They're hardly likely to be nosing round my bedroom.'

'There might be a fire,' her mother retorted. 'And the fireman rescuing you would find out. And then where would we all be?'

Dora was unable to persuade her that the fireman would be concentrating on either extinguishing the fire or rescuing her. 'Nobody could ignore that book,' her mother declared angrily. 'Nobody. It's absolutely disgusting.' She put her hands on her hips. 'And you don't even wear a hat to work. The neighbours can see *that* all right.'

'Nobody wears a hat to work any more, Mum.'

'In decent streets, they do. You're letting yourself down, and you're letting me down.'

Dora was used to grumbling. Her parents often declared that 'They shouldn't 'a' let it happen', or

'They ought to do something'. 'They' referred to the Government or the authorities, which Dora's parents simultaneously criticized and respected. The people who smoked, drank and gossiped at Maud and Bertie's talked about plays, books, films, politics and ideas, unlike her parents who talked about Royalty, the War and what everyone else in the street was up to.

Bertie didn't just complain, he wrote articles, corresponded with MPs and ministers and urged the whole household out to demonstrations and on marches. He held passionate views, which he constantly dared Dora to challenge, about comprehensive education, racism, women's rights and British cricket as well, but most of all he believed that the twin constrictions of deep Victorian shame about sex and the straitjacket of the class system were strangling Britain.

'Well,' he declared, sweeping into the office one day. 'Are you going to demand a modesty board or a pay rise?'

'What?' Dora was learning that he started conversations on the assumption that you had just read exactly the same article as he had, but still found it hard to keep up. She tried to read a copy of *The Times* upside down under his arm.

'It's the latest thing with you girls,' he said. 'If your employer doesn't provide a modesty board in front of your desk to stop all the young sales reps looking up your very, very short skirt, you can ask for a pay rise. What do you think of that? Are we going to have a piece of plywood in front of the kitchen table or face ruin?'

Dora was uncomfortable at the implication that Bertie might be contemplating looking up her skirt. 'I don't think that's . . . er . . . necessary.'

'Why not? You deserve your rights. It says so here.' He waved the paper at her.

Dora flushed, and turned back to her work. 'I think that's like saying that you can pay to look up girls' skirts. If you turn it the other way round.'

His broad grin confirmed that she'd made the right deduction. 'Clever girl, Dora. This smacks of exploitation.' He whacked the paper down on the table. 'While apparently aimed at protecting women, it's typical of a society where women's sexuality is commercialized.' He began to pace up and down. 'The thing is, who's exploiting whom . . .' By lunchtime, his musings had turned into a newspaper article, and by the following day, another furious correspondence was triggered off for the letters page.

Soon Bertie was getting Dora to check the newspapers for him for issues that might interest him, and passing on review copies of books to her, quizzing her afterwards on whether they were worth reading. Her first shock was *Room at the Top*, which had revealed to her, for the first time, that women could, and did, enjoy sex. The memory of the sordid, painful episode with the man in the hotel became less shameful. She could see, once again for the first time, that everybody might be allowed a few mistakes in life. And in any case, having to take dictation while Bertie stormed up and down the room saying things like 'masturbation is a perfectly normal part of sexual development' gradually inured her to shock.

'I don't think, Bertie,' she'd venture, 'that *The Times* will let you talk about masturbation.' She was blushing as she said the words.

'What? Why not? They should, they should. That's what's wrong with society today . . .' He'd stop and look at her. 'Dear Dora. As ever, you're right. More fool them though. Now let's see how we can word it so I can say what I want . . .'

Back in the twenty-first century, Dora finally bundled up armfuls of old newspapers, which had accumulated under her bed in yellowing piles, now stiff and fragile with age. She blew the dust off them and sneezed. These she would burn in the garden, on the patch at the end, where she usually stacked the autumn leaves. She didn't need them under the bed any more. She would never forget Bertie.

12

The world is newly minted at six o'clock in the morning in summertime, thought Lily as she opened her eyes. Anticipation tingled in her veins. The first day of the holidays. At last.

Vicky had promised to arrive early, so that they could leave town before the traffic and get to the Boathouse at low tide. Lily whirled round in a fever of activity, packing the car and getting ready to leave her dear little house for six weeks. It already looked forlorn, as if ready to summon up dustballs and mould the moment she locked the door behind her.

At exactly six-forty-five, framed by the sunlight, Chris and Natasha stood in the door. Natasha carried only the tiniest shoulder bag.

'Is that all you've got?'

Natasha smiled. 'Possessions are not important.'

'Oh. Right.' Perhaps such statements sounded better in Swedish.

'This is very good of you,' said Chris. 'Mind you behave yourself, Natasha.'

It was an austere departure for a father. Natasha looked, for one moment, desolate. Then she turned to Lily with a toothpaste-advertisement smile. 'Here I am! Ready to look after children!'

The children squabbled. The clock inched round. Several times, Lily went outside to the front garden, ostensibly to pull up a few last weeds before nature took over in her absence. What could have happened to Vicky?

The peace of the early morning evaporated with the mist. As the buzz of the city rose in the streets, car-exhaust fumes turned the skies a dull, pewter blue. The heat began to weigh heavily on Lily, draining her of energy.

'When are we going to go?' demanded Daisy. 'Ouch. Stop that! Mumm-ee, Billy's hurting me-e-e.'

'When's Harley coming?' asked Billy, surreptitiously kicking Daisy.

'Soon. Stop that! *Don't* hit Daisy.'

This dialogue was repeated, with remarkably little variation, a dozen times over.

By the time Lily heard the low rumble of a taxi at the door, her head ached and she could feel sweat running down beneath her clothes. The idea of a long drive no longer excited her, and she'd lost sight of the idea of the Boathouse as a sanctuary. Dora's warnings began to rattle round her head like a loose marble.

Vicky emerged in a tangle of luggage. 'Darlings. I'm so, so sorry. Nightmare morning. First the gardener was late, and then the cleaner, and it was simply impossible to find a taxi. Then Harley forgot his puffer and we had to go all the way back. Never mind.' She hugged Lily, who was trying to be welcoming rather than resentful. 'We're here, and you're off. You're a star.'

And she disappeared in a cloud of taxi fumes, calling, 'See you the last two weeks in August. Cam and I will be down to help.'

Lily spent the first hour of the drive having a conversation in her head, thus missing several turnings. The conversation, which she was not enjoying, and would have liked to have with someone else – although she wasn't sure who, as she wouldn't have quite dared to have it with Vicky at whom it was undoubtedly directed – went thus:

'Surely the gardener and the cleaner weren't coming that early? Couldn't she have got here first? And if she can afford a gardener and a cleaner, why didn't she get another nanny? Why am I taking her child away for the summer?'

'Because you offered. You wanted to. And temporary nannies cost the earth. Much more than gardeners and cleaners. And you thought it might help Billy.'

'Yes, I know, but in that case, why did she have to leave me waiting for an hour and three-quarters? When she knew it might mean that we miss the tide. Couldn't she do something about the gardener and the cleaner – I don't know, get Cameron to sort it, or whatever?'

'Cameron's hopeless. And she didn't know they were going to be late. Anyone can be late once. People living in cities don't remember things like tides. It's not worth making yourself miserable over.'

'I can't help it. I don't like sitting in stationary traffic just because someone else couldn't be bothered to organize their house properly.'

'Deal with it. Get your mind on to a higher plane. Vicky's a warm and wonderful person. You're lucky to have her as a sister-in-law. And you're on holiday. Time doesn't matter. Think about something intellectual. Use your brain. Stendhal and Proust couldn't have written like they did if they'd spent their time getting upset about trivia.'

'I bet Madame Stendhal and Madame Proust dealt with all that. And what about Flaubert? You don't write *Madame Bovary* without spending an inordinate amount of time obsessing over other people's domestic detail.'

'Ha, they never married.'

'Well, servants . . .'

Eventually she ran out of variations on the theme and reminded herself that she didn't want to turn into one of those madwomen who talk to themselves in cars. The warren of clogged roads and stop-start traffic lights gave way to a motorway, which raced past in a panoramic sweep of rolling green.

It crossed her mind that she was angry at Vicky because she was angry full stop. She had always vowed not to be one of those divorced wives or husbands who let their bitterness eat away at their lives like acid. She and Tom had done so well so far.

Let it go, she told herself. Just let it go.

*

As the miles inched slowly away, the sky grew darker and rain began to spatter heavily on the windscreen. By the time they reached Devon, it was like driving underwater, the windscreen wipers wearily slapping the water away for no more than a few seconds at a time. She was stiff from hunching over the driving seat, and aching muscles drilled columns of pain into the back of her neck, from tension or tiredness.

When she'd last been down these narrow, twisting roads, Chris had been at the wheel, competently negotiating the high banks and hedges. Now she could hardly see a few feet in front of her. Her hands tightened on the steering wheel, gripping in panic as the car slewed around the tight corners. On either side, the banks turned the lanes into Victorian fairytale tunnels of doom, with tendrils of dark, tangled vegetation reaching out to scrape and entangle the car. When a large van appeared, suddenly, from the other direction, she almost skidded into it, finally stopping a few inches from the van's bumper, her heart pumping.

'That was quite close, I think,' said Natasha pleasantly. 'Only two more inches and we would have had a big dent.' She laughed.

'Only two more feet and we'd have had to be cut from the wreckage,' muttered Lily. 'If they could have got the Fire Brigade down this lane.'

The other driver signalled that there was a passing space behind her. Reversing in restricted spaces had never been Lily's forte. She reversed, went up the vertical side of the bank, wheels spinning, and the car tilted perilously. She shot forward to correct it and finished up almost back under the van again. The driver and his friend settled in for the duration. They had, presumably, seen it all before. Watching tourists getting stuck was probably a local spectator sport.

In the end, Lily had to back cautiously down a steep incline, trying to convince herself that the car wasn't going to roll over or slip and kill them all, before finally wedging the car into a passing place. The two men waved at her, looking furious at the delay.

'If we were in London, I suppose I'd have been a victim of road rage by now.'

'If we were in London,' Natasha pointed out, 'the road would have been wide enough.'

Lily wasn't sure how many more Blinding Glimpses of the Obvious she would be able to take.

Nevertheless, a long journey changes you, she thought. You are not the same cross, tired person who set out five hours earlier. That is why people travel. To leave behind the parts of themselves they can't live with.

But they had missed the tide. The water was almost lapping over the pub car park, and the last few strands of seaweed on the edges of the beach were shifting, ready to float off.

They would have to go in the back way, over the cliff and down. Bloody Vicky, muttered Lily, promising herself that tomorrow she would become a nicer, less resentful person.

The track was steeper than she remembered it, and narrower, which must, she supposed, be the effect of the summer's growth in the hedgerows. Nettles, cow parsley and red campion rustled against the sides of the car, and the wheels strained in the mud as she tried to accelerate uphill.

Even Natasha was apprehensive as they bumped down the last, seemingly perpendicular, section of lane. Tree branches met overhead in a thick, dark mesh. The sun, thought Lily, rarely shines here.

'Is it really this far? I think this is a footpath,' ventured Natasha.

Lily fumbled with the padlock on the gate, weary with driving, and got back in to park the car under the gloomy mantle of spreading fir trees. She was already exhausted and defeated. Chris had been right. This was madness. They were town people. They would stay for the weekend, she thought, and would go back afterwards. As she pulled luggage from the boot, several large drips of water from the branches above landed on the back of her neck, trickling icy fingers into her collar. She shivered. At least it had stopped actually raining. For the time being.

'Look at the sky,' breathed Natasha, striding to the edge of the wood and stretching.

'Sky?' asked Billy. 'Can we get Sky down here?'

'No TV,' said Lily, wondering if she could stick to it.

'NO TV?' he roared. 'But that's impossible.'

'In my mother's house in the woods in Sweden, we do not have television,' said Natasha, as if that was the final word on the matter. 'We have television in the city. Not in the country.'

Billy, surprisingly, seemed to accept this.

'Here, everybody,' ordered Lily. 'Carry as much as you can. It's a long way down, and we don't want to have to come back up again.'

Grumbling, they obeyed, and set off down.

'Be careful,' she warned. 'The steps are very steep.'

As if to demonstrate, her foot slipped under her and she skidded down, dropping her bags. Groceries scattered down the hillside. Scrabbling to regain her balance, she saw a box of half a dozen eggs bounce neatly down the steps and a loaf sail out of its thin plastic bag to land in a large, muddy puddle.

There was a worried silence from the children. Lily slithered around retrieving the food, and, knees trembling with the effort, reached the Boathouse safely.

By the time she'd rummaged in her bag for the keys, praying that she hadn't forgotten them, then finding them tucked into a zipped pocket she hardly ever used, she was so tense that the key jammed in the lock. She tried to turn it one way, then the other, took it out and inspected it. Could it be the wrong key? Or perhaps it fitted another door. She tried again, but it stood stubbornly fast.

'I'm hungry,' said Billy. 'This bread is sopping wet.'

'I'm tired,' moaned Daisy.

'This is because Mercury is in retrograde,' observed Natasha. 'It causes many things to go wrong. It is well known.'

'Well, it had bloody well get out sharpish,' hissed Lily, wondering if she dared break a window, and if so, whether she'd fit through the shards of broken glass. Behind her, the sea looked cold and grey and the waves breaking on the beach foamed like dirty detergent.

'Shall I see if I can pick the lock?' offered Harley unexpectedly.

Lily didn't even want to think what lay behind this suggestion. It was hardly the kind of skill you'd expect from a tenderly nurtured scholarship boy. 'Let me try one more time.'

The door opened suddenly and she shot into the dark, cold interior.

Their brief day at the cottage had left no impact on the silence of thirty years. Even their scrubbing and cleaning seemed superficial, as if the building was too self-contained to be affected by twenty-first-century bleach. With the doors and windows closed against the weather, Lily could no longer feel the freshness of the sea and salt air drift through the quiet white rooms. A chill settled on her heart. It was very, very cold.

'What's for supper?' asked Daisy.

Lily opened the egg box. The eggs were still there but they were all cracked. 'Scrambled eggs.'

'On toast?'

'Perhaps.' She wondered if you could dry bread out, and, if so, whether anyone would notice the taste of mud.

The sound of water running down the hill made them shiver.

'The fire! That'll cheer us all up.'

The four children looked at her in disbelief.

But Lily had never lit a real fire before. Tom had done that, brushing her aside, telling her she was hopeless. Anyway, they'd always had log-effect gas fires that turned on at the tap and blew back in your face in a sudden whoosh of flame.

How hard could it be to light a fire? Lily felt her town-bred inadequacy once again. She looked at the logs Sarah had laid in the fireplace. 'I think you need paper.' They didn't have any. 'Natasha?'

'Only my old copy of *Vogue*. But I have read it.'

'I'll buy you the latest issue tomorrow.'

They scrunched up the shiny pages.

Matches. Lily sat back on her heels. Oh, no.

'I've got some.' Natasha handed over a flimsy piece of card with the name of a fashionable restaurant inscribed on it.

They wobbled and bent when Lily tried to strike them, failing to light as she scraped the tips furiously against the strip. Occasionally a spark flickered.

She got the last match alight and touched the edge of a piece of *Vogue*. After a few doubtful moments, it began to burn. 'There! We'll soon be warm.'

Daisy's lips were almost blue. Lily took off her cardigan and wrapped her in it. Most of their clothes were in the car. As the sky darkened to the colour of mud and raindrops began to crash like pebbles on the roof, Lily could scarcely bear the idea of climbing the endless, slippery stone steps again.

Then she heard Natasha's teeth chatter.

'Stay round the fire, you lot, and warm up. I'll be back soon with some more clothes.'

The steps up went on for ever and left her out of breath, her heart pounding in her ears. It began to rain again.

When she got back down once more, soaked to the skin and clutching as much as she could manage without slipping, four pale faces looked round at her in despair. 'The fire's gone out,' said Daisy.

'Don't you need smaller sticks and bigger ones as well as logs?' said Harley. 'My dad makes a pattern with them when he does a fire.'

Lily was too tired to answer. 'I've only got two towels.' She handed them out. 'Get as dry as you can and then we'll have supper and bed.'

They ate in exhausted silence. The wind howled around the trees and the water crashed against the jetty, jagged and arrhythmic. Daisy and Billy looked uncertain, and even Harley seemed nervous. Only Natasha appeared oblivious.

'It is also windy sometimes in Sweden,' she said.

Lily wished the sea didn't sound so like someone trying to break in, and had to remind herself that city fears were different from country ones. Human malice was different from the impersonal violence of nature. She opened the door and forced herself to look out, buffeted by the wind, but all she could see through the heavy grey air was the spray crashing against the rocks.

Natasha appeared behind her. 'It is very ghostly, don't you think?'

'I'm not worried about ghosts.' Lily closed the door again. She thought of Chris's words – that it was a dangerous place – and suppressed a shudder. She'd said she could make the Boathouse happy again, but she hadn't realized how small and powerless she was against the immensity of the sea and the sky. 'I just hope the building will withstand the storm.'

'I do not think it will be blown away. It has been here for many hundred years, I think.'

You had to be young to have that much confidence, thought Lily.

The thunder came after they'd all gone to sleep, crashing into Lily's consciousness like a series of explosions. She turned the light on, determined to convince herself that it couldn't hurt her. The Boathouse, she told herself, was built of thick, ancient stone, and was a part of the bank, low and solid enough to survive the wind and waves.

A bolt of lightning cracked nearby, and the lights went off. Daisy screamed.

'I'm coming. I'm coming. It's all right.' Lily,

shaking with fear, felt her way in the dark towards the children's room, illuminated by occasional stabs of lightning. Every few seconds a dark, small shape swooped and vanished, like a ghost across the corner of her eye. Bats. Chris had said there might be bats. Harmless bats.

'I'm here, Daisy.'

Daisy and Billy were crying, although Harley appeared to be asleep. There was no sound from Natasha's room either. 'I don't like the dark,' sobbed Daisy. 'I'm frightened.'

So am I, thought Lily, taking them back to her bed. So am I. Living with street lights, I had forgotten how black the dark could be.

Billy's small, bony arm reached out around his mother and sister. 'If Daddy was here, it'd be all right,' he whispered. 'But if anyone comes in, I'll hit them very hard.'

She drew the children close to her. He felt so small and thin and young. She was no good at being on her own, and neither were the children. Perhaps Tom was right. For better or worse, they all belonged to each other.

As she struggled to stay awake, ears straining for the sound of danger but only hearing the thud of her own heart, she slipped into multi-layered half-dreams, where she clung with the children to the side of a dizzyingly steep cliff as the water sought to knock them off. She dreamt she woke to find a faceless man in black pacing the house, searching for them all with a torch, and from that she woke to hear the sound of thumping on the door of the Boathouse.

Fully awake at last, she lay motionless, in liquid terror, too afraid to find out what a bang on the door in a storm, in such a remote place, might possibly mean.

This has been a terrible mistake, she thought. Chris was right. We shouldn't be here. She struggled to keep her eyes open, to remain aware so that if something – she wasn't sure what – happened, she could protect herself and the children. She owed it to them to stay awake, to remain on guard. She wouldn't let catastrophe catch them all asleep.

As the children folded into the curves of her body, a heavy weight seemed to press on her chest, and, through the hallucinogenic semi-consciousness of exhaustion, she struggled to breathe as if the ghosts of the cottage were trying to stifle her.

13

The telephone rang in Dora's house, startling her. She must have dozed off.

Sighing, she went to answer it. These days it would be some market researcher, wanting to take 'a few minutes of her time to answer one or two questions' or a kitchen company who 'just happened to be in the area' and could give her a free estimate.

'Dora?'

It was Cameron. Her heart jumped for joy. An old, worn simile, she thought, but so exactly appropriate. She had felt a little leap inside her, and a bolt of happiness.

'Dora, can I come and talk to you? About Dad and what really went on in the old times.'

'Of course.' She tried to tell herself that her legs had begun to tremble because she had got up too quickly after dozing. 'Whenever you like.'

'It's this TV programme.'

Dora's legs felt steadier. She took a deep breath. 'Ah.'

'It's called *Voices of the Sixties*. You see, they seem to think that although Dad was a good writer, and gave parties where influential people met each other, and advised the Government on the arts and all that, they're really only interested in what he wrote about sex. They say he was one of the leading voices of the permissive society.'

'That's all anyone was ever interested in,' said Dora. 'Whenever he mentioned sex the editor was swamped with mail. There were even questions in the House, once, I think. And I remember when *Time* magazine called London "the Swinging City", the telephone rang all morning. Bertie went down to Broadcasting House twice that day.'

'I need to write all this down.' Cameron sounded eager. 'Can I come round now?'

'Of course.' Dora could think of nothing better in the world than to see Cameron as soon as possible. 'I can give you some supper if you like.'

She heard a brief confabulation with Vicky. 'Great. About three-quarters of an hour. Can you run it all through your mind? Go over everything in case you remember something you've forgotten?'

Dora smiled as she put the phone down. She mustn't talk too much. Life was something that slipped by, until someone said, 'Do you remember *Z Cars*?' or, 'In my day, Spam was a pink luncheon meat,' and then you couldn't stop. It was boring for the young.

Cameron bowled in through her front door with the energy of large dog, and wrapped her in a hug. The other two, Tom and Chris, always pecked her cheek with sedate, austere kisses, but Cameron's greetings were whole-hearted and reminded her how rarely anyone touched her these days. It was the generosity of the loved baby, she told herself. The child that everyone wanted. Nothing more.

But we loved them all, she reminded herself. Chris and Tom were loved, too.

Cameron ranged restlessly round her small galley kitchen as she prepared a salad. 'How do you find anything in here, Dora?' He opened a biscuit tin. 'Can I?'

She checked it quickly. Sometimes she forgot about things like biscuits, and they grew mould, or attracted ants. Not, fortunately, in this case. 'Help yourself. Actually, I'm having a clearout.'

He laughed.

'It's taking me a long time,' she admitted.

'So.' After they'd eaten, he perched, as if about to fly away, on a stool. 'Dad. The sixties. The permissive society. Tell me everything.'

'It was Profumo that started it,' said Dora. 'For me, anyway. That photograph of Christine Keeler sitting naked on a chair. I couldn't believe it. In a respectable magazine.'

The Profumo affair was the first time that Dora had really talked, in public, about sex, as opposed to its romanticized form, True Love, which she and her girlfriends had puzzled over since they were thirteen. The confused tangle of who-slept-with-whom-and-said-what seemed to generate a heaving, libidinous, ever-increasing fog of sexuality, which continued to seep in everywhere long after the affair was over, as if the dam of respectability had been terminally breached. It faced her all the time like a personal challenge: even the serious newspapers and magazines debated over whether the pill would mean the collapse of society and morality, and there seemed to be constant advertisement of the nuts-and-bolts of the act through the long, farcical obscenity trials of *Lady Chatterley's Lover*, *Fanny Hill* and *The Naked Lunch*. Far from suppressing anything, thought Dora, censorship and the law seemed intent on coming together to make coitus the chief preoccupation of the day.

Especially at Maud and Bertie's house.

'I mean, it's obviously all right for educated people like us to read pornography,' said someone with the absurd name of Hugo Twistlethwaite-Smythe, over dinner. 'But I agree with the Lord Chancellor. It would destroy the moral fibre of the working classes if absolutely anyone was to be able to get hold of anything.'

Bertie's eyes turned into hard, dark pebbles. 'Why should that be?'

'Well, they're not used to handling sophisticated information. They're childlike. They must be protected. It's our duty.'

There were murmurs of assent. Bertie banged his hand on the table. 'Don't talk nonsense. People who *happen* to have a lot of money are no more able to handle information responsibly than people who *don't* happen to have a lot of money.'

'You're just a dyed-in-the-wool Communist, Bertie, that's what's wrong with you,' shouted someone else, and Dora saw a wife or girlfriend nudge the speaker. Occasionally she could see their friends remembering that, although Maud was a lord's daughter, Bertie, if not actually working class, came from decidedly lower-middle origins, even if he had been to Cambridge and refined his accent. As a watcher – someone who had always stood on the fringes without ever properly belonging – she quickly realized that the new egalitarianism was an eggshell-thin veneer of superficial change rather than a fundamental shift in attitude. Prejudices didn't get swept away that easily, and Bertie wasn't quite as careless of what other people thought as he liked to pretend.

Maud fizzed with fury at anything that she interpreted as an attack on her beloved Bertie. 'It's disgusting,' she said. 'If you've had the privilege of a good education, you ought to know better. I simply can't wait for private schools to be abolished. If we don't end that kind of prejudice in those they turn out, I'll . . . I'll . . .'

Bertie kissed her, passionately and publicly. 'You'll what, my little duchess?'

'Oh, Bertie. You made me forget what I was saying. You are awful.' She always took politics rather personally, and occasionally ran out of arguments, but there was no doubting the passion of her beliefs.

And it also took Dora a while to get used to the way these ideas were bandied around with such enthusiasm, with everyone calling each other fools, morons and Communists, only to leave at the end of the evening with slaps of bonhomie and: 'Bloody good dinner, Maud, as usual. Christ, I don't know how you do it on the fourpence a week that wastrel husband of yours earns.'

To which Bertie would reply: 'Sod off, you old reprobate, and never darken my doors again.'

They would both roar with laughter and agree to meet up next week. If anyone had called her father a fool, or, worse still, a Communist, there would never have been an end to it.

There were three kinds of guests around Maud's chaotic but generous dinner table. There were doe-eyed fawn-like dancers and models, who were an androgynous collection of beings and might as well have come from outer space as far as Dora was concerned. Then there were the movers and shakers: the boutique owners, property developers, publishers and writers and those who worked in new, exciting professions like advertising or television. And, finally, the old guard, who were mainly politicians and senior management of newspapers, all of them men. She found the newspapermen and politicians predatory and overbearing, and the models and music friends too stoned and pretentious – they were inclined to ponder for hours over pronouncements such as 'every fallen leaf has a meaning' – but began to make her own friends in the middle category. Mr and Mrs Dawlish became David and Christabel to her. Christabel Dawlish was always 'doing up a house' and selling it on to pay the school fees, and David complained that he never had builders' dust out of his hair. Maud, Dora and Christabel thought they might start a boutique together. Anything seemed possible.

Even sex. Or perhaps love. Dora was still in a muddle over them both, because of Simon. Simon was in advertising. He had a big-boned, strong face and heavy-lidded eyes, and he watched Dora like a cat watches a mouse. Covertly, she watched him back as he smoked, holding his cigarettes between the third and fourth fingers of his right hand. He wore tight, figure-hugging frilly shirts and velvet trousers and the hair trailing over his collar was an unlikely pale honey-blond. The contrast between this feminized, self-indulgent beauty and his obvious maleness – he had big rough-looking hands with nicotine-stained fingers and broad shoulders – made Dora self-conscious. If her father had ever met him, he would have ejected him from the house on the grounds that he was 'a poofter'.

Dora herself at first thought that Simon might be homosexual, and only interested in her as a cover, to provide an alibi if he ever got arrested for being gay. She didn't mind that, but she didn't want to fool herself and fall for someone who had no interest in her.

She met him at the Boathouse at one of the Full Moon parties. People appeared from nowhere, it seemed, by car and scooter and even motorboat. Suddenly the quiet jetty was roaring with shouted confidences and high heels wobbled on the decking.

'Tynan's just an old-fashioned spanker. The other day he told me . . .'

'Forget about two-dimensional painting, today's about counter-cultural images in art . . .'

'The sort of person who smuggles their own bread over when they go to France . . .'

'Oh, no, not the Cavalry Club, the Hungry Horse. Or Grumbles in Pimlico . . .'

Dora let it all drift over her. She was simply happy to be here, even if the smoke from Turkish cigarettes was like a curling stain in the clean fresh air. Someone was playing on the guitar. She was aware of a voice singing softly in her ear. 'Hi. I'm Simon.' He offered her a fat, crumpled joint.

She took it and tried a short puff, coughing.

'You don't have to, you know.' He sat down beside her. 'Nobody's going to think you're square if you don't.'

Dora had never felt entitled to male interest. She had grown up stooping, with her head slightly bowed, avoiding the pity of men in the street and assuming that male glances were for more delicate and feminine women. It was only now, with all six foot of Veroushka sprawled across the pages of *The Sunday Times Magazine*, that she'd learnt to stride down the King's Road as if she owned it, and look back at men when they stared. She still couldn't quite take it for granted.

'You and me,' Simon said to her at the end of that evening, as people pulled sleeping bags out under the trees or stretched out on sofas. 'We're both refugees from the Class War.'

'Are we?'

'Yup. Born into one thing. Making damned sure we end up in another.' He waggled his cigarette at her, indicating the night sky. 'You know exactly where you're going, and so do I. Up.'

Cameron wouldn't want to hear about Simon, though. He would want to know what Bertie had written about the pill, about abortion, nudity and homosexuality.

They had marched, she remembered. Bertie had expected them all to act, not talk. The whole family – Bertie, Maud, the children and Dora – went on marches, sit-downs and sit-ins. Bertie even got taken away, once. He was lifted by two policemen, still cross-legged, from the end of Whitehall during a sit-down against the Bomb. It was entirely good-natured, and he merely clambered out of the van at the police station and rejoined the sit-down again at the other end.

The pro-abortion march was different. Dora sensed stirrings of danger. Even with Bertie's arrogant, protective presence, she was frightened. The sheer weight of people pressed in on her, and the police, theoretically employed to protect the marchers, didn't think that nice young ladies marched, particularly not for issues like abortion.

'Slags,' hissed one policeman in her ear. Shocked, she turned, and Maud turned with her.

'What did you say?' Maud spoke in her best cut-glass tones.

He spat at her. 'Slags. That's what you are. In spite of your hoity-toity ways.'

It was only seconds from the spittle landing on Maud's cheek to her hand flashing out to slap his face.

She was arrested for assaulting a policeman, and Bertie had to bail her out.

'Have you come to spring me?' Maud asked, in her brittle, social way, when Bertie was finally allowed to see her. 'I thought prison would be a nice rest. I was looking forward to catching up on my reading.' Even so, she couldn't quite conceal her relief when Bertie persuaded the police to let her go. It was against her personal code to show fear or surprise, but Dora thought that beneath the brave, frivolous talk, Maud was very vulnerable.

'You gave me a fright,' Bertie told her. 'Don't do that again.'

'He called Dora a slag,' said Maud. 'I had to do something.'

'Yes, well, next time take his number and report him. Use the system, Maud, don't fight it. It'll crush you.'

Maud stuck her chin out, and fizzed with outrage. 'That's not how you work.'

That was the end of going on marches and sit-ins.

Bertie decided he could make more difference in print. One day the paper wanted him to write a column on the mock elections being held in schools around the country. Each school had to vote on whether they would return a Liberal, Labour or Conservative candidate.

'Look, Dora.' He waved the paper at her. 'Here's a public school, a real bastion of privilege, the sort of place with playing fields that won us the Empire, actually voting to put a Labour candidate in power. Naturally, all the other little Lord Fauntleroys have voted the way their parents would, but things *are* changing. At last.'

'Well,' said Dora. 'Maud will be pleased. After all she went through with her family to marry you. She'll be glad the children won't have to suffer that kind of prejudice.'

'Mm.' Bertie looked mischievous. 'I wonder what she'll do now? Now that she doesn't have that particular banner to carry.'

Like so many of his remarks, Dora didn't understand what he meant, but knew that he didn't really require a reply.

'Anyway,' he continued. 'The real breakdown in the class system will be achieved when people really can have sex with whom they like, when they like.'

'Your father,' Dora said to Cameron, 'believed that sexual repression was used as a method of controlling people. The Government and the Church, he always said, knew how to get a man by the goolies. If he's under control sexually, you don't have to worry about him. A rather old-fashioned view, in my opinion, but there you are.' She leant forward to pour herself some more coffee. 'You see, he grew up in a society where you had to get married if you wanted sex. The nice, stable set-up devised for Noah's Ark, where the animals came in two by two, was the foundation of Britain in the fifties. Along with the class system. Sex was controlled by the Church, and everything else was controlled by class. So everybody stayed in their place and did what they were told. Bertie tried to open people's eyes to what they could achieve if they broke down those barriers. He wrote about sex as a way of rebelling.'

'Not as a personal thing?' Cameron was surprised.

'Oh, no,' replied Dora. 'I don't think he thought about sex as a personal issue at all. For him it wasn't about a man and a woman. It was about ideas and values and social mores.'

'Do you think he was right?'

Dora was jolted. No one had ever asked her if she had agreed with Bertie. She had typed out his opinions, and knew more about them than anyone. 'I think there was some truth in what he said. Especially then.' She spoke carefully. 'But I didn't wholly approve of it, to be honest.'

She felt, after forty years, a deep disloyalty at admitting it, but Cameron's smile was her reward. 'Good old Dora. Always independent-minded.'

'I'm afraid your father would have said I was small-minded if I'd ever said that to him.'

Cameron bent over his notebook. 'He had lots of famous friends, didn't he? I think they're going to want to talk about those. Everything's about celebrities these days.'

'Well, let me see. He knew Ken Tynan. And Laurence Olivier. And Mary Quant. And some of those rather dodgy businessmen that hung around Harold Wilson, but you don't want to go mentioning them. He met Mandy Rice-Davies a few times, and thought she was lovely. He got around to meeting most people who mattered, in fact, although I don't know how many of them were really what you'd have called friends. He was just there, at every party, in every nightclub, table-hopping at every restaurant.'

'How did he ever find the time to write?' asked Cameron, who was also gregarious.

'That was the problem.' Dora could hear the regret in her own voice. 'He always believed he could write the Great British Novel, and, of course, he never did.'

'He wrote at the Boathouse in the summer, didn't he?'

Dora hesitated. 'I think it might be best if you didn't talk about the Boathouse. It was . . .' She tried to think of a good reason why not. 'It was his private place. He . . .' She wasn't making a very good job of this.

'He what?' asked Cameron.

'Well, it was very much . . . a private thing,' she

repeated. 'I mean, I don't think you should let them film there or anything.' She hoped Cameron couldn't see the tiny quiver in her hands, or that, if he did, he would assume that it was nothing more than the tremble of an old woman.

He thought for a while. 'Oh, OK. I'd rather they filmed in London anyway.' He grinned wickedly. 'In my studio preferably, with my paintings in the background.'

'Oh, yes.' Dora could hear the sudden warmth in her voice. 'That would be much the best.'

'Are there any papers or anything?'

Fortunately, thought Dora, there weren't. 'He never kept a diary. But I've got some newspapers upstairs that I was going to throw out. They're full of his columns and articles. You can have those if you like.'

'Could I?' Cameron jumped up, ready to get them immediately. 'You're fantastic. Keeping everything like that.'

'Not for much longer,' she warned him. 'I'm going to start a new life.'

Cameron paused at the bottom of the stairs. 'Good for you. So am I.'

What? When? How? The questions hovered on her lips as he bounded up to the first floor, but she'd lost him.

'Are you working at the moment?' She managed to slip in one question as he piled the old newspapers into the back of the car.

He straightened up. 'You sound just like Mum.

When am I going to get a proper job? Am I earning anything? You know I'm not like Chris and Tom, I'm not a salary man.' He drew breath. 'But I'm working on something. Now, Dora, stop worrying about me. I'm fine.'

She waved him off from the side of the road, and he tooted farewell. After eleven o'clock at night. An angry head appeared at a window to protest and she hurried inside.

She would always worry about him.

14

When Lily woke up, the sunlight was bright on the water, and the children had gone. She could hear their happy voices chirruping outside.

Ten o'clock. First day at the Boathouse. Lily remembered the freezing misery of the night before and raised her head. She could see right across the bay without even leaving her bed. Cotton-wool clouds scudded against a cobalt sky and the cliff-sides framed the windows, dropping down to the beach. There was no trace of the storm. Pink and purple foxgloves poked out of the wild herbs and the tall, swaying grasses stood proudly refreshed by the rain.

Nothing is as bad as what goes on in your mind, thought Lily. Nothing is as destructive as your own dreams. Had that knocking been part of the hallucination, too? Surely no one would have come here in the middle of the night.

Daisy raced in. 'There are ducks, Mummy, and swans. Can we give them that bread you dropped in a puddle?'

Lily sat up. Her head ached, like the day after exams. 'Why not? But wait for me.' She pulled on her jeans and a T-shirt and followed the children outside, feeling the satisfying smoothness of wooden boards under her bare feet.

The air was crisp and clean, yet soft against her skin, like the finest linen laundered with lavender. A single outboard motor puttered across the water, setting off concentric circles of ripples across the stillness. At the edge of the jetty, two majestic swans, followed by a dutiful line of half-grown cygnets, conducted a royal progress, turning their graceful heads from right to left in search of titbits.

Billy leant forwards, aiming the bread towards them with as much accuracy as he could muster. Seeing the intensity on his face, she reflected that what he really needed was something like this to be involved in, something that wasn't a computer game.

Within moments every other bird in the estuary seemed to have heard about the free breakfast.

'Now I know where the phrase "pecking order" came from,' she murmured, as they screeched, flapped, quarrelled and hovered with frustration only a few yards away from them.

'Look,' cried Billy, 'there's a little one there that hasn't had anything.' He threw a piece towards it, and several bigger birds cawed in fury.

'Look how white their breasts and necks are. As if they're wearing starched shirts,' said Lily. 'They must use the best washing powder on earth. Perhaps they could give me laundry tips.'

She was amazed at their perfection, and the differences between them. There were speckled grey feathers over the white breasts and formal black plumes on tails. Brightly coloured legs poked out from the plump bodies like scarlet or yellow stockings. They all seemed very smart and prosperous, and reminded her of a flock of white-coated doctors and black-robed barristers, all arguing furiously amongst each other in some medical negligence case.

'Can we get a book of birds?' asked Billy.

It was so long since he'd asked for anything except a takeaway pizza or a PlayStation game.

She ran her hand over his head, and drew him to her. For a second, he stayed, before twisting away again. A second was better than nothing. She carried the warmth of that tiny gesture around with her for several hours, like a spark of hope.

After fiddling with the lock of the pontoon, they were able to get the car over at low tide, and bring the rest of their possessions in.

'Look,' said Natasha, opening up a big cupboard under the stairs to put away coats. 'Hats.'

There was a row of pegs, hung with hats, as if their owners would be back soon. There was Bertie's panama and his tweed cap, a floppy lace hat she'd seen Maud wear in photographs, and several frayed wide-brimmed straw hats. There was even a bowler. Natasha placed it on her head and began to dance.

'I'm Ginger Rogers. Or Fred Astaire. Don't you think?'

Lily laughed. 'You won't get much dancing here,

I'm afraid. Just old ladies and tourists eating vast crab suppers.'

'I can find dancing anywhere.'

The boys discovered a little dinghy, apparently in perfect condition, except for its peeling red paint, tucked under the eaves of the veranda. Lily traced her finger across the name. *Enchantress.*

'I wonder whose this was.'

'I think perhaps it was Grandmother Maud's,' said Natasha. 'She was a very beautiful woman.'

Lily felt her loss like a sudden punch, a sharp, astonishing indrawn breath of pain. The realization that she would never see Maud again seemed as fresh as it had the first time she heard the news of her death. 'I'm surprised that people of your age ever think that older women can be beautiful.'

Natasha smiled. 'It is only our bodies that grow old.' She flicked her blonde hair back in a graceful arc. 'She had inner beauty, I think.'

They began the holiday ritual of unpacking, imprinting the sunny cottage with their own personalities.

Natasha set out crystals along the window sill.

Daisy colonized the tree house with little scraps of material and toy horses.

Billy refused to do anything, so Natasha unpacked his little bag of clothes and set out his board games in a neat pile on a bookshelf.

Harley set out a library of impressive books on the shelf beside his bed, and stacked balls and bats in the cupboard.

Lily's domain was the bedroom that had belonged to Maud and Bertie, a long, low room with a glass door opening on to a narrow balcony, facing the sea. You could lie in bed and watch the birds and boats going about their business.

She pulled open the drawers of a tall chest. There was a faint smell of cedar and old dust, but they were empty. Lily wondered about summer clothes unpacked and laid out by other hands over the years, and picked up the newspaper lining the drawers. Nineteen sixty-seven. Wasn't that the Summer of Love? There was a photograph of three toothy women in beehive hairdos and thick eye make-up, who were, apparently, the Carnival Queen and her attendants. She skimmed the editorial. Should dinghies sail from Beesands beach? 'We allow horses and dogs on the beach,' wrote one correspondent. 'How can we turn away dinghies and trailers?' Another article implored people not to play their transistor radios outside. She folded the newspaper away in the drawer again, and laid her T-shirts and jumpers on top.

She opened the window, and let the breeze shimmer through the air. The thick white walls seemed to whisper to her as the faded curtains fluttered. It was strange that somewhere so empty could feel so resonant of old memories.

'Time to go shopping,' she informed the children, adding, 'I mean exploring,' at the sight of their faces.

Reluctantly, they plodded back up the hill. 'I want to stay behind,' grumbled Billy.

'Another time. When we all know the Boathouse well enough, then you can stay behind. If Harley or Natasha are here to look after you.'

'Shopping is fun,' Natasha added. 'Perhaps we will find sweets.'

'I hate shopping.' Billy kicked the back of the car seat as Lily set off.

'You hate everything,' said Daisy, for which she was rewarded with a slap. She burst into noisy wails.

'For God's sake!' shouted Lily. She turned. 'Just be quiet, will you, Billy? You ruin everything, for everybody, all the time.'

Billy slumped angrily into the seat, and stared out of the window, occasionally quietly kicking the back of her seat again. She ignored this.

Failed again. However you should have dealt with that, as a parent, she thought, she had not.

They stopped at the Post Office on the way out of the village. A tanned young Australian eyed Natasha's endless legs and tiny shorts with interest.

Natasha ignored him; she was busy studying the noticeboard. It proclaimed Summer Solstice Dances, Womanspirit seasonal gatherings, a Dance of the Seven Veils course of bellydancing, Tantra for Women and a Clowning course aimed at relieving anxiety. Perhaps I should do that one, thought Lily.

'There is so much going on here,' murmured Natasha, taking down a few numbers.

'I can show you around, if you like. I'm Pete.' The Australian offered to shake Natasha's hand. She looked at it absent-mindedly, as if not quite sure what it was, then shook it with a brief hello. She doesn't realize how beautiful she is, thought Lily.

'Do you have echinacea?'

'We have most things, but not echinacea. You could try Diana Henry just out of the village. She sells odd things.'

'Is it a farm shop?' Lily had visions of a roadside shed filled with fresh leeks and carrots, and pick-your-own strawberries. Were there fields of echinacea in Devon?

'Not really. She does Women's Self-discovery courses and some healing, along with pottery. Second left out of Salt Creek. Down the lane, follow the signs to the pottery and on your left again. Or she's got a little shop in Totnes.'

They bought enough basic provisions to last the day.

'We can order for you,' said Peter. 'Free-range local meat, organic wines . . .'

Lily, feeling that it was important to support local produce, placed an order for the following day.

'Send the kids up to get it,' advised Pete. 'Quite safe for them here. We can keep you a tab.'

Natasha said goodbye politely, but without warmth. Peter's eyes followed her out of the shop.

Oh dear, thought Lily. I'd forgotten that this is what it's like for young girls. The constant bombardment of male interest. Natasha seemed coolly able to take care of herself, though.

They drove along the coast without any real sense of where they were going. Natasha rolled down the car window and her long, corn-coloured hair whipped around her shoulders.

The cliffs vanished, to be replaced by crescents of smooth, golden beach, with waves ruffled by white sea horses. Swathes of wild mustard blew in the wind, their frondy tips echoing the yellow shingle. Lily stopped the car by a memorial.

'Look, boys, here's where the American army trained for the Normandy landings. In the Second World War.' The boys read the inscription and looked down the beach. Harley began to run down towards the sea and back again. 'It's harder than you think. To run on the sand.'

Billy couldn't resist a challenge. 'Bet I can do it.'

'You'd have had packs on your backs,' warned Lily. 'All your kit and ammunition.'

'I'll take the shopping.' Billy seized two carrier bags from the back of the car.

'You can be the Germans, Daisy,' said Harley. 'And we'll attack you.'

'I don't want to be the Germans.' Daisy pushed her lower lip out. 'They got beaten.'

'I'll be the Germans with you,' offered Lily,

deciding that the shopping would probably survive.

Billy stomped off down towards the water, scattering pieces of shingle with his feet.

'You could be the Germans, too,' Lily cried after him, determined not to be seen as siding only with Daisy.

He didn't turn to look at her. 'Don't be stupid,' he shouted into the wind.

'Girls can be Germans.' Natasha settled herself brightly next to Lily and Daisy, her back against the concrete sentry post. 'Boys are the Americans.'

Lily got the impression that Harley wasn't entirely pleased by being outnumbered. Still, it showed that Natasha knew how to handle them all. Lily's back sank into the hard concrete behind her in relief and she turned her face to the sun.

Harley, like Cameron, she thought, always wanted to be in the thick of it all. Or perhaps, like Vicky, he always wanted to win. Natasha's act had switched the balance of power from the Americans to the Germans, and Harley hadn't liked it at all.

The game petered out, and they returned to the Boathouse to swim. As the tide came higher up towards the jetty, the children waded in deeper and deeper, with shouts of excitement. Lily, first shocked at the iron quality of the cold, waded steadily in, leaning against the weight of the water, before turning, with a final gasp at the chill. The temperature settled to perfection, and she drifted, floating on the salt, her last anxieties seeping away into the sea.

'Salt water is very good for you,' Natasha informed her, swimming out with determination, her hair spreading around her like a halo of seaweed. 'The salt in the water is very like the minerals in our bodies.'

'Mm.' Lily had already discovered a bowl of rotting gunge in the fridge which Natasha claimed to be her fruit face pack.

As they returned, wet and exhilarated, to the Boathouse, it settled around them in comfortable folds like an old blanket. We belong here now, thought Lily, revitalized by the water. For now, this is our home.

That evening, as they spooned up pasta, there was a knock on the door. She looked at Natasha, who shrugged.

'Perhaps it's a ghost,' offered Daisy. 'Someone who died here long ago.'

Lily tried not to think of Bertie.

'I'll get it,' said Natasha, whose bright, Scandinavian helpfulness seemed to be permanently turned on to maximum.

'Hello, there! I heard that the Devereauxs were back.' The man who stood at the door was in his early fifties, his face weatherbeaten with sailing and beer. He was wearing, only slightly unfortunately, shorts and deck shoes.

'The next generation.' Lily indicated Billy, Daisy and Harley. 'And this is Natasha, Chris's daughter.'

His eyes flickered to Natasha's studded belly button, and the hand he extended to shake waved around uncertainly between her and Lily. 'Roger Henry. Old friend of Chris and Tom's. From way back when. Thought you might all like to come round for a neighbourly drink next week.'

'That's very kind of you.' Lily rescued the hand before it wrapped itself around Natasha's honey-coloured midriff, and shook it.

'We could get these chaps sailing. I run a sailing school. Children a speciality.' He indicated Billy and Harley. 'Is the old *Enchantress* still here? I could have a look at her if you like. Check she's seaworthy.'

'I'd like to go, too,' said Daisy.

'Good for you, young lady.'

'Have you got children?' asked Lily.

'All grown up now, ha, ha. Off in London earning lots of money. Well, you have to these days, don't you? Not like me. I married a local girl. Diana. Another old friend of Chris's. You two will get on.'

'Diana Henry of the pottery? They told us about her in the Post Office.'

'The very same.' He looked around. 'Ah, it's good to see the old place opened up. I used to come here in Bertie's day. Happy Valley, he called it. There was always a drink. Or a party.'

'We're rather dull, I'm afraid,' apologized Lily. 'But would you like some tea?'

'How kind of you.' He settled himself at the table. 'I heard that Chris was going to sell.'

'The Boathouse is owned by all three of them,' Lily pointed out. 'It's not just Chris. The others want to keep it.'

'Quite. Quite. Anyway, if they do decide to let it go, let me know. I'm sure Chris would want to give locals first dibs.'

Everybody wanted the Boathouse. 'I'll tell them.'

'Now then, what about next Tuesday? Around seven o'clock. Bring everybody. We're at Halfcross Farm, about three miles beyond Salt Creek. Named after an old stone cross at the end of our drive. The Early Christians set it up at the crossroads, and it lasted there for about two thousand years, but people in cars kept crashing into it. So they put it at the side of the road. I suppose that's progress for you. From here you go straight through Fore Street, or rather Foreplay Street, as I always call it, ha, ha . . .' He set about giving her a complex set of directions, punctuated by lots of 'you can't miss it' and 'if you see an old barn, you've gone too far'.

'And stay for a bite, afterwards, why don't you?' he asked Natasha's small, pert breasts.

'That's very kind, but—'

'Thank you so much,' interrupted Natasha. 'I have offered to cook some nights, so I think you may have rescued me.'

'Well that's that.' He straightened up. 'Just thought you might need to know a friendly face nearby.'

'That's very kind of you,' said Lily.

'See you next week,' chorused the children.

He pinched Daisy's cheek affectionately. 'And mind you help your mother out, you little rascals,' he said. 'If you're good, you can have ice-creams after your sailing lesson.'

Lily phoned Tom, to tell him they'd settled in.

'We've met a Roger Henry. He says he's an old friend of yours.'

'Roger?' Tom was vague about names. 'Roger? Oh, Roger. Roger Henry, you mean.'

'That's what I said.' She was often irritated by Tom. 'He says he's married someone called Diana who used to be a friend of Chris's.'

'Mm. Chris's first girlfriend. Absolute stunner. I was about eleven and she was the first girl I actually noticed. More than noticed.'

No trouble in remembering that name, Lily noticed. 'Did Roger pinch her off him?'

'No, not really. There was some dreadful row over her, but . . . er . . . anyway, I can't remember now. Still, I wouldn't mention her to Chris if I were you. He goes all dark and terse if you do. You know what he's like.'

'I don't suppose I shall be speaking to Chris.' Was this desire to sell the Boathouse an exceptionally long sulk over a girlfriend? If so, it seemed rather self-indulgent and spoilt.

'He wants to buy the Boathouse,' she added.

'I know. When Maud died, he asked about it in his letter of condolence. So sorry to hear about Maud, what about selling me the Boathouse.'

'No!' She was pleasantly scandalized.

'When it comes to property,' Tom said, 'people will stop at nothing.'

'We're invited to Halfcross Farm next week for supper.'

'Chris always used to call it Doublecross Farm. Diana's family have been there for generations.' Tom laughed. 'But Roger's pretty harmless underneath it all. Unless you're female.'

'He was slobbering over Natasha a bit.'

'Well, you be careful, too,' said Tom, an edge in his voice. 'He's not called Roger for nothing.'

'*I* don't have affairs with people who are married.' Even as she spoke them, she knew the words sounded unnecessarily aggressive. Their conversations so easily swung round from pleasant chit-chat to argument in a few seconds.

'I think it's time you let go.' There was an edge of anger in Tom's voice. 'There's nothing to be gained from going over the same old ground. You've got to move on.'

'I have moved on.' Lily thought about her peaceful day. Perhaps, if she lived here all the time, she could feel that peaceful all the time. That would be moving on.

Tom ignored her last statement, as if to deny it. 'Can I speak to the children?'

'Fine.' Her voice sounded clipped, even to her own ears. 'Daisy! Billy! Your father wants to speak to you.'

Daisy, who was playing with a jigsaw on the floor,

looked up, her eyes suddenly shadowed with wariness. 'Daddy!' She took the phone from Lily and turned away, as if to confide secrets.

Lily left the room angrily, shouting Billy's name.

'I haven't done anything!' he shouted back.

Lily took a deep breath. 'I'm sorry, Billy. I wasn't angry at you. I was . . .' Too late she remembered that it was important not to criticize the absent parent. 'I was angry at myself,' she concluded.

Billy crouched, hostile and disbelieving, almost a wild animal, halfway down the bank.

'Billy. You have to be careful climbing. You know Grandpa Devereaux was killed there.'

'I'm careful. I'm careful. I'm careful,' he screamed at her, leaping down the bank.

'Your father's on the phone.'

He rushed past her without acknowledgement, grabbing the receiver from Daisy.

She let it happen. Anything was easier than another round of confrontation, and she'd already lost this one when she lost her temper with Tom. 'Your father', she thought, sitting on the side of the jetty and letting her feet dangle above the water. Those were angry words. Not 'Dad'. Shouting at the children because she didn't like what Tom had said to her. Putting her eight-year-old daughter in a position where she had to whisper to her father in secret. How much am I to blame for all this, she asked herself? Was I wrong?

She watched the rosy stripes of sunset settle in

the sky. The smoke of the Boathouse's log fire, now burning without difficulty, hung on the still air, perfuming the night with the scent of Darjeeling tea. Across the water, a few lights twinkled in distant houses. Were they filled with happy people?

You can't run away from your problems, she thought. They come with you. Tom was right: she had to move on, rather than remaining entangled in the same old mesh of anger, accusation and resentment. For the children's sake, if not for her own.

She remembered a saying. Those who cannot remember the past are condemned to repeat it. If she understood what had made Tom, what motivated him, and why he had come to behave in the way that he did, she might be able to forgive him. And she knew that until she was able to forgive Tom, she'd never be able to forgive herself.

'Natasha?'

'Mm?'

'You don't mind sleeping in the children's room if we have visitors, do you?'

'I am very happy to sleep anywhere,' replied Natasha.

Lily picked up her mobile and began to climb the steps. When she reached the top she took a deep, clear breath of air, and dialled Dora's number.

'Dora? It's so lovely here. Why don't you join us for a week or two?'

As she walked back to the edge of the jetty, she heard the knocking sound that had woken her in the middle of the storm. Boom. Soft and firm, like a single blow on a heavy door.

She looked towards the cliff. It was the water, banging an occasional giant wave against the rounded interior of a cave. Boom. The water sprayed out, and the wave sagged back.

Once you know what something really is, you are no longer frightened. She turned the thought over and over in her mind, like a smooth, shiny pebble.

I 5

Dora took the train to Totnes. Arriving at the pretty Victorian station was like going back in time. Or stepping on to the set of a BBC costume drama production. She almost expected to see people in top hats and crinolines, but there was only Lily, waiting for her in the car park, looking better already, Dora noted.

She was worried about Lily, and Tom, too. She suspected one or both of them was having second thoughts. Good. Of course. If they got back together, Dora, for one, would be delighted. But an idyllic summer at the Boathouse might distort that decision. It was easy, she knew, to fall in love with a family, rather than a man, and the Boathouse wove its own magic. You found yourself doing things you would never normally have done.

The steep Elizabethan streets and ornate clock towers of Totnes gave way to winding green lanes peppered with wild flowers.

'I remember thinking,' said Dora, 'when we buried Maud: Oh, good, it hasn't changed.'

'It's very well preserved.' Lily spoke cautiously. 'But underneath I think it's all very different. Lots of wealthy second-home owners and blow-ins running consciousness-raising courses, and you get a better choice of organic balsamic vinegar than you would in Notting Hill Gate.'

Dora smiled. 'That's survival for you. They always were a canny lot down here. Don't be fooled by the mañana attitude.'

Lily laughed. 'I love it, actually. I used to fume in London if I got into a slow supermarket queue. Now I think: Oh well, what does it matter? Mind you, that's easier if you're not working.'

They swooped down alongside the coast, where the drifts of wild mustard guarded the sand.

'I went fishing here once with a boyfriend,' said Dora, and caught the surprise in Lily's eyes. She had always been good old Dora to them, never a young woman with her own doubts about love.

All the talk about sex made it seem more like something that you might actually do. Without shame, even. And if Dora was going to actually do it, she sensed that Simon was the most likely candidate. She and Maud had discussed whether he was gay or not, and Maud had said definitely not, or if he was, he undoubtedly swung both ways.

Maud and Bertie conspired to ask Simon round as often as possible. One evening there were eight of them mopping up one of Maud's delicious coq au vins with crusty bread. They discussed Freud and whether the clitoral or the vaginal orgasm was the more mature.

'What do you think, Dora?' Simon's voice cut across the chatter.

She froze, as everybody looked at her with the polite, indulgent fascination accorded a child. Or a social inferior or a zoo animal, she thought, with one of her few flashes of bitterness.

She made herself laugh. 'Who wants a mature orgasm? Sounds like something you might get at a Women's Institute meeting.'

They all laughed, and her heart sang to think that she was now, truly, a part of the witty swinging scene, the one that foreigners and provincials read about in newspapers. She, too, could make jokes, and talk about sex, and, she thought, from the way Simon raised his glass to her when no one was looking, that she could now accept that she had an admirer.

When she gathered up the plates and went out to the kitchen, he followed her.

'I love the unawakened act.'

Her sophistication abandoned her. 'Sorry?'

He took her chin between his thumb and fore-finger and turned it towards his face, studying her. 'You're one sexy lady. And I don't suppose you even know it.'

Dora fidgeted, which was not what sexy ladies did, she suspected.

'Have you ever had an orgasm?'

Innately truthful, she moved her head, turning her face away from him.

He gently took hold of her chin and drew her face

round, so she had to look into his eyes. 'I think that's a no.'

She disentangled herself and began to wash up.

Simon folded his arms. 'I can promise you one. No strings. No expectations. No guff about love. Everything cool. Whenever you want.'

She refused to acknowledge him for a few moments, and scrubbed the chicken off the plates. Sex on her terms. It sounded . . . possible. Less frightening than sex with love. Not as messy and difficult as sex with desires and emotions. And wasn't that what mattered? Being honest. Not trying to trap men into marriage the way her mother's generation had.

'I'll think about it.'

He looked amused, and went back to join the others.

'Here.' She called him back. 'Make yourself useful. Take in these plates.'

He paused in the doorway. 'There's no reason why you or I should be their servants. Not any more.'

'We're not. We're their friends. And friends help out. Maud made this syllabub. I'm bringing out the plates so that we can eat it.'

Simon took the bowl from her, dipped a finger in to taste the creamy concoction, and shrugged. 'Mm. OK. Because it tastes good. But I think they're using you.'

That evening he offered to drive her home. She knew that was a euphemism. If she arrived back in

Stockwell late, reeking of cigarettes, good food and wine, her parents would come downstairs in their dressing gowns – her mother with her hair in curlers – and screech abuse at her until they realized that the neighbours might hear.

She was determined to shake off the tyranny of what the neighbours might think, and make her own decisions. She accepted Simon's offer.

'Your place or mine?' He had a Jaguar E-Type parked outside Maud and Bertie's house.

His flat was strewn with girls' underwear and tights, hung out to dry over chairs and on a rack over the bath.

'Caroline and Jilly,' he said, carelessly. 'My flatmates. And before you ask, no, I don't sleep with them. It would spoil a beautiful relationship.' He pulled her down on the sofa. 'Let me give you a tip. If you decide to share a flat, go for men. We use the laundrette or take it back home to our mothers. Women leave things soaking in basins, then hang them up to dry beside the fire so that the room always feels damp.'

She nodded, aware that he was trying to make her relax with inconsequential talk. His eyes weren't talking about the laundry.

'Brandy or Scotch?'

She swallowed a large swig of some fiery liquid, hoping for courage, and looked around. The rooms were big and dusty, and filled with cheap, hideous rental furniture.

'So.' Simon assessed her. 'Virgin?'

Dora tried to stop her teeth chattering, and shook her head. Simon's flat was freezing cold, and she was frightened.

'Oh, God.' He raised an eyebrow. 'One or two gruesome experiences, then, I take it?'

She nodded again, wondering if she ought to run away now. But he'd sounded so confident when he'd talked about giving her an orgasm, and she suspected that this was her only opportunity to find out what it was like.

'Well, I like a challenge.' He took her by the hand and led her into his bedroom. As she sat nervously on the bed, he lit the gas fire, removed two damp pairs of tights dangling from the mantelpiece and chucked them out the door ('They get in everywhere, those sodding things, like some sort of awful fungus'), unzipped the back of her dress and began to massage her shoulders. 'Calm down, baby. I'm really not going to hurt you.' He put his mouth to her ear, so that she could feel the warmth of his breath on the side of her neck. 'Just relax. Leave it to me. And any time you want us to stop, say so. This is about pleasure.'

And she did, and, surprisingly, it was.

The difficult, intimate aspect of the night was spending it in the same bed together. Simon's bed was huge, but the bedclothes kept slipping off, and bits of her froze successively in turn. When she woke up, stiff, aching and hungover, and realized that her eye make-up and false eyelashes had rubbed off, and she was back to her pale skinned-rabbit look again, she turned away from him. He drew her back

This time, without the protection of her eye make-up, she felt much more truly his. But he had offered her an orgasm, not a relationship.

Relationships weren't cool. Sex was. She got dressed.

'Like we said. No strings, babe? OK?'

Dora laughed. 'I'll be the first with the scissors. At any signs of string.'

He winced, and she saw respect creep into his eyes. 'I was right.'

She stopped at the door. 'What?'

'You're one helluva foxy lady.'

She smiled and closed the door behind her. 'Goodbye.'

So that was that. Sex no longer frightened her. She could get on with her life without worrying about it. A bit like having your tonsils out, or explorers having their appendixes removed before going into the jungle, she supposed, so it wouldn't pop up and be a nuisance when you least expected it.

Yet, for someone who claimed an aversion to meaningful relationships, Simon lifted the lion's head knocker of the Devereauxs' blue front door surprisingly often.

Dora let him in.

'Hi, doll.' He kissed her on the lips.

'I'm still working.'

'I'll be downstairs. You can come out later with me if you like.'

Sometimes they went to a pub, after which she'd take the late bus back to Stockwell. Or they'd join other people and drift, like an eddy of fallen leaves, from nightclubs to parties and back again. She rarely knew the hosts of these parties, and neither did Simon, and sometimes there didn't seem to be any host at all. People would mill around on the street and cluster on staircases, grinding their cigarettes on the carpets, and drinking from the bottles they'd brought, until someone was sick down the stair-well or suggested somewhere better to go. While Simon carefully avoided any formal link, such as 'girlfriend', he made it clear that Dora was under his protection. He bought her drinks, looked across the room or down the staircase occasionally to make sure she was 'all right', and took her home to his flat at the end of the evening, although she would never have been surprised to find another girl in his bed as well. That, in this day and age, she thought, was as much as you could expect from a relationship.

'At least . . .' Dora modified her possession of Simon to Lily. 'He was as much of a boyfriend as one had in those days. It was uncool to demand anything of anyone, like fidelity, or even that they'd turn up when they'd said they would.'

'I don't think I could stand that,' said Lily. 'Surely

you couldn't have gone out with him knowing that he might be sleeping with someone else?'

'Men called you bourgeois if you worried about things like that. Or heavy. Mind you, I think that was so they could sleep with as many girls as they liked without having to feel any sense of responsibility. I'm not sure how much women got out of Free Love. Although Simon had a flatmate called Jilly who happily romped in bed with any number of men and seemed perfectly happy about it all. I rather admired her for it.'

Lily lapsed into an abstracted silence, and Dora's mind, always ready to slip into the past these days, returned to the time when Bertie asked her if she wanted to take a week off.

'You can borrow the Boathouse. Take Simon if you like. Or any of your friends.'

'I . . .' Dora wondered if he could read minds. Until recently, it hadn't occurred to her to think about holidays, as she was no longer expected to join her parents on their annual fortnight in Ramsgate. Simon and his friends were beginning to talk about package holidays in Spain, which she couldn't afford, although they were very cheap. Simon, she thought, would go off with Jilly and Caroline – who'd just come back from hitch-hiking to Greece with plans for more of the same – and there would be girls in bars, and girls in his bed. She reminded herself that jealousy was an outdated emotion, and irrelevant to the sixties, but it still hurt.

'Come on. We work you hard enough.'

'OK. I'll see what Simon thinks.'

Simon said he didn't mind if they went. Maud handed her the big old key and Dora settled herself in the passenger seat of Simon's car, tying on a scarf to protect her hair and wedging on a huge pair of sunglasses. He accelerated out of the city and down to the coast.

'I love summer,' she shouted over the wind.

'I love you,' he shouted back.

She thought she'd probably misheard.

It took them all day to drive down, stopping at a pub on the way. The further west they drove, the more she was aware of people looking at them. It was like being a film star. You could tell they came from London, from the King's Road, the place where everything that mattered happened. They might as well have had the words 'we are hip' emblazoned on the side of the E-Type. Dora affected not to notice, but was secretly thrilled. She wore a sleeveless shift dress she'd made herself: short and tight and flowery. He wore a dark paisley tunic with a Nehru collar and a Ban-the-Bomb pendant nestling among several strings of beads. His hair was longer than ever and so were his sideburns. Dora's father would have been horrified, but there was something about the wildness of the bay when they reached the Boathouse that made the most outlandish clothes seem tame and ordinary. Compared to the vivid cobalt sky, the flame-colour blaze of rhododendrons at the edge of the cliff and the frothing white caps of the waves, they were specks of dull, man-made neutrality.

'Hey.' He was speechless at the sight. He pulled her to him. 'Far out. Really. Far out.'

She disentangled herself. She'd always thought that the bay was full of eyes, watching, and she knew Simon's inventiveness about sex. She was not an outdoors girl in that respect, she thought firmly.

She remembered that week as a time apart from the rest of her life. A kind of dream. It was like playing house. In London she'd always had the feeling that Simon was looking over her shoulder for the next good party or groovy chick. Here, he and she slotted together as if they'd been made for each other. They woke up early, as the sun hit the sea outside, then lazed in bed until one of them could be bothered to get up.

'Last one into the sea makes breakfast,' shouted Simon.

Dora threw a pillow at him to slow him down, and skidded past, screaming. She raced into the icy water. 'Bacon and eggs for me.'

Simon had other things on his mind. 'You're so sexy with your hair wet.'

She pulled away. 'Stop it. Someone might see.'

'Like . . . ?'

'Beast. Sex-obsessed beast.' She tickled him and tried to run away over the waves.

'Oh, no, you don't. Wait 'til I catch you.' They collapsed in the water, shrieking with laughter.

In the evenings they ate freshly caught crab, mackerel and lobster, bought straight from the fishermen, pulling a table out on to the deck in front of the cottage, wedging a candle into a Chianti bottle and talking until the moon cast long, silver shadows over the water.

Simon shared the cooking with her. Dora was amazed. She'd never heard of a man who could cook.

'I'd never have thought it of you.'

'I have hidden shallows.'

They fished off Beesands. Simon caught three mackerel, and was too delighted even to pretend to be cool when he also bagged a sea bass.

'This is it, babe.' He laid the fish down on the ground and beat his fists on his chest in a mock drum-roll of triumph. 'You don't get finer than this.'

'But, Simon . . .' Dora gesticulated.

'Sh.' He kissed the tip of her nose. 'I am going to photograph . . . No, *you* are going to photograph the Master Fisherman of All Time. With a sea bass.' He rummaged in Dora's basket for his camera. 'And then we have a fish dinner you'll always remember.'

'Simon!'

'Don't interrupt a man when he's on important work. And nothing's more important than fishing.'

He straightened up. 'Why are you hopping about like that?'

Dora let out a cry of anguish, and he turned to see the sea bass and all three mackerel borne away by a fleet of cunning gulls who had been circling them intently.

'Oh, no!'

For a moment his face clouded and then he began to laugh. 'Oh, Dora.' They clung to each other, gasping hysterically. 'I'll just have to take you out to the best restaurant around, won't I?' He wiped his eyes.

They never made it to the restaurant, though. They spent the rest of the day in bed, and when Simon cooked up some scrambled eggs on toast for them to eat on the jetty, Dora thought it was the best meal of her life.

16

'Does everybody know why Tom and I split?' asked Lily as they sat out on the jetty, having eaten supper and put the children to bed. Natasha had gone out to the pub.

'Why you're divorcing? Not exactly.' Dora stretched her legs out to feel the warmth of the dying day against her skin, sighing with gratitude to feel the sunshine seep into her bones. 'Do you want to tell me about it?'

'It seems, in a way, too trivial, especially after what you've said about . . .' Lily waved a hand to indicate possibly 'sex', possibly 'love', possibly 'life'.

'It wasn't trivial to you.'

'No. He had an affair.' Lily paused, as if searching Dora's face for shock.

Dora had guessed this, some time ago. 'I see.'

'It was at work. The way these things are. After Daisy, we were both busy and tired, and I'd started at Dotcombomb and was working very hard, and, you know . . .' She stopped, remembering, perhaps, that Dora didn't know. 'Well, we didn't, I admit, make love very often. Not as often as we should have done, maybe. But he never complained, or talked to me about it. I would have . . . I could have . . . or maybe I couldn't, but at least I'd have *known*. Instead I went on trying to get everything right, not realizing that I was missing the point. I knew it wasn't perfect, but I thought it wasn't bad. Not that bad, anyway.'

'I don't think men do talk. Not about that sort of thing anyway. And it wasn't necessarily your fault. Or bad.'

'Maybe not. But when I did find out, it was too late. I'd look at him and think: He's slept with her. He'll compare me with her. Was she thinner? Did she do different things? I know I should have been putting my marriage back together but I literally couldn't bear him to touch me.'

'And what did he do?'

'Begged, wept, pleaded, promised, broke it off with her, did all the washing-up for about a year. There isn't a hoop he didn't jump through. I can't blame him for not trying, but all the time I was sitting there, feeling frozen inside, thinking: I can't do this. I can't find the way back. It was as if something had broken between us. I don't know if I should have tried harder but I didn't see how.'

Dora feared that anything she said would sound like a platitude. She looked across the bay. It seemed untouched by time, with its huge expanse of water fringed by the same distant thickets of blackthorn, oak and pine along the shoreline. The tide had receded, leaving a promising slice of sand at their feet, where oystercatchers and greenshanks were busy picking out plump, juicy worms from the sand pools. The occasional crow, the beach's undertakers, hopped between them, black and straggly.

Lily's voice steadied. 'After a while my lack of response became a problem in itself. Tom started to accuse me of being cold, I shouted back, and it all slid away from there. A very ordinary story, I expect.'

'No, Lily, not ordinary. It happens, all too often, but it's never ordinary.'

'If we'd lived in the sixties, like Maud and Bertie, perhaps I wouldn't have taken it so seriously. Maybe I was just being heavy, or whatever they used to call it.'

'It still hurt. Even in the sixties. I remember, here, on this bench, just after we arrived one summer when the boys were young . . .'

Dora realized that she shouldn't be breaking a confidence. But did it count if everyone was dead? 'Well, Bertie once told Maud something that made the light go out of her eyes. For years, really.'

Dora hadn't heard what Bertie had told Maud on the bench at the Boathouse. Maud, only ten minutes later, walked back into the kitchen and gave Dora the smile of a clockwork doll.

'Are you all right?' asked Dora, feeling a sense of deep apprehension.

Maud opened a kitchen cupboard and stared vaguely into it, as if she had no idea what she was doing. 'I'm absolutely fine, Dora, thank you.'

'Can I get you another drink?'

Maud looked at her with a blank, shocked expression on her face. 'Honestly, I'm absolutely fine.' She picked up the whisky bottle and sloshed some into a glass. 'A little top-up for you?'

Dora shook her head, and, for one moment, she thought Maud might be about to cry.

But Maud breathed in and laughed a light, social, brittle laugh.

'Dear old Bertie's been confessing. Really, it's all too silly for words. This is the sixties. If he wants to' – her voice changed, dropping hard and low – '*fuck* a silly little model, then I hardly need to be kept informed of it.' Her eyes glittered with tears. Or anger.

Dora looked quickly outside. Bertie was striding out along the beach. She put a hand on Maud's arm. 'Maud! How awful.'

Maud raised her chin. 'Really, Dora, you are sweet. But it's all too boring for words, I simply can't be bothered to discuss it.'

Dora barely slept that night. She'd never, ever thought that Bertie would be unfaithful to Maud. They all talked about sex, incessantly, when people dropped in for drinks, dinner or coffee; they read about sex; and even, in Bertie's case, wrote about sex – as a commentator, the obscenity trials were meat and drink to him – but she'd never taken any of it seriously. Maud and Bertie were to her what the King and Queen had been to her parents. Beings that belonged together divinely. The following morning she woke up and told herself that Bertie had obviously slipped up, just once, had confessed all to Maud, and begged her forgiveness. Everybody can make one mistake, after all, and if Maud wasn't worried, well, who was Dora to judge?

For the rest of the holiday, Dora never felt that Maud was quite with them. It was an imitation of a perfect summer, not the real thing. Dora worried about it for a few days, then tried to push it all to the back of her mind. Maud and Bertie didn't follow the rules. They made them.

Several months later, back in Chelsea, Dora let herself into the house as usual. Neither Bertie nor Maud woke early. She always picked up the post from the mat and lit the fire in the study. It had a tiny marble fireplace converted to gas, which gave out a feeble, flickering heat. From time to time a man came from the Gas Board, shook his head at it, pronounced it a 'death trap' and went away again.

There were two desks: Bertie's handsome leather partner's desk, and the former dining table for Dora, with a huge typewriter on top. The days of four and five-course dinner parties hauled up on the dumb waiter were over, Maud had declared. Everyone could muck in around the kitchen table now.

Dora's first task was to open Bertie's post and lay it out for him to read. She then typed out his copy, which he scrawled, in a loose, spidery hand, across reams of lined paper. He'd throw this at her, asking her to 'type it out in rough', after which he edited it in pencil, swapping round paragraphs, altering words and adding or crossing out whole sections. This procedure was repeated dozens of times over.

If she took him at his word and typed it out 'in rough', he'd toss it back at her, telling her that mess was unprofessional, and he couldn't think straight faced with a piece of paper like that. If she took too long, arranging column headings and paragraphs carefully, and correcting typing mistakes, he'd ask her what the hell was going on and why there was such a delay.

He was equally contradictory about the letters. Dora opened them all, dividing them into two piles for 'business' and 'personal' after she'd checked their contents, and putting the most urgent first.

One day, he received a thick four-page hand-written letter, on lilac paper. 'Dearest Bertie,' it began. 'It was so wonderful to see you again at last on Sunday. I can't live without you, and I know, deep down, you feel the same. You don't mean it when you say it's over. I proved that on Sunday . . .'

The letter almost fell from Dora's fingers as she read the words. 'I wonder if the others guessed that, only a few feet away from them, you were making passionate love to me. I'm not ashamed of it. In fact, it gives me a thrill to think that anyone – even your wife – could have walked by, looked past the hydrangeas and seen me with your . . .'

Dora could see words that she had never read before,

or never read in a woman's handwriting, short, four-letter, physical words that spoke of urgency and sweat and animal noises. She flipped through to the signature, dizzy with shock. It was from a girl called Camilla, a model who drifted in and out of the house in an ephemeral way; she talked in a childlike voice and ignored Dora completely. Dora remembered that Maud and Bertie had spent the previous Sunday lunching at a friend's house and that Maud, sounding tired and slightly drunk, had said that Camilla had turned up. She was the daughter of a stockbroker in Virginia Water.

Dora's heart thumped as she placed the letter, trembling in her hand, on its pile. So it was still going on. It wasn't a one-off mistake. There was something about Bertie being unfaithful to Maud that felt like Bertie being unfaithful to Dora. Her face burnt, and she bent over her typewriter, making mistakes that she never usually made. She was, almost for the first time in her life, profoundly and genuinely scandalized, and felt physically sick.

She thought of Maud's pale, tense face over the summer, and the way she often seemed far away from the conversation, giving herself a little shake and smiling brightly if anyone addressed her.

Yet Maud had always agreed with Bertie at dinner parties when he proclaimed that sexual fidelity was irrelevant. 'You're letting yourself be dictated to,' she'd told one woman. 'By the Church and the State. Think for yourself.'

*

Bertie strolled in and sat down at his desk. 'Morning, Dora.'

She muttered something.

She could tell, from the room's complete stillness, exactly the point at which he picked up that letter. He ran through it quickly and folded it up. 'Did you read this, Dora?'

'What?' Her voice croaked. 'Only the first line to see whether it was a business letter or not.'

'Hm. Well, when a letter is obviously personal, kindly don't open it.'

Dora was too frightened to ask how she could tell from the envelope. Only a few people typed their envelopes, and the rest were usually hand-written.

'Oh, and that girl Camilla. She's completely stoned. Or mad. I don't know which. Doesn't know what she's doing or saying most of the time. If you open the door to her' – Bertie avoided Dora's eyes – 'say we're not in.'

He filled his pen from the inkwell he kept on the desk and cleared his throat. 'I did tell Maud, you know. I don't keep secrets from her.' As if that made it better.

Dora didn't reply.

'Dora,' he said. 'This Camilla girl means nothing to me. I ended it in the summer, and she, sort of . . .' He raised his arms helplessly. '. . . came back again. Just the once, on Sunday. I . . .' He flung down his pen. 'Goddamnit, I don't have to justify myself to you.'

'No, of course not,' whispered Dora.

'But it is definitely over now.' Bertie sounded more confident, more like his old self. 'Maud understands.' His expression changed again. 'Although perhaps we won't mention Sunday? It was a complete aberration.'

Dora shook her head vigorously, and began to leave letters in their envelopes if the writing looked particularly feminine.

'For God's sake.' One day, he threw a letter written on pink paper across the desk. 'This is from a maker of sanitary ware. They want me to write about their bidets. I write about major social shifts and Government policy. Not lavatories and washbasins. Can't you filter things a bit better? I'd prefer not to have this stuff on my desk at all, but if, for some reason, I do have to read it, the least you could do is to open the envelope.'

'I thought that as it was hand-written and on pink paper . . .'

'Well, I don't pay you to think. I pay you to open my post.'

And so it went on. The compensation was being a sounding board for his acute brain, and hearing about what this minister or that captain of industry had said, and getting a different view of life from the one printed in the papers. And he often asked her opinion, and she learnt to give it frankly. When the paper wanted him to write a column on whether the availability of the pill would put prostitutes out of business, he asked her what she thought.

'I mean, if anyone can have sex any time they like, then there won't be any need to pay for it, will there?'

Dora hesitated. 'Er. Only if the only reason for saying no is being frightened of getting pregnant.'

Bertie's eyes met hers in a complicity that was more intimate than any physical experience she had ever had with a man. 'Of course, Dora. Of course. How could I, of all people, be so stupid?'

She wondered what he meant.

He scribbled on the piece of paper again. 'Mind you, it'll be different when unmarried women are allowed it. That'll change things. And it'll happen. They can't get the genie back into the bottle now, especially not now we've got a Labour Government at last.'

Dora wondered if Camilla had got a supply somehow. You could pretend to be engaged, she'd heard, although it didn't always work. Camilla was the sort of girl who knew how to circumvent rules and laws. She'd even got past Dora a few times.

'I found out later that Camilla had threatened to tell Maud all about their affair,' said Dora to Lily. 'Bertie had owned up, but waited until they were at the Boathouse. I don't know why – maybe he thought she couldn't run away at the news from there, or he thought it would all be easier to handle if they were on their own instead of in the middle of

London. He'd ended it, he said, and it had meant nothing to him.

'Maud felt very threatened by Camilla. She couldn't see that she was the kind of young, pretty, slightly dotty girl that entrances men until they see that she's genuinely unstable. Then they run a mile.

'You see, Bertie loved Maud, he really did, but they lost each other, for several years. He was getting very well known – he was always on radio or television doing things like *Just a Minute* or *Start the Week*, and one of the St John Conroy books was made into a film, so he suddenly started to do rather well again, and girls like Camilla thought he was up for grabs. They took no notice of Maud's status as a wife at all. Wifedom, suddenly, wasn't cool.'

'That doesn't excuse his behaviour, though.'

'Is that what you think I'm doing? Perhaps. There was a certain reverence, in those days, for the male sexual drive. Men were supposed to need *it*' – Dora's voice italicized the word – 'at least twice a week or their health might suffer.' She began to giggle at the thought. 'It was as if they were attached to some massive out-of-control hormonal warhead that might go off in the wrong direction if it wasn't regularly serviced. There wasn't as much idea of individual morality in the matter as you might think. Although, of course, divorce was very shocking.'

'Perhaps that's why Tom thought he could do it. Because his father got away with it.'

Dora placed her hand on Lily's. 'No. The boys never knew about that particular episode. I doubt if they even noticed there was anything different. They still don't know.'

'Don't you think you ought to tell them, then?' Lily's voice was taut. 'They're all — even Chris, I think — trying to live up to some impossible ideal of marriage, because that's what they thought their parents had, and now you tell me it was a complete fraud?'

'It wasn't a complete fraud,' said Dora, gently. 'It was just harder than it seemed on the outside. And they didn't know about that, but they knew about . . . Well, they knew it wasn't perfect. Whatever Tom lets himself believe now.'

'You should still tell them, though.'

'That's what I keep asking myself.' Dora got up and smoothed her dress down. 'But one thing will lead to another, and . . . well, once you start unravelling secrets, you can't always predict what will happen next.'

17

When Lily rang Roger Henry to find out if Dora could be included in the invitation, he barked with laughter. 'Dora Savage? Good God. Is she still alive? Must be about ninety now. Will she be able to manage the stairs?'

Lily reassured Roger that Dora was only seventy-four, and Roger said they would love to have her.

The Henrys lived down a narrow lane lined with hedgerows, their farmhouse nestling in a dip in the hills as if it had grown out of the earth. It looked Georgian, or perhaps older, grander at the front than at the back, and ramshackle, facing a courtyard surrounded by barns. There was a shady tree in the middle with a table and chairs under it. A notice propped against one of the barns proclaimed it to be a 'Studio and Gallery Café'. 'Coffee and organic cake', it said, was '£1.60'.

'It was just a muddy farmyard when I was here last,' said Dora. 'It looks like a cappuccino bar now.'

'A very rural one, you must admit,' said Lily, taking in a little vegetable patch to the side with its compost heap and the tumbling flowers everywhere.

'It's like a secret place,' said Daisy. 'And there are horses.' She rushed to the side of the field where a shaggy pair of ponies eyed them curiously. 'And hens! Mummy, this is lovely.'

Roger opened the door to them. 'You're here. Good. Good. Splendid. Wonderful.' He took their coats. 'Dora Savage.' He raised his voice, as if addressing someone slightly deaf or senile. 'You're looking well, dear. It's nice to see you down here again.'

'I am well,' said Dora crisply. 'You're looking a lot older, Roger.'

'Good, good,' said Roger, obviously not listening. 'Now what's your poison? Squash, young lady?' Lily saw Daisy beaming. Children, she had noticed last time, liked Roger.

Roger ushered them all into what, until you noticed the wind chimes and straggling money plants, looked like a classic English sitting room, puffed up with chintzes and strewn with books, magazines and flowers. Every surface toppled with papers and objects. Two small, yappy dogs scurried to inspect the newcomers and a shapelessly fat cat draped itself over the back of an armchair, emanating languid disapproval.

'Now, this is my lady wife, Diana. Diana, Lily Devereaux, and Natasha, and all the little Devereauxs.'

Lily had the impression of one of the thinnest women she had ever seen. Her eyes were a startling aquamarine, but the rest of her was a skeleton, with overtanned skin stretched tightly over high cheekbones. There was a fine mesh of lines around her eyes. Lily could see her eyeing Natasha warily, and wondered if she starved herself to retain Roger's attention. She wore a full, flowing canvas skirt, and her hair was plaited around her head as if she were dressing up as a member of the Bloomsbury group, or auditioning for the part of Maria in *The Sound of Music*. Lily was transfixed.

Diana took one of Lily's hands in both hers. 'It's lovely to meet you. And I really mean that.' She continued to hold Lily's hand, looking intently into her eyes, until Lily longed to twitch away. 'What delightful children,' she added.

'This is Natasha, my niece. Chris's daughter.' Lily indicated the others.

Diana released her hand and clasped Natasha's. This time the interest was less mannered, as if Diana was genuinely fascinated.

'I can see that.' Diana traced her finger along Natasha's cheek. 'You have such a look of Chris. Although, of course, you're much more beautiful.' She laughed. 'I find it extraordinary, don't you, seeing my friends' faces in their children's. Like shadows from the past.'

'I know what you mean.' Lily did.

Diana released Natasha's hand and looked round at the others. 'Well, you're all very different, but I can see Devereauxs in all of you. And Dora. How lovely to see you. After all these years.'

Lily could feel one of the terriers trying to hump her lower leg and tried, unobtrusively, to shake it off.

'Don't take any notice of her,' said Roger, bearing

down with a glass of red wine. 'This year she's into all this Wiccan stuff — faeries, angels, personal development, the lot — and she talks a lot of nonsense as a result. Last year it was turning the barn into a gallery-cum-coffee shop. Not that anyone ever comes down *here* for a cup of coffee. Down, Boozer! Off!' The last remark, accompanied by a swipe, was addressed to the terrier, who yelped, but scuttled off, looking indignant. As Lily took the glass she thought she felt Roger's hand caress her bottom. It was a light touch, like a spider weaving a cobweb against her trousers.

His breath, smelling of beer and crisps, wafted in front of her nose. 'Boozer and Bagshot are a pair of rogues and thieves,' he declared. 'The cat's Falstaff. Only interested in the cat equivalent of wine, women and song.'

The dogs nosed around the floor in search of dropped crisp crumbs, entrancing Daisy, who had refused to go with the boys, as urged, to find the ping-pong table in one of the barns.

'Tell them about your pottery, Diana,' boomed Roger. 'She does a good line in grockle bait.'

'Grockle bait?'

Diana's transcendental smile never wavered. 'I'm afraid Roger is an utter philistine. "Grockle bait" is craftwork designed to appeal to tourists. I tried,' she sighed deeply, 'to renovate local craft by starting up a gallery, but I soon realized that there are more important things in life.' She lowered her voice as if confiding a secret. 'You know,' she whispered, 'there just aren't enough hours in the day.' The blue eyes bored into Lily. 'My real work is healing.'

'That is so neat,' said Natasha. 'Do you know anything about Reiki?'

'My dear.' Diana turned to Natasha again, with excitement. 'You've come to *exactly* the right place. Totnes has been a centre for natural medicine for, oh, nearly two hundred years. It's a place that I'd really describe as . . .' She sketched out wonder with her hands. '. . . quite, quite magical. I've got a little shop there, in fact, so if you'd like to pop in one day, I'd love to show you round.'

To Lily's relief, some of Diana's intensity drained away in the warmth of the candlelit kitchen. She spooned out a vegetarian casserole and passed a plate of chick peas round. Her face, without the trowelled-on welcome smile, had deep lines of sadness etched down from nose to mouth. She and Roger, Lily noted, never looked at each other.

Billy and Harley passed the chick peas quickly on, and tried to hide the casserole under their forks.

'Brown bread,' said Billy in tones of disgust.

'Sh,' hissed Lily, nudging him. 'How pretty.' She indicated the flowers on the table. 'Are they wild?'

Diana nodded. 'I know that conservationists don't think you should pick wild flowers, because their seeds will be lost to the future, but I throw these on the compost heap afterwards so they do get a chance. And I think there *must* be a middle way between conservation and moving forward, don't you? I mean, do you agree? Or not?'

Lily hadn't given it much thought. 'Well, yes . . .' Out of the corner of her eye she could see Dora whispering to the children, obviously conspiring to help them conceal the food.

'Perhaps you think we should just conserve?' Diana's tone implied that it mattered, very much, what Lily thought.

'Well, I just don't know . . .'

'You see, that's the trouble. If you don't mind my saying so, not you, of course, but people don't *think*. They just do what they like. And our hedgerows are being *lost*.' Her voice rose at the end as she focused on Lily.

'Oh, dear, er . . .'

'A hundred years ago, each farm labourer was allocated his own stretch of hedgerow to manage.' As Diana leant forward, the freckled skin of her cleavage crinkled against her T-shirt. 'It was the perfect way of keeping it in good repair. The labourers took out what they needed: wood prunings for firewood or small cuttings for tool handles. They'd let one or two trees grow to full length and cut them down eventually to carve into furniture. You'd even grow a tree for your own coffin, and by the time you cut it down, your grandson would have planted his own coffin tree. It was a cycle.' She gesticulated a circle in the air. 'And they made jams with the berries in autumn, *of course*, and used the wild flowers in their remedies.

'Now, I'm all for modern medicine, believe you me, but I do think that such a lot of the old wisdom has been lost in this drive for—'

'Do shut up, Diana,' said Roger, amiably. 'Nobody cares about hedgerows.'

'That's the problem, Roger,' Diana replied in a tight voice. 'Nobody does.'

'Yes, well.' He sounded irritated. 'You don't have to bore our guests with it, that's all.'

'I am not bored,' said Natasha. 'I would like very much to hear more.'

'She gets worse,' said Roger to no one in particular. 'Another mad idea every year. It frightens me, it really does.' He poured himself another glass of wine and left the room. Lily wondered if one of them should follow him, but Dora shook her head.

'There's at least one farmer round here, you know' – Diana leant forward towards Natasha again – 'who swears he keeps his vet bills down by managing the hedgerows in the old way with lots of wild flowers. The cows and sheep use it as a kind of medicinal dispensary . . .'

Lily tuned out, letting the words flow over her.

'You can often tell the old uses by the names.' Diana picked a purple blossom out of the vase. 'Houndstongue. Used against dog bites. And other skin diseases, of course. And this . . .' She touched a marigold-like flower. 'Yellow fleabane. Against fleas and midges. It really works.'

Lily wondered if there was one called Mistressbane,

which could be used to keep your marriage safe. It would be scarlet, with a twining habit, perhaps. Diana could use some, she thought. She could see Roger, outlined in the late summer twilight, on his mobile phone in the garden.

'Tell me.' Diana turned back to Lily again. 'Is Chris coming down?'

'I don't think so.'

'Give him my love if you speak to him.'

18

They got back to the Boathouse just before midnight.
The moon had turned the trees silver, casting grey
shadows across the path. Lily carried a sleeping Daisy,
and slipped her into bed, while Billy and Harley, having
demanded to stay up, fell asleep without a murmur.

'There's a bench which has a wonderful view of the
bay,' said Dora, making herself a coffee. 'Maud used
to call it the Moonlight Bench, because it's best to sit
there at night under the full moon. Otherwise you'd
come a cropper trying to get up there in the dark.'

'Let's try it, then.' Lily looked at the full round
disc in the sky. 'It must be about the full moon now.'

They picked their way cautiously up the steps and
off the path, round through the rough grass, their
clothes brushing against dewy, fragrant leaves, then
catching on the sharp prickles of dog roses. Lily felt
the ground slip beneath her feet several times, and
wondered if Dora could manage it.

Dora sat down painfully, breathing hard. 'Well, I'm
glad I can still make it.'

The sea was a sheet of battered pewter in the
soft, clear light. 'How much nicer only to be able to
see this occasionally,' mused Lily, 'when the moon
or weather is right. No garden lights or anything.

Just lucky chance, like a shooting star. Out of our control.'

'Yes. That is what makes it special,' agreed Dora. 'And the fact that it's the only truly dangerous bit of the cliff.' Dora indicated a rail a few feet ahead of them. 'Although the steps seem pretty lethal, I don't think you'd get anything much worse than a twisted ankle if you fell down them or anywhere else on the hillside, but there's a sheer drop down to the rocks from here. This is where Tom went over, the first time we came. That's why they had the railing put up.'

'What happened?'

'Tom used to follow Chris around like a little dog. We hadn't warned the children about going too close to the edge, and Chris was very adventurous. They were playing King of the Castle up here. Then Tom just tumbled over.'

Lily looked at the rocks forty feet below her. Even on a quiet night the waves thudded against them, booming as they hit the inside of the cave. 'Was the tide up?'

'No. But he landed on that ledge, there.' She pointed to a few feet of rock, jutting out around ten feet down, with a tree growing out of the hillside.

'The trouble with toddlers is that you can't *tell* them to stay still. Or to grab hold of a rope. Or anything, really. Tom started to cry, and before we knew it, he was having a fully fledged tantrum, with drumming heels. He was likely to go over the edge at any moment. It would have taken us too long to drive to the village and get the coastguard. Maud screamed when she saw what had happened, and Bertie came out of his office. "Back," he shouted. "Back. Or you'll all fall."

'That's when Chris slipped down the side as well, shouting: "I'll get him. Don't worry."'

'Oh, no.' Lily visualized a six-year-old slithering down towards the ledge.

'I felt awful about that,' said Dora. 'One of us should have gone, not Chris.'

Lily craned her neck to see. 'An adult weight could have dislodged everything.'

'It could have done. But the ledge is still there. So it wouldn't have. I remember seeing Chris's little body edging and bouncing down towards Tom, and the way Tom clutched at him, nearly sending them both spinning over the edge. I thought that if we lay down we could almost reach them. It's not so very far, after all.'

'Far enough.' Lily judged the distance. It wouldn't have been quite possible for an arm to reach a small hand stretching up.

'I know. But Bertie managed to find a rope from the boat, while Maud and I called to the boys, telling them that if they kept absolutely still we'd give them a packet of Smarties each. And ice-creams. I don't think Tom really understood, but Chris kept his arms round him and calmed him down. Still, if Tom had lost it again, he'd have pitched them both off. Eventually Bertie got a rope tied securely round a tree and dropped it down to them, instructing Chris how to tie Tom securely on.'

'Six is a bit young, isn't it? Were you sure he could understand?'

'We didn't have any choice. We pulled Tom up very slowly and carefully. I made silly faces and clapped my hands, to attract his attention, to stop him wriggling or starting another tantrum. We knew Christopher's knots would be unlikely to hold against one of those. It seemed an age until he was safe in Maud's arms, and we could drop the rope again.

'The worst of it was that Bertie was angry with him. Angry. With Chris. For playing such dangerous games with his brother. He never mentioned the rescue. Never praised him. And Chris was so brave. So very small and so very brave. Much more than any of us. Maud and I told him how wonderful he'd been, but you could see he didn't believe us, because his father was angry with him. Bertie was so very, very hard on his sons.'

Lily wondered if this was a kind of plea bargaining for Tom, a petition for understanding. 'Was it Bertie who had the rail put up?'

Dora nodded. 'He was determined that there wouldn't be any more accidents.'

Lily surveyed the cliffs around the bay. They dropped away sharply, but you could probably scramble down them safely, and in many places they'd been terraced, by the Edwardian gardeners, she assumed. There was no other dead drop. 'Was this where Bertie himself fell over?'

'No one really knows,' replied Dora. 'Well, I must be off to bed.'

Lily looked at Dora's coffee in surprise. She'd hardly started it. Bertie's death, of course, she remembered. They hated to talk about it. All of them.

'Oh, do wait a few moments,' she said. 'Tell me . . .' She thought quickly. 'I know, about the boyfriend you brought here. Didn't you ever want to marry him?'

Dora, half out of her seat, relaxed. 'He used to say that marriage was bourgeois. It was his favourite word. He was determined to reject everything that his parents had been.'

Funnily enough, she remembered, thinking back, so had she.

Something caught at Dora's throat when she and Simon packed the car to return to London on their last morning at the Boathouse.

'Here,' he said. 'For you. To remember me by.' And he handed her a shell, not a remarkable one, but so perfect in its speckled exactitude and its blush ceramic underside that she could hardly believe it had ever weathered the sea.

'It's beautiful.'

'So are you.' Simon could never resist the corny one-liners.

Dora wrinkled her nose up and tried to smile. 'We'd better go.' She didn't want to look back. She thought

Simon would return to his city persona, declaiming philosophies about the stuffy middle-class nature of fidelity.

But back home, nothing changed. Bertie still fumed about politics and sex, Maud seemed more rudderless than ever, and Simon continued to turn up at the door at the end of the day.

One evening, she finished tidying Bertie's desk and sealing up the last post, and went downstairs to where Simon, Maud and a stoned-looking girl were rolling a joint at one end of the kitchen table. At the other end of the table, Tom, his tongue sticking out of the corner of his mouth in concentration, was doing his homework.

Bertie followed her down. 'What's this, Maud?'

Maud lit up, inhaled deeply and blew three careful smoke rings. 'What's what, darling? This, here, is a bottle of Hirondelle. White wine. Not, perhaps, quite as classy as Daddy's Pouilly-Fumé, but perfectly drinkable. One must cut one's coat and all that. And that, there, is your favourite Scotch. And this artistic ceramic work here is an ashtray . . .'

'You know what I fucking well mean.'

Only Maud could look him in the eye when he spoke in that way. 'You're such a square, Bertie.' She giggled. 'The great columnist and author is a square. Positively cuboid.' She passed the joint to Simon who concentrated on the ceiling, screening out the impending scene.

Bertie stood there.

'Oh, all right. It's pot, darling. You know. A reefer. A joint. *Cannabis sativa*, perhaps you'd prefer to call it. As you're so educated. Not like silly little me.'

Bertie grasped Maud by the wrist and dragged her up the narrow basement staircase. Dora could hear a hissed argument upstairs, until Bertie shouted: 'You've got two still very young sons, for heaven's sake. Do you want them to see you taken away in a Black Maria? What good is it going to do them if their mother's in prison? You can't just do what you want when you have children.'

She laughed her privileged, high-society fifties laugh. 'That doesn't stop you, darling. You do exactly what you want. Regardless of the rest of us. We're talking the famous double standard here, don't you think? You're allowed to behave like an unneutered tomcat, while—'

'I don't behave' – Bertie spelt out the words slowly and clearly – 'like an—'

'There was that—'

'Just once.'

'Once! Oh, yes, once.' She laughed again. 'I'm not a fool, you know.'

'Sometimes you behave like one.'

'I suppose you're going to tell me that it's my fault. That if I only put my make-up on before breakfast and cooked you your favourite meals, you'd be the perfect husband for the perfect wife. My God, I'm glad I don't have a daughter to be brought up as a second-rate citizen toiling over a kitchen stove while her husband screws every pretty girl he meets.'

'You've got to get over that, Maud. You can't go on crucifying both of us in this way.'

They couldn't hear her response, but the next thing Bertie added was: 'And I don't see a lot of toiling either. Over a kitchen stove or anything else.'

There was the sound of a slap, and a low scream.

Dora darted a look at Tom, but he was bent over his books, having apparently not noticed what was going on.

They heard the sound of footsteps from above, followed by Chris's voice. 'Don't hurt Mum.'

'I'm not effing hurting her.' Bertie's voice was resigned.

Simon caught Dora's eye. 'Fish and chips? And the Purple Pussycat?'

Dora nodded. Nobody would want spectators at this kind of scene.

Maud came down the stairs, slightly unsteadily, with Chris protectively behind her.

'Don't bogart that joint, Simon. Let . . . Sorry, I've forgotten your name . . .' She tried to focus on the girl sitting at the table next to Tom. 'What is your name?'

Both women giggled, for some time.

'You're in my kitchen, and I don't even know your name.'

'I'm always in your kitchen and you never remember my name.'

Maud leant over and kissed the woman full on the

lips. 'I've always thought I should have a go at lesbianism. You should try everything once, they say, except pot-holing.'

The woman giggled again. 'Pot . . . holing . . . get it?'

They both spluttered with laughter. Maud passed the joint to Dora, who passed it on. She thought she might need a clear head. But Bertie was off, striding up the stairs. The front door slammed as he stormed out.

'Simon and I are just off, Maud,' murmured Dora. 'Unless you want any . . .'

Maud waved them away. 'Young love. I remember that. Magical times. Magical times.' She blew another smoke ring, inhaling with flared nostrils, while Dora tried to think of the right words for: 'No, nothing like that, absolutely not, no strings . . .'

'Mum, I can't work out this maths.'

'I'm no good at maths . . .' Her voice was thick and dreamy. 'Ask your father. He passed exams in maths. Nobody even thought I should take them. No point, they said. So you're stuck with him. Not that he's here, mind you. Not being here is something your father is very, very good at. But if he were here, he'd be good at maths, too. You can't say I don't give him credit where credit's due.'

Simon, who had stood up, leant over Tom. 'Let's see . . .'

Ten minutes later, when Simon had sorted out

Tom's homework, they slipped out, as Bertie, his face grey with anger, strode back in.

'Phew,' muttered Simon once they got to the safety of the King's Road. 'It's like being the last man out of a besieged city before the enemy troops take over.'

'Do you think we should have stayed behind? For Tom and Chris?'

He put an arm round her. 'You're not paid to worry about Tom and Chris. And what you are paid for – very inadequately, I might add – finishes at five o'clock.'

Simon often took her to the Purple Pussycat, a basement nightclub. It was like stepping into a womb, with deep purple carpeting all over the floor, the ceiling and the walls, and even the curving banquettes that wound round a tiny parquet dance floor.

One evening, Dora, contemplating the thick fog of cigarettes, dry ice and incense, saw a small, slender woman in a short black shift dress and bare feet, dancing through the sweetish, smoky air in a dreamy, self-contained way as if she were completely alone. Until a man blocked Dora's vision, and she saw the woman raise a fragile bare arm, and loop it around his neck. Everyone else was jumping around, shouting 'Wild Thing', but this couple revolved with almost stately precision, probably, she thought, because the man was holding the woman up. He nuzzled her neck.

When the record segued into 'Satisfaction', the

man steered them towards an empty banquette, and the woman stumbled, before righting herself, and looked up at him. He bent his head to hers for a long, searching kiss.

When she detached herself, she looked around like a frightened animal checking for predators, and Dora saw her face. It was Maud.

She tugged Simon's sleeve, and he followed her eyes.

'So?'

'But . . .'

He laughed, and placed a reassuring hand on her arm. 'Cool it. People aren't into faithfulness and cleaving to one another exclusively until death them do part any more. It's bourgeois.'

'But they've got children.'

He shrugged. 'So what? They'll grow up knowing about life. What a great start. Come on, Dora. Think of you and me. We're not worried about what we do with other people.'

Dora was distracted. Was this a conversation about 'us'? She decided not to say that she wasn't doing anything with anyone else, in case he took fright at the prospect of fidelity, however accidental.

'Shit!' Simon almost dropped his drink.

'What?'

'Bertie. Over there.'

'I thought you said they were cool. About everything.'

'Bertie,' he hissed, 'is not cool. About anything. He's freezing cold. Like an iceberg and just about as dangerous. Oh, God. We'd better stand by to pick up the pieces.'

'Really, Simon, if I didn't know better, I'd think that there was a decent man under all that crap, struggling to get out.'

'Don't get me wrong. I'm only out for what I can get.' But he watched Maud and Bertie intently, as Bertie grabbed her arm and Maud snatched it away. Eventually Bertie, tugging her by the elbow up the stairs, propelled her out of the club.

Simon sighed. 'Oh, well. I think it would probably make things worse if we interfered.'

'You don't think he hits her, do you?'

Simon shrugged. 'If it came to court, I think the judge would say she'd deserved it. Not that it would. I don't think much has moved on since Dixon of Dock Green said that if he arrested every bloke in Dock Green who clipped his wife, he'd be working overtime.'

'Mm.' Dora didn't watch much television. 'They weren't always like this, you know. They used to scrap occasionally, but they always made it up. As if they really meant it. Sometimes they were so involved with each other, you knew they'd forgotten you were in the room.'

'It's you I'm worried about,' added Simon. 'You've got to get out of there.'

'Oh, I couldn't do that . . . I can't let them down, not now.' But she had been thinking about it, feeling horribly disloyal. 'What else could I do?'

'Be someone else's secretary. There're plenty of jobs around. Work in one of the boutiques on the King's Road. You've got the body for it. Saw some ads in one of the windows this evening for sales assistants. Nine pounds a week for chicks, twelve for men. Not bad money at all. Might throw in my own job.' But he was joking. Simon, in his own words, always had loads of bread. Being an advertising manager obviously paid well.

'And another thing.' He twisted his fingers comfortably around hers. 'You're miserable living with your parents.'

'I know. But I really can't afford to rent a flat, not even sharing.'

'That's the whole point. You need to sort yourself out. Get a decent job, save up some money and buy somewhere. Your own place. Stop being at the mercy of everyone else.'

This was a startling piece of advice, because she'd never heard Simon admit to planning ahead before. 'You forget. Single women can't get mortgages. Building societies don't like lending to them.'

'Oh. Yeah. So they can't.' She got the impression that she was expected to say this. He swigged back his drink. 'I can, though. What say we get a mortgage together? Two salaries and all that. Even if you did stay with the Devereauxs. Two can live as cheaply as one, they say.'

She was astonished. 'We'd have to be married.'

'Well. What of it? We could go to a Register Office.

A piece of paper doesn't have to make any difference to us, does it?'

She was perplexed. 'I thought you said property was theft. And marriage was bourgeois.'

He grinned wickedly. 'Not all property. And not every marriage. What about it, then?'

Dora shook her head, afraid to believe him. 'You're drunk. And stoned.'

'And you're right, as always.' He finished his drink. 'Come on. Jilly said there was a party in Sidney Street we could crash.'

There was a restraint in their lovemaking that evening. Simon had always looked directly into her eyes, maintaining contact between his flesh and hers in as many places as possible, so that she felt utterly joined to him. But now he looked at the wall above her head, and turned her over so that she felt like a piece of meat.

Six months later, he married Jilly. 'For the mortgage, you know,' he told her with a wink. 'Doesn't have to stop you and me.'

'Oh, yes it does.' She was surprised at how much it hurt to say so. 'I don't have affairs with married men.'

'Yeah, well. I guess you're right. Well, anyway, the party's coming to an end. Mark my words.' And he hoisted his jacket over his shoulder, and strode off. The swagger in his gait was even more pronounced than usual.

*

All Dora said to Lily, though, as they watched the inky waves thud and whisper, in and out, in their eternal timeless rhythm, was: 'He did ask me to marry him once. But I thought he was joking.'

She hadn't dared say 'yes'. In case he was.

19

After ten days, Lily woke up to the noise of running water. She pulled back the curtains to see rain sheeting past the window, beating down the blossom and running in red-tinged rivulets across the jetty. The mud coursing down the cliffs was the colour of old blood, and reminded her of the rhyme about the Dart. Every year it takes a human heart.

But it was soothing to return to the big old bed and lie there, listening to the water drumming against the window outside, as if none of it could reach her. Nothing and nobody, she thought, could penetrate the cosseting layers of comfort.

Except that it reminded her of the end of summer. She would have to think and plan. Since waking up that first sunny morning to see the sea spreading out before her, a weight had lifted off her back, a thick foggy morass of anger, guilt and exhaustion that had prevented her from seeing clearly. If she went back, would the weight descend again? Had it come from leaving Tom, resigning from her job, leaving London, or simply being on holiday? Perhaps she needed to change her life completely. Perhaps she should start again, somewhere new? Or maybe, once rested by the break, she should stay where she had friends and support? The options revolved in her head like the chambers of a pistol in Russian roulette. If she chose wrong, then what? What sort of damage might she do?

Eventually she was forced up by the shouts of the children. Stifled by the warm wet weather, Harley, Billy and Daisy were playing an endless game of Monopoly.

'It's not fair!' shrieked Daisy. 'Not fair!'

'Cry-baby,' shouted Billy.

Daisy raced into Lily's arms.

'Sh, sh.' She tried to make herself heard above the sobs. 'You have to learn to be a good loser.'

'But I don't want to be a loser,' sobbed Daisy.

Lily could see her point.

'And Harley cheated,' said Billy.

'No, I didn't,' growled Harley.

Billy picked up the board and threw it across the room, scattering the paper money and tiny plastic houses in a hundred different directions.

'Billy! Stop that.'

'I think we should take them out,' suggested Dora. 'The rain here can go on for ages.'

'I don't want to go out.' Billy raced upstairs. Harley ostentatiously picked up a book and began reading it, as if he didn't care. The title said something about music theory.

'I want to go home,' whispered Daisy. 'I don't like it here.'

'Yes, you do.' Lily was perplexed. 'Devon is much better for children than London is.'

'Don't care,' muttered Daisy. 'I want Daddy.'

Lily hugged her, but noticed a bruise on her leg. 'What's this?'

Daisy seemed vague. Lily hoped that it hadn't been at Billy's hands.

'Shall we go into Totnes?' suggested Natasha. 'I should like to see Diana's shop.'

It seemed better than hanging around getting on each other's nerves.

Boozer – or it might have been Bagshot – yapped a warning as they stepped into the shop, and both dogs scuttled over to sniff their ankles with the intensity of wine connoisseurs assessing a vintage. Diana had abandoned the Heidi look, and had tied her hair back in a leopardskin chiffon headscarf. Although there were unopened boxes all round the shop, she was perched on a stool, engrossed in a book. She hastily removed her reading glasses when she saw them.

'Darlings. How lovely to see you all. This is *so* fascinating. Did you know that knapweed was used by country girls to foretell their future lovers? Don't you think that's absolutely wonderful? Would you ever have guessed? Really?'

'I didn't know anything about knapweed at all,' said Lily. 'What did they do, boil it up and drink it?'

Diana squinted at the book again. 'It doesn't say. Perhaps it's a he-loves-me-he-loves-me-not system. Here.' She handed Natasha something that looked like a bunch of brilliant purple thistles without prickles. 'Why don't you take these home, and let me know if you suddenly divine the name of your future lover? You, too, Lily,' she added, in a distracted way.

'I think we want a herb that keeps children happily occupied,' laughed Dora. 'If you have such a thing.'

'Pack them all off to Roger's sailing school,' replied Diana. 'He's brilliant with children. Even in the rain.'

A plump girl behind the till was talking about her wedding on the telephone. 'No, I don't want orange flowers,' she shrieked. 'Everything pink.'

Lily wondered how Diana ever sold anything. Even allowing for the fact that the shop was too small for three adults and three children to stand around talking, it was chaotic. 'I think we'd better get out of here, or your customers won't be able to get in.'

'Oh, don't worry about that,' said Diana. 'No one's been in all day. Except a German tourist asking for directions.'

Somehow, looking at the clutter, Lily wasn't surprised. Natasha tried to study the noticeboard behind the door, placed so that anyone looking at it would be flattened by the next person coming in. Lily caught sight of various flyers entitled: 'Do you love your body?' 'Are you plagued by self-doubt?' and 'What makes love work?'

If only she knew. The girl at the till was talking about shoes now. 'I'll have to practise walking on a reely high heel.' Lily felt like tapping her on the shoulder and saying: No, you'll have to practise making love work. And even then it might not.

'This is Gem.' Diana waved a hand in the girl's direction when she eventually put down the phone. 'Gem, darling, do you think you could possibly sort some of these boxes?'

Gem looked baffled. 'What exactly do you want done with them?'

'Oh, I don't know. Books on the shelves, I suppose. Wherever you can fit them. And any you can't find a place for in the store cupboard?' She sounded doubtful.

'I will help,' said Natasha. 'If you like.'

Diana gave the rest of them directions to the sailing school, and asked them round to Sunday lunch.

'Oh, no, you must come to us,' said Lily.

'We will. But another time,' promised Diana. 'I'd love to see the Boathouse again. We had such wonderful times there.'

The rain had stopped by the time they got back, releasing the children to race about in the woods.

'Knapweed isn't the easiest flower to arrange,' said Lily. 'A bit stalky.'

'If we add some grasses . . .' Dora took over. 'And a few leaves.' With a few deft movements, the wild flowers fell into place.

'I wonder how they did foretell their lovers from it,' she mused.

'You've made it look like something from a Bond

Street florist,' said Lily, winding a stray stem round her finger in a ring. 'I'm going up to the Moonlight Bench to get reception for my mobile phone.'

She also wanted a moment to herself. She took a few moments to breathe and let the soft greys and blues of the sea wash across her vision, merging with the sky in wisps of chiffon and smoke.

Her mobile, amazingly, rang. 'Hello?' She twisted the knapweed ring around her finger.

'You were going to ask me down,' said Chris. 'I'm waiting for my invitation.'

Lily thought he was probably joking and laughed. 'Any time.'

'All right.' There was a pause. 'I'll be down next Friday. I've got a prospective deal to look at in Somerset, so I'm going west anyway. Unless you have anyone else staying.'

'No, no. Dora's going back after the weekend.'

'See you around suppertime.'

Well. What was that about? Was he checking up on her? Lily was uneasy.

She dialled Vicky, who, frustrated by the lack of a fixed phone line at the Boathouse, had asked to be kept in touch with Harley's progress. She tended to fuss if she wasn't called every evening.

'It must be heaven down there,' she said. 'You're so lucky. London is sticky, smelly and sweaty. Really vile.'

'Do come. Any time. I wouldn't mind the chance to go off exploring, so you could have my room.'

'The minute I can get away, I'll be there. Still,' said Vicky, 'some of us must toil. How is Harley today?'

Lily decided not to mention the cheating at Monopoly. It was only on Billy's say-so, anyway, and probably nothing serious.

'He's fine. Absolutely fine. Though I think he misses—'

'It's so lovely for him to have an ordinary summer with other children. He's usually just focused on his music and reading. Is he doing his practice, by the way? We like to keep it all nice and normal, and not put him under too much pressure, so an hour a day is fine, with perhaps another half-hour or so before bed if he feels like it.' She laughed. 'He usually does, of course.'

'Er . . . mm.' Lily hadn't seen him bring out an instrument.

'We saw Chris and Sarah last night, by the way. I must say' – her voice always changed whenever she mentioned Sarah – 'I think it's a bit much of her to expect you to take Natasha for the whole summer. I mean, a teenager is quite a responsibility.'

'It was Chris who asked me to have her. And I think Sarah's done what she could, but Natasha is nothing to do with her, after all. Anyway, she's a help with the children, except that she keeps blocking up the tiny fridge with natural face packs then forgetting to clear them away so they go all green and pungent.'

'I just hope she doesn't get pregnant or turn to

drugs.' Vicky snorted. 'Sarah wanted her out of the way, you know. She's determined to get her hooks into Chris, and she can't do that with his daughter about.'

'Chris is coming down next weekend.'

'With Sarah?'

'He didn't mention her.'

'Well, she doesn't let him out of her sight, so I'd cater for an extra if I were you.' Vicky giggled. 'And that doesn't just mean buying an extra tin of baked beans. It's nothing less than Gary Rhodes and Marco Pierre White every night for Princess Sarah.'

Oh, dear. If they came as a couple, Lily would have to swap bedrooms and give them the big one. Not to mention the problem of finding food delicious enough for Sarah to eat. She hoped he was alone.

Outside on the jetty, Dora waved to her.

'I've got a tin of old photographs,' she said. 'Would you like to see them?'

'I'd love to.'

Dora reached for an old red biscuit tin she'd placed on the table. It had a battered lid depicting two kittens playing with a ball of string. 'I've been clearing out, and I found these. I always meant to put them in a book, but now I wonder if the boys might like them. If they're interested in the past.'

'I'm sure they are.' Lily craned forwards.

'Look,' said Dora. 'This is Diana. At seventeen.'

Lily studied it, searching for early signs of the

sadness that now marked Diana. She was tall and slender, wearing bell-bottom jeans and a cheesecloth shirt with flowing sleeves, and there was a flower tucked into the side of her head. 'She's very beautiful,' she commented. Diana's face glowed with sunshine, but there was an unlived-in look to it, as if anything could happen. It seemed very bland compared to the Diana of today.

Suddenly, Lily was worried about Chris coming. 'Look, ought I to keep Diana and Roger out of the house when Chris is down? Tom said something . . .'

'Did Tom tell you what happened?'

'Not really. You know Tom. He always pretends everything's fine.'

'Mm,' said Dora. 'Well, I don't know if I should tell you, but I don't see what harm it can do. You might understand how Bertie was with those boys.'

'I would like to know. If it was part of Tom's past.'

Dora hesitated, clearly trying to make up her mind. 'Well,' she said, eventually. 'Diana was seventeen, three years older than Chris, and so, in theory, light years out of his league.' She handed Lily another photograph, of Chris, looking gangly and skinny, sitting on the beach with dark hair flowing past his shoulders. He was wearing Bertie's panama hat and looked almost Mexican.

'But she used to turn up at the house looking lovely, wearing skimpy bikinis and very short shorts. Although it was one of the most dismal summers I can remember. Partly because Maud wasn't there.'

'Why not?' asked Lily.

'Oh.' Dora's voice was casual. 'She left Bertie for a few months. In nineteen sixty-seven.'

In spite of what Simon had said, the party wasn't over. The world around Dora grew more vibrant every day. As she walked down the King's Road, she was assaulted by fluorescent green, red and orange, candy pinks and sherbet lemons and tangerines, by flowers and beads, slogans and badges proclaiming peace and love, by music blaring from every shop, and strident, beautiful, confident men and girls who seemed to know exactly where they were going.

Inside the little house in Chelsea, it was quite different. Coming to work was no longer an adventure. As she closed the door behind her in the morning, she had to resist the temptation to switch the lights on, even in the thin spring sunshine. She knew that she had to leave, to find her own way, and to grasp some of the opportunities that tumbled out of the shops, pubs and offices.

Maud was literally vanishing under Dora's eyes. She spent the morning in bed, coming down at about two p.m., looking ravaged, to sip black coffee, smoke cigarettes and shiver. She would get completely involved in a simple, unimportant task, like refilling the cigarette boxes on the tables in the drawing room, slowly stacking up Turkish cigarettes on one side of the divider and filter-tips on the other. Bertie remained closeted in his office, and demanded that it be kept absolutely tidy. The relaxed, easy-going, broad-minded, left-wing commentator of the newspaper columns stormed round the house, picking up a piece of laundry here and a newspaper there, shouting demands to know why this had been left or that had been broken and who was going to do anything about it. Maud turned her face away, and Dora, in the interests of peace, cleared up after them both.

She applied for a job as a PA to a friend of Simon's, who worked in television, and knew that if she got it, she could look for a flatshare in *The Times*. At the end of the interview, he asked when she could start. It seemed a terrible betrayal.

The following morning Dora opened her front door to be greeted by a thick, viscous yellow fog. The soft silence was punctuated by the occasional low rumble of a bus or taxi, as if London had been muffled in an old blanket the texture of curdled cream. The buses would be late, so she walked – carefully – hardly able to see the buildings on either side of her, and arrived too late to talk to Bertie before he started work. He was already completely wrapped up in what he was writing.

'Sorry. Couldn't get a bus.'

'Mm? What? Oh, there you are.' He scribbled across the pad and leant back in his chair, scrutinizing what he'd written. 'Damn stupid, damn stupid.'

This didn't, she knew, refer to her, but it was no good trying to get through to him in one of these moods.

She decided to talk to Maud first, but it was usually very difficult to get her alone. She wasn't likely to be up till lunchtime, and it was around then that people began to drift in and out. Maud always urged them to stay for another drink. So did Bertie. It was as if they couldn't bear to be alone.

But today Bertie had an appointment at Broadcasting House, and left early to be sure of getting there in the fog, which also seemed to have deterred any casual callers. Presumably nobody wanted to get run over or to breathe in the foul air if they didn't have to. The house was like a ship adrift on a silent sea, isolated in its own mists of unhappiness.

After Bertie had left, she went downstairs to find Maud floating around the kitchen in a distracted way, prodding the washing-up as if it were alive. Which it might well be, thought Dora.

'Do you want some help with this?'

Maud collapsed down in a kitchen chair and began to cry.

Dora drew up a chair beside her and put a hand on her arm. 'What is it?'

Maud went on crying for several minutes, and then blew her nose. 'Just, you know. There isn't any point to me.'

'What do you mean?'

She sniffed. 'He doesn't love me any more, you know.'

'Who? Bertie? Maud, don't be silly . . .'

'Oh, he's fond enough of me. But he doesn't love me. Not the way he used to.'

'Love changes,' said Dora, although she was uncertain as to whether it did or not. 'That doesn't mean it's gone.'

'I haven't changed. But he . . .'

Fascinated, Dora watched Maud's nose literally dribble with misery.

Maud picked up another hanky and blew hard. 'He's so cold to me. It's like talking to a man from the Ministry of something. The Ministry of Indifference. It's like being absolutely alone on a dark night in a country I don't know. I see his eyes light up when Camilla talks, and the way he laughs when Christabel tells one of her dirty jokes, and . . .' She snuffled again. 'Even you, Dora, he thinks more of you than he does me. He relies on you, and respects you and listens to what you have to say, and notices what you wear. I'm just a piece of wallpaper in his background. A wallpaper that needs replacing, probably.'

Dora was horrified. 'Really not, Maud. You've got it quite wrong. You're everything to him.'

'I was. Now I'm nothing. Bertie's a well-known writer. You're his PA. Christabel Dawlish does up houses. Even that bitch Camilla models. I don't do anything.'

'You're a mother.' Dora couldn't believe that Maud didn't realize how she was driving him away with her behaviour. If I had Bertie, she thought, disloyally, I'd take such good care of him that he wouldn't want anyone else.

Maud grimaced. 'I'm a servant. Bertie's servant. Not even a very good one.'

Dora couldn't think of anything soothing to say to that, and a part of her thought that Maud could have tried harder. You married someone, and you looked after them. That's the way it was. The alternative was to be left on the margins of life.

Maud looked at the sodden handkerchief with distaste, then wiped her tears away with her hands, leaving dark smudges across her panda eyes and sooty watermarks on her fingers and cheeks. Her Queen Nefertiti eye make-up couldn't withstand a crying session. 'You see, when I married Bertie, I gave up everything else.'

Dora knew that. Money, privilege, a life of ease, and what had presumably been a loving family. But how loving could they really have been if they'd allowed her to stay estranged like this?

'My father said he hoped I knew what I was doing. He said the man's only after your money, and I'm disinheriting you to protect you. If he knows there's nothing, absolutely nothing, coming his way from us, then perhaps he'll leave you alone. When Bertie did marry me after all, I thought we'd proved Daddy wrong.'

'Did you think your father'd come round?'

Maud shook her head. 'Yes. No. I don't know. I didn't really think. He died last year. They never told me. I read his obituary in the papers. And they've divvied up the estate. I don't suppose there's going to be a prodigal daughter's welcome for me, because they'll assume I've come back for my inheritance, don't you think?'

Dora then said something that she would regret for the rest of her life. 'Not necessarily. They might be waiting for you to make the first move. Perhaps they've been very hurt, too.'

'Do you think so?' Maud looked thoughtful. 'You see, I only wanted Bertie, and I didn't care about anything else. But maybe Daddy was right. Perhaps he did think I'd inherit, all along. But I bet he wants to marry Camilla now. She's stinking rich, after all, and her parents wouldn't care if she married a divorced man. They're frightfully broadminded, you know.'

'He doesn't want to marry Camilla,' asserted Dora. 'He loves you.'

Maud shook her head. 'It's not as easy as that. I thought that love was the only important thing in the world, but now I've found out that not having any money can even ruin that.'

'No, it can't,' urged Dora. 'Of course it can't. People in my street don't have much but they still love each other.' Although she wondered if that were true. Her best friend at school, Molly, had had two proposals of marriage, from different men, and had openly admitted to Dora that she'd deliberately chosen the one with the best job. Dora had been shocked, but Molly had told her that she was being naive.

'It was fun at first,' reminisced Maud. 'Do you remember when we used packing cases instead of kitchen chairs?' She laughed, but there was an edge of hysteria in her voice. 'And when I got so furious with him for buying the television rather than the table and chairs we really needed?'

'I know things are tight, but . . .'

'The point is that if I walked out today, I couldn't survive on my own. You're so lucky. You can. That's the difference between us.'

'But Bertie does love you, honestly, and . . .'

Maud gave a short, bitter laugh. 'Like he'd love a faithful dog. He pats me while he's talking to one of his important friends or thinking up the next meaningful thing to write, and I'm supposed to wag my tail, and fetch his slippers like a good girl, and that's supposed to be enough.'

Dora suppressed impatience. Bertie did expect everything to be done for him, immediately and without question, but that was no different from any other man she'd ever met. David Dawlish was possibly the only one who treated his wife as an equal partner — she knew he discussed things with Christabel, after which they would decide on them together, but he had to live with builders' dust in his hair, so she didn't think anyone else would be following his example in a hurry.

'I did think that if I were less dependent on him,

he might be more interested in me again. But married women can't work. Or if they do, it's like saying their husbands are the most frightful failures. I know that's what Bertie's thinking when I suggest something, although he dresses it up by saying the children need me. He doesn't want people to say that he's obviously not doing so well after all, and has to send his wife out to work. That really touches his middle-class pride.

'And the children don't need me. I'm a lousy mother. I've never been any good with Tom.'

'But Tom's only eleven.' Surely there was no such thing as being 'no good' with an eleven-year-old? Surely a mother was a mother, equally important at all ages?

'I know. You see, Christopher was part of the original enchantment between me and Bertie. We couldn't believe we'd made this marvellous, unique human being, and we couldn't believe that he was really ours. It was fun when we were first in this house, too. It was like playing grown-ups. I used to take the baby out for endless walks while Bertie wrote. And when I got back, he'd talk to me about the latest article he was writing, and I'd make suggestions while he gave baby Christopher a bottle.

'Until Tom came along, when it suddenly seemed like terribly hard work and Bertie was always in his study with the door shut. Tom was always a difficult, colicky baby, and I realized how lucky we'd been with Chris. And then . . .' Maud's eyes filled with tears again. '. . . then the baby that died came along too soon afterwards. That was when I really lost Tom. He seemed like someone else's child to me when I finally came home from hospital, one who'd been absent-mindedly left here by someone who was as awful as I was. I felt he'd be better off having no mother at all than having me.'

'That's not true. Simply not true.' Dora remembered those long, dark days and Bertie closing the door of his study against having to deal with them.

'And I'm not trained for anything. People tell me I should write a book. Or paint. Or do interior decorating. But it would just be another wife justifying her existence. You have to have a better reason than that.'

The problem with Maud was that she was intelligent. And not educated enough. Her quick brain flitted about illogically, like a moth fluttering towards the light. It crossed Dora's mind that if she left for the television job, Maud could begin helping Bertie again, and that this might be exactly what she needed. 'I—'

'Do you know what he said today?'

Dora shook her head. 'Bertie?'

'He said that women were second-class citizens. Like slaves.'

Dora was perplexed. 'Why did he say that?'

Maud, sniffing, shrugged. 'I don't know. He said that he thought I ought to be a little more in touch with reality. He pretends to have all these liberal views, and to believe that everyone's equal whatever their class or race or sex and all that, but underneath he's exactly like every other man. He wants his house and children looked after, his dinner on the table and sex whenever he feels like it without any trouble.'

Well, of course, Dora felt like saying, wondering if aristocratic mothers ever told their daughters anything.

'You have to, don't you?' asked Maud. 'Even if you don't want to.'

Dora was lost. 'Have to what?'

'You know. Men. Sex. You have to. Or it'll be your fault if they get it somewhere else.'

Dora hesitated. That was certainly what her mother and her friends had always agreed, in their carefully coded conversations. Men had appetites, they said. It was dangerous to thwart them. Not good for their health. A woman only had herself to blame. And so on. But it was probably different for the upper classes. Adultery was part of the game for them, she'd understood from books. If Maud was no longer sleeping with Bertie then, surely, she had to take at least some of the blame if he seemed cold towards her?

'Look, Maud, I think if you did something you really wanted to do, you might get your self-respect back. And then you'd see that Bertie does love you after all.'

'What *do* I want to do? I don't know. No one's ever asked me before. I've hardly even asked myself.' The intensity in her eyes surprised Dora. 'What do *you* want, Dora? Do people *know* what they want? Does anyone?'

'I want . . .' Dora thought about the job she wanted. 'I want to share a flat with some other girls.'

Maud looked resigned. 'Oh, well, that's easy enough. You should be able to do that all right. We can look in the papers tomorrow.'

'In fact, that's something I'd like to talk about—'

'But what I want,' interrupted Maud, 'is the moon and stars. To be extraordinary to Bertie. Like we were. For him to look at me again and think: You're amazing. Always to put me first and I'll always put him first; and when we make love, it'll always be like the first time because we'll touch each other's bodies as if they were precious and unknown. I want it to be magic, the way it was. Not a hideous, demeaning duty that you have to do twice a week to stop your man from looking for it elsewhere.

'But I don't think I'll ever have that again. With anybody. You only get it once and when the stars fall to earth you realize they were only sparks after all. They were never for ever. I'll never be special again.'

'Look.' Dora tried to reach her. The reference to sex made her uneasy. She really didn't want to know their bedroom secrets on top of everything else. 'Bertie does love you. A great deal. The children are wonderful. And they love you so much, too. And you've got a fab home, and lots of friends who think you're smashing, and . . .' She trailed off.

Maud gave her a watery smile. 'I know.'

They sat in silence for a few minutes, while Dora tried to work out a good opening to talk about the job.

Maud sighed and squeezed her hand. 'I will pull myself together, I promise. I'd better tidy my face so he doesn't know I've been crying. It irritates him frightfully. How long is he out for?'

Dora looked at her watch. 'Probably a couple of hours. He usually goes into the BBC canteen and has lunch with the producer. So maybe not back till four.'

'Oh, good, masses of time.' Maud scrabbled around for her handbag and stuffed her hanky away. 'Thank you, dear Dora. And I'm sorry for being such a drip.'

Maud's aristocratic slang always made Dora smile.

'I know.' Maud brightened. 'I shall have a huge, lovely clear-out. He'll be pleased about that. He's getting awfully fed up with having my clothes piled up in every corner of the bedroom. I shall take a whole suitcase of them to the charity shop.'

Dora was relieved. It looked as if Maud was adopting Cynthia Savage's solution to all marital problems – cleaning – but the house was incredibly untidy, and Maud with a project was definitely better than Maud slumped in the corner of a room drinking. And not that she worshipped tidiness the way her mother did, but she did think that Maud would feel a great deal better if she pulled her finger out and got the house straight.

*

Bertie came back at around four, looking happier than she'd seen him for ages. 'It looks as if there might be a series in the offing. With me as presenter. Let's have a drink. Where's Maud?'

Dora looked up from her typewriter. 'Gone to the charity shop with a suitcase of old clothes.'

He frowned. 'In this fog? She must be mad. Never mind, it's high time I got to see the bedroom floor. I think there's rather a nice little chair under the mound of stuff in the corner which I'd like to use again. Oh, well, we might as well get a few letters done.'

Chris and Tom let themselves in from school, and at five, Dora went down to see to their tea.

'I expect she's feeling so pleased with herself for tidying up that she's treated herself to something new on the way home,' said Bertie, jovially. 'Time for that drink, now, I think.'

They stayed down in the kitchen with the boys, talking and laughing. The atmosphere in the house was lifting, she thought. As soon as Maud got back she would tell them both about the job, and she would buy *The Times* tomorrow, and start ringing round. She longed to move on. It would be so exciting.

Suddenly Bertie checked his watch. 'Where's Maud? The shops close at six. It's half past.'

Dora looked up to see fear on both boys' faces. Chris, she could see, remembered people talking about the dangerous smogs of his babyhood. She remembered that four thousand people had died in a few days in London, not so very long ago, it seemed.

'Let's go and look for her,' said Chris.

'No.' Bertie sounded distracted. 'I'm not having you out in that. You can hardly see ten feet in front of your face. You stay here. In case she's forgotten her key. I'll go.'

'Dora.' Bertie's voice floated down from the bedroom a few minutes later. 'Could you pop up here for a moment?'

'Back in a minute, boys.' She was now practised at sounding calm in front of them during a Maud-and-Bertie crisis. It must be like being a simultaneous translator, she thought, with one kind of message coming in through your ears, and having to alter it beyond all recognition by the time anything came out of your mouth.

The bedroom looked wrecked, as if it had been burgled, although this wasn't so very different from its normal state. Bertie stood there with a letter in his hand. 'She's gone.' He sank down on the bed, and ran his hand through his hair. 'She's gone.'

Dora sat down beside him. 'I'm sorry. I should have realized . . .'

He shook his head. 'How could you? No, this is my fault. I said something to her this morning . . .'

'I know. She told me.'

'Do you think that's why she went?'

Dora couldn't think of a safe, satisfactory answer.

'So bloody stupid. I can't believe I was so bloody stupid. I only said it because I thought she needed a bit of a shock. I meant that unless women like her pulled their fingers out, women would always be second-class citizens. That she can't just sit on sofas drinking and crying over soppy novels.'

'Does she?' Dora was distracted. She hadn't noticed the soppy novels.

'Where do you think she's gone, Dora?'

'Has she got any money?'

Bertie looked bewildered. 'I don't know. I don't know anything about her any more.' He sank his head into both hands. 'Please God she's safe.'

Dora didn't know what to do. She pushed the bedroom door shut in case the boys came upstairs, and waited in embarrassment.

'At least she took a suitcase,' he murmured. 'At least she took a suitcase.'

She realized that Bertie believed Maud capable of suicide. People walked into the fog and never returned, or their bodies were washed up in the Thames a few days later, and you never knew if they'd jumped or fallen.

'Shall I phone the hospitals? And friends? Or would you rather?'

Bertie's face was more shadowed than she'd ever seen it before, his skin rough and stubbled. 'Could you, Dora? Thank you.'

They looked at each other in a moment of

shocking honesty and she knew what they both wanted to say. She may have gone to a man.

'She hasn't,' said Dora. 'She really didn't sound as if that was in her mind.'

And Bertie nodded, as if he'd asked her the question out loud.

'I think she's gone back to her family.' Dora spoke without thinking. 'Just to see them again.'

Bertie threw himself back on the bed. 'Oh, God. I've lost her then. I always knew she'd go back one day.'

'She won't have gone for ever. Just to see them again. Perhaps . . .' Dora hoped she wasn't wrong. '. . . she has to forgive them. Maybe it's part of why she feels so bad about herself, this thing with her family.'

Bertie ran his hand through his hair. 'They despise me, you know. In the early days, when I was invited over the threshold – very reluctantly, I might add – I was having dinner there once, when they were talking about some politician who had defrauded someone. Maud's father looked straight at me and said: "Of course, I've never trusted any man who buys his shoes from a shop."' At Dora's puzzled glance, he added, 'He got his hand-made at Lobb's, of course.'

'But that was a very rude thing to say,' said Dora. 'Shouldn't an aristocrat have better manners?'

Bertie laughed. 'That sort of aristocrat thinks they make the manners. And that manners are something for one's own social class.' He mincingly imitated the tones of his father-in-law before reverting to his normal voice. 'Or a way of ordering the peasantry around without getting their heads ultimately chopped off in a revolution. They couldn't bear what they called the "middle classes". They thought I was after Maud's money.'

'Well, I think that's horrid,' said Dora. 'And you've proved you weren't after the money. And they're both dead now. And the world is a different place.' She sat on the bed beside Bertie and seized his hands. 'You've got to go after her. Don't you see? She thinks you don't love her any more. I'll look after the boys.'

'Oh.' He almost laughed. 'If only everyone in the world was as nice as you. You really do see the best in anyone, don't you? The world, my sweet Dora, still turns exactly as it ever did.' He rested his head lightly on her shoulder, and she thought he was hiding the despair on his face. 'Dear, dear Dora.'

There would always be another job in television. Probably a better one. She couldn't leave now.

20

'We spent that summer, Bertie and I, down here at the Boathouse,' said Dora. 'Until Maud forgave him.'

Lily raised an eyebrow. 'What about the children?'

'The children?' Dora's eyes followed the butterfly flash of a gull as she swept low, skimming the water with the tips of her claws and screeching *kitti-w-a-a-k-e*. 'When I hear those birds, I can almost smell Bertie's cheroots and Maud's wonderful garlicky cooking.' She laid her drink down. 'Oh, Lily. I just want them back. I want them back so much.'

Lily placed a hand on Dora's freckled one. 'I know.' They sat in silence for a few minutes.

Dora resumed her story. 'The boys stayed in London at first. When Maud came back from Yorkshire and Bertie offered to move temporarily down to the Boathouse, they, of course, had to finish the term at school, so they stayed with her, in a rather accidental sort of a way. People didn't think children really noticed things in those days, so they assumed that provided the boys were in the same house and going to the same school, then there wasn't any reason to worry about them any further. And then when the end of term came, Maud sent them down here without any warning.' She took a sip of her drink. 'I sound rather critical of her, don't I? I don't mean to. She was my dearest friend, as well as my employer's wife, and she was desperately unhappy. But I sometimes think that unhappiness makes people selfish.'

'Tell me,' asked Lily. 'How did Maud, and all the other women whose husbands have affairs, manage to forgive them?'

'I think it helped,' said Dora carefully, 'that that was how it was, then. There weren't any other options, or not easy ones anyway, and there was far more of an emphasis on duty than there is now. In many ways, it was a question of survival.

'Bertie's earnings had paid for the house, so it was deemed to be his. There was no recognition, in law, of a woman's contribution to a family home until the early seventies. So she'd have had nowhere to live, and, because it was difficult for a single woman to get a mortgage, very little chance of her buying something else anyway. Maybe she could have rented, but what with? She wasn't trained for anything, and would have had trouble earning. Without a house, she probably wouldn't have been granted custody of the children. And that's without even starting on the kind of social exclusion that divorce still carried even in the sixties. So needs must glued you together, and sometimes that glue stuck you properly. I don't think that's the case now. If anything, you're forced apart by this in my opinion very destructive emphasis on personal happiness. But then I would say that, wouldn't I?'

'So, in the end, it was partly about money?'

'Not exactly.' Dora smiled. 'It was a little more complicated than that. Maud was very wild. And she loved to make grand, seemingly impossible gestures. I mean, she seemed like a nicely brought-up girl, very sweet and demure when you first met her, but underneath she was a romantic. She was deeply passionate and needed a cause to champion, something heroic that would make her life worth-while. At first, that was Bertie, the grammar-school boy outside the society she'd been brought up to conform to. Loving Bertie was a rebellion against her parents, a shining ideal that she could wave a moral sword for.

'But when he became successful and the old social structure began to break down, that seemed less impor-tant. Don't get me wrong: the sixties was never a class-less society, apart from a brief spate of it being very fashionable to be working class, but that never went much further than London and didn't last long. Where you belonged in the strata was still critically important to most people in a way that would seem quite in-comprehensible today. But her little rebellion – being an aristocrat married to someone from the middle classes – no longer seemed exceptional.

'And she was more hurt and frightened by the rejection of her family than she ever admitted. They had tried very hard to persuade her not to marry him, and had assured her it would never last.' Dora gave a small, brittle laugh. 'Maud told me that her mother came into her bedroom one evening for a serious talk which went along the lines of: "One could understand it if you were interested in some honest John Thomas on the estate, a decent working-class man with dirt on his hands. There's always been a certain amount of that around, after all. But the middle classes. My dear! They're just too ghastly for words, with their jumped-up manners and the way they try to avoid saying 'toilet' and watch one like hawks to see which knife one's using. It just doesn't make for a happy marriage."

'That's why the affair with Camilla terrified her. She'd actually been brought up to believe that affairs were fine, provided that everyone was married and no one disturbed the status quo, but, of course, without her family behind her, there was no status quo, especially as a few people they knew were just beginning to get divorced. It was no longer unthinkable. Her father had always claimed that he'd cut her off because Bertie would leave her once he knew there wasn't any money in it, and she started to believe it herself.'

Lily was thoughtful. 'But it wasn't Bertie who left.'

'No,' said Dora. 'He was difficult, and took her for granted, the way lots of husbands and wives do after nearly twenty years together, and he was unfaithful, and careless of her feelings, but he would never, ever, have left her. It stunned him that she could go like that.'

*

Dora saw that Bertie, without Maud, was only half the Bertie she'd known. He reminded her of an abandoned mongrel. Now, when he bumped into friends in the village, he no longer suggested that they drop in for a drink, and when he called London from the telephone box, he never emerged with the news that 'such-and-such is coming down to paint for a few days' or 'so-and-so's having a bit of woman trouble, we'll be scooping him up while he mends a broken heart'.

The Boathouse seemed empty, and slightly chilly, not so much because it was the second dull, damp summer in a row, but because Bertie had lost his energy for chopping logs and building fires.

But Chris, in that seesaw way of fathers and sons, seemed older and more vibrant. Now it was his friends – Roger, Diana and other local teenagers – who appeared, peering in and tapping at the window, and Chris who dropped the newspaper to usher them upstairs to the top room. The sound of 'Lucy in the Sky with Diamonds' would filter down under the closed door, or out through the window, and Bertie would glare at the noise.

'How can I work with this racket going on?' he'd mutter.

Secretly, Dora thought he rather liked it. He hated to be alone.

At the first sign of the sun escaping from the misty clouds, Chris and his friends would emerge, clustering together on the beach around a tinny transistor radio for a few precious, goose-pimply minutes of sun. It was a missed summer: not cold or hot, and as bland as half-melted ice-cream.

Bertie tried out his jokes on Dora.

'Really, Dora,' he said, rattling the paper. 'In the world outside British troops are fighting in Aden, there are massacres in the Congo and Mick Jagger's been arrested for smoking hemp. And what are the headlines here? "Dartmouth waiter in stolen car." And here's another one: "Dartmouth waiter steals five pounds but gives it back". Nobody else ever seems to commit crimes. Do you think the Devon constabulary are conducting a vendetta against waiters?'

'Perhaps the waiters are short of money,' Dora suggested. 'Even the *Gazette* admits that there's nothing for anyone to do here, and that they've got a tourist crisis.'

'Hmph.' Bertie rattled his paper again. 'Everyone's going to Spain now, you know. Or France. Where they can drink all day, and not get chucked out by landladies after breakfast. The British have only themselves to blame.'

Dora continued to unpack her shopping basket. 'Betty Brown's has closed. I saw when I was in town today. That's three cafés gone this year.'

'More waiters on the streets to turn to crime,' murmured Bertie.

But there was no conviction in his voice, and he couldn't take a joke, twist it around and make it last, the way he used to do. It often fell rather flat.

The heavens opened in one of Devon's torrential downpours. Chris and his friends dashed in from the beach screaming and shrieking.

'Dad, there's a rally in Hyde Park this weekend. Can we go?'

'How would you get there?' Bertie, who, only a few years ago, would have been writing impassioned pieces urging his readers to support or refute whatever was at stake, sounded bored.

'Hitch-hike,' said Chris.

'Over my dead body,' replied Bertie. 'And over yours, too, I expect. It's extremely dangerous.'

'For God's sake, I'm not a child any more,' growled Chris. 'I'm nearly six foot.'

'You're only fourteen. And that's the end of it.' Bertie folded up the paper and turned back to his typewriter. A few moments later he pulled out the twentieth sheet of paper that morning, read it, sighing, and crumpled it up. He still dictated his journalistic pieces to Dora, but had become protective about his novel, picking away with two fingers. Dora, working in the kitchen, would hear tap-tap. Tap. And then a long silence.

'Christ, Dora,' he said a few weeks later, after half a bottle of whisky. 'I feel impotent. Literally. I used to think I could make a difference, but it's all an illusion. You're born, you tinker about and you die. And that's it. Nothing changes. That idiot Ginsberg, you know, the one who gave a flower to the policeman who collared him for playing a mouth organ in Hyde

Park, what does he think he's achieved? Apart from his photograph in the papers? He might as well have stuck the flower up his own proverbial.'

Jealous, thought Dora then. Once it would have been him.

Outside, the downpour continued. Diana wandered downstairs, in a tiny gingham bikini, her hair twisted in a tumbling pile on top of her head. Her smooth, brown skin was puckered with cold.

'Bertie,' she cooed in her throaty voice, moving so close to him that her bare thigh brushed his arm. 'You'll think me frightfully silly, but I can't quite understand this . . .' She showed him a piece of folded-up newspaper.

'Diana,' shouted Chris. 'Diana, where are you?' He came scrambling down the stairs, all legs and arms, his eyes burning with the raw, bittersweet intensity of youth. And love, thought Dora, who had never seen him look at anyone in quite that way before. 'Oh, there you are. Didn't you hear me shouting?'

'Sorry, Chris. Your dad was explaining this.'

Chris stood there, hands on hips, his hair shaggy on his shoulders, while Bertie spelt out how the miners' strike and the rail workers' redundancies interacted.

Diana flapped huge false eyelashes at him, like a cartoon cow, thought Dora. 'Thank you so much. I'd never have worked that out on my own.'

'Diana, we're waiting for you,' said Chris.

'Coming.' She treated Dora and Bertie to a luminous smile before following Chris upstairs with a languorous tread.

'Most girls of seventeen would regard a boy of fourteen as beneath them,' said Lily.

'Chris has always seemed older than his years,' Dora replied. 'And he was — is, I suppose — very good-looking. In the same kind of gipsy-raffish way that Bertie was. They were very alike. Perhaps that was part of the problem.' She sighed. 'Anyway, Chris and Diana. He was clearly infatuated with her. She seemed to respond, although it was harder to tell. And I think they made love. In fact, I'm sure of it.' She handed Lily another photograph, a grainy one of the beach with four or five teenagers on towels. Chris and Diana were sitting close together, laughing.

Lily nodded.

'But one day, she turned up when Chris was out, so she said she'd wait. I was in the spare room typing, so I don't know exactly what happened, but I know that Chris returned earlier than expected, and found her in a passionate embrace.'

'Roger,' said Lily.

Dora shook her head. 'No. It was Bertie.'

Lily was silent.

'You have to remember,' added Dora. 'Sea and sun and sand and idleness make a powerful cocktail. It can befuddle anyone's senses. And Bertie thought he'd lost Maud. I think he regarded Chris as just a puppy and Diana as a fully-grown woman, so he didn't take their relationship seriously. Although perhaps it was helped along, too, by the friction between the middle-aged man who thinks he's getting less attractive and the son apparently flaunting his sexuality.'

'What was Bertie's excuse?'

'He never made one. "Never excuse, never explain." That was his motto.'

'What happened then?'

'Chris went up to his room, and came down again, slamming all the doors and storming out of the house. Bertie said he'd cool off in time, and pretended not to care, but by ten o'clock that evening you could see he was worried.'

'He's probably over at Roger's house.' Bertie reread the same page in his book over and over again.

Tom cleared his throat and looked at his watch. 'He's, er, gone back to London.'

Bertie threw down his book. 'Why the hell didn't you say so before?'

'He told me not to. Not until he'd had time to get well away.' His voice squeaked when he was nervous.

'Is he hitch-hiking?'

Tom swallowed and nodded.

'For Christ's sake. Hitch-hiking at night. Who the fuck does he think he is? Come on, Dora, we've got to find him. We'll take turns to drive. And you, Tom, can bloody well be lookout.'

'It was the longest, most hideous drive. We never took our eyes off the side of the road, and Bertie checked every petrol station and café on the way, in case Chris had been dropped off there. We hardly dared go to the house in Chelsea, but, as Bertie pointed out, if he hadn't reached home, we'd have to notify the police. We got there at six-thirty in the morning, Maud opened the door to us and saw . . .' Dora stopped.

'Saw what?'

'Oh, saw, almost immediately, I think, that we really couldn't cope without her. Chris had got there a few hours before, but clearly hadn't said anything about why he'd left, except that he wasn't getting on with his father. And then the rest of us appeared, and she made us scrambled eggs.'

'Just like that? They got back together as if there'd never been a Camilla or any of those lunching women?'

'Well,' said Dora. 'Not quite.'

Lily had the impression that she was choosing her words now, picking through the story carefully and checking herself, in case she accidentally said more than she intended.

'But more or less.' Dora resumed her tale. 'I remember them going to *Così fan tutte* a couple of weeks later, and Maud coming back full of the beauty of the music and saying: "It was so lovely, Dora, it was just like us. All about how it's so much better to love someone knowing all their faults than living in some sentimental dream." And Bertie said, "My darling Maud, you don't have any faults. Except that you're an incurable romantic." I remember Maud kissing him then, and Tom, who was revising on the kitchen table, saying, "Per-lease, I am trying to eat a biscuit, you're making me feel ill." We all laughed. With relief, I think. We hadn't heard them tease each other for such a long time.'

'But what about you, Dora? How did you feel about all this?'

'Me?' Dora responded sharply. 'Why do you ask? It had nothing to do with me.'

'Oh, I just wondered what it was like being in the middle of it all. You never talk about yourself.'

'Well . . . I was relieved. Of course. As I said. I knew everything would be all right at last.'

There was something missing, Lily thought. She tried to identify it. 'What happened then? Did you all go on as if nothing had happened?'

'Not exactly.' The wariness in Dora's voice was audible now. 'I'd always intended to get another job, though, at that point, but . . .' She stopped.

'But what?'

'Oh, it never happened somehow.'

Beyond their feet the rising tide lapped against the shore, rustling softly against the banks, and over their heads, a titanium moon threw a silver cobbled pathway to heaven across the water.

'Bertie wasn't a good father,' said Dora suddenly. 'But I think he was a good man, in some ways. He was one of the people who helped change the way people thought, by his writing, and part of the freedom we have today is because people like him cared passionately about ideas and principles, even if they lost track of how to live their own lives as a result. They tried to throw out all the old prejudices and . . .'

'Any minute now,' said Lily, 'you're going to say that none of us is perfect.'

Dora raised her eyebrows. 'We're not. The question is: Can we forgive ourselves? Or other people?'

'Did Chris tell Maud?'

'I'm sure he didn't. He was very close to her, and always tried to protect her. And, remember, like every child, he wanted his parents back together again. Whatever the cost.'

Lily was sure that that, at least, was a dig at her and Tom.

'I'm sorry, Lily, I didn't mean to lecture,' Dora apologized. 'Except for a period of a few years, they did have a . . . a very close and loving marriage, but I think all marriages, perhaps . . . well, some anyway . . .' She looked frustrated. 'I'm not telling this very well, but let's say that their relationship had a . . . a hole in it at the time. And, although Tom was only about eleven or so, he did know that everything wasn't perfect. So I'm surprised if he really portrays it that way.'

'It was just little things, like telling me how they used to make a Christmas stocking up for each other. Or how the holidays at the Boathouse were such paradise for them all. It seemed as if our holidays never quite measured up. I felt inadequate.'

Dora regarded her with compassion. 'Some of that may be in your own head, my dear. But Tom has always tried to pretend that disagreeable things weren't there, that I have noticed.'

'What about Bertie and Chris? Did they make it up?'

'I don't think Chris has ever really trusted anyone properly since. He once told me that it was a huge advantage in the world of property-dealing, and that that was why he'd become so successful. He was only half joking.'

They continued to sip their coffee in silence, as Lily thought about the betrayal of an older brother and a mother from the perspective of the eleven-year-old Tom. Bertie couldn't have loved either Chris or Tom, to do that, surely.

It was only Cameron, born after they got back together, who, everyone always said, had been their father's favourite.

'So Cameron was a reconciliation baby?'

'You could call him that, I suppose. He was certainly a very important part of the renewal of their relationship. Look.' Dora scrabbled around in the tin again, and dug out another photograph. 'Us all at Cameron's christening. I'm his godmother, you know.'

Lily studied the photograph of Dora, wearing bright pink trousers, with a matching jacket and hat, holding Cameron. Maud and Bertie, both smiling, stood on either side of her. Chris stared out of the photograph, defying anyone to ask him to smile, and Tom, on the other side of the family group, had an anxious, lop-sided grin.

'Trouser suits were absolutely the latest thing, then,' said Dora. 'Look, Maud's was a shade of tangerine that we would think quite hideous today, and as for that head-to-toe cerise outfit of mine, well! But we thought we looked the bee's knees.'

'Chris's hair is so long,' said Lily. 'And look at Tom. He looks as if he had a bird's nest on his head.' She handed the photograph back to Dora. 'So. Another baby. Would that be your prescription for a happy reconciliation?'

'Absolutely not. Cameron was . . .' Dora paused again. '. . . not intended. At first it looked as if he might be . . . one more problem for them. But he turned out to be a huge, marvellous bonus. Against all the odds.

'No, the truth of it was that they really did love each other enough to forgive each other. Maud used to tell me that she had missed Bertie terribly. "However angry I am with him, Dora," she said to me, more than once, "and I promise you I'm simply furious, life seemed colourless without him."'

Lily thought for a while. Had life been 'colourless' without Tom?

She had another thought. 'It must have been quite worrying, Maud having a baby so late? After the problems she'd had. Especially in those days.'

'Yes,' said Dora. 'We were all very . . .' The pause was so long that Lily thought Dora might have lost track of her thoughts. '. . . worried . . . about Cameron's birth.'

'So forgiving Bertie all of a sudden was Maud's grand gesture,' said Lily. 'It somehow doesn't seem quite enough. That you all turning up in the middle of the night and a few lines from an opera could explain her change of mind.'

Dora patted her hand. 'It really is time for bed now, you know.'

21

Dora stayed at the Boathouse for a week. It was sunny for four days and rained for three. 'At least the weather hasn't changed,' she joked to Lily.

The sea, too, swished in and out as it had always done, in thousands of restless variations of blue, green and grey, occasionally whipped up by the wind to crash down on the jetty or, even less often, apparently pausing for an hour or so, as still and peaceful as a lake.

In Salt Creek, the holidaymakers opened up their cottages, one by one. These cosy, picturesque buildings now had a sleek, well-fed but somnolent look to them, as if they had slept all winter and only came alive in the summer to the sound of tourists. Conservation had preserved thick stone walls, low beams and thickset windows — beautifully — but Dora couldn't ignore the differences underneath. The Post Office stocked organic brown bread, designer ice-creams and extra virgin olive oil instead of margarine, sliced Wonderloaf and plain choc ices. Large, glossy cars struggled to manoeuvre through stone-walled streets that had been built for people to walk or ride along. Nothing had changed, yet everything had.

We're so afraid of change, she thought, watching the children chasing each other along the sand from her window. We do everything we can to hold it back, but I'm beginning to realize that if we stopper it up in one place it flows more quickly somewhere else, and may burst out with all the destruction we'd feared and more.

Perhaps closing up the Boathouse had been Maud's way of holding back any more change in her family. She'd been afraid that she would lose someone else to its seductive beauty. Perhaps Chris was right. Cameron and Tom needed the money and while the Boathouse linked the three Devereauxs they couldn't be free of each other. And free of Bertie.

Everyone has to move on, she thought. Chris, in particular. And Cameron. She sighed. Please God, he was happy. Please God that it would all work out for Cameron.

She could hear Daisy, Billy and Harley pouring into the house, chattering and shrieking, calling for lunch, and decided to walk the half-mile across the beach to the pub to be alone with her thoughts.

'Can I get you anything from the Post Office?' she asked Lily on her way out.

Lily pushed her hair off her face. She looked younger than she had in London, thought Dora. She was less tired, and the fresh air had taken away the grey tinge to her skin, restoring it to peachiness. She always reminded Dora of a girl in a Renoir painting, soft, pretty and gentle. 'A couple of pints of milk would be great. If you don't mind.'

When Dora arrived at the Salt Wind, she saw, with pleasure, that she was early enough to get one of the two tables by the huge window overlooking the bay. The dark, wobbly bentwood chairs and the thick oak tables were probably the same ones she'd sat on with Bertie, she thought, leaving her bag on one to keep her place.

'Half a pint of cider, please.'

The publican was a young man – oh, fortyish, perhaps fifty. How terrible to be calling fifty young. She smiled at the thought.

'Staying locally, are you?'

'Up at the Boathouse. Round the corner of the bay.'

He nodded. 'About time that was opened up. Nice little cottage. They're not thinking of selling it, are they?'

'Why, do you know someone who might want to buy?'

'I know most people in the area. And they'd all like to buy it. Not that many of us could afford it now, mind. But it's a waste to keep it closed up. I mean, if they don't want it, they should rent it out.'

Dora smiled, thinking of his custom. A stream of drinkers from the Boathouse would always be very welcome. 'How long have you been here?'

He steadied the glass in his hand, and handed it to her. 'Fifteen years now. Came down from London with my wife.'

'I used to drink here in the sixties,' she said, despising herself for being the kind of lonely person who takes her memories to pubs.

'Not many left from that time,' he said. 'But sometimes there's the odd one from the old days who pops in and asks for people they knew who lived here. What's your name?'

'Dora Savage. No one would ask for me. But they might ask for the Devereauxs. Who own the Boathouse.'

He thought. 'Devereauxs. Devereauxs. Doesn't ring a bell. But, do you know . . . ?' He went to a small door behind the bar and shouted up the stairs. 'Karen! Karen!'

A plump woman with straggly hair bounced down the stairs. 'No need to shout.' She smiled at Dora. 'Hello, love.'

A Londoner, too, thought Dora.

'You know that man who comes here every spring. Elderly gent. Nice fellow. Pleasant wife. Always asks if anyone's at the Boathouse. Asks after someone who used to be here in the sixties.'

Karen thought. 'Ooh, yes, I do recall . . . Greying hair. Very smart.'

'Was it Dora Savage he was after?'

'Well, now you mention it, I think it was. Are you Dora Savage?'

Dora was amazed. 'Yes, but I can't think who would want to find me.'

'His name was Simon. And his wife was . . . what

was it, Karen? They're real regulars, they are. Come in every Easter. Like clockwork. Ever since I've been here.'

'Jilly.' Dora's heart began to bang in her chest. She hated the fluttery feeling it made and tried not to get excited. She imagined Simon and Jilly bringing their children to the beach when they were little, then coming back alone when they'd gone to university, a little fatter and greyer, a slightly uneven gait, perhaps, from a bad knee or a worn hip, but still stylish. And prosperous, of course. Simon would always be the one who bought houses ahead of the property boom, or shares when they were about to go up. They would walk down the bay at low tide, and Simon would remember, occasionally, that he'd spent a week in the amazing cottage that everyone wanted to buy. With a girl called Dora. Jilly might remember Dora, too, and she could imagine them wondering, perhaps just once or twice, what had become of her. Simon would probably say, hopefully, that wherever the Devereauxs were, there was always a party. Perhaps they'd even walked up the slipway and knocked at the door, peering in the window for signs of life, hoping that Bertie Devereaux would come out waving a bottle of whisky and asking them why'd they been so long. Perhaps they hadn't heard of his death.

'Did they come this Easter?' she asked.

'He did. Just popped his head in the door. I don't think they'd taken their usual cottage. They used to rent one of the Henrys' places up on the ridge. You could ask Roger. He'd have their address.'

It was the cider making her heart thump, she told herself. And the idea of seeing old friends again was exciting. She'd avoided Simon and Jilly after they married, but now it would be different. All those old emotions had been swept away, like debris on the beach after the tide has washed over it.

Now she would love to see them both again. It would be good to talk about the little things they'd all known. She remembered Jilly as an exotic creature in turbans and pale pink frosted lipstick. Sometimes she'd piled her hair on top of her head like a Walnut Whip. They'd all gone in gangs to nightclubs together: the Ad Lib and the Purple Pussycat and others whose names she couldn't remember. It seemed extraordinary to think of her in tweeds, with lines on her face, perhaps sitting on the parish council of somewhere, or as a magistrate, as if she'd never smoked any joints herself. Would Jilly have turned out like that? And Simon? Had he continued to keep an eye out for the main chance, or had that gentle, sympathetic side of his character that Dora had only occasionally glimpsed emerged? She longed to know. She would love to sit around a table with them again, recalling the days of dry martinis, the tyranny of false eyelashes and the depressing inevitability of tights hung out to dry over the radiators. It would be like coming home.

22

Lily dreaded Chris's arrival.

Natasha and the children went sailing every day, leaving her alone with the gentle throb of the sea and the whispering silence of the woods. The Henrys came to dinner on Wednesday, and Natasha cooked something creamy and Swedish, with anchovies and potato. Diana told them how to use wild borage against snake bite, sadness and melancholy.

'You and I,' Lily heard her say to Natasha, 'have an *intense* sensitivity to other people. Don't you think?'

Roger snorted, and turned to Lily. 'They're doing well, the children. Billy will make a fine little sailor one day.'

Lily's heart leapt to hear someone speak warmly of Billy.

'He's a great little chap,' added Roger, 'very brave.'

Lily thought she might seriously fall in love with him, in spite of his hairy ears.

'Harley and Billy are sailing the Laser now, but I'm keeping Daisy in the Wayfarer with me.' Roger slurped back his wine and his eyes drifted across to Natasha. 'Harley is a bit . . . how can I put it? Strong, I think. Yes, he's a bit strong for someone little.'

Lily vaguely wondered why it wasn't a good idea

to partner up someone strong with someone small, but assumed Roger knew what he was talking about.

She went to a family quiz night in the Salt Wind, with Natasha and the children, on Thursday.

'Any of your friends here?' she asked her. Natasha had been down to the pub on her own several times.

Natasha flicked back her glossy hair and looked round. Several men eyed her covertly over their pints, but she ignored them.

'No,' she said. 'The boys are not here. I think there is a party down in Dartmouth.'

'Oh, Natasha.' Lily wondered if she'd made Natasha change her plans. 'You should have said.'

'It is fine.' Natasha was tranquil. 'I can go to parties any time.'

The practical side of life had become natural. Lily had learnt to light fires and mastered the rhythm of driving down the narrow, twisty roads. Every journey was like a dance: swoop up, down and round to the right, then down, up and round to the left, face the car coming in the other direction as if it were your partner in a minuet, then three steps back, and then start again with up, down and round. If you had to spend almost as much time in reverse as you did driving forwards, well, there was plenty of time. She began to anticipate the sharpest turns and look forward to the sudden glimpses of sweeping land-scape between the high-sided hedges.

The Boathouse had started by feeling difficult and even dangerous, yet within days, she had found a sense of belonging, a routine, a few people to talk to. It had become home.

And she liked the closeness to the weather and the tides. Once just a monotonous weathercaster's drone or a pattern on a TV screen, they now ruled her day. When it was sunny, the children sailed or roamed, only returning, ravenous, for meals. On a wet or cold one, she was forced to drag battered games – packs of cards, Cluedo, Monopoly and Scrabble – out of her suitcases and be the circus ringmaster to Harley, Billy and Daisy. A few months ago, in her office, the thought of such an afternoon would have filled her with dread and boredom. Now it was part of the gentle rhythm of her life. She had nothing else to do, except read or walk. She explored the bay, and devoured novel after novel, gorging on time.

Even watching the sea and sky was a meditative joy, as it changed from the soft metallic silvers of dawn to a bright, almost garish, contrast of blues and greens at midday and through to the dusky rose tints and lavender blues of the evening light.

But, occasionally, she spotted the end of the summer, like a cloud darkening the valley. She must decide what to do, where to go, whether to return to Tom. If she went back, they would probably keep the Boathouse and she could return here, to feed her starving soul, every summer. And Billy could grow up good at something, instead of being the child in trouble all the time. And gradually, like Maud and

Bertie, she and Tom would learn to forgive each other and love again. The cloud tracked her overhead as she returned from Totnes on market day, sweeping above like a mythical bird of darkness, turning the emerald fields to olive green and the bright white cottages a dull grey.

Just as she thought she might never be free of it, she swung round a tight corner and accelerated up an incline, and a fiery streak burst through the clouds ahead. The road snaked towards it: a narrow strip of sunlight on the crest of a distant hill, forging a gold band between earth and sky. Her heart soared.

'The Valley of the Shadow,' she said to herself. 'That's where I am now. But there's sunlight ahead.' She was getting as bad as Diana, she thought, seeing omens where there were only coincidences.

She was struck by the same shot of pleasurable surprise, an impetuous, irrational feeling of unexpected warmth and happiness, when Chris walked in the door on Friday evening.

Harley, Billy and Daisy were all spooning in spaghetti as if they'd been starved for a fortnight, and regarded him with tomato-spattered interest.

'Dad!' Natasha got up to greet him, hugging him lightly in a ladylike way, and air-kissing both cheeks. She sat down again.

He took his jacket off and unbuttoned the top buttons of his shirt, as if shedding his unapproachable city skin. Pulling out a chair, he relaxed into it;

leaning back, he looked at Lily, amused. 'Phew. I always forget how long the journey is. You look as if you're running an orphanage.'

She wondered why, in spite of her misgivings about this weekend, she was actually glad to see him. Perhaps everything, even Chris, seemed better at the Boathouse, or, possibly, Dora's story had made him seem more human.

'If you want to dump your stuff, you're in Natasha's room, the one Dora always used to have. Tash is sharing with the children. Have a drink.' She pushed a bottle at him and fished a glass out of the cupboard. 'Is Sarah with you?'

'She's in New York.' He poured himself a glass. 'So how have you all been?'

'We've learnt to sail,' said Harley.

'Roger taught us. He's nice,' added Daisy.

'I have been with Diana and Gem.' Natasha tucked a blonde strand behind her ear, nervously, thought Lily. 'Learning about wild flowers and herbs.'

Lily hoped the mention of Roger and Diana wouldn't flip him back to the terse, irritable Chris that they all knew so well, but he seemed easy.

'Have you been out in the *Enchantress*?'

They shook their heads. 'Roger said better use his boats. He wasn't sure if the *Enchantress* was seaworthy.' Harley's voice had recently acquired the uneven up-and-down growl of a teenage boy.

'Oh, I think she's pretty sound. I'll check her

tomorrow morning and then perhaps we can all take her up the creek.'

'I am going out,' announced Natasha, clearing away the dishes.

'Where?' For the first time, Chris sounded like a father.

'To the Salt Wind. The tide is out now.' She shrugged. 'Then I'll come back through the woods with a torch. It will be quite safe.'

Chris hesitated. 'Well, I suppose you can't come to any harm here. But be careful.'

She shot him a look. 'I am always careful.'

'Do you think it's all right?' Lily had been anxious about Natasha's disappearances, but she'd always come back safely.

'Well, I wouldn't like her wandering around in the middle of the night in London,' said Chris. 'But she should be OK here.'

'Yes. Although there are police notices in the car parks saying: "Thieves operate here".'

'I don't think they do,' replied Chris. 'I think they just like putting them up. Gives them a sense of achievement.'

'It's taken me a while to get used to looking complete strangers in the eye and saying good morning,' admitted Lily. 'If I did that in Camden, I'd probably either have my face bashed in or be asked for a quid.'

'Would you?' Chris looked troubled. 'Nobody ever bothers me. That's why I find it so difficult to assess the dangers for Natasha. Being precipitated into teenage fatherhood, particularly with a daughter, without any experience of what went before, is like taking an exam without having been to any of the lessons.'

'Well, I think all parenthood is like that, if it's any comfort. Diana says . . .' She hadn't meant to mention Diana's name again.

He looked at her intently. 'I gather from the way you've gone pink every time Diana's name is mentioned that Dora has told you the sorry story of the last holiday I spent here.'

'Well, er . . .' She didn't want to drop Dora in it. 'I was asking about Maud and Bertie, actually, because . . .' She might as well tell the truth. 'Well, we've been talking about them quite a lot. I think Dora thinks—'

Chris looked amused. 'Hang on while I catch up with that one. Yes, now go ahead. You think that Dora thinks . . .'

'That Tom and I ought to get back together the way Maud and Bertie did.'

Chris flung back his head and gave a shout of laughter. 'I'm quite sure she doesn't.'

'Well, you know. Forgiving affairs and so on.'

'Ah, yes. Forgiveness.' He studied her carefully. 'A very good thing, of course, but rarely everything it's cracked up to be.'

Lily was stung. 'Well, you would say that, wouldn't you?'

'Would I?'

She thought she might have overstepped the mark, but was determined to continue. 'I mean, did you ever forgive your father?'

'What for?' Chris's voice was icy.

'You know. Diana . . .' Lily's voice trailed off.

'Oh, Diana. That. God, yes, ages ago. I'd probably have done the same in his position. No, if you've got Roger and Diana coming round this weekend, you really don't have to worry about getting me out the back door while they come in the front.'

'I haven't.'

'Good.' He grinned. 'I find them both rather boring. Or did when I last saw them. Years ago. I can't remember where.' He began to shave slices off the cheddar she'd set out on the table. 'Mm. This is first-class. But what about you? Do you want to forgive Tom?'

'It would be easier,' she admitted.

'Easier,' he repeated, with another thoughtful glance at her. 'No, I don't think you're right there. Forgiveness isn't easy.'

Lily poured herself another glass of wine, and refilled Chris's glass. He studied her over the debris of the empty table as if she were a specimen under a microscope. 'Lily?'

'Yes?'

'Do you want to go back to Tom?'

Lily thought about the empty, lonely nights, and the almost tangible dent in the sheets where he had been. She thought about the hole in her life, the times she wanted to turn to him and tell him something the children had done, and how often she reached for the phone, only to drop it again after dialling half his number.

But she thought about what it would be like if he was back: the nit-picking rows; the tug of wills between them; the sudden explosions of his temper and the fractured air it left in the family; the scar of his affair; and then sex . . .

'Not as things stand.'

Chris nodded.

It was only half the truth, thought Lily, but it was, she hoped, the better half. They were both fencing, she thought, making little lunges, and feinting and parrying the other's questions. It wasn't quite communication, but, on the other hand, was more than a polite exchange.

He stood up. 'Did you know that if you go down to the rock pools on a moonlit night and watch very, very quietly, you can see limpets swim?'

She laughed. 'I don't believe you.'

'Want to bet?'

She got up. 'But it's not fair. I wouldn't know what a limpet looked like, swimming or not.'

'Good,' he said. 'I like unfair advantages.'

23

They argued over the limpets. Chris pointed one out to her, swearing he could see it swimming, but Lily said that it was the shadow of a scrap of seaweed, floating across the sand.

'You're so stubborn,' he said. 'You won't take anything on trust.'

'Trust! Look who's talking.'

He didn't comment on this. They walked along the moonlit sand, and Lily hugged her arms to herself.

'Cold?'

'I'm fine.'

'You're shivering.' He took off his jacket and put it round her shoulders.

'Now you'll be cold.'

'I don't notice it. Too many years camping in houses I was doing up. Before I hit the big time. I spent most of the seventies living in almost derelict houses then selling them on.'

'Couldn't you have lived at home?'

'I could have. I didn't want to. I didn't get on with my father. Not that that was anything special – I don't know anybody who got on with their fathers in those days.'

They padded along silently, while she thought

about the jigsaw of Bertie and Maud, and the pieces around them that were herself and Tom, fitting it all together.

'Tom always talked as if you all grew up in the perfect family. But when I say so, he says I'm imagining it. Now, judging from what I hear from you and Dora, it was anything but.'

'Oh, it was happy enough. Like most families. Mum and Dad changed after Cameron was born. It suited Tom. I was older. I was hoping to be grown up enough to join the party, and then I got there and it seemed the party was over. As it were.'

Lily thought she could hear the faintest inflexion of a betrayed, confused teenager in his words.

'Mum was pretty old to be having a baby – forty-three – although "afterthoughts", as they were called, were quite common in those days because the pill had only just been invented. The doctors were appalled. They said that she had to have total rest, and she certainly wasn't going to get that at home or at the Boathouse, so she and Dora went to a friend of Dora's in France for six months, while Tom and I were packed off to boarding school. It was all very sudden – it was as if the family had been torn apart like a piece of paper and thrown away. We went in the middle of the term, and everyone else had already made all their friends. Still, Tom loved it. I think he adored the routine and the sport and the camaraderie and everything. I hated every minute of it. I couldn't believe the petty rules and restrictions. I'd more or less done what I liked for the past five years, and suddenly I was being made to go to bed at nine-thirty p.m.'

Lily perched on a dark grey rock and stared at the stars. 'Tom never mentioned his schooldays, except to say, usually when we're arguing about Billy, that he'd been sent away to school at eleven and that it had done him a lot of good. He seems to want Billy to be sent away.' It was one of the reasons, she realized, why she didn't want to discuss Billy's problems with Tom.

'Poor Billy.' Chris sat down, too, propping himself up on one elbow. 'It was the utter, blank misery of the place that got me. All I can remember is relentless rain, the sick-making, lumpy food, and a bit of mild but terrifying bullying. Thank God, I only had two years of it. I remember thinking that I never wanted to be dictated to by anyone else again. I was never, ever going to stick to someone else's rules if I didn't have to to survive.'

He didn't speak for a while, and she could see that he'd gone into that abstract, distant part of himself where he stored memories.

'And then Cameron was born, and nothing was ever the same again.'

He's really bitter, she thought. It's as if it was all Cam's fault.

'You must have been quite old to have a baby brother.' She wondered if she could get him to talk about it.

'Sort of. It was quite rare, but not unique, so I wasn't the only teenager with an afterthought baby in the family. Dad was besotted with him, and Mum . . . well, she'd been advised against having any more children, so she kept referring to him as a "miracle baby". Over and over again.' His smile was self-deprecating. 'I'm sorry, I sound like a spoilt brat. I didn't mind them all loving him. He was really cute. All chubby and blond and happy. He used to come staggering after us, nappy trailing off, face covered in dirt, arms outstretched for a hug.' He glanced at Lily. 'You could say,' he grinned, 'that he hasn't changed much. He's still a mess.'

It was unusual to hear Chris speaking affectionately of Cameron.

'I didn't blame Cam,' he added. 'But everything changed so much, so suddenly. Then the sixties ended, and the long, dark seventies began.'

'Tom doesn't seem to think they were dark.'

'Oh, he was very settled. And I suppose I had quite a good time, too. But I meant they were, literally, dark. Lots of brown and purple in the shops, and power strikes all the time. But to Tom, it just meant having our parents back together again, and, because he'd been so young during the party years, he hadn't enjoyed them. He preferred the comfort of routine, the quieter and more predictable way the house was run, and, because there was a baby in the house again, my mother did really make an effort to be like other mothers. And my father tried to be more of a father, going to matches and all that. I just got out as soon as I could.'

'Were your parents really happy then? Or was it all an act?' Lily ground some wild thyme between her fingers, smelling the sweetness it released in the air. She handed him some. 'If you make a tea of this, it cures bad dreams. And the scent gives strength and courage. Diana told me.'

'We all need some of that.' Chris took it from her fingers and inhaled. 'Yes, my parents were happy. I remember what they were like before, always arguing, and my mother used to get very drunk. I hated that. Now it was as if they'd both grown up at last. They seemed like proper parents, responsible and contented and balanced. Not the people I knew before. Not at all.'

Perhaps that was how it was done.

'Are you thinking of you and Tom?' He was perspicacious.

'No,' she lied.

'We're rather alike, you and I,' he said. 'We keep ourselves to ourselves.'

'I don't,' she flashed.

He stretched up with a great barrel of laughter. 'Lily.' One arm came down and hugged her, strong and warm and solid. 'Lily, Lily, Lily. What am I going to do with you?'

'But you're much more secretive than I am.' She was embarrassed, blurting it out without thinking.

'Ah,' said Chris. Before she could respond, he stood

and pulled her up. 'Two in the morning. We'd better get some sleep. Tomorrow we can all have some adventures.'

The wild thyme bestowed its magic. Lily thought she would lie awake, puzzling over what Chris had exactly said, but as soon as she laid her head on the cool, crisp pillow, she fell asleep, and the restless, anxious dreams that sometimes haunted her were absent.

24

Lily, wandering outside with her cup of tea the following morning, found Chris standing on the jetty, looking out at the sea and sky. They shimmered in metallic shades of white and grey. He was wearing a towel wrapped round his waist and dark hair traced a mackerel pattern down his stomach. He seemed to be all bone and sinew.

'Another glorious day.' He stretched. 'A silver start usually means good weather. Let's all go for a walk.'

'A walk?' Harley came out with a bowl of cereal in his hand, munching through his disgust. None of the children believed in walking.

'Walk,' said Chris firmly. 'Have you got some paper, Lily?'

'Oh, er, I think so.' She scrabbled around in her drawers and came back with several sheets, which Chris began to write on as the children looked on in interest.

'Right.' He handed a sheet to Harley and began a new one for Billy. 'There are ten things you have to find or see on this list. I'll give you fifty p for each one.'

Harley cheered up considerably. 'A fiver. Cool.'

'Spiders, gross,' said Billy, reading over his shoulder.

'That's bribery and corruption,' said Lily.

Chris grinned. 'I've always found it very effective.' He handed Billy his sheet and began one for Daisy.

Natasha put her hands on her hips. 'And me, Daddy?' she enquired, ironically. 'Will you be doing me a list for fifty p an item?'

He gave a short bark of laughter. 'It would be more like ten pounds an item, I suppose?'

'Yes, please!'

But Chris handed the sheet to Daisy and got up. Lily couldn't tell if Natasha was disappointed or not.

'Right,' he said. 'The old lady who owns the estate is expecting us. She is called Miss Dean. I phoned her butler yesterday. The big house is about three miles' walk away, through the woods and gardens, and when we get there, her housekeeper will give you all home-made lemonade and you can play with her croquet set while your mum and I talk to her in private. She says she's too old to see more than one new person at a time, and much too old to meet children. Now just give me a chance to have a bath and we'll set off.'

Lily had occasionally seen the old lady being driven to town in an ancient Daimler, shrouded in the back seat, like a character from an ancient fairy tale.

Chris packed a small rucksack methodically, with water for them all, some bars of chocolate he produced from nowhere, suntan lotion and spare socks, a towel and a mobile phone ('Not that these things ever seem to work here'). His self-sufficiency was daunting, as if he didn't need anybody else.

They set off, turning out of Salt Creek halfway through the village, as the hill inclined sharply upwards. Chris opened a farm gate marked 'Strictly Private' and led them all up a narrow path fringed with ferns and brambles. The blackberries were small and green.

'We used to come up here at the end of summer,' said Chris, 'and gorge on these. No one else knew they were there.'

Lily's thigh muscles, even after weeks of the Salt Creek hills, were almost cramped with the effort. 'Mm,' she murmured, wondering how soon they might be allowed to sit down.

But Chris walked steadily on, up to the brow of the hill and down, beyond the field and into the shady mystery of the old Edwardian gardens. They had been laid out in a series of interlinked terraces, up and down the sides of the hills, with wild, wooded dells, walled lawns and huge clumps of massed trees and shrubs. These jostled each other and anyone venturing along the overgrown paths and crumbling steps. Oak and chestnut trees towered over their heads, and the exotic geometric outlines of palm and Japanese cherry framed the sea behind in jagged shapes. Wild flowers peppered the hillsides, and, occasionally, a secret stream bubbled to the surface in a miniature waterfall. Lily settled into a rhythm with the children chattering behind them, and Natasha, unusually quiet, bringing up the rear.

Chris noticed her breathing heavily, and slowed down. 'Sorry. I'm not used to walking with people.'

Lily thought of Sarah and the other polo blondes. 'Do you walk a lot?'

'Mm. I go walking once a year, somewhere in Britain, on my own. I have done ever since I left home. For five or six days at a time. It clears my mind.'

'Really?' Lily hadn't heard about these holidays before. 'Does the family know this?'

He shrugged. 'Perhaps. I usually tell my office, in case anyone wants to get in touch with me. It was funny, when you said, if you don't know your own country, you don't know yourself, I thought: Well, if there's someone who really ought to know themselves, it's me. I must have walked every walkable bit of the British Isles.'

'I think I was just being pretentious,' said Lily. 'But do you know yourself?'

'Pretty well.' He laughed. 'At least you could say that I haven't given myself many surprises in recent years. I know what I want, and how to get it. That's knowing yourself, wouldn't you say?'

It was certainly an advance on Lily's frame of mind. She had no idea of what she wanted, and still less of how to get it. Most things were hedged about by their suitability for the children.

'Do you think Sarah will come with you in the future?' This, thought Lily, was an even better test than the house-decorating one.

'I wouldn't dare ask her,' he admitted. 'Unless *Vogue* did a feature proclaiming the Pennine Way to be the new Bahamas.'

'I don't think that's very likely. Although the old seaside resorts have come back into fashion.'

'Yes,' he said. 'Fashion. Very unpredictable.'

He was thinking about selling the Boathouse, and, here, folded into the verdant green of the Devon hills, with no sound except the cooing of pigeons and running water, Lily was saddened. These winding trails belonged to a lost world, one that glossy magazines and fashion would change if they swept in in their four-by-fours. Equally, though, without the money from tourism, these places would die. There was nothing in Salt Creek that did not ultimately rely on visitors arriving, being bewitched and spending their money.

Chris stopped by a rusted gate and opened it. 'Here. The secret walled garden.'

Daisy was enchanted. 'Just like the book!' The boys stopped totting up their fifty p's and ran across the shaggy grass. Natasha shook herself out of her mood and followed, competing with Daisy as to who could do the best cartwheels.

It was an overgrown glade of meadow grass, studded with daisies and clover and ancient orchard trees, surrounded by a moss-encrusted stone wall. The air was still and quiet, as if dreaming in the hot sun, and in the corner a tumbledown shack framed an old stone bench. 'In the spring this is ringed with flame-coloured azaleas,' Chris said. 'It's said that their scent could drive a man mad.'

'Have they driven you mad?'

'No,' he said. 'I'm afraid I'm horribly sane and rational. Not an ounce of romance in me anywhere. Look, have a seat. The gardens were designed so that each view or corner or individual garden has its own place to sit and think. Not that the Edwardian gentry did a lot of thinking, I don't suppose. They were too busy eating enormous meals and changing their clothes four times a day.'

They sat down on the stone bench, and watched Natasha and the children make daisy chains in the long grass.

'She's a good girl,' said Lily. 'She's been an enormous help with the children.'

'I know,' Chris replied. 'I wish I was a better father to her. But I've no control over the relationship. Ingrid decided to have her. Ingrid decided to keep her in Sweden, miles away from me. At very irregular intervals Ingrid decides it's time for me to be a father and puts her on a plane. What I think and feel seems irrelevant.'

'Is that what you need in a relationship?' asked Lily. 'Control?'

He was silent for so long that she thought he was offended. 'It's a fair question,' he eventually replied. 'I don't know the answer. All I know is that I'm no good at loving.'

'I don't think you should say that. Distance is a terrible problem.' Lily tried to make excuses for him, to offer him a way out of his bleak view of himself. 'That's why I can't move too far from London. They both need their dad, especially Billy. Although Billy really needs the open spaces, too. He's a different boy when he's got a chance to work off all that energy, and has a focus like sailing.'

'You've obviously thought of it, though.'

She shrugged. 'I do more than think about it. I went to an employment agency the other day. They didn't know how to slot me into a category. "I see. No degree? Management responsibility? Exactly what was your job title?" And so on. And it's not as if there are all that many suitable jobs round here.'

'No, I suppose not. Rather a large retirement community. Speaking of which' – he looked at his watch – 'the old lady's expecting us. That generation are very punctual. Tash, can you keep an eye on everyone down here for about half an hour?'

Natasha waved and smiled. Chris took Lily's hand and pulled her up through a broken gap in the wall. 'Careful. There used to be steps here, then the wall collapsed on top of them.'

'You still know every inch of it, after all these years.'

'Of course,' he said. 'It never changes. It just slowly crumbles.'

They pulled an old-fashioned bell-pull, which resonated inside the house. After a long wait, a wizened old man in a butler's uniform struggled to open the massive front door.

'Mr Chris. How good to see you, sir.'

'And you, Bentley. And you. How are you?'

'Mustn't grumble, sir, but very creaky.'

'I'm sorry to hear that. And Mrs Bentley?'

'Passed away, sir, three winters ago.'

'I'm so sorry.' Chris touched the old man on his sleeve. 'She was always so kind to me. And she made the best apple crumble in the West.'

'The best apple crumble in the whole of Britain, if you don't mind me saying so, sir.' A tear gleamed in the corner of the old man's eye. 'But come on in. Miss Dean is waiting for you.' He turned to Lily. 'Mrs Devereaux, is it?'

'Yes,' replied Lily. 'But I'm Tom's . . .'

He had turned away and was hobbling ahead of them, clearly too deaf to hear unless he could see her lips. The high, panelled corridors were lined with stags' heads, watching them, Lily thought, as if they were intruders who might steal the spoons. Huge doors on either side were shut and Lily had the impression of silent, empty rooms waiting to be opened up.

Eventually Bentley pushed open a door at the end and announced them.

'Mr and Mrs Devereaux,' he said.

'I, er . . .'

Chris touched her arm. A large, sepia-brown room filled with furniture spread out ahead of them.

'Open the curtains, Bentley,' quavered an imperious voice from a big armchair. 'I want to see Chris's girl properly.'

'I'm not . . .' But it seemed churlish to continue.

Bentley struggled with the strips of fading, fraying velvet at the window, tugging them ineffectually to left and right. A little more light crept into the dingy room.

'That'll do, Bentley, that'll do. We don't have all day.' She rapped her cane on the floor. 'You're getting old, Bentley, old and slow.'

'We're all getting old, madam.' Bentley bowed and shuffled off.

'The man's impertinent,' said Miss Dean, before he'd left the room. 'Now let's have a look at you, girl. Sit there, sit there, where I can see you. Christopher has never brought anyone here before. Not that you've been often enough recently, you naughty boy.'

'I've been busy.'

'Hmmph. But he writes good letters, doesn't he, Lily? I may call you Lily, mayn't I? These days we're all so modern.'

Lily murmured agreement, and wondered when she was going to be able to say that she wasn't that Mrs Devereaux. Chris was standing with his arms folded, looking amused.

'Stop fidgeting, Christopher, and pour us some tea. 'Now, then.' She took Lily's hand. 'You're very pretty, my dear. Don't be embarrassed. I'm an old lady and I can say what I like. You will look after Christopher, won't you? Because he needs it.' She patted Lily's hand as if that was all that needed to be said, and turned to Christopher to talk about the Right To Roam.

'People knew their place in my day,' she said, sharply. 'Still, I suppose I must move with the times.' Chris gave his advice gravely, and promised to look a few things up.

When Bentley saw them off from the large panelled door, Chris took Lily's arm.

'As we're married, I think we should walk off arm in arm. To make Bentley happy.'

She could hardly wrench herself away, not with Bentley gazing fondly down the drive after them. The weed-strewn gravel crunched beneath her feet. 'I hope Natasha's all right with the children.'

'Bentley sent the housekeeper, who is even older than he is, down to the walled garden with some lemonade and biscuits. They're a bit more organized here than they look.'

'It's a wonderful place.'

'You've seen the end of an era. Miss Dean won't last much longer, and it'll all go to a nephew who doesn't care. He'll sell up. It'll be flats and yuppie homes in a few years' time. And the gardens will go. There'll be building. Even here.'

'How sad.'

'There's one more thing I want to show you before we go back to the children.'

They took an overgrown path to their left, and scrambled upwards for a few minutes, until Chris said, 'Look. Here.'

On the crown of the hill, Miss Dean's Edwardian ancestors had built a stone gazebo, commanding a dramatic sweep of the sea for miles around. The water foamed in a distant froth against a clump of rocks jutting out just beyond the shore. A single white yacht, like a Matchbox toy, hove to, and seagulls circled it, hoping for scraps. Below them the garden terraces fell away in a jungle of different leaf colours and shapes, with drifts of red and purple blooms fighting through the dense greenery in splashes of vivid colour. The civilized veneer of a great garden had cracked, and grown up wild and wonderful.

'This view is why Miss Dean's grandfather bought the estate.'

Lily was awestruck. 'I thought you said you weren't a romantic.'

He didn't answer and they stood there in companionable silence for a few moments, watching eternity spread out in front of them.

As they walked down to find the children and go on to the house, Lily felt that a promise had somehow been forged between them. She couldn't define it, but it was there, an invisible skein of silken happiness binding her to Chris and to the ruined garden on the hilltop.

That evening, with the children asleep in bed, and Natasha in the pub as usual, Chris returned to the question of what she wanted to do with her life.

'Well, being here has made me realize some things,' she said. 'When I find an old local recipe for hedgerow jelly written up in a church leaflet, or I chat to someone who does something special and local, like cider-making or carving walking sticks from coppiced wood, I realize that what makes places special are all these different things, and that, unless we keep them all alive, everywhere is going to be exactly the same in fifty years' time. I'd like to do something to help that. But what? Then I think about the children, and Tom, and maintaining the links between them . . .'

When she lay in bed, and thought about the children and Tom, her mind paced restlessly round a range of options. Stay here, living modestly and doing something – waitressing, anything – to give Billy the space and hobbies he loved. Get back with Tom and persuade him to move jobs, so that they could all live down here or somewhere near the sea or a lake. That seemed a little more practical. Go back to Tom, stay in London but spend the holidays at the Boathouse. That was a real possibility. If she stayed with Tom, they, with Vicky and Cam, could afford to buy the Boathouse off Chris.

Or get finally divorced, go back to London, find a decent job, and struggle on with life as normal without the Boathouse.

'Sorry. I was miles away. It's so difficult to work out what's best for Billy. And Daisy, of course. And their relationship with their father.'

'What about what's best for you?'

'That's part of it, of course. Tom's in London, the

children's schools are in London, and my best prospect for work I can do part-time is also in London. And I like London – I've got lots of friends there.'

'But you've changed.' Chris poured her a glass of wine. 'Here, I mean. You seem . . .'

Lily tensed.

'Softer,' he concluded. 'Less angry.'

'I am less angry. That's why I came. Don't you think that where you are makes you see things in another way? Isn't that why people travel? To get away from their ordinary selves?'

'Or to be extraordinary?' he offered. 'We all want to feel that we're special in some way.'

'Where will you find yourself this year?' She studied his face, tinged with the glow that comes from a day's sunshine and fresh air. 'A tropical paradise in Nantucket style? Or what about the eco-safari?'

He tweaked her cheek in affection, leaving his hand on her face for a few seconds. 'Don't tease.'

She leant her face against the warmth for the brief comfort of feeling a male touch again. 'I didn't mean to be bitchy.' But she did, she knew. Sarah had suddenly become the enemy.

Oh dear. They looked at each other in silence for what seemed like an endless second.

He took his hand away. 'It was nice being married to you today.'

'Ah, well, we didn't have time to get on each other's nerves,' she joked uneasily. 'Or argue about trivia.'

He raised an eyebrow. 'So that's what marriage is like, is it?'

'I don't know,' she said. 'I only know what my marriage was like. And I don't think we should talk about it.' She tried to change the subject. 'Look, shall we go up to the Moonlight Bench before it gets too dark?'

Chris hesitated.

'Or not?' she supplied.

'No, no, that's fine. Come on.'

Lily scrambled after him, trying to balance her drink without falling over. 'We don't have to go up there,' she shouted, breathlessly, 'it's not compulsory, you know.'

But Chris was too far ahead to hear.

When she reached the bench, he was standing by the railing, facing the sea, as if he'd forgotten that she existed. She waited quietly, trying to concentrate on the magic of the sea glittering across the horizon, and the graceful sweep of the birds below them, as she watched Chris's knuckles whiten against the rail.

He turned round. 'There's nothing here. I thought there would be something, some little thing, but there isn't. You can go through all that, and there's nothing left. Nothing to show for it.'

Lily held herself very still. 'Is this where your father died?'

'Yes.' There was a short pause. 'At least, that's what the police think,' he added. 'No one knows exactly.'

'Do you want to talk about it?'

He sat down beside her and picked up her hand, absent-mindedly. 'I don't believe in all this talk business. Things happen. You survive. That's all there is to it.' He curled her hand round in both of his and kissed it. 'You're cold. Here.' He took off his jacket and put it around Lily's shoulders, then leant back with his arm around her. 'Can I stay married to you for a little bit longer?' He indicated the sea. 'It's so, so big, and so, so beautiful, and we are hardly relevant to any of it at all.'

Lily didn't want to speak. His body burnt beside hers, etched into her side as if it belonged there for ever.

'You see,' he said. 'I thought that what I felt about this place was about it itself: the sea and the jetty and the thick stone walls. But it isn't. You take it with you wherever you go.'

'Tom was like that.' She groped to understand his words. 'I think the Boathouse was this place in his head, the only place he could really be happy.'

'And yet he never brought you here.'

'Perhaps he knew we would never be happy.'

'Don't be bitter,' he said.

'I won't.'

'I am surprised.' Chris looked out to sea again. 'That he didn't come. He could have, if he'd really wanted to. I think he knew it wasn't really derelict.'

'Something stopped him,' said Lily. 'I don't know what. Memories of your father, perhaps.'

'And yet' – he indicated the bay – 'it's just an empty house. There's nothing left of Bertie Devereaux here.'

'I wish you would tell me what really happened.' Lily spoke softly.

The gap between them opened up.

'I wish you would come to bed with me,' he said.

Lily let go of something she'd been carrying in her head for far too long. She turned her face to his. 'Yes.' She was amazed at herself, that she could just say 'yes', like that, without any debate, any courtship, any discussion of what would be right or wrong.

'It's all right now,' he murmured. 'Everything will be all right.' His arms closed round her, and he traced the line of her cheekbone with his finger, down to her lips. 'Dear Lily.' He kissed her, gently at first until her body folded into his as if they had been carved out of the same mould. She felt her body responding to his in little flames of desire, licking up deep down inside her. For a moment she paused, expecting the usual 'stop' mechanism in her head to come down like a barrier.

'What is it?' asked Chris.

'Nothing,' she said. 'Really, nothing.'

'I would never hurt you,' he said.

'I know.' She could taste the scent of freedom on the pine and salt air, on the red wine of his kisses and feel it in the huge vault of stars overhead. The tangled nets of guilt and duty, of love and pain, that had enmeshed her and Tom, catching them more tightly every time they turned and twisted to get away, had gone, blown away on the night air, like cobwebs.

25

It wasn't until Chris took her hand and led her back down to the Boathouse again that she thought of Tom.

This, she thought, is what he was looking for. Barely being able to breathe for desire, the electricity of a strange new touch on your skin, and the feeling of coming completely alive after years of being half-sleep.

This, she thought, is why he did it.

And then she forgot everything when Chris pulled her into the bedroom, wedging the door closed against a stray child with a nightmare, and kissed her again.

'We've got all night,' he said.

At some point, he got up and came back with wine and tea, and they propped themselves up with cushions and pillows, and talked, intertwining their limbs. Lily traced the mackerel pattern of hair from Chris's navel.

'I wanted to do that this morning.'

He laughed and kissed her shoulder, delighted. 'Really? I've wanted you . . . oh . . .' He looked at her, teasing. 'Well, ever since you set foot in the Boathouse.'

'Not before?'

'Before, you were Tom's wife.'

The shadow of the family hovered over them for a second and dissipated. 'But not here?'

'Here, everything is different.'

Lily stretched, luxuriating in every point where Chris's body touched hers. The honey-coloured beams striping the ceiling above seemed richer and warmer than they had been before, and the scraps of red check curtain flapping in the breeze had the charm of tattered perfection.

They dozed. The curtains fluttered with ghosts, and, at one point, Lily sensed a presence moving through the room. She felt a benediction, and, then, like the wind, it had gone. The tide drew in, and the sea wiped their footprints from the sand.

She woke up to find Chris watching her. 'I told you, Lily, I'm no good at loving.'

'You can't say that. Loving isn't something like . . . well, tennis. Or chess. That you can be good at.'

'What is it, then?' asked Chris. 'You see, I don't know.'

'What about Sarah?'

'Sarah isn't my brother's wife.'

'Neither am I.'

Chris's dark eyes penetrated her consciousness as no other eyes ever had. 'I think there's been enough betrayal in this family already, don't you think?'

He was right. Not just Tom, but Daisy and Billy. They didn't deserve more complications.

'But if . . .'

He touched her lips with a finger. 'Don't think about if.'

Lily could see the first coral tendrils of dawn, snaking, delicate and stealthy, across the sky. 'Tom expects me to be something I'm not. And to me, that's not love.'

'Are you sure that's fair?' He understood the change of subject. 'I think he loves you for what you are. Lovely, unusual, brave Lily. Lily who-makes-me-laugh.'

'Do I?' Lily didn't want to admit that she wasn't brave, not in the slightest.

He laughed and kissed her. 'You judge him, too, you know. Everybody judges everybody else. Usually without knowing the full story.'

Lily turned away, softening the movement by wedging the curve of her back against him. 'Perhaps.'

Chris's hand circled her stomach, and she could feel the warmth of his breath in her ear. 'You've got to face it. Either there is something to save in your marriage, in which case you do probably need to "put up with" the memory of Tom's affair, or there isn't, in which case you should let it all go. Including his unfaithfulness. You've got choices my mother didn't have. Use them.'

She twisted back to face him. 'I know. Do you think I'm being silly about it? In this day and age?'

'No,' he said. 'Infidelity always means something.

Not necessarily the same thing in every case, of course.'

'That's it.' She stroked his chest, liking the difference between his skin and hers. 'Perhaps that's what I haven't quite worked out yet. What it all meant.' She tried, and was unable, to suppress a dizzy intake of breath as he touched a nipple, very gently.

'Come here.' He shifted his weight so his face was above hers, very close, very tender.

'I am here.' She laughed out of sheer, abundant pleasure. 'I could hardly be closer.'

'Oh, I don't know about that. I think . . .'

'Don't think,' she murmured, pulling his mouth on to hers.

An hour later, she slipped out of bed and stood at the window. A yacht headed out to sea, busy and purposeful, and a fishing boat fussed around, bobbing on the waves and throwing out lines in search of prey. The water was waking up. 'We don't have much more time.' She turned back to him. 'The children will be down soon.'

He swung his legs over the side of the bed. 'Damn.'

She crossed the room and sat down beside him. 'Will you marry her?'

He knew she meant Sarah. 'We're talking about it.'

So not 'no', then. Her heart, she thought, might freeze over.

'I promised myself I'd never come back here,' said Chris. 'Beautiful places are dangerous. I told you that.'

'Couldn't this have happened in London?'

'What do you think?'

She thought about it. What had Dora said? Sea and sun and sand and idleness make a powerful cocktail. Without the warmth of the air in the moonlight and the sense of being as free and wild as the sea and the sky, they would have carried on being their normal, polite, civilized selves. 'No,' she said.

'No,' he agreed. 'Although I would always have wanted to.' He took her hand and kissed it. 'Dearest Lily. I'm sorry. I wish it were otherwise. But Sarah wants what I want. A good life. Comfort. Luxury. A rewarding career. We've talked about children. She can't have them. Some illness when she was twenty. I don't think I'd be a good enough father. I've seen what bad fathering can do, and I don't want to pass it on.'

Lily tried to speak.

'Sarah's accepted it,' continued Chris. 'She won't want to adopt or anything. None of the others really believed me. They thought they could change me. I could see that in their eyes. Sarah knows what I have to offer and its limitations. I think I would make her happy, and that she would . . .' He stopped. 'I'm sorry to say this, but I think she would make me happy, too. Insofar as I'm able. I'm a difficult beast.'

He kissed her face, over and over again, gently and slowly, as if he were still hungry for the feel of her skin against his lips. 'You, Lily, will never settle for second-best. And that's all I can offer, I'm afraid.

Any time we spent together would have to be a secret that can never ultimately be kept. We'd still make Tom unhappy when he eventually found out. Upset the children, pulling them apart all over again.' He got up and began to dress. 'I'll go now.' He fetched his clothes from the spare room in silence, and was soon buckling up his case.

'Tell Natasha I said goodbye. If she cares.'

'She does. I'm sure of it.' Lily wanted him to hurry up and go. It was too painful to watch him pack.

'Really,' he said, as he stood at the door. 'What choice have we got?'

She shook her head and followed him out on to the jetty, wrapped in her white cotton robe, hugging herself for comfort.

'I'll always think of you here, as if you belonged. It's so much better than—' He stopped.

'Better than what?'

He shook his head. 'Lily?'

'I could try. To settle for second-best.'

He stared down at her. 'Never change. Not for someone else. It doesn't work.'

She thought of herself and Tom. They hadn't managed to change to fit each other better. The problems that had been there at the beginning, the little snapping disagreements that she'd discounted as wedding nerves, or something that would go away, were still there.

'Lily,' he repeated. 'The last few hours. They were real, though, weren't they?'

'Yes.' She was too tired to do anything other than acknowledge the truth. 'They were the best.'

There was regret in his smile. 'It was the closest I've ever got.'

She watched his long legs stride up the steps with a sense of relief. She was glad to see him go. Now she could get on with the rest of her life. Love only slows you down, and trips you up.

The sun inched up in the sky like a searchlight, blinding her against the white of the waves. It was too bright and too hard, like a tasteless joke at a funeral.

26

Lily went back to bed and slept. When she opened her eyes, a bolt of physical pain shot through her, the almost tangible pressure of loss on every sensitive nerve end in her body. She wanted to curl up in a ball and shut the world out. The sun was offensively bright, and the seabirds sounded piteous and desolate. Everything reeked of Chris. Last time I woke up, he was here, she thought. This time yesterday he was mine and I didn't know it.

She needed to get away. The cosiness of the Boathouse was claustrophobic without him, and the isolation, for the first time, felt like loneliness. In London she would have called a girlfriend, and she could, she supposed, do that now, sitting on the bench overlooking the bay, from her mobile phone. But what would she say? I've fallen in love with my brother-in-law, but he's going to marry someone else?

Yeah, right, as Billy would say.

She had to go out.

On the other hand, running away was what she'd done last time. She was only here because of her hurt and anger over Tom. What next? Jump on a plane to Indonesia to get away from this one? There wasn't far enough to go, unless space travel suddenly became a reality. Wearily, she got up. It would have to be faced.

Daisy wandered into her room, looking forlorn and clutching a teddy. 'Mummy?'

'Yes, darling.'

Daisy clambered into her bed and snuggled down. The warm, soft body of her daughter soothed her. She stroked Daisy's silky cheek and marvelled at her sheer perfection. So pretty and gentle and generous. This was what love meant. This steady, endless tenderness. Not the dreadful yo-yoing contradictions of passion.

I was perfectly all right without a man, she muttered to herself. I was absolutely fine on my own. Now I've got to go through all this again.

'Sweetheart, what shall we do today?'

'Can we get Daddy?'

'No, darling.' She stroked Daisy's face and kissed her. 'Daddy's a long way away. Working.'

'I miss him.' Daisy put her thumb in her mouth, and Lily gently took it out again.

'Bad for your teeth.'

Daisy flashed her a smile, and slipped out of bed, Daddy apparently forgotten.

'Toast? With Nutella?' She knew when to take advantage of a weak moment. Lily hoped that her negotiating instincts would survive into adulthood and earn her a happy place in the world.

'Just this once. And not too much.' She sighed. The day must be got through somehow.

The view, which had calmed her ever since she'd arrived, would now be tarnished with the memory of Chris. Every bright little boat would be etched with his name, and when the gulls cried it would be as if they were calling 'Lily' in his voice. It would hurt, she knew, to climb the cliff in the invisible tracks they had left when they had set out to walk to Miss Dean's, and her heart would be seared when she pumped up the pontoon, recognizing only now that there had been such tenderness in the way he'd teased her about it that first day, when it was all before them. She knew now that she had been under his protection, in an indefinable way, ever since then, and that this protection must now be withdrawn.

In the end, everything was, as usual, easier in the sunshine. Lily found herself at nine o'clock in the evening surprisingly quickly, wishing that Chris had phoned to say he'd arrived safely. Long drives on too little sleep could be so dangerous. Natasha had slipped off to the pub, as usual, and with the day over, and the kitchen table cleared of supper, there was nothing left to do except think.

Lily couldn't bear it.

'Harley?'

He was sprawled, with Billy, over a massive game of Monopoly. Daisy, thumb in mouth, was already asleep, her hair blonde and her skin brown from the sunshine. Lily stroked her head and gave her forehead a soft kiss. 'I thought I might go for a walk. Can you look after everyone here for about an hour?'

He barely looked up, but nodded.

'I don't *need* looking after,' said Billy, angrily.

She ignored that. 'Bed, after that game. It's late.' She set out with a torch up the slippery steps, across the pine needles and bracken, and carefully picked her way along the grass spine of the track to the car. It had been a ghost of a road when they'd come, but now, even in the dark, she could see two distinct grooves carved by her car wheels. It made her feel slightly better. She'd left some impression on the land.

She drove around. Should she go to the pub? She felt like talking to people. Jack, the publican, was always friendly when she popped in with the children at lunchtime, and so was Karen, his wife.

But after the silence and darkness of the walk, the lights and noise of the pub assaulted her brain. It was too sudden an immersion in the world of social life, and she blinked, stunned.

Jack grinned. 'Don't often see you here in the evenings.'

'Not like my niece, Natasha, I suppose. Is she in?' She was sure that Tash had said that she was off to the pub. Perhaps it might be nice to have a drink together.

'Who?' asked Jack.

'You know. Natasha. One of your regulars. Swedish girl with long blonde hair.'

A ruddy-faced man leaning on the bar chortled. 'Wouldn't forget her in a hurry.'

Jack's face was a mask of discretion. 'I know who you mean. She comes in occasionally with the Henrys. But, no, she's not here tonight.'

'Comes in with Roger more like,' cackled the man with his pint. 'Bit of luck for him. Don't know how he does it.'

Lily froze.

'Be fair, Will,' said Jack. 'She comes in sometimes with Diana, too.'

'And that knacky baggage that works there,' added the old man.

'Oh, Gemma Conway, you mean. But if you're worried that she's drinking too much' – he turned back to Lily – 'you've got no worries there. She's hardly ever here, and when she is she sticks to mineral water.'

'I seen her waiting at the end of the road, and being picked up in Roger's car,' said Will. 'More'n once.' Another filthy chuckle emerged from his lips and he took his pint to the window, still muttering, 'Wouldn't mind being in Roger's shoes, I wouldn't.'

A shiver rippled up Lily's backbone. It was a repellent thought. And if Natasha wasn't here at the pub, where was she, and where had she been all those long evenings? Lily tried not to panic. Natasha always came home, sober and cheerful.

'You're looking a bit peaky,' said Jack. 'Looking after all those children on your own. You need a bit of life for yourself, you know. What's it to be?'

'Oh, I'm all right.' But she wasn't. She wasn't sure. She'd fractured into a thousand more pieces since Chris had gone. 'I think I'll have a glass of house white.' House white. She felt even more trivialized. Another woman, the brave woman that Chris had painted her as, would, in her situation, be drinking Turkish coffee with nomadic tribesmen. Or vodka with Russian peasants. Or whatever.

Thank God Vicky and Cameron were due down for a couple of weeks. It wasn't the work she minded – Tash had been very helpful with washing-up and tidying – but the relentless responsibility she felt as the only grown-up. Lily needed some time to herself, meeting friends in wine bars – in London if necessary – and generally letting go. Then she'd have to draw up some kind of battle-plan for more work. She would have another couple of months' money when she got back, but after that she needed to start earning fairly quickly.

But before she could take any time off, she had to sort out Roger and Natasha. It was a possibility. It would account for why she never brought any of her pub 'friends' back to the Boathouse, and why no gangly young men were ever seen hanging around the jetty.

Lily felt sick. Challenging Roger and Natasha might drive their affair, if there was one, underground. She needed to think.

As Lily picked her way back to the Boathouse, she told herself that she couldn't make assumptions.

She decided to wait for Natasha to come home, sitting out on the jetty with a glass of wine. There must be a simple explanation.

When Natasha arrived, some time after the pub had closed, she seemed dishevelled and breathless.

'Nice evening?'

Natasha nodded, but continued to walk past her.

'Who was in the pub?'

'All the usual ones.' She shrugged. 'The boys. They are fun, but silly.'

'So no one special, then?'

Natasha looked up. 'Nobody. Just the crowd.'

'Were they late? Did you have to spend time there on your own?'

Natasha looked at Lily as if she had gone quite mad. 'No. I go in there. My friends are waiting. We drink, maybe three, maybe four drinks together. Then I leave. I walk home alone.'

'Oh.' Lily tried to think of another innocuous question she could ask. 'Was Roger there? He told me that he pops in occasionally.'

Natasha pretended to stop and think. 'No. I don't think so. But perhaps he was in the other bar. I do not go in there.' She hesitated. 'Why do you ask?'

'I wanted to ask him for an address.' Lily turned back to her drink. 'Where did you sit in the bar?'

Natasha looked incredulous.

'I just wondered if you'd enjoyed a good view.'

Tash rolled her eyes. 'I did not think about the view. We all stood, you know, the way you do. The tables had all gone.' An edge of exasperation crept into her voice. 'So all night, we stand by the bar. A group of five, maybe six, of us. Except when I go to the Ladies. Once.'

She was not only lying, but also, Lily thought, taking the mick.

'Is there anything else you'd like to know?'

Lily decided that she would have to ask her outright. 'I'd like to know if you were having a drink with Roger Henry.'

'Roger?' Natasha began to laugh. 'Why would I have a drink with Roger?'

Lily could feel herself going red. 'Well, I just thought . . .'

Natasha shrugged and went to bed.

She hadn't specifically denied it, and she was definitely telling porkies. Something wasn't quite right.

Lily reviewed her options. Option one. Call Chris. That could be humiliating. He might think she was finding excuses to ring him. Or he might be angry that she hadn't looked after his daughter more carefully. She didn't think she could bear either reaction, and it would hurt even more to hear tenderness in his voice.

Option two. Ring Sarah. But she would put Chris on the line, and Lily wasn't sure she could stand an exhibition of how close they were as a couple.

Option three. Well, option three was dealing with it herself, and talking to Natasha about it again. But would she listen? Natasha was very self-contained and, although she appeared eager to help and malleable, Lily had never felt she'd really got to know her properly. And what could you say? Roger had been teaching them all to sail, and Natasha could easily have had a few drinks with him to say thank you. It could all be quite innocent.

Option four. Ring Vicky. She needed another woman's view. But Vicky was critical enough of Sarah and Chris leaving Natasha here in the first place. Bringing Vicky in would escalate it to the level of a family row. If possible, she needed to sort this out before Vicky and Cam arrived.

Option five, the last one, the one she least wanted to take, was to ask Tom what he thought about it all. Because at least Tom would be sensible. For all his faults, he did think things through. If he thought she should deal with it herself, he'd say so, and he'd tell her if he thought she should really call Chris. And if Chris was angry, he'd defend her.

If Chris had been a better father to Tash, she might not have looked for a father figure in Roger. Lily was uneasily aware that she was allowing her own children's connections to lapse, and that they were suffering from it. Tom hadn't seen his children in three weeks, and Billy, who had blossomed in the sunshine and the water, was beginning to get sulky and difficult again. And Daisy's eyes filled with tears at the slightest setback.

You can't get away from it, murmured Lily. You

can't let the tide cut you off indefinitely. It was time to call Tom.

She dialled. Nobody answered at first, but just as she expected the machine to cut in, he said, 'Hello,' sounding breathless.

'I haven't woken you, have I?' Lily whispered, although she knew no one could hear her. Around her, trees rustled, and the heartbeat of the sea brushed across the sand.

At Tom's end, she could hear music in the background. Perhaps he was with someone. She was surprised to feel a tweak of pain at the thought, which penetrated the dull ache that Chris had left.

'No, no, of course not. I'll just turn the music down. Don't hang up. I'll go into another room.'

He sounded flustered. So there was someone else. She almost pressed the button to cut them off, but reminded herself that this was about Natasha.

'Have I disturbed you?'

'Not a bit,' said Tom heartily. 'No trouble.'

She told him about having been in the pub, and Natasha being secretive.

'Hm. Tricky. It may not be anything, of course.'

'No.'

'There may be a completely simple explanation.'

'Do you think so? I could ask him.'

They both giggled at the manoeuvres she'd have to go through to get that conversation going in an apparently normal way.

'I could have Roger and Diana to supper again.'

344

'In the end, it has to be down to Chris, but you know what he's like. He'll swoop down on her in a rage, and anything could happen then. She might run away.'

She hadn't thought about that. Chris coming the heavy father with Natasha might make things worse. 'Oh, no. I'd never forgive myself if she disappeared, let alone if she did a bunk with Roger. Do you think it would be better to pretend I haven't noticed and let it run its course? Even if we are right, they're hardly going to spend their lives together, are they?'

'Well, I don't think middle-aged men leave their wives for teenagers.'

'They might. Although Roger is what I'd call all mouth and no trousers. I'm sure he'll scuttle back to Diana at the first hint of trouble.'

Tom chuckled. 'The thought of Roger without trousers is more than I can bear on a full stomach. I may have to be sick. But I know what you mean. Do you think we should tackle it at the Roger end?'

'One of us tell him to stop?' Lily couldn't imagine what such an interview would be like. 'Shall I call round, back him into a corner by that absurd padded bar-thing he dispenses drinks from and tell him to lay off?'

'The trouble with men like that,' said Tom, 'is that they don't respect women. In any way. He calls them "ladies" and takes absolutely no notice of what they say. I'm sorry, I'm not saying you can't handle it, but I think he'll just flirt hideously with you, deny everything and be more careful about where he's seen with Natasha.'

Lily's first instinct was to rebut this, furiously, but she paused. 'You're probably right. Much as I hate to admit it.' Her flesh crawled at the thought of the confrontation, with Roger's eyes running up and down her body, and the little, snide suggestions he might make about him preferring 'a real woman' rather than 'a chit of a girl'.

'Shall I come down? And have a word with him? If that doesn't work, we can tell Chris. I'd like to see the children anyway.'

Lily knew that she ought to handle this on her own, like the independent woman she was, or intended to be, but the thought of Tom fixing it, the way he'd fixed the bathroom door and the tap washer, was tempting. 'Oh, Tom.' She couldn't keep the relief out of her voice. 'Would you mind?'

'I'd love to.' His voice was warm. 'I've got to change a few arrangements, but there's nothing much on at work so I could be down by Tuesday evening and make nearly a week of it. I could go back Sunday evening. If you don't mind,' he added.

Five days of Tom. Lily was amazed to realize that she didn't mind. Not only that, but it seemed like a good idea. Everything between them was so much in the past, and she longed for some company. And comfort.

'Apologize to your girlfriend. I didn't mean to mess up her evening. Or next weekend.' If Tom had got a girlfriend . . . No, don't think like that. She decided to tease him. 'Firstly you leave her on her own while you have a long conversation with your wife and then you bugger up your weekend together.'

'Yes,' said Tom. 'I'd forgotten how you can see down a telephone line. It's just something I'll have to deal with.'

They both laughed guiltily. After all, thought Lily, whoever the poor woman was, she had every right to her date and her weekend.

It was only as she turned the light out, the edges of her pain about Chris fractionally soothed and blunted, and her anxiety about Natasha stilled, that she realized she'd called herself Tom's wife. Not his ex-wife.

It was only a slip of the tongue. Tom probably hadn't noticed.

27

She slept until ten o'clock the following morning, and, when she woke, the leaden stone that Chris had left in her heart seemed to have shifted. Not by very much, but enough to make it worth opening her eyes. She hugged the memory of him to her. It wasn't as if she'd never see him again. He would always be part of her family, although they could never be lovers again. Did that matter?

Well, it did. Very much. But it was time to get on with life. She still had three more weeks at the Boathouse before the children went back to school, and then she would have to find a job. Back into the world of computers? The thought depressed her.

A part of her mind had always assumed that this six weeks off would provide a whole raft of answers; it would soothe away her pain and hurt; it would be, above all, a rest. She'd thought that it would give her a chance to think about what she really wanted to do, or that serendipity would somehow step in. She had imagined seeing an advertisement in a little shop for someone to help a local company with their computing, and that it would all fall into shape. She would escape the rat-race to a life of fresh air, a larger cottage with a garden for the children and meaningful friendships. But this was holiday world; there were few enough permanent jobs for locals out of season. And the property prices almost matched London. People were friendly but they knew she was temporary. Things don't just fall into place, she realized. She had to plan.

And time, which had started the holiday as infinite as the merging of the sea and sky outside, was almost lapping at her feet. The six weeks were half over.

The door creaked open, and Daisy tripped in for her morning cuddle, jumping up on the bed and trying to bounce on Lily's stomach. 'Wakey, wakey, wakey. *We've* got visitors.'

Lily suppressed a wild hope that Chris couldn't live without her and had driven back overnight. 'Who?'

'Diana. Natasha offered her toast and Nutella and she started talking about food in a very funny way. I don't think she likes Nutella.' Daisy bounced on the bed, using it as a springboard to jump to the floor again. 'I think that's very silly of her. Don't you?'

Diana? Downstairs with Natasha? Aargh. Lily leapt out of bed.

'Two minutes.'

The sky outside was already shimmering in the heat, and she pulled on a swimsuit, a pair of flip-flops and her shorts, dragging a brush through her hair and quickly doing her teeth. There was a strained atmosphere downstairs.

'Sorry, Diana. I was having a lie-in.'

Diana's eyes looked bruised with tiredness. 'Lucky you.'

Lily had never seen Diana with anything other than a radiant smile indicating pity for those who overloaded their systems with toxins.

Natasha looked up from buttering bread. 'May I take the children out in the *Enchantress*? I thought we could go up river.'

'Can you manage on your own?'

'Oh, yes.' Natasha sounded offended. 'I have been in boats all my life, and Roger has taught us all well. And we're only going on the river.'

'Fine. Be careful.'

Diana accepted a cup of coffee as the door closed behind them.

'Roger's been so kind to them,' said Lily, making conversation.

'He's a very special man.' Diana always spoke of Roger as if she'd recently been anointed as his high priestess.

Lily cleared away the crusts that Natasha had left behind, putting away the butter and jam, and beginning to bag up the rubbish. Should she say something?

'Are you all right?'

Diana looked distracted. 'It's just that I'm not sleeping very well.'

'Anything special?' Lily sat down.

'Well, I don't know if I should talk to you about it.'

'You can talk to me about anything,' Lily reassured her.

Diana hesitated. 'You know that men get better-looking as they get older, but it's the reverse with women?'

Lily repressed a shudder at the thought of Roger's ruddy face and lobster-tentacle eyebrows. 'It depends,' she said, cautiously. 'I think you're much more attractive than Roger, for example.'

'Do you?' Diana's face lit up, and she held Lily's hand fractionally too long. Lily got up, ostensibly to wipe down the work surface, because she still found Diana's intensity difficult to deal with. 'I do know,' added Diana, 'that he's a very attractive man, and I have to accept that . . .'

Lily reached out, indignant. 'He's lucky to have you.'

'Oh, you're terribly kind. But all the women round here—'

'What?' Lily tried not to screech. 'There is no way that he deserves to lick the toes of your boots in terms of attractiveness!'

'Well, he's never unkind. Really, he's a very good man.'

Lily was reminded of Dora talking about Bertie. Were all women like this? Had she overreacted to Tom's affair?

'I've always known that I'd never have a faithful marriage.'

Lily's heart plummeted. 'Oh, dear.' She wondered

if Diana had propelled herself into a self-fulfilling prophecy, picking out the man who would be most likely to confirm some pre-selected belief pattern. And it all seemed to be confirming everything she and Tom had thought last night. She'd hoped it was her imagination working overtime.

'I was very wicked when I was younger.' Diana plucked at the tablecloth. 'I suppose I'm reaping the benefit now.'

'We're all wicked when we're young. Of course you're not.'

'I did something very dreadful.'

'It can't have been all that bad.'

'Please don't be shocked.'

'I couldn't be. I promise.'

Diana managed a weak smile. 'Thanks, but I was once . . .'

'Beautiful.'

'Not beautiful, not exactly, but all right. In those days, you could really stand out by being the most fashionable, most outrageous girl in town. Fashion mattered – it defined exactly who you were, and if you looked "it" people turned their heads to look at you in the street. It was a kind of power, and I'm ashamed to say I relished it. I was the first with everything: the shortest skirts, the beads, the hipster jeans, everything.'

Lily nodded.

'My mother used to storm into my bedroom in the morning,' continued Diana, 'and whip open the curtains, and say, "It's a lovely day." Then she'd add: "And you can get any goddam man you like because you're young and beautiful. And I can't. Because I'm fifty. Not that it'll help you in the long run. You'll find out when you get to my age."

'My father was having an affair, you see, and it was killing her inside. It was so lonely at home, but the idea of a gap year didn't really exist then, so I helped out at tables at the local restaurant, and saved up for clothes, and waited for university to start. I was totally and completely miserable.

'Bertie and Chris changed all that. Once the Boathouse was open that summer, I could always go there. Nobody shouted at anyone. Everyone was always pleased to see me. Chris was younger than me, but I liked talking to him, and Bertie, well, he was like my dad was before he had the affair, only more glamorous. He was really exciting. He was famous.

'So I decided that if Dad could have an affair, then so could I. That would show him. I targeted Bertie, I'm afraid, I really did. Whenever I knew Chris would be out, I called round, and did everything I could to get him to notice me. He was always very kind, but it was no-go. He was always saying things like, "Darling Diana, you are the most beautiful girl in Devon, you deserve to have some exciting chap whisk you off in his sports car, not to waste time talking to an old married man like me." And I'd tell him he wasn't old, and he'd laugh and tell me I was sweet.

But even if I went up close he'd tap my arm affectionately and move away. I began to get obsessed by him. I knew Maud had left him, and thought I could be the one who would understand him.

'And then one day I was feeling great about myself because I'd had the first bubble haircut – it was called the Harpo Marx look, and was literally a huge halo of big round curls all round your head. I walked down the street and got the most gobsmacked looks you could imagine.' She giggled. 'I felt confident and wonderful and brave and in charge of my destiny, all those stupid things. I was too young to know that it was only a haircut.

'And I liked the way Chris looked at me when I arrived. For the first time I thought about him as a man, not as a gangly, lovesick schoolboy. He said he had some great new dope – heaven knows where he got it from down there, his father, possibly – so we opened all the windows in his room to let the smell out and sat on his bed smoking joints. You might think it was stupid of me to smoke joints on a boy's bed, but I suppose I was stupid. Very innocent, certainly. We started to hold hands. I'm not quite sure how it all happened, because until that day I was so involved in getting Bertie to notice me that I hadn't thought about Chris except . . .' She blushed. '. . . well, to use him to get more invitations to the Boathouse. I knew he'd always ask me to come again tomorrow and so on. Anyway, we started kissing, and it was surprisingly nice . . .'

Yes, it was, thought Lily.

'I should have told him I wasn't interested, but I just wasn't thinking. I feel really bad about that now. I was too involved with everything that was happening at home, and it felt so good to have someone's arms around me, and the dope and the haircut all made me think I should get this sex business over with. Just do it. Whether it was right or not.'

Lily must have been looking horrified, because Diana added: 'It wasn't Chris's fault. But I wouldn't have done it if I'd been thinking, or if we'd been wearing more clothes, but there we are. Our first time. You know, one minute it hurts and the next it's all sticky and messy, and you feel dirty and embarrassed and think: Oh God, why did I *do* that?' Diana's face was twisted with distaste, and Lily, desperately and unsuccessfully, tried to suppress a lightning bolt of jealousy.

'I hated it,' said Diana softly. 'But I couldn't tell Chris that, could I?'

'No.'

'It was just an accident, something that got out of hand. Neither of us knew what we were doing,' added Diana. 'In my class at school, of thirty of us, only two had ever "done it"; one was snidely referred to as "the village bicycle" and the other had been going out with her boyfriend since she was eight and was already engaged. Everybody else didn't. We all talked about being virgins when we married. Most of *them* were.' She put a hand on Lily's arm. 'You must think I'm such a tart.'

'No, not at all. Just unhappy. And it wasn't an awful thing to do. At all.'

'It was then.' Diana looked sad. 'For me. In the newspapers and in London, it was actually called the Summer of Love. That was a joke in Devon, where a few newspaper headlines don't erase generations of so-called decent behaviour. If you read the *Daily Mail* you saw photographs of men and women wearing flowery shirts and bells and beads lying on floors looking cool. Down here in the *Dartmouth Gazette* it was still all Carnival Queen and Bonny Baby contests.

'As I walked home to Mum and Dad, I prayed that everything would be normal there, just for once. Tea on the table and everyone talking nicely to each other. I wanted life to be like it used to be like.

'I opened the back door to hear them screaming at each other as usual, and this time Dad really did walk out. The dog, Susie, went chasing after him, and he picked her up, and said, "I'm taking her, too."

'But he didn't say that he wanted to take me. He just went, with Susie. I went back to the Boathouse immediately, on my bicycle, partly as a kind of homing device, because I knew they'd be nice to me, and partly because I wanted to be honest with Chris and say that it couldn't happen again. But only Bertie was there.'

She stopped.

'What happened then?'

'Bertie asked me how I was. As if he really cared. And I told him. Everything. Even roughly what had happened with Chris and how bad I felt. And I cried. I told him that my father had taken the dog, but not me. It was the worst thing that had ever happened to me. Bertie put his arm round me, and . . .' Diana blew her nose again.

Lily thought that no parent should have to listen to the story of their son's first sexual experience. No wonder 'never excuse, never explain' was Bertie's motto. She now understood the reason for his silence.

'He said that taking a dog was treating it as a possession,' continued Diana. 'And that no man who loved his daughter would treat her like a possession. The way he explained it made it feel all right. And he told me that everyone's first time is a bit frightening or a bit of a disappointment and that it's nobody's fault. Just nasty old life teaching you that all the fairy tales are just stories. So I'm afraid I kissed him. And he held me tightly. And then, well, we did kiss properly. And Chris came in. I felt terrible about that. Because that was my fault, too.'

By now Diana had torn the paper napkin to crumbs and had started on the next. It was like a lethal game of consequences, thought Lily. From Diana's father and mother to Diana and Bertie and Chris, and even perhaps, in some way, to her and Tom, and, from there, the baton of unhappiness would be handed to Billy and Daisy unless she could find a way of breaking the cycle. 'Did you explain that he was only comforting you?' It sounded pretty weak.

'I tried to, but fourteen-year-old boys are very

sensitive. And I honestly hadn't realized how much he cared. I don't think he and Bertie spoke to each other for ages after that. I feel so guilty.'

'It wasn't your fault,' Lily pointed out. 'Bertie was in his late forties and you were just a teenager. He should have been the one to behave responsibly. He shouldn't have kissed you.'

Diana shrugged. 'I was vulnerable. But I knew he was vulnerable, too. I'd been chasing him for weeks, remember, not that I knew what I was up to. You don't, do you? Sex isn't real until you've done it.' She suppressed a shudder.

Lily thought about it. 'I know. More coffee?'

'Have you got decaffeinated?'

Lily rootled through the cupboards. 'No, but there's some ginger and lemon herbal if you like.'

Diana nodded.

Lily filled the kettle again. 'It was an upsetting experience, but I don't think it's necessarily relevant to anything that might or might not be happening now.' She still wasn't quite sure why Diana had chosen that moment to tell her the story.

Diana looked extremely worried. 'I don't think I've explained it very well. You see . . .' She stopped. 'I think Roger's up to something. He flirts a lot with women, and I've got used to that, but I think that whatever's going on at the moment might be serious.'

Lily stirred her tea. She couldn't think of a reply.

'I need to take a stand,' continued Diana, 'but until

I get my head together, I can't make sense of it all myself. Look, thank you for listening.'

'Do come round. Any time. I'm always here.'

Diana hugged her, holding her so close that Lily thought, for a moment, that she was hiding tears.

When she'd left, Lily tried to decipher the conversation, and decided that Diana was saying that there was another insecure, unhappy, vulnerable teenager looking for a father figure at the Boathouse.

28

Tom arrived late the following evening, rumpled, grey and exhausted. Lily remembered her own face in the mirror when she'd first arrived. Now her skin was burnished to the shade of creamy honey and dusted with freckles, and her hair, shot with streaks of sunlight, escaped into curling tendrils.

'You look great,' said Tom, after his first mouthful of wine. 'I like the blonde.'

Daisy clambered on to his knee. She, too, had turned into a honey-coloured sprite, with a cascade of white-blonde corkscrew curls. 'Daddy, do you know how to sail?'

'Of course. When I was your age, Uncle Chris and I used to go out in the *Enchantress* all on our own.'

Lily frowned at him. She was still afraid of the combination of children and water.

'And once we were very, very silly, and went too far out and the tide began to go out too, and it dragged our boat further and further away from the shore . . .'

Daisy snuggled into his chest and put her thumb in her mouth.

'We soon realized that if we got swept away into the sea, we might come across great big waves which could turn the boat over, and even if the boat didn't turn over, it would be very difficult for anyone to find us. It's a very, very big place.'

Lily put her hand over her mouth, thinking of two small boys in a tiny boat, tossed about by enormous waves.

'What happened?' Billy, who had been off-hand when his father arrived, pretending to prefer another game of Monopoly with Harley, crept closer to hear the story.

'We managed to get close enough to one of the buoys and Chris and I hung on to it to stop ourselves being dragged out any further. We clung on until the tide changed.'

'But that would have been at least six hours,' gasped Lily. 'What sort of weather was it? Weren't you freezing?'

'Freezing, starving, boiling, terrified, desperately thirsty, bored, yes . . . all of those things.' Tom sounded almost wistful. 'Then we sailed back in and pretended to have been fishing up the river bank all day.'

'What did Granny say? Wasn't she frightened?'

Tom winked. 'We never told her. Best not tell Mummies things that frighten them.'

Lily decided to avoid a row and suppressed a sense of unease. She'd always carefully instructed the children to tell her anything and everything.

'Suppertime. Chops, everyone?'

'Yes!' Billy often refused any food she suggested. 'I'll have three!'

'I don't think you will.' But she smiled.

Tom went over to the Monopoly game by the fire. 'Who's winning?'

'I am,' said Harley.

'Right. Perhaps Billy and I ought to form a partnership.' He sat down on the sofa, with Daisy still curled up in his lap and began conferring with Billy. The shadows left her son's face, and tranquillity stole across the room.

Family life, she thought, as she placed the chops under the grill and tossed a salad. This is family life. Tall stories, cosy partnerships, lucky escapes, minor deceptions. All the little ingredients that make up the sum of happiness. The safe harbour after the heaving, monumental waves of passion that can so easily overturn your small boat.

On Thursday Lily decided to call Vicky to finalize the plans for the fortnight after Tom left. It would be nice to settle Vicks and Cam in, and then get away for a bit of exploring or a few indulgent trips to old friends.

'Hi, dearest.' Vicky sounded evasive. 'I'm so glad you phoned. Now, we've got the teeniest little problem about next week . . .'

Lily's heart sank.

'Cam's exhibition really seems to be going somewhere, and the most awful bore of it is that they've laid on a whole load of extra events. He's got dinner with some advertisers and some sort of art day to do with sponsorship; I don't know the half of it, but I really feel I should be there to support him.'

'Oh, of course.' Lily suppressed her own selfish desire for some support. Be nice, Lily, she told herself. Share. 'But that's marvellous, isn't it?'

'Well, hardly. It is my holiday, and I don't see why I should give it up. But at least you're there, so we don't have to worry about Harley, and, if we came down this weekend, then we could stay, oh, until Wednesday at least.'

'Tom's here this weekend.' Lily felt like adding: And it is my holiday, too.

'That'll be lovely,' said Vicky. 'Just like old times.'

'It's just that there are only three bedrooms. I can let you and Cameron have the big one . . .'

'That does seem to make sense. If it's got the best bed. My back's giving me hell. You are an angel. I just can't wait to see you. We'll have such fun.'

'. . . but that would mean I'd have to tip Tom out of the small one.'

'Oh, he can sleep on the sofa. It'll do him good.'

'Well, I'm not sure that the sofa is quite man-sized. I suppose I could sleep on a put-you-up with the children . . .'

'That's a good idea. Anyway, you're much better than I am at all this planning and I've got a report to write. See you about eightish tomorrow evening then. How exciting! I really need a break.' And she put the phone down.

'Bugger,' said Lily. 'Cameron and Vicky are coming

down tomorrow and I feel I've got to give them the decent double room, as they're a couple and I'm not. But that leaves you and me to fight over the small spare and the sofa.'

Tom grinned. 'You do get bogged down in detail, don't you? Why don't we share the big bed? Cameron and Vicky can take the standard double in my room. That way you don't have to move your things.'

'Tom.'

He held his hands up. 'I really am not suggesting anything. You can put a pillow down the middle between us if you like. But we've shared a bed quite chastely for many years . . .'

'That wasn't intentional.'

She could see he was enjoying this. 'That wasn't what you said at the time.'

'Oh, for God's sake. Why do I have to be the one to worry about where everyone is going to sleep? Romantic heroines just waft through life. They don't have to juggle sheets and supplies and run houses like Boy Scout camps.'

Tom laughed. 'I had no idea you visualized yourself as a romantic heroine. I'd have polished up my Rhett Butler act if I'd known.'

'Oh, shut up.'

'Look,' he said. 'Vicky is a spoilt, manipulative cow who expects everything and everyone to revolve round her. Give her the goddam second-best bedroom. It's about time she realized that we can't all dance like puppets on the strings she pulls.'

'Tom.' Lily was astonished. Part of the Devereaux family legend was that Vicky was a warm, wonderful person who nurtured the wayward, immature Cameron. Her role in the family was that of put-upon breadwinner, emotional rock and perfect mother. 'What on earth do you mean? I thought you liked Vicky.'

'I like her well enough. But she's selfish, and she's careless. Careless of other people's feelings, their time, their possessions . . .'

Lily thought of Vicky arriving late the day they'd left. It wasn't the first time she'd been late. But some people were punctual and some weren't. 'That's not fair. It's Cameron who's the careless one. The irresponsible baby brother whom everyone has to look after.'

'Look more closely. Vicky gets exactly what she wants by being very charming, and, if necessary, very vulnerable. Cameron looks after her, not the other way around.'

'Why are you so against her?'

'I'm not. I just don't like to see you being used, that's all. Or Cameron. She subtly gets at Cameron for not earning, but she was the one who screwed up his career when Harley was first born.'

'I don't believe you.'

'Don't then. But she claimed to have terrible postnatal depression and used to ring up in the middle of jobs and demand that he come home to change Harley's nappy.'

'I'm sure you haven't got that quite right,' said Lily. 'Post-natal depression is pretty serious. People aren't rational. And other people don't understand.'

'No, we certainly didn't understand. But Cameron danced to her tune, and the jobs dried up. She likes being the chief earner. It gives her control.'

Lily shook her head. Vicky had obviously said something tactless to Tom. Perhaps he felt that she'd taken Lily's side over the divorce. That was probably it, although there was also a glimmer of truth in what he said. Just a glimmer. No one is perfect, after all, and she'd often been irritated herself by Vicky. But, in the end, faced with her warmth and the way she managed to juggle so many balls, you had to forgive her.

'Well, I think she has quite a tough time. Perhaps she has to be a bit selfish just to survive.'

It had been easy to identify the Devereaux family roles from the first time she'd met them all together: Chris, the ruthless but responsible bastard who controlled everything; Tom, the regular nice-guy in the middle; and Cameron, eternally the baby, the favourite, the one who had to be protected. Vicky and she had fitted their own temperaments around this blueprint. That was how the family – any family – worked, wasn't it?

It was when Tom had strayed off the Happy Families script that she'd stopped playing. But, funnily enough, she no longer cared about that. It seemed like a long time ago, and irrelevant.

'Let's not argue.' He put his arm out, and, just for a moment, because she felt so miserably lonely, she allowed herself to lean into his embrace. His body felt warm and strong, and more solid than Chris's sinewy frame. 'Look,' he murmured. 'You run away if you want to. Leave me to cope with Vicky and Cameron. You've done enough.'

She nodded. 'I might do that. Let's just sort out the Natasha situation first, though. I don't want to go away leaving everything hanging in the air. I feel responsible for her.'

At the end of the day, she and Tom took their drinks out on to the jetty, and watched the stripes of sunset slowly dissipate over the horizon and sink into the blue darkness. Cotton-wool clouds edged in iridescent rose marked the last few rays of sun.

'Well, what do you think?' She didn't have to complete the sentence. Tom knew what she was talking about.

He looked worried. 'I drove past the Henrys' place on the way back from Totnes today, and saw your car there. It wasn't you, was it?'

Lily shook her head. 'I've been here all day, and I did lend it to Natasha. But she's been very friendly with Diana.' She remembered Diana's strained face and the story about infidelity. 'Until recently, anyway.'

'Mm. Anyway, when I saw Natasha later, I asked her about her day, and she never mentioned the Henrys. Later on, I asked her about Roger's boat hire, and pretended to have lost the number of his office. She gave it to me, and told me that he wouldn't be there today. So she's pretty well informed about his movements.'

'None of it really adds up to anything.'

'But it doesn't disprove anything either.'

'What shall we do?'

'Call Chris?'

Lily thought about hearing his voice again. She didn't think she could bear it. 'I think we have to. But I'd rather not, if you don't mind.'

'I don't blame you,' said Tom. 'He's likely to go ballistic.'

Lily tried to group the pinpricks of light scattered across the inky space above. They made no sense to her. They weren't the same stars that she and Chris had lain and watched. Everything was different. 'I don't see why he should. He's the first to say that he's not as close to Natasha as he should be. He's got no right to come the heavy father after hardly being a father at all.'

'He won't see it that way. He'll just see that his daughter is threatened. And that he's responsible for her. And then he'll charge in there without thinking anything through.'

Lily sighed. 'He's still the only one who can deal with it, though. Unless he calls Ingrid and gets her back from her nude sunbathing in the Arctic Circle or wherever she's gone.'

'Wish me luck.' Tom got up and strode up the

steps to get a signal, returning, breathing heavily with the effort, only a few minutes later. 'Oh, dear.'

'What?'

'You know Chris. He's tearing down here, tomorrow, to get Natasha.'

'I didn't expect him to be that quick.' Lily suppressed the wish that he was tearing down to get her.

'He said he had a meeting first thing tomorrow, and he'd be down after that because he and Sarah are going to St Barts on Sunday morning.'

'But there's nowhere for him to sleep. Cameron and Vicky will be here.'

Tom shrugged. 'You try stopping him.' He handed her the mobile.

She dialled.

'Yes,' shouted Chris.

'Sorry. It's Lily.'

There was a silence.

'You can't come down. At least, you can, but there isn't anywhere to sleep.' Lily felt every inch the mundane housewife, obsessed by trivia. She felt like screaming: This isn't me, I'm not a person who normally can't get their brain any further than whether everyone's got a pillow or not, but nobody else round here is going to do it.

'We'll get a room at the pub.' Chris switched off.

We. Of course. We. A horrible, smug little word, we.

'Sarah's coming, too,' she said, bleakly, to Tom.

He raised his eyebrows. 'Mm. Well, she's pretty

much living there at the moment. And I think they're sneaking off to the Caribbean to get married on a beach, if you want my opinion.'

It hurt. It really did hurt. 'Why do you think that?'

'Just little things they've said. Or, rather that she's said, and he hasn't contradicted.'

She sighed. 'I know this sounds very mundane, but it looks as if we're going to have to get some supplies in. Nothing is worse than a lot of hungry, tired, drunk people without anything to mop up the alcohol and anger.'

Tom helped himself to another glass of wine. 'You're right. And could you add some beers to that? Oh, and I've run out of toothpaste.'

29

The following day dawned to a fierce whiteness.

'It's going to be hot,' said Tom. 'Very hot.'

Even at ten o'clock, Lily could feel the weight of the sun on her back as she mounted the steep steps, although the woods were still fresh and cool. It will be stifling in town, she thought.

The road into Dartmouth was slow, clogged up with a tractor and too many holiday cars, curving round from one temporary roadworks sign to another, jamming over the hump-backed bridge and tailing back out of the town, so that all the parking spaces were gone by the time she arrived. Lily usually enjoyed picking out fresh fruit and vegetables, calculating special twists she could give to dishes, and chatting to the butcher about the best cuts of meat. Today, it was too warm to think about food. The shopping stretched out ahead of her, slow, heavy and frustrating.

Enough grumbling. It's a lovely day. Ahead of her, an old lady picked her way carefully in the heat, moving swollen, distorted limbs slowly and painfully. Think how lucky you are, Lily. Don't tempt the gods. Here, beside the sea, they can be very vengeful.

Lily stopped to transfer the shopping from one

arm to another, hoping to make the load feel lighter, but there was no escaping the sheer weight of food required to keep a household of ten people for the weekend. It was past one when she arrived back, limp and tetchy, to find Tom stretched out with the papers.

He jumped up. 'Let me take those.'

She waved at the direction of the woods. 'There's more in the car.'

Daisy appeared. 'When's lunch? I'm hungry.'

Lily struggled not to snap at her. 'In a minute.' The sea, as still as a photograph, shone into her eyes every time she looked out. It seemed suspended in time, burning slowly off the horizon. She sat down, drained. 'Do you think there's a storm coming?'

Tom shrugged, handing her the groceries. 'I don't know. I think it's just hot.'

Lily began to pack the fridge, fitting the awkward items in with jigsaw puzzle accuracy, and the afternoon stretched out ahead of her in an almost endless succession of tasks. Bed-making. Clean towels. Flowers. No, not flowers. Nothing unnecessary. Because even the simplest of food would need slicing and chopping and washing and clearing. And at the end of it all would be Chris. With Sarah. On the way to their wedding.

Cameron and Vicky arrived first, with the late-afternoon low tide, Vicky driving confidently over the glistening sand.

'Darlings.' She folded Lily in a hug. 'I'm knack-ered. But what heaven to be here.'

Harley, self-contained and serious, came down the steps from the garden as if he was greeting his head-master on speech day.

'My baby!' she shrieked. He disappeared almost entirely into Vicky's voluminous cotton frock. 'Let me look at you! So tall and brown! You look gorgeous.' She frowned. 'When did you last wash his hair, Lily?'

'I, er . . .'

'Never mind. I'm one of the most laid-back moth-ers I know!' She planted a smacking kiss on both of his cheeks, and Cameron put an arm out to greet his son.

'Hi, Dad.'

'Hi.' They looked at each other. Cameron held out his arms, and Harley wrapped himself around his father.

Billy, as wild as a woodland creature, shot out from behind the jetty, shouting.

'Hey,' said Cameron, joking. 'What about hello?'

Billy stared at the ground and muttered. Cameron dropped down on to his haunches to talk to him directly. 'Has it been a good summer so far?'

'Yeah.' Billy looked away.

'Billy,' remonstrated Lily, and he tensed, angry and aggressive.

Tom put a hand on his son's back, and the boy looked up at him, and then Cameron. 'Brill summer,' he added, quite calmly.

'Good,' said Cameron, touching him on the shoulder.

Billy smiled back, and, for one moment, was an adorable ten-year-old boy. 'We've got a tree house,' he said. 'Will you come and see it?'

'I'd love to,' Cameron assured him. 'I used to play there, too, when I was your age. I could teach you how to use a catapult.'

Billy smiled again, and raced off with Harley and Daisy.

Both Tom and Cameron were so much better with Billy than she was. Lily felt her own inadequacy. It was clear. He needed a man around. For Billy, she should go back to Tom. They should be a family together. There was no doubt about that.

Cameron stood up and stretched out his arms, surveying the steep hillsides with their rambling flowers and grasses, and the woods at the top. 'I haven't been here since I was five. I always remembered it as this magical place where I was always happy. Hi, Lil, you look fab.' He hugged her. 'How are you surviving?'

'More than surviving,' she assured him.

Vicky, meanwhile, was pulling treasure out of the back seat. 'Wine. Cheeses, choccies . . . our contribution.' She handed over a vast box of Godiva chocolates, and three bottles of champagne. 'I'll pop them in the fridge, shall I?'

She emerged from the cottage a few minutes later,

looking baffled. 'Oh, dear, is that the only fridge there is?'

'Don't worry.' Lily took them. She would have to repack the fridge. Chocolate, in this heat, would melt and bloom, and the champagne needed cooling too. Once, she thought, she would have enjoyed the champagne, without thinking about such details. Where had that laughing girl gone?

Vicky handed Tom the overnight bags. 'Tom, dearest, would you mind taking these to our room? I've got to take the car back to the car park before the tide comes up.'

Tom took the bags. 'A pleasure, Vicky.'

Lily followed him in. 'Where are you going?'

'Where do you want them?'

She hesitated. 'In the hall. While we decide.'

Tom put them down. 'Oh, shit.'

'What?'

He was looking out of the window, across the beach. 'That's Chris's car.'

Lily took a deep breath and went out to greet them.

Chris got out, looking as if he hadn't slept for days. His eyes were bloodshot and he had a thick growth of stubble on his chin. He looked extremely tired.

'Hello,' said Lily. 'Did you have terrible traffic?'

'Not too bad.' He looked down at her, challenging her, refusing to do the trivial kiss on the cheek.

She was glad. She couldn't have borne the sense of him so close, the herby, acrid notes of Acqua di Parma and sandalwood.

'Darling!' Sarah hopped out of the other seat, spry and vigilant, planting an air-kiss to the left and right of Lily's cheeks. 'And look who we've brought.' There was a note of pleading in her voice, as if this was their only possible contribution to the crisis.

'Dora!'

Dora got out of the car stiffly. 'I hope it's not too soon to see me again.'

'Of course not. It's lovely.' Lily took a deep breath, to find the words to ask why.

'We've all got rooms at the pub,' added Sarah brightly. 'It's the sweetest little place.' Sweetest, judging from her tone of voice, was not entirely a compliment.

'Hi, Cam, have you been here long?' Chris thumped his brother on the back, a little harder than was strictly necessary, thought Lily.

Cam thumped him back amiably. 'Not long,' he said. 'Thank you for allowing me back here at last.'

Chris's eyes were dark and unfathomable. 'You could have come back before. If you'd wanted to.'

Cameron laughed.

Lily decided to go inside, to put baked potatoes in the oven.

Dora, familiar with the workings of the house,

quietly laid the table. Vicky took a book out on to the jetty. 'Sunset at the Boathouse,' she murmured as she went through the kitchen. 'I've heard so much about it. Paradise on earth. You're so lucky to have six weeks of it.'

Sarah looked tired, too, Lily noticed. 'Have you had a late night?'

'I was up late packing. We'll probably drive from here to the airport. That's why Dora's here. She's going to take Natasha back to London.'

'Will Natasha go?'

'I think she'll have to. It'll either be that or a plane back to Sweden, and, as we're going to the airport, Chris won't have the slightest hesitation in enforcing it. He's determined not to leave her here with this Roger man.'

'Shouldn't Chris try to find out what's going on first?'

Sarah shrugged. 'I don't know. Once he's made up his mind, it's very difficult to get him to change it. He's awfully stubborn, don't you think?'

Lily didn't want to discuss him. 'You look exhausted. Why don't you have a drink on the jetty with Vicky?'

'If you're sure there's nothing . . .'

'Darlings . . .' Vicky rattled her glass. 'If you're coming out, would you bring a teeny-weeny top-up. It's such heaven to be here. You wouldn't believe what an awful week I've had.'

Sarah poured her another glass of wine. 'Thank

you *so* much,' said Vicky. 'You're an absolute angel.'

But Lily could hear the dislike in her voice.

Once Sarah had been pushed, reluctantly, out to 'enjoy herself' with Vicky, Lily made a salad dressing.

'Want someone to wash the salad?' asked Tom.

'You weren't like this when we were married,' replied Lily. 'Then you expected your dinner on the table.'

'Did I?' He sounded surprised. 'Sorry about that.'

'You weren't that awful.' She smiled. 'At least you did the washing-up. Sometimes.'

'It's quite difficult, you know, to know who should be doing what. In a marriage.'

'Yes. I know. I imagine your father did absolutely nothing.'

He grinned. 'Nothing whatsoever. Mum and Dora did it all. And no one thought it was odd. So we don't have any kind of blueprint to go by.'

'Your father was lucky.'

'Not necessarily. I don't think he knew us the way we know our children.'

'Speaking of our children, how do you think Billy is?'

'Better,' he said, cautiously. 'Not as wild. But life's never going to be easy for him.'

Lily put the large, colourful salad bowl on the table. 'Do you think we ought to try to find him some professional help?' It cost her a great deal to suggest that. She could hardly bear the thought of experts prying into their lives, making judgements on them.

'I think it might be a good idea.' Tom spoke gently. 'We can discuss it when you get back.'

Lily felt her chest ease, as if she had put down something heavy. Through the open door, she could see Sarah and Vicky facing away from each other on the jetty.

'Why does Vicky hate Sarah so much?'

Tom raised his eyebrows, with a short, sharp laugh. 'Because of Chris, of course.'

Lily's heart stopped, for one second. 'Chris?'

'Oh, yes. Vicky pursued Chris before she took up with Cameron. She managed to be the kind of platonic girlfriend-who's-just-a-friend that would make most men run a mile. He didn't seem worried, although he certainly didn't capitulate either. He just went on being nice and friendly. In fact, I think he liked her company, and she was quite clever about organizing little events that she knew he'd enjoy. But when it came down to it, he refused to take it any further, and Cameron's such a softie that he picked up the pieces. To tell you the truth . . .' Tom paused in his opening of a bottle of red wine and looked her in the eye. 'I never believed she loved Cameron at all. I think she only married him to stay close to Chris.'

'But why didn't anyone tell me?'

Tom gave her a curious look. 'Why should they? There was never anything specific, and it was ages ago. I mean, you couldn't have called her a girlfriend of Chris's or anything. And, in fact, whatever my original misgivings, she and Cam do seem to suit each other. I'd more or less forgotten all about it.'

Lily had a thought. 'Did she have a go at you before Cameron?'

Tom went rather pink. 'Not really. Nothing you could put your finger on, anyway.'

She couldn't help laughing at the thought of Tom fleeing an intense Vicky. 'Sorry,' she added. 'I couldn't help it.'

'Yes, well, I couldn't help it either. I don't like rapacious women.'

Only last week she would have asked him if that meant that it was he who had done the running with that girl at work and what that meant in the context of his affair. And they would have argued, intensifying their bitterness with things that should never have been said.

But she merely smiled. 'Me neither.'

Daisy, trailing her favourite security blanket, tugged at her. 'Can we have supper with you?'

'Sweetheart, you've had tea. And there isn't room around the table.'

'I want to eat with Daddy.'

'You can eat with Daddy tomorrow.'

'Could we have a midnight feast? Take crisps and things up to our room?'

Lily sighed. The endless portioning out of food was exhausting. 'If you must. Here. Off you go.' She handed her daughter a packet of biscuits and some crisps, and Daisy, detecting impatience, scampered off.

Vicky stood in the doorway. 'Now then. I must unpack. You know me, I can't relax until everything's completely sorted. The last person to sit down, that's me.'

Lily suppressed the observation that she had been reading, with her feet on a chair, on the jetty for two hours while Lily, Dora and Tom prepared supper.

'Are you out of the main bedroom yet?' added Vicky.

A flash of anger shot through Lily. 'Actually,' she said. 'Tom and I've decided to stay there. It seemed silly to bother everyone by moving stuff out, and the wardrobe's already clear for your things in the little room.'

Not a muscle in Vicky's face moved. 'Tom.'

'Tom.' Lily was firm.

'Oh. It's just that my back has been giving me quite a bit of trouble over the last week. I've just had a quick peek, and the double in your room looks nice and firm.'

'Hard beds are the worst possible thing for backs,' Lily assured her. 'And you aren't here for long, after all.'

Vicky's face was white, accentuating great shadows under her eyes. She looked tired. Lily felt sorry for her, just for a moment, and then reminded herself that she'd been looking after Vicky's son for four weeks.

'We can always stay at the pub, darling,' said

Cameron, standing behind her and resting an arm on her shoulders.

Vicky moved a few inches away from the arm. 'You're sweaty, darling.'

'There are only two rooms at the pub,' said Sarah's voice from the other side of the room. 'I particularly noticed,' she added.

Lily imagined Sarah running Chris's life as comfortably as Dora and Maud had run Bertie's, never allowing him to run out of clean underwear, or think about who had to sleep where. She would always notice how many rooms were available and where the best steak could be purchased.

'Anyway, we can't afford the pub.' Vicky looked as if she might be about to cry.

Lily stifled her guilt at the thought of the huge box of chocolates and the three bottles of champagne. Lovely, but more than the cost of a night at the pub. And there was the gardener, and the cleaner. It occurred to her, somewhat late in the day, that Vicky used their alleged poverty as a way of manipulating people.

Vicky raised her chin in defiant defeat. 'Oh, well. Never mind.' Her voice was hard.

'Sarah and I are going to find Natasha.' Chris, in the darkness of the stairway, must have heard it all.

Nobody else spoke.

'Supper will be ready at about eight,' said Lily, eventually.

30

Lily, whose feet hurt and head ached with the combination of heat and cooking, decided to go to bed
first, as the last pink and golden streaks of cloud
glimmered and vanished over the distant horizon.
The brothers and Vicky took drinks and coffee out
on to the jetty.

As Lily filled a glass with water, she heard Sarah's
footsteps behind her.

'That was a lovely meal, thank you.'

'Oh, I'm glad you liked it.' She couldn't meet Sarah's
eye.

'Do you think it would matter if I slipped away?
I've got rather a headache.'

Lily felt sorry for her, trapped in the middle of a
family that might soon be hers, but ruthlessly
excluded by Vicky. 'Of course not. Just do whatever
you like. It's a bit hot for late nights.'

'Yes. Although it's lovely here.'

They were trying to reach out to each other,
thought Lily, but not quite touching. The effort of
the day had left her too drained to respond. She would
try harder some other time. If she did go back to
Tom, and Sarah married Chris, they would be sisters-
in-law. 'Beautiful,' she agreed, hoping that might be

enough to send Sarah to bed satisfied with the exchange.

'Really beautiful,' echoed Sarah, looking out of the kitchen door at the jetty. 'Body language is extraordinary,' she added, a few minutes later.

'What?'

Sarah indicated the group of drinkers on the jetty. 'Cameron. It's always Chris and Tom together, isn't it? And everyone else out on a limb. Especially Cameron.'

Lily followed her gaze. Chris and Tom were relaxed back in their chairs, their heads close together, their body positions mirror images of each other. Now that Sarah had pointed it out, she realized that they always sat like this, communicating by glances and slight movements that others could scarcely detect, let alone interrupt. Chris and Tom had met every Saturday lunchtime in a pub throughout her marriage, even during the sleepless nights and screaming babies phase. She hadn't queried it.

Cameron was opposite them, hunched forward in his chair, as if trying to make a point. Vicky was slightly set back from them all, a referee or an observer, not committed to either side.

'He's so much younger.' Lily knew she was making excuses.

'Was it difficult for you, though? Being married to a man who was so close to his brother?'

Lily was rooted to the spot. 'I never thought about

it.' She looked out at the silhouettes. 'Perhaps I should have done.'

Sarah, she thought, would quietly but ruthlessly, strand by strand, sever the relationship between Chris and Tom. If she thought it was necessary.

'I think Cameron's angry,' observed Sarah. 'At being left out.'

'Cameron?' Lily was astonished. 'He's the most laid-back member of the family.'

'Oh, he hides it well.' Sarah turned away. 'Well, if there's nothing I can do . . .' She indicated the kitchen.

'It's mostly done, don't worry. And I think Tom will wash the rest up.' Lily thought about the rage that had burnt inside her, and how destructive it had been. Was it anger that prevented Cameron from getting his act together? Was he taking revenge on anyone who expected anything of him? On the other hand, she wasn't sure she believed in trite psychological observations.

Her own anger had burnt itself out completely, she realized, in spite of Chris. Or, perhaps, because of Chris. Maybe no other emotions could exist in the cold, Arctic world of loss. The Dart, she thought, had claimed its human heart for the year. But at least she could now make a real decision on what she should do with her life. She no longer pored over the same old, humiliating details any more, or rehearsed in her mind what she should have said or could have done, or picked over their past in a desperate attempt to make sense of it. It all seemed a very long way away.

Oh, it was too late, and she was too tired.

'Goodnight, Sarah. Sleep well.'

'And you. We're going to talk to Natasha in the morning. She said she had a Bodymind Attunement session tonight.'

'Ah. Yes. She does quite a lot of that sort of thing.'

'Yes. Well. It can't hurt, I'm sure. I mean, it's not culty or anything, is it?'

Lily was ashamed to realize that she didn't know. 'I'm sure it isn't. There's quite a lot of it down here, I think.'

'Mm.' Sarah fidgeted, as if she wanted to ask something. 'Well. I'd better go then.'

'Goodnight.'

'Goodnight.'

The bedroom was stifling, and the sheets twisted under her, warm and crumpled. Lily couldn't find a comfortable position. Eventually she drifted off into a half-dream.

She was woken by Tom stumbling around as he got undressed, unfamiliar with the layout of the room. She could hear his breathing. The bed sagged as he got into it, and she tried not to inhale the odours of wine and coffee as he leant over her.

She kept very still, forcing herself to breathe evenly.

He kissed her cheek. 'Goodnight,' he whispered. 'I love you very much.' His voice was slurred. He wouldn't remember it in the morning.

Lily couldn't even turn over now, in case he realized she was awake. She counted, to a hundred, then to two, and heard him begin to snore.

Slowly she slid out of the bed. It was too hot. She couldn't bear it. Her skin was slippery with sweat, and her cotton pyjamas clung to her, scrunched up with heat and sleep. Out on the jetty it would be cooler.

The air, though, was still and soupy. The tide was out again, and the sand seemed luminescent in the moonlight. Lily lay flat against the slatted wood of the jetty, stretching her arms out.

'Can't you sleep?' It was Chris's voice, harsh and low. He was sitting in the dark, with a bottle of wine. He must, by now, be very drunk. You couldn't hear it in his voice, though.

Lily sat up defensively, turning away from the voice. She didn't want him to smell the sleep on her. Her body was sticky and leaden. 'No.'

'So you're back with Tom again?'

She couldn't say 'yes'. She didn't want to say 'no'. She curled up tighter, in a ball. 'Does it matter?' she asked eventually.

'Of course not.' Chris sounded impatient. 'I was only asking.'

'So. You're on your way to the Caribbean to get married?' She tried to make the query sound light.

'Yes, we are.'

'Congratulations.' She forced the word out.

'Thank you.' His voice, as usual, sounded ironic.

'Well, I'd better be off.' He stood up, then looked down at her.

Lily tried to keep the rage out of her voice. 'Is it a secret? You and . . . ?'

'I suppose not, but . . .'

'Vicky.'

'No. Vicky might not like it. She'll have to get used to it, though.'

'Sarah will have to keep you locked up.' Lily was suddenly overwhelmed by bitterness. 'Or you might turn out like Bertie, after all. Having to have everyone.'

'That's not true.' Chris spoke gently. 'There really was nothing between Vicky and me. She loves Cameron.'

'That doesn't stop her watching every new girl-friend of yours like a competitor. It must have been another reason why you and I couldn't . . .'

'Lily,' he said, gently. 'It wasn't like that.'

'What was it like, then? Don't you have any problem at all with sleeping with me when you were committed to marry someone else? Doesn't that strike you as just a tiny bit . . . well, disloyal? Am I the only one in this family who values fidelity?'

'Firstly.' Chris's voice was steely. 'I wasn't commit-ted to marry Sarah when I came down here last time. We'd talked about it, but I'd already told her that I didn't think it was necessarily the right thing to do . . . We'd booked this holiday anyway. Sarah managed to get the wedding tacked on. We didn't want any fuss.'

'That really makes me feel special.' Lily stood up. 'I'm going back to sleep now.'

'You don't understand . . .'

'No, I don't, but I'm sure you could explain it all very fluently. However, if you'll excuse me, I'd rather not hear it. I'd prefer just to hear the truth, but somehow I don't think that's on offer round here.'

She was trembling as she walked back inside.

'Lily,' Chris called out to her. 'You've gone back to Tom. How is that different?'

She had the sense that someone else was moving around in the Boathouse, but perhaps it was only the wind, fluttering a curtain.

Back in her bedroom, Tom had turned over and was no longer snoring. The air hung heavy and still, stale with sleep, and Lily lay down, her eyelids like sandpaper. If only it weren't so hot.

31

A breath of cool air, hardly more than a shadow on the rising sun, touched the Boathouse just before dawn, and everyone slept. When Lily woke, no one else was up. She crept quietly down to make herself a cup of tea, luxuriating in the warm stone under her bare feet and the tranquillity of the water outside. The tannin crept through her system, reviving her, as she listened to the birds outside quarrelling. She might even swim, she thought. In a minute.

Cameron, in jeans and a denim shirt, appeared beside her. 'Hi. You the only one awake?'

She indicated the kettle inside. 'The water's hot. Do you want some tea?'

He reappeared a few minutes later and sat down beside her, dangling his legs over the edge of the jetty. A black-headed gull eyed him in interest from the rocks.

'Where did Dad fall from?'

Lily looked around. 'Oh, I'm not sure, up there somewhere, I think.' She waved vaguely in the direction of the Moonlight Bench.

'Mm. Quite a climb for a very sick man.'

'Sick?' Lily was surprised. She was sure no one had ever referred to Bertie being that ill.

'He had motor neurone disease.'

'Really? I had absolutely no idea.' Lily was disconcerted to think that Tom had kept something like this to himself. She had thought they'd told each other everything in the early days. Everything that mattered.

'I presume it wasn't very far advanced, though,' she added. 'Or he couldn't have got down the steps, let alone up to the Moonlight Bench.'

'I don't know. He seemed quite weak to me. But memory's a funny thing.'

'And you were only six at the time.'

'Mm.' He sounded doubtful.

'Anyway,' said Lily. 'I suppose it was lucky, then. To fall like that, and die quickly. He faced a horrible, lingering death.'

'I think it may have been suicide,' said Cameron. 'Although no one ever admits it.'

'Oh.' No wonder they all hated talking about it. 'Not even now? After all, the stigma has gone, I'd have thought. Gone entirely. In that situation.'

'Well, even if anyone knows the truth, I don't suppose they'll tell me.' Cameron looked at the hillside thoughtfully. 'I'm not to be trusted, apparently.'

'Is there any breakfast?' Harley appeared, followed by Billy and Daisy.

'Just a minute.' Lily jumped up. The self-indulgent swim would have to be deferred. 'Cam, do you want some toast?'

'That'd be great.'

She opened the fridge to see that Vicky's chocolates had been torn open carelessly. Most had gone.

'Billy? Have you taken these chocolates?'

'You always accuse me!' he screamed. 'Why me?'

'Don't shout,' said Lily, sharply. 'I was only asking. And did you?'

'I hate you.' He pushed past her and ran out of the door, scrambling up the hill.

She put the chocolates back. It wasn't worth making a fuss.

'Shall I go after him?' offered Cameron.

She sighed, overwhelmed with a sense of defeat. When she'd been alone with the children, they'd hardly had any of these encounters. As soon as other people came, Billy went back to his usual suspicious, disruptive self. She'd so hoped that this summer would offer permanent answers. 'Don't ask me. Whatever I do is wrong in his eyes. No, he'll be fine. He can't come to any harm.'

'I was like that,' said Cameron. 'That's what Chris and Tom say. They say I was incredibly badly behaved. They used to accuse Mum and Dora of spoiling me. But perhaps it's genetic. Still' – his voice was bitter – 'I don't suppose that's much comfort. You wouldn't want Billy to turn out like me.'

'I would.' She smiled at him.

'Well, Tom wouldn't,' said Cameron, bitterly. 'Both he and Chris think I'm a complete failure.'

'No.' Lily touched his arm. 'That's not what they think. I'm sure of it.'

'Anyway.' Cameron jumped up. 'I've got a surprise for them. Later.'

As the sun mounted in the sky, the Boathouse, tucked into the fold of the cliff, baked in its sheltered position. Constructed to take full advantage of the sun, its thick walls gradually absorbed the heat of the day, failing to release it each hot, airless night. The cumulative effect was to turn it into a brick oven. Outside the flowers and grasses parched and were turning the colour of fading blonde hair. It was too much effort to move, except at the slowest possible pace. Lily's feet, climbing the steps towards the car, had leaden weights dragging her down.

Vicky was stretched out on the sun lounger declaring, loudly, that the room had been like the black hole of Calcutta last night. She had, she informed everybody in turn, slept appallingly badly. 'Cam snored. And Harley got into our bed, so there were three of us in a standard double. It was absolutely steaming, I can tell you.'

Guilt and the heat of the stone steps leached all hope from Lily's bones.

Should she have let Vicky have her bed, after all? And was Vicky different or was it her imagination? Everything she did and said grated. I should stand up to her, thought Lily. But, as Vicky said, she worked hard and had very little time to herself. Lily, rich in her weeks and weeks of holiday, could surely spare the time and effort to give Vicky a decent weekend.

If the situation were reversed, Vicky would have done the same for her. Or would she?

When she returned, Vicky was nearly asleep. 'Oh, hi.' She shaded her eyes with her hand. 'Cam, Tom and Dora have taken the children off to Dartmouth Castle. Did you have a good time shopping? Dartmouth is really sweet, isn't it? A friend at work told me not to miss all the little gift places and that alternative crafty stuff.'

'Just food,' replied Lily. Inside, there was a trail of toast and coffee across the table. She began to clear it up and prepare a salad for lunch.

Vicky wandered in forty minutes later. 'Is there anything I can do to help?'

Lily looked at the table, set out with salads and cheeses. 'It's fine, I think. We can eat as soon as they get back.'

'Well, just let me know.'

She was, after all, making an effort.

'Let's have a drink,' offered Lily, determined to match it.

'You bet.' Vicky's face brightened. 'I think we deserve the champagne, don't you? After all, we're the ones who do all the work. Princess Sarah et al are just going to swan up and sit down, I presume.'

'They're spending today with Natasha,' replied Lily. 'They won't be here till this evening.'

'Oh, rather her than me. Poor kid.' Vicky popped the cork with a practised twist and passed a glass to Lily. 'To us. And to the Boathouse. Cam's got a plan.'

'Was that what they were talking about last night?'

Vicky shook her head. 'Just memories. You know what men are like. One of them tells a story, and then the next one tells another. It's like passing a parcel round. They hardly even bother to listen to each other. But tonight, he's determined to sort everything out once and for all.' She sighed. 'God, it's hot. Too hot to eat, really.'

'I think it's even too hot to swim.' But Lily fantasized about simply walking into the cool of the sea and letting her troubles drift away for ever.

At lunch, a raucous rabble of children and adults grabbed what they could and smeared a layer of food and dirty crockery around the Boathouse kitchen.

'Don't just leave your plates, there, boys,' Lily begged. But they'd gone, slender brown bodies flashing up the hillside. Daisy, serious and helpful, balanced plates and cups on top of each other and carefully brought them to Lily.

She kissed the top of her daughter's head. 'Thank you, sweetheart. But you shouldn't do it all.'

Was she going to bring up another generation of women who did the chores and men who slipped away when anything needed doing? 'Off you go and play with the boys, darling.'

'I don't want to,' said Daisy. 'Harley's too rough. And Billy copies him.'

Lily frowned. Harley had certainly got louder and brasher since Vicky and Cameron had arrived. He must have been missing them. Unless some of Billy's antagonistic character had worn off on him after so many weeks together. She felt guilty. Again.

Dora placed a hand on her arm. 'Lily. You've done enough. I'll do that. The tide's out. Why don't you go for a swim with Daisy?'

But Daisy shook her head, and scampered off to read a book in Lily's room, where Tom was sleeping lunch off.

'It's nice for her to have some time with her father,' said Dora. 'I think she really misses him.'

'Yes.' Lily shaded her eyes to look across the bay, and picked her swimsuit off the peg. 'It is rather difficult. Now, are you sure you're OK with that?'

Dora waved her away.

Lily walked across the sand and let the water lap around her ankles, then her knees, and finally, tentatively, cast off into the choppy green water, relishing the brief pleasure of goosebumps across her skin. After a few minutes, though, the sea acquired the texture and temperature of tepid tea and the heat above drained her energy, making each stroke a monstrous and impossible exertion.

It will always be like this, thought Lily, floating and screwing her eyes up against the fierce light on the water. There is nothing left except pain and loss and heat. The sun drummed down, and she wearily waded back to the Boathouse and found a shady corner of the jetty where she could switch on the radio, and let the world drift through her brain.

Old people were dying in the heat in France, she

heard, and there was news of forests catching fire in England. Crops were roasting in the sun, ripening too early, and farmers would be made bankrupt. Motorways were jammed with people fleeing the cities, and holiday companies issued statements about holidaymakers staying unprofitably at home, in their own sunny gardens. So many apparently contradictory problems. She looked out over the bay. Should she lie on her own bed, next to Tom and Daisy? Or should she and Tom lock the door and rediscover each other again?

But her skin slithered with perspiration beneath her fingers. It seemed pale, ugly and doughlike against the brightness of the water and the sky. His fingers would be heavy and hot against her flesh.

She stood up and looked at her face in the mirror. It glistened. No one could call it beautiful. She had grown old that summer, old and resigned.

She wouldn't go to Tom, not just now. But she would, soon, she decided, settle for good enough. She would learn to forgive. She had learnt what happened when you flew too close to the sun. You burnt, not with the impassioned fires of hell, but with the slow, relentless desolation of the desert.

32

Sarah, Chris and Dora – who'd gone back to the pub to change – scrambled down the steps just as the evening high tide heralded a breeze from the sea. They all turned their faces eagerly to it, like shipwrecked mariners in search of rescue, but it died down, and the dinghy sails crossing the water fluttered and drooped.

Chris went inside with Tom to get a beer.

Sarah flapped a newspaper at her face. 'Do you have a fan here?'

Vicky laughed. 'I think you're mistaking the Boathouse for the sort of holiday home you do up.'

'Did you have any luck with Tash?' Lily interrupted, before Sarah could retaliate.

Sarah looked frustrated. 'It was all very odd. She told us she was helping out in Diana's shop, so we agreed to take her out for lunch, but there was the most godawful ding-dong between Diana and Roger, and Diana rushed out in tears. Followed by a furious Roger. So Tash couldn't leave, and we couldn't exactly begin the conversation properly because we didn't know if one or the other was going to come back at any moment. In the end, we bought her a sandwich and said we'd see her tonight.' She looked at her watch. 'Really, I wanted this to be sorted by now. I was hoping to leave by six, and stay near the airport.'

'Well, we've cooked for you,' said Vicky. 'So don't worry about that.'

Lily refrained from correcting her. Vicky had spent the afternoon in Dartmouth getting Harley some school shoes and a haircut. 'I'll never have another opportunity,' she'd said. 'You remember what it was like being a working mother.'

The words 'school shoes' reminded Lily that she would have to think about real life soon. The thought terrified her. What could she earn a living at? Perhaps she should have stayed at Dotcombomb after all? Who else would offer her a deal that would give her any chance of being with Billy and Daisy? And what, she thought, looking at Billy racing round the cliffs with the other two, all whooping and shrieking their heads off, would Billy be like once he was confined to a small, city house and a tiny back yard again?

Vicky's forehead furrowed at their yelling. 'Lord, I remember that stage of motherhood. Everything at maximum volume. Never a moment's silence. I suppose it's lucky there aren't any neighbours to be disturbed. Still, we've all been there, so one can only sympathize.' She topped up her glass.

Lily and Dora went inside to put final touches to the meal: dressed crabs from the harbour, cold chicken, new potatoes and salad, followed by strawberries with thick, rich Devon cream.

'Delicious,' said Vicky, when they were called to the table. 'I don't know why anyone bothers with fast food. This sort of thing is about as instant as you get, healthy and no trouble at all, is it, Lily?'

Lily knew it would sound petty if she said that salads still needed washing and that a no-cook menu didn't mean a no-shop one. She looked at Vicky with new eyes, seeing spoilt petulance rather than generosity in the pouchy face.

'You sit here, Chris.' Vicky sat at the head of the table and tapped the seat beside her. 'And Cameron on the other side of me.'

She always avoids sitting next to Tom, thought Lily. She remembered all the times that Vicky had dried her tears, poured her a glass of wine and promised her that Tom just wasn't good enough for her. Had there been animosity between her and Tom all along? Tom, after all, was the Devereaux brother who had offered neither friendship nor love. Vicky might have minded that very much. To what extent had Vicky, in her friendly, cosy way, actually undermined her marriage? Or was she being paranoid?

'I don't believe in this silly rule about husbands and wives not sitting next to each other, do you, Sarah?' trilled Vicky. 'We hardly get time to talk to each other as it is. Oh, sorry, Sarah, of course, you aren't exactly husband and wife, are you?'

Sarah affected not to hear.

'Dora, why don't you sit next to Cameron?' Vicky

smiled at the older woman, and, for the first time, Lily saw traces of condescension in her manner.

'Where's Natasha?' asked Chris.

'She'll be here any moment now,' said Lily hastily. 'Oh, look, Tash, there you are.'

Tash's gazelle-like frame was outlined in the doorway. There was someone behind her. 'Diana is with me. I said she could come. It's all right, yes?' There was a note of pleading in Tash's voice, and Diana looked as if she'd been crying.

'Oh, of course,' Lily assured her. 'There's plenty. Just bring in a chair from the jetty, Tom, would you, and squeeze Diana in beside me?'

Lily was beginning to think that Natasha was deliberately avoiding a confrontation with her father.

She decided to reassert herself over supper. Vicky was giving every impression of the hostess who was chairing the meeting, and, suddenly, Lily wasn't prepared to put up with that.

She looked at Tom. 'Tom, why don't you sit on the other side of Sarah?' Was this a power struggle or just a table plan? She slipped into the seat at the other end of the table. She and Vicky faced each other like rivals. Vicky poured herself another drink.

This heat, thought Lily. It's too hot to think straight.

'Well,' said Cameron. 'The family. All together again.' He raised his glass. 'To everybody.'

This took them all by surprise. They scuffled for their glasses and murmured a ragged, muted: 'To everybody.'

'And to Lily, for putting up with us all,' said Dora. 'She's worked very hard to make us all welcome.'

'To Lily.' There was an even more embarrassed murmur.

Lily's cheeks burnt.

'And now.' Cameron leant back in satisfaction as everyone began to dissect their dressed crab. 'I have a rather exciting proposal. Although my exhibition hasn't started yet, there's been a lot of interest from the glossy magazines, and I've already got two ad campaigns booked.'

Vicky looked surprised. 'What, both of them booked you in the end? Why didn't you say? I thought you didn't believe in commercializing your work.'

'I wanted to surprise you. You knew about our plan for the Boathouse, Vicks,' continued Cameron, 'but I kept the best news for now. We can do it without extending ourselves to ridiculous levels. When you're paid a lot' – he grinned wickedly – 'I don't call it commercialization. It's Art. With a capital A.'

There were murmurs of 'well done' around the table, but Lily noticed that Vicky seemed anxious. 'Darling, I don't want you to do anything you feel is wrong. Not just for the money. We can struggle on.'

Cameron squeezed her knee briefly, but carried on. 'Anyway, the three of us – that's Tom, Vicky and I – have been talking, and we've got a proposal for you, Chris. We can raise the money to buy you out if we value the Boathouse at three hundred and ninety-five thousand, which, looking at properties in the area, seems reasonable. We've got the mortgage arranged, and—'

'We've already had a better offer.' Chris cut across Cameron. 'Sarah's middle-European prince has offered six hundred thousand. I met him when I was down here last weekend, and he means it. It's well above its true value – we'd be mad not to take it.'

Lily, astonished, looked at Chris for the first time that evening. He avoided her glance. That's why he'd been down to the Boathouse. To sell it. She burnt with fury. He must have left her on Sunday morning and gone secretly to meet the prince. Traitor, she thought. Judas. He never told me. She suppressed the thought that she had told Tom, too, not to include her in the decision-making. She felt like a tenant. She struggled with the childish desire to cry because she'd been left out.

'How strange.' She tried to keep her voice steady. 'I've been here all the time, and I haven't seen any European royalty anywhere near the place.'

'He doesn't need to see inside. He's sailed past. It's the location. He's got great plans. To extend it, turn the old sheds into staff chalets, landscape the hillside, put in a proper landing stage for bigger yachts, everything.'

'He wants it for drug-smuggling, I suppose. Or perhaps he's a people-trafficker.' Vicky's voice was dismissive. 'How could you, Chris? How could you?'

'He's not a drug-dealer or a people-trafficker.' Sarah's voice was cool and clear. 'He has a completely legitimate business and he needs somewhere totally private. Where he can entertain politicians and other businessmen without the paparazzi training their lenses on them.'

'I suppose Sarah gets the contract to do the place up with chintzy frills,' flashed Cameron. 'My God, the pair of you deserve each other. It's all money, money, money with you. Well, I have no intention of accepting.'

'Cam,' said Tom. 'Two hundred thousand each is a lot. That's what we'd get out of it. It's an awful lot.'

'I don't give a fuck,' replied Cameron. 'It's here that matters. Look at it. It's special. You can't just go into an estate agent's and buy what we've been lucky enough to be left by Dad. And Mum. We owe it to them. Dad would have wanted—'

'What do you know about what Dad would have wanted?' Chris interrupted him again. 'You . . .' He stopped, as if to force self-control on himself, shutting his eyes briefly. 'You haven't been down since you were five,' he concluded.

Lily was sure that he'd originally intended to say something quite different.

'Don't give me that,' shouted Cameron. 'It's like I don't really belong to this family because I came later than the rest of you. Well, I have news for you. I have every bit as much right to the Devereaux family memories as you have, and—'

'Really, Cameron, no one has said anything about

your not having the right to family memories.' Chris leant back, now languid and superior. 'I was simply observing that you have spent much less time here than either Tom or I have.'

'You two make me sick,' said Cameron. 'You and Sarah. Well, you've met your match at last, Chris. Someone like you who will put a price on anything, and knows the value of nothing.'

'I'm not bothered about getting an apology from you, Cameron, because I'm not interested in that sort of thing, but I do insist that you apologize to Sarah. She has acted entirely honourably in—'

'Oh, yeah? Well, if Sarah can assure me that she does not, in any way, stand to gain materially by this sale, that she isn't getting, or even likely to get, the contract for refurbishing the Boathouse, I'd be only too delighted to apologize to her.'

Sarah's cheeks burnt. 'Currently I have the contract for all the prince's work. But if he didn't buy this place he'd buy another, and I'd have the contract for that instead. So, no, this isn't a way of getting myself more work.'

'What a clever little answer,' sneered Cameron. 'Well, Tom, can we raise our offer to Mr and Mrs Moneybags over there? We could rent the place out, get more of the mortgage covered . . .'

Tom's brow furrowed. 'I'm not that keen on having holiday tenants. It's a lot of extra work and organization, and—'

'Don't tell me you're siding with Chris as usual.'

'I'm not *siding* with anyone. I'm giving my opinion. I think we've offered Chris as much as we can afford to. With the offer Chris has put on the table we could all buy our own holiday homes, maybe in France or Cyprus, which we wouldn't have to rent out . . .'

'I know several excellent rental agencies down here,' replied Cameron. 'One specializing in the South-West, so we can rent out the Boathouse, we can—'

'I don't think there's much point in discussing trivialities like the rental agency you intend to use when we haven't taken a decision on the property itself,' said Chris.

'Jesus Christ,' exploded Cameron. 'I don't believe you. I really don't believe you.'

'Lily has worked hard to give us all a nice meal,' said Dora. 'It seems a shame to spoil it by arguing. Do you think that we could perhaps ask everyone to sleep on their various offers and we could reconvene when everyone's calmed down.'

'We ought to sort this out before we go,' said Chris. 'And I need to talk to Natasha, too.' He flashed a glance at his daughter, who gazed back with guileless blue eyes.

'But the flight's tomorrow morning,' squeaked Sarah. 'At nine.'

He glared at her. 'If we have to miss it, we miss it.'

She stared at her plate. Lily thought she could see her carefully manicured hands shaking, and felt a dash of pity for her.

In spite of her quietness, though, Dora commanded respect, and a stilted silence followed. It was like, Lily thought, a seventies French art film. All she could hear was the sounds of the waves, the cries of the seabirds and the children's shouting, intermingled with the clatter and scrape of knife and fork or the gurgle of poured wine. Sweat trickled down Tom's forehead, and Lily could feel her clothes clinging to her body with heat.

'So.' Sarah, with her usual bright insouciance, clearly couldn't bear silence. 'Isn't it lovely here? Where's everyone sleeping?'

No wonder she was so good at producing hampers full of picnic goodies, thought Lily. She was a logistics woman through and through.

With a sudden gesture, Chris got up and walked outside. Sarah watched him anxiously.

The children's screaming had changed, she realized, with a prickle down her back. The happy yells were shot with pure terror.

'Christ!' Vicky jumped. 'Can't anyone control that boy?'

There was something in the tenor of their screaming that cut through Lily's consciousness like a knife. You know when it's playing. And when it isn't. She knocked her chair over as she stumbled to get up, moving far far too slowly to get to the door on time. There'd been a fall. Like the one that killed Bertie. Or something more unexpected – a shark, perhaps? The Dart had not, after all, claimed its human heart this year.

Chris, standing in the water up to his knees, held a weeping, choking Daisy over his shoulder while trying to part Harley and Billy with his other hand. Billy, shouting at Harley, was punching and kicking him, as Harley screamed in pain.

Harley fell, with a grunt, into the water and began to cry in jerky, adult sobs. Billy ran out of the sea as Vicky waded in, kicking off her shoes and tucking her skirt into her knickers.

'My baby,' she screamed. 'My baby! What has that horrid boy done to you?'

Billy raced up the hillside, as swift and sure-footed as a wild goat. They'd never catch him now.

'Billy,' called Lily. 'Billy, come back.'

Chris strode through the water without seeming to notice it, and handed Daisy to Lily. 'There you are.' He spoke to her as if she were a tiny child. 'Safe and sound and back to Mummy.' He gave her a brief kiss on the top of her head.

Tom stood in the doorway. 'What happened?'

'Billy attacked them,' shrieked Vicky. 'He's really hurt Harley, and look at Daisy! She's in a terrible state.'

'Is that true?' Lily whispered to Daisy, whose sobs were subsiding. Daisy burrowed into her neck and murmured something incoherent. She was very frightened, thought Lily. Very frightened indeed.

'He needs professional help,' said Vicky. 'This kind of thing is intolerable.'

'It's just kids fighting,' said Tom defensively.

'Chris stabbed me with a penknife once when we were that age.'

'Rubbish,' said Chris. 'I was holding the penknife in front of me and you ran into it.'

'Tom used to bang my head against a wall when he got angry with me,' added Cameron. 'And he was so much bigger than me, it really hurt. Anyway, I'll go up and find Billy, shall I?' His eyes scanned the top of the hillside. 'I thought I saw him up by that bench. He might come with me.'

'I did not bang your head against walls,' retorted Tom. He took Daisy gently from Lily and carried her indoors.

'Never mind that now.' Vicky was impatient. 'Things were different then. And this wasn't normal horseplay. It's all your fault, Lily. That boy is completely out of control. He's got real problems. Everyone says so. You need to send him to someone before he becomes completely delinquent. He'll kill someone one of these days.'

'It takes two to have a fight,' said Lily. 'Perhaps we should find out what happened first. You may be right about Billy, I don't deny it, but Harley may have contributed something to the situation, too.'

'Harley's a scholarship boy. He's in all the school teams. His reports are excellent . . .' Vicky paused. 'Billy is a disaster. A walking disaster. Almost an animal.'

Lily opened her mouth to reply, but Vicky went on.

'But you won't face up to it, will you, because you've always got to be the best, the favourite, the nicest, haven't you? Maud used to go on about you, how wonderful you are. She never saw any of your faults, of which you have many.' She gasped for breath, as if choked by a lifetime of resentment. 'And I've always had to be second-best in the family, the one who neglects her children and has a career. Maud used to watch me and say, "That boy needs you," then: "Lily works part-time, I think that's marvellous, don't you?" Lily this, Lily that. Lily has a cold, poor Lily, she works so hard, and yet when I had pneumonia, she more or less told me I was faking it . . .'

'Vicky . . .' Lily was terrified at the volume of hatred and jealousy that was spewing out. This wasn't just a knee-jerk reaction to a boys' fight, it was obviously something that Vicky had thought about deeply, probably even discussed with Cameron and heaven knew who else. A credo that she had formulated over the years, not an opinion given away in minutes.

'Even your children have to be the greatest in the family. Harley's always had brilliant reports, been brilliant, and nobody's ever taken any notice. But when Billy learnt to read, everybody had to hear about it. Even though Billy's clearly educationally subnormal. But I can tell you, unless you sort him out, you can say goodbye to finding another man. Nobody's going to stick around if they have to deal with that kind of behaviour all day.'

'He's not educationally sub-normal.' Lily was so winded by the attack that she was barely able to respond. 'Whatever that is.'

'And now you're after the Boathouse. That's what this summer is all about. Making this place yours, and keeping me away from it.'

'That really doesn't make sense at all, Vicky. I only hoped that if all the children had a good summer, then Chris might think it was worth keeping after all, and you could all enjoy it again. I never wanted you to stay away. I asked you down . . .' Lily was frightened. Had Vicky gone mad?

'Don't expect me to believe that you meant it. You don't want me down here messing up your little kingdom and taking the best bed. You're setting out to be queen of this family, but I've got news for you. You don't even belong to it any more.'

'Vicky, I don't think you know what you're saying.' Chris's voice, from the water, was commanding, but Vicky took no notice.

'You think you're so fucking great,' she sneered. 'But you've lost it. You've probably been having it off with some fucking man who thinks you're fucking Madonna because you can make spaghetti bolognese for three children, and have given up your redundancy money and time to look after them . . . but you haven't a fucking clue what's been going on in their heads.'

'Vicky,' said Dora. 'This has happened. Blame won't change anything.' She took Harley's hand. 'Come along, young man, there's no need to cry. Let's get you dried off.'

'It's all right for you.' Vicky seized Harley's hand from her. 'You don't understand. He isn't your son. You don't know what it's like to be a mother, to be responsible, day in, day out. To love somebody the way a mother loves a child.'

'I'm afraid you're completely wrong about that.' Dora's thin frame was rigid and upright and two bright spots shone on her faded cheeks.

'Dora.' Chris jumped up on to the jetty, appearing not to notice that he was drenched in seawater from the waist downwards. He put his arm round her shoulders, protectively. 'Don't you think it's time you told us all the truth?'

'Chris,' said Sarah, in a tight voice. 'Those shoes are suede.'

33

'Very well.' Dora stood still and, for a moment, she looked fragile. Old, for the first time. 'But not now. You, Chris, have to have your talk with Natasha so that you and Sarah can catch the flight. My story will wait.'

'I'll just take Harley inside and give him some toast.' Vicky's voice was subdued.

'OK.' Chris looked at Dora steadily, as if to seal a promise, then turned away.

Lily looked at the ground, trembling with shock. Was she, perhaps, this terrible person that Vicky had portrayed? Was she manipulating the Boathouse and the children for her own ends? It was like looking in a mirror and seeing her own face, horribly distorted, only to realize that it was real. 'I'm going inside to see if Daisy's OK.'

She bathed Daisy quickly and carefully, looking for bruises. 'You will tell me, won't you?' she whispered. 'If Billy gets too rough?'

'I don't like telling tales.' Daisy snuggled down, tired and secure, and gave a little sigh. 'I'm glad Daddy's here.'

Tom came in. 'I'll finish off here,' he murmured. Guilt and inadequacy curdled together in Lily as she went back to where Natasha and Diana, having done the washing-up, were on the jetty with Chris.

'Is Billy back?'

'He's up with Cam. On the Moonlight Bench. Look, you can just see them both.' Dora pointed out the two dark shadows far above them.

Chris cleared his throat. 'Natasha. I want a word with you in private.'

'We can talk here,' said Natasha, her voice betraying only the slightest tremble. 'I have nothing to hide.'

'I think I'll go and pack the car,' interrupted Sarah. 'It'll save time.'

Chris nodded at her absent-mindedly, never taking his eyes off his daughter. 'For God's sake, Tash, I'm a perfectly reasonable man, you know. I'm not going to be angry with you. Anyone would think I hit you or something.'

'I hope not. But I would prefer to talk in front of people.' She indicated Diana, Dora and Lily. 'I do not want any more secrets.'

Chris folded his arms. 'I'm not in the slightest bit interested in secrecy, one way or another. As far as I'm concerned, the whole thing can go in the bloody local paper, if that's what you want. But, for your own sake, and for Diana's, I strongly suggest that we talk in private.'

'I agree with Natasha.' Diana's voice was low and throaty. 'I don't know what you want to say to her, but she has something to say to you, and she would prefer to say it in public.'

Chris flashed her a look of fury. 'For God's sake. All right. And do you want Sarah back? Shall we call Cameron out of the undergrowth? The *Dartmouth Bugle*, perhaps?'

Natasha sat down on one of the wicker chairs on the jetty, and pulled Diana down to the chair beside her. 'Just Lily and Dora. And Tom.' She looked up as Tom came back. 'That is enough. Sit down, Daddy.'

Daddy. No one had ever heard her call him that before, except as a joke It seemed to have slipped out, somehow.

Chris fetched an upright chair from inside the Boathouse, as if to assert himself, and Tom followed his example. Dora, looking worried, dropped into the remaining wicker chair, and Lily sat on the edge of the jetty and dangled her legs. As the sun sank behind the water, a single indigo boat puttered across the bay.

Chris poured himself another drink and pointed the bottle at Lily. She shook her head. She'd drunk enough, and Natasha obviously wanted to get on with talking. She'd never seen her look so nervous before, licking her lips and biting at them.

'What is it, Tash?' she asked, because Chris seemed to have settled into a moody silence and was glaring at her like a prison warder expecting an escape.

Natasha folded her arms. 'I have decided to go travelling.'

'On your own?'

'No, with Gem, from Diana's shop.'

'I thought Gem was getting married?' Lily

remembered the girl behind the counter, shouting about wedding dresses and matching flowers.

'Not . . . now.' Natasha allowed herself a small, impish smile.

'Well, I don't have a problem with any of that.' Chris sounded surprised. 'Provided Ingrid doesn't mind, I certainly don't. As long as you don't go anywhere dangerous, of course. Why all the fuss?'

'We're lesbians,' added Natasha in her pedantic, northern way. 'I think it is important to be clear on this point. I do not wish to live a lie. I am sorry, Lily.' She turned to her. 'I have not been very truthful while I have been here. But that is not how I like to live.'

'So you're not having an affair with Roger, then?' Vicky, who had appeared from the doorway, sounded astonished. Lily wondered who had told her.

Natasha burst into a peal of laughter. 'Why would I have an affair with Roger? He's too old, and he's a man. I don't like men. Not in that way, anyway.' She gave a little shudder.

Diana blew her nose, and then smiled at everyone. 'I'm afraid Roger's having an affair with a woman in Sidmouth, and he's left me. It's been a great shock . . .' She reached for Natasha's hand. 'But Natasha's been marvellous. Such a comfort. She's explained to me that you don't need men.'

Everybody leant fractionally forward, looking worried.

'Or women, of course,' added Diana hastily. 'Not

in that way, anyway. Really, I think I'm going to be absolutely fine on my own. Much nicer, really, than having to deal with a . . . husband. I'll be able to do what I think is right. Like making the holiday cottages holistic.'

What was a holistic holiday cottage? Lily's brain caught on the trivia. 'But Billy,' she said, 'Roger was training him up for the Dartmouth Regatta at the end of the holidays. He's looking forward to it so much.' She stopped. She was being selfish.

Diana smiled serenely. 'There is an excellent sailing school at Dittisham. Far better than Roger's.'

Lily bit back the retort that Billy was awkward and difficult with new people. Roger, for all his faults, had brought out the best in him.

'I've asked Natasha to stay,' added Diana. 'Until she and Gem go off.'

'So you've been conniving at this . . . absurdity,' fumed Chris. 'Natasha is only seventeen. It's all very well you deciding what to do with your own life, but I think that, whether you're a man or a woman, influencing such a young, impressionable girl is potentially—'

Natasha let out another peal of laughter. 'Chris. Dad. Whatever you want to be called. Diana does not influence me. Nor does Gem. I influence her. She is not my first affair.' She squeezed Diana's hand like a reassuring aunt, then released it. 'I am the one who showed *Gem* what she really is.'

'You're too young,' said Chris. 'You don't know

what you want. Dora, you must take her straight back to London. Or we'll put you on the plane to Sweden. This is madness—'

'She knows,' interrupted Diana. 'You have to admire Natasha for being that sure at seventeen. I knew you were supposed to want men when I was her age, and I tried terribly hard, but it never clicked. Now that I've faced up to it, I can't believe what a relief it is that Roger's gone. Although scary. That's what I was trying to tell you the other day, Lily.'

There was another silence. 'Sorry, Chris,' she added. 'Nothing personal.'

'If the first woman you make love to subsequently says she's never liked men, you can't help feeling it's a bit personal,' he replied.

'It is time for everybody to stop lying,' said Natasha, flashing a glance at Lily, who looked back at the sunset again. 'You think that because I am foreign, an outsider, that I don't see things. But I see things other people don't see.'

'Natasha is a very, very perceptive person,' murmured Diana.

Nobody spoke. Chris ran his hands through his hair. 'Well, I suppose it'll have to do,' he murmured. 'I don't see what more I can say.'

Cameron and Billy, hand in hand, came scrambling down from the Moonlight Bench.

'Here he is,' said Cameron. 'Safe and sound. And we've had a little talk. Up on that bench up there.' He went inside.

Lily felt the full force of Billy rushing towards her. 'Mummy,' he whispered. 'I'm back. Don't be cross.'

She hugged him to her. He would never allow himself to be cuddled normally, and as she clung to him, she could feel the thin bones of his hot little body. 'I love you, Billy,' she whispered, suppressing her first instinctive desire to be furious with him. 'I love you so much.' She wrapped her arms round him. They hadn't done this for so long, since all their lives started going wrong. She held him tighter, and he buried his face in her neck. 'So very, very much,' she whispered again.

'I didn't start it, I promise,' he said. 'But I thought you wouldn't believe me.'

'I do believe you.' What was she believing? She didn't care. She held him, quietly, while the others chatted, rocking him as if he were younger than he was, and watching the last of the sun slip behind the horizon.

'Vicky,' said Cameron from the doorway fifteen minutes later. 'I've spoken to both boys and Daisy. Harley was holding Daisy's head under the water to see how long it would be before she passed out. And Billy was trying to stop him.'

Vicky's hand flew defensively to her mouth. 'Nonsense. You can't believe anything Billy says. The boy's a pathological liar.'

'I'm afraid all three children confirm it. There's no doubt.'

Lily's heart shrank at the horror of it, and she held

Billy to her. 'Well done, sweetheart,' she murmured into his ear. 'Brave boy.' She could feel a pulse in her neck, thudding away in terror. What if Chris hadn't heard, what if Billy hadn't succeeded? What if? thudded the blood in her head. What if?

'Well,' said Vicky. 'Lily's in charge. She shouldn't have let it happen.'

Chris stood up. 'We're all in charge, Vicky. We're a family. We're all responsible for each other.'

'But she's right. I shouldn't have let it happen.' Lily heard the unsteadiness in her own voice. 'I was in charge, and I got tired and my attention slipped. I'm sorry.'

Tom came over. 'I'll put Billy to bed.' He took the boy's hand and tucked a strand of Lily's hair behind her head. 'We're all adults. We should all have known. One person can't keep an eye on everything.'

Lily, numb, nodded.

'I'll be back in ten minutes,' said Tom. 'But, Dora, don't say anything until I come back.'

'And I need to talk to you, Vicky.' Cameron's voice was more authoritative than Lily had ever heard it. Vicky looked as if she might explode, then she shrugged and got up.

Natasha's smile was dazzling. 'Thank you, Lily, for letting me stay with you.' She got up. 'And goodbye. I wish to go with Diana now. I hope that being honest has not been a shock for you. If you ring my mother,' she continued, 'she will tell you that I have had girlfriends, not boyfriends, since I was thirteen.

She sent me to England to find some nice English boys. I knew I was never going to change my mind. But I would like' – she turned back to Chris again – 'your blessing. Your goodwill.' Her voice cracked a little. 'Your support.'

'Fine,' said Chris in a hollow, tired voice. 'It's fine by me.' He looked at her, standing above him. 'But I'm sorry. I'm sorry I wasn't a better father. Maybe, if I had been . . .'

'This is not about you,' said Natasha. She turned to go into the house.

'Stop,' said Dora. 'What about Lily? She's been here looking after Harley, Billy and Daisy, and you, too, Natasha, don't forget, and she needs your help. You can't just walk out on her.'

Natasha hesitated. 'I didn't think about that.'

'You go.' Lily waved her off, swallowing to keep her voice steady. 'Honestly, I can manage.' How often had she said that? I can manage. Don't worry about me. Let me do it. She heard the words of her childhood reverberate in her ears. 'Only children are always selfish . . . They don't know how to share.' She had been trying to be needed and loved by other people ever since. Too hard, perhaps.

Vicky and Cameron were having a hissed conversation. Vicky broke away and ran into the house.

Cameron came up to Lily, and squatted down on his haunches by her chair, touching her arm. 'I'm so, so sorry about all this, Lily. Vicks has had a bit too much to drink, she's absolutely exhausted, and she's been very tense about my exhibition. She didn't mean any of that.'

Lily, numb, merely shook her head. 'It's fine. Don't worry about it.'

'I think that I should take her and Harley away for a couple of days and sort everybody out. If it's not letting you down. And we can take Harley back to London with us afterwards, and organize a rota with friends. If that would be better.'

'It's fine,' she repeated. 'Absolutely fine. Whatever suits.'

'Or I can stay,' said Dora.

Lily thought about Dora's quiet, steadfast, unfussy ways. 'Would you really, Dora?'

'It would be a pleasure, my dear.' Dora beamed at her.

'And Dora,' said Cameron, walking back to the house and drawing Vicky out gently by the hand, 'Natasha has been honest. Now it's your turn.'

'I thought that because it happened so long ago,' said Dora, 'it might be better if I went on keeping this all a secret. But it's obvious that Chris knows a little of what happened, and I think it's better that I should tell you all, rather than have you discover bits and pieces, and maybe draw all the wrong conclusions.

'Your mother, as you know, left your father for a short time.' Her voice was clear and sweet. 'In nineteen sixty-seven, to be precise.'

34

Dora and Bertie sat on the edge of the bed together, hands clasped, staring numbly at the floor, wondering what to tell the boys downstairs in the kitchen. Maud had left, with her suitcase. She might be anywhere. She might be dead.

Dora felt his hand in hers, stiff and uncomfortable. She knew so much about this man's mind, but the touch of his hand was that of a stranger.

After a few minutes, she got up, smoothed down her dress, and went back downstairs to see to Tom and Chris.

'Where's Mum?'

'She's gone to stay with a friend.'

'Why didn't she say goodbye?' Tom's eyes accused her.

'You were at school.'

'Has she had a row with Dad?' Chris was the difficult one to answer, because he was so nearly grown up. Fourteen was old enough – or was it? – to understand that adult life wasn't always smooth.

Dora's innate honesty struggled with the ingrained belief that children should always be protected from the truth. They were better off not knowing, that was what everyone always said.

'She has,' said Chris. 'Don't bother lying to me. I always know.'

'Everyone has arguments sometimes. It's part of life.'

'Mum and Dad argue all the time,' said Tom, sounding worried.

'No more than anyone else,' said Dora stoutly, wishing it were true.

'Will they divorce?' asked Chris.

'No, of course not.' Dora was shocked. 'People like your parents don't get divorced.'

'It's our fault, isn't it?' asked Tom. 'We make too much work for her.'

'No, of course you don't,' said Dora.

But they didn't believe her. She had already told too many lies to protect them from the reality of Maud and Bertie.

'Finish your homework. And I'll make you some supper.'

It was the waiting that was so terrible. You could hardly report a woman of forty-three as missing, merely because she was home a few hours late.

Dora and Bertie poured themselves a glass of whisky, and sat in the kitchen, ears straining for the telephone.

'Can you ring her family? Do you know the number?'

Bertie shrugged. 'I presume that the dreadful elder brother has inherited the estate. The phone number is probably still the same. But I'd be fobbed off by some supercilious butler. The name of Devereaux is about as hated as that of Harold Wilson in that house. Or that stately home, I should say.'

Harold Wilson. Dora seized on the name to distract Bertie. She tried to talk about politics with him. Would the pay freeze work?

Bertie didn't rise to the bait. He gazed at her from a long, long way away. 'Of course not.' He didn't sound as if he cared.

Her unease deepened. She'd never known him indifferent to politics. He poured her another whisky and looked at his watch. 'How long do you think it takes to get there?'

Dora didn't dare say. Maud had been missing, she thought, for about five or six hours. Whether that was long enough to get to York, and then on to a branch line, and then to find a taxi that could take her to a remote, hostile, splendid estate, she had no idea.

'What do you think, Dora?' Bertie was already slightly drunk. 'I've been a fool, haven't I? A careless, irresponsible fool who couldn't see what was right under his nose.'

Dora still thought that Maud had something to answer for, too. She couldn't have been easy to be married to for the past couple of years. Her mother had always implied that a marriage was woman's work, and a man could hardly be blamed for its collapse, provided that he wasn't violent and earned enough to keep the household going.

'No,' she said. 'Of course you haven't.'

Bertie took her hand and squeezed it. 'You're so sweet, Dora. So terribly, fundamentally sweet. I don't think you've ever had a nasty thought in your head.'

They waited, and waited. The seconds stretched painfully slowly to minutes, and the minutes, every hundred years or so, eventually added up to hours. They finished the bottle of whisky between them, and Dora began to feel the world swim beneath her feet. When she heard the rattle of the telephone bell, it seemed to come from far away, from a dream.

'Yes?' Bertie picked it up immediately.

It was a woman's voice on the other end, but Dora couldn't hear what was said, or who it was.

'Please don't.' He spoke with all his heart.

But the voice stopped. Dora heard a male voice bark down the phone.

He replaced the receiver. 'It's over, Dora. She's not coming back. You were right. She's with her family.'

He stood there, shattered, and Dora walked over to him, and took him in her arms.

'We simply went to bed and fell asleep,' said Dora, thirty-six years later, on the jetty. 'But we woke up at about four o'clock and it seemed so normal and so right to . . . well.' She twisted her hands in her lap. 'To do what men and women have done since time began. It was comfort, I know, and circumstance, and, of course, drink.

'Then I opened my eyes a few hours later, thinking

I would have a terrible hangover, and went downstairs to make myself a cup of tea. It was cold, the sort of crisp day that crunches under your feet and cuts your breath with a knife. I looked out of the window and saw the outline of the church spire against the sky, as frosty as a snowflake, and everything suddenly seemed very, very clear. Maud would be back, and he belonged to her and to the boys. I would see them through this crisis, and then, finally, I really would leave them. If necessary, I would leave London. Or even emigrate. This sounds immensely old-fashioned, but Maud and Bertie had made each other a binding promise in the presence of God and their friends, and even if you break a promise you can still go back and try to mend it again.'

'What about Bertie?' asked Lily. 'It was more his fault than yours. Surely, he should never have . . .'

Dora smiled. 'Oh, no, I'm afraid I don't agree with that at all. Remember, I was a fully grown woman of thirty-eight. I knew my own mind. Bertie didn't inveigle me into anything. I don't believe in this modern tendency to blame other people all the time. You have to take responsibility for your own actions in this life. And if it all goes wrong, well, you must do what you can to make it right.'

She stopped, as if exhausted with remembering.

'But that wasn't the end of it, was it?' interjected Chris. 'What happened next, Dora?'

She began to smooth one hand out with the other, as if she could rub out the marks of age and ease the distortions of her joints. 'I think you know very well, don't you, Chris?'

'It's your story, Dora. No one else can tell it.'

'Very well. I just hope it won't make things worse.' She took a deep breath. 'The following day a massive oil tanker called the *Torrey Canyon* ran aground off Cornwall. The images of dying seabirds coated in oil haunted the newspapers and television news. We thought it might reach the Boathouse. Could we do anything to stop it? Of course, we couldn't. We'd thought we could do anything, and now we realized how powerless we really were.'

'It's over, isn't it?' said Bertie, picking up *The Times*, day after day, with the resignation of an old man. 'The party. The free lunch. The dream we all had of making the world a better place?'

'No, it's not.' Dora couldn't see why he was so depressed by a single event. 'Accidents happen. There've always been shipwrecks.'

'Not on this scale,' he replied. 'Not this much damage. Everything in the world is getting bigger. And it's only the beginning. I want to get away. Out of this filthy city.' He sighed. 'Maud's written to me, you know. She wants the house. And the children.'

'What are you going to do?'

'I don't have to give her anything I don't want to, legally. As far as the law is concerned, she can rot in the North on a small allowance.'

Dora held her breath. On the front page of the

paper, a cormorant, caked in thick, black, viscous oil, lay huddled and lifeless on a blackened beach. She remembered the cormorants at the Boathouse, swimming and diving in the bay, then standing on the side, wings outstretched to dry in their graceful heraldic stance.

'If you and I went down to Devon,' said Bertie, 'we could leave Maud here in Chelsea with the boys. She might . . .' He trailed off. 'I don't really know what would be best.'

'I think being kind is always best,' Dora reassured him. 'And it would definitely be best for the boys.'

'That's it, then.'

'But it was a lost summer,' said Dora. 'I felt so tired all the time. I thought it was the cloudy weather. And the general lassitude everywhere. London was happening. If you were young, really young, like nineteen, the world was opening up. But everyone else and everywhere else was on fringes. There were hardly any holidaymakers in the town, because people preferred to get on planes to hot places where they could drink all day. You saw "closed" signs everywhere, even in the height of the season, peeling paint, and only those too old or ingrained in their habits moving slowly across the beach or eating sandwiches in their cars. It was dull and sad and slow, and so was I.'

'So you were pregnant?' Vicky's voice, shrill and accusing, broke into the narrative. 'Or what?'

'Yes. I tried to get an abortion but it wasn't legal.

It was funny that — a few months later and it would have been easy. Just a few months. But at that time it cost a lot, and was very painful and dangerous, and I couldn't do it. And you couldn't be an unmarried mother. You just couldn't. Landlords wouldn't let you rent, building societies wouldn't lend you money. There was virtually no childcare available so you couldn't work. Unless you had a family who could step in, it just wasn't practical. And my parents would have died of shame. There really was nothing.

'But it's extraordinary how you can lie to yourself. I was very tall. Nobody noticed me thickening at the waist. I ignored . . . other physical symptoms. I never, ever allowed myself to think the worst. Until we followed Chris back to Chelsea and Maud opened the door to us, and saw, immediately, the change in my shape. I suppose it helped that she hadn't seen me for months, while Bertie and the boys saw me every day. But perhaps you saw, Chris.'

'I saw it,' said Chris. 'But I didn't realize what I was seeing until years later, when I said something to you like: Oh, Dora, you've never been fat. Then I had this sudden vision of you that summer, very solid in the body and softer and fuller in the face. It was when Lily was expecting Billy, and I thought: Ah, like Dora. Those changes.'

Lily's heart warmed at the thought that he had been watching her for years.

'Surely Maud was absolutely furious?' queried Vicky. 'She must have felt so betrayed.'

'No. She was amazing. While some women would have been angry, and turned straight round, she simply said, "Oh, Dora. I'm so sorry. It was my fault, wasn't it? For leaving like that, I mean."

'Of course, it wasn't. Nobody has to take the responsibility for another person's actions, but she couldn't see it like that. "I've grown up now, Dora," she used to say to me. "I think I know what love means. A bit late to find out, but there you are."

'So she devised a plan. We would both go to stay in the depths of France, and in the muddle over where we were, the baby would be registered as hers. Things were a lot less organized in those days. She'd always longed for another baby, she said, after the little girl that died, but the doctors had said it was impossible. So she and Bertie would bring him or her up with his brothers.'

'Cameron,' said Vicky.

Dora nodded.

'Maud suggested it?' Lily was shaken.

'Yes,' said Dora. 'Maud wanted to do something amazing. To do something that nobody else could ever have done. Something that would blow Bertie away with its magnificence. And that was Cameron. To bring up Bertie's son as her own.

'You see, Maud had to have a cause. If she'd been born a few hundred years earlier, she'd probably have gone into a convent. A few decades later or into a less fossilized family, she'd have had the education and the freedom to become somebody in her own right. As it was, her first cause was Bertie, the grammar-school boy, and then, when he didn't seem to need her any more, she was lost until Cameron came along.'

'Anyway,' interrupted Tom. 'Everyone was more easy-going about fidelity, then, weren't they? I mean people believed in Free Love and all that? Didn't they?'

'In theory,' replied Dora. 'But, remember, I was there when Bertie first told Maud that he'd been unfaithful to her. It shattered her, in spite of everything she declared about sex and being free over the dinner table in London. It takes more than fashionable phrases to stop you feeling betrayed. She tried to pretend she wasn't hurt. But she was, terribly.

'But while everybody else merely sang along to "All You Need Is Love", Maud really believed it. She thought that love should transcend sex. Not that sex was nothing, but that love was more. We all did. We were surprised when it didn't turn out that way, that people got hurt and marriages got broken, and by the time the terrible diseases came along, much later, of course, everybody had realized it was always going to be more complicated.

'But basically, All You Need Is Love was the credo for our lives then. And Maud had lots and lots of love to give.'

'I always knew I never belonged in this family,' said Cameron.

'Don't be absurd,' snapped Chris. 'Of course you

belong. You always have. Maud loved you. Everybody loved you. It's sheer self-indulgence to pretend otherwise.'

'You didn't love me.' Cameron stood up. 'You resented me.'

'That's not true,' said Chris.

'You blamed me,' retorted Cameron. 'I was never good enough for you and Tom. Never.'

Lily thought again about the part that each brother played in the family. Chris the dominant oldest child, Tom the peacemaker in the middle, and Cameron, the favourite and the youngest. No wonder the roles had been so carefully protected until Maud died.

'Chris loves you,' she said to Cameron. 'He just has a strange way of showing it.'

Chris didn't contradict her, and she saw Cameron's shoulders relax, just fractionally.

'Were you ever going to tell him?' she asked Dora.

'I don't know,' replied Dora. 'We didn't talk about the long term at the time, because we were too occupied in getting through the day. And then, well, Maud died so suddenly. I always meant to find out what she wanted, but somehow there was never time. I felt that if I raised the subject, it would be as if I were claiming Cameron back, and often I thought, in a way, that she really had forgotten that Cam wasn't biologically hers.

'I thought, probably, that it would be best for the secret to die with me, but there's the genetic issue. Suppose someone had to have a DNA test at some point? And would it have shown up, and then perhaps Cameron might have thought that Vicky'd been unfaithful? Or anything like that. I don't know enough about it, but I couldn't guarantee that someone down the line, perhaps someone who isn't even born, wouldn't be left with an important puzzle, something that might affect their lives, that they couldn't solve. And I didn't want to leave it in a letter or a diary because I'm here, to talk to you all; I knew what happened. I can answer your questions. You can't just write it down and run away. At least, I don't think you can.'

She looked at Cameron and Vicky. 'Most of all, I wanted to tell you how much you mean to me. Even if that's selfish. And how much you meant to Bertie and Maud.'

35

Nobody spoke.

The quiet rustling of the bay was shattered by Vicky, who let out a shriek. 'Darlings, it's so, so romantic.' She jumped up and hugged Dora. 'Just too exciting. I can't believe it. Can you be Granny Dora?'

'I can *be* Granny Dora.' Dora looked pleased. 'But heaven forfend you ever call me such. Plain Dora is fine, thank you very much.'

Vicky sat down in a swirl of bangles and flowing skirts. 'I can't believe it,' she repeated. 'Can you, Cam?'

Cameron shook his head. 'It makes a weird sort of sense.'

'What do you think, Tom?' asked Vicky, turning up the intensity of her voice. 'Aren't you absolutely, I mean, totally blown away?'

'Sort of,' he said. 'But I suppose, like Cam, in a strange kind of way, I'm not surprised.' He touched his brother briefly.

'So,' said Chris. 'I'd better be getting back. Sarah's worried about missing the plane.' He looked at his watch.

'I'd be grateful if you could stay for a few more minutes.' Cameron spoke formally. 'There is something else I would like us to talk about.'

Vicky opened her mouth to protest, but Cameron touched her on the arm, and she turned away, pulling a packet of cigarettes out of her bag.

Interesting, thought Lily. Vicky rarely smoked.

Chris sighed.

'The *Voices of the Sixties* programme is coming out next week,' Cameron continued. 'I've seen the previews. There's quite a lot of Bertie Devereaux in it.'

There was a small, tense silence.

Only Dora had the courage to break it. 'They didn't ask how he died, or anything, did they?'

'It's perfectly obvious how he died,' said Cameron. 'To anyone who comes here. I saw that when I was up at the Moonlight Bench talking to Billy. So now I can see why it would be better for us all if we sold the Boathouse.'

Vicky's foot, in its jewelled shoe, swung angrily. 'Well, I can't. We agreed—'

Cameron took her hand and wrapped it in his. 'Sh.' His voice was tender. 'Dad's death has hung over this family for long enough.'

Dora sat very still. Chris looked over the bay, stony and remote. Tom's brow was puckered.

'But it's over now, Chris,' said Cameron. 'Tell your prince we accept his offer.'

Chris's eyes, turned on Cameron, were very dark. The knuckles of his left hand shone white in the moonlight as he gripped the arm of the wicker chair. Cameron's hand, broader and darker, stretched out to cover it, and they remained, silently, long enough for Vicky to strike another match, and puff a short, furious blast of smoke into the still, night air. 'Well,' she said. 'That seems to be that, then, doesn't it?'

'At least I understand,' continued Cameron, 'why no one has ever been allowed to come back here.'

'Not so much not allowed,' interjected Dora. 'And I don't think . . .'

'Ah, but Maud, as I suppose I should call her—'

'Call her what you've always called her,' said Chris sharply. 'Nothing has changed.'

'Well, Mum, then.' Cameron swallowed, and repeated the word, as if it were new to him. 'Mum made it clear that anyone going down to the Boathouse would be treading on her precious memories and that she couldn't cope with that. You know how we always thought of her as so fragile. You couldn't get beyond her looking all frail and fluttery every time anyone mentioned the Boathouse. I know, I tried.'

'Did you try, Tom?' Lily asked.

He shook his head. 'No. I remembered it as such a magical place. I didn't want to . . . well, to think about it too much.'

'So we're saying it was suicide?' Vicky leant forward, jangling her bracelets.

'Yes—' said Dora quickly.

'We're not saying anything.' Tom interrupted her. 'No one has said anything. And no one will. Ever.'

'Well.' Vicky sounded sulky. 'That's not such a big

deal these days, is it? I mean, it's not as if there was any insurance fraud to worry about or anything, was there? And he'd just been diagnosed with the most horrible illness. It all seems quite sensible to me. I don't know why you've all made such a fuss about it when we could have been bringing the children down for their holidays all along.'

'Vicks.' There was a gentle warning in Cameron's voice, a note that Lily had never heard before.

Leaning forward for a sip of coffee, Lily intercepted a look between Dora and Chris. He was, she thought, surprised – astounded, even – by what he read in Dora's face. Or perhaps she was imagining it.

She felt excluded. They know, both of them, she thought, and they still think it's better not to tell us. Even though we've guessed. Tom was staring into his glass, avoiding everybody's eyes. Perhaps they were protecting him. He hated any talk about death or difficulties.

Vicky must have realized that she'd gone too far, because she threw the cigarette down on the jetty. 'These things are vile.' She ground the burning tip with her shoe.

'It's all right, Vicky.' Cameron stroked her hair back from her face, as if she were a difficult child. 'We'll find a boathouse of our own. Somewhere different and special.'

Vicky seemed doubtful. 'I looked in estate agents' windows today, and there was absolutely nothing—'

'It doesn't matter, Vicks. We're going to sell.' Cameron leant back. 'To a man who knows nothing about any of us, and will change everything completely anyway. And then we will all be able to forget about it, and remember the good side of Dad.'

Chris stood up and stretched, dropping his hand casually on Cameron's shoulder. Cameron's own hand went up to meet it. Chris sighed, and tightened his grip.

Their silhouettes were motionless in the darkness for a few seconds. Lily heard the soft plop of a fish breaking the water and the distant hoot of an owl.

Chris released Cameron's shoulder and walked to the edge of the jetty. He looked out over the water. It was still and quiet in the heat, shimmering in the moonlight.

The click-clack of Sarah's heels echoed on the stone steps as she descended from the woods down to the beach. The plush, peachy notes of Mitsouko drifted in the heavy air as she came closer, mingling with the scent of sea and wild garlic.

She had changed for the journey, and was luminescent in white – a floaty shirt and principal-boy trousers – as if everything that was wrong in the world could be bleached and ironed away. In the light of the moon, she looked as pure as a bride, untouched by the darkness that surrounded the Boathouse.

'Chris.' The delicacy of her outline made Lily feel lumpen. 'We ought to be off. I've packed the car.'

'I'm over the limit,' replied Chris, walking back to the table and pouring himself another glass of wine.

'I'm not.' She spoke calmly, like a mother soothing a child. 'It's a four-hour drive to Heathrow and check-in's at seven. We can catch a nap in the First Class lounge.'

'OK.' He finished the wine in one gulp. 'See you all. Cam, good luck with the Private View. I'll catch the exhibition as soon as I get back.' He paused. 'And thanks. Tom, we'll talk.'

Tom nodded, staring into his glass.

'And Vicky. Look after yourself. And Cam.'

'I always do,' said Vicky defensively, wrapping him in one of her operatic hugs. 'Have a wonderful, wonderful . . .' She stopped. '. . . holiday, darlings. Both of you. Come back lovely and brown and relaxed.'

Dora got up to embrace him briefly, and then Sarah. 'Bon voyage, my dears.' She paused, with her hand on Chris's arm. 'And Chris?'

He looked down at her, as wary as a cat, thought Lily.

'I know you're doing the right thing. You always have.'

'Goodbye, Dora.' He kissed her forehead. 'See you in London.'

'Lily.' Chris stopped, as if he wanted to say something but had changed his mind. 'Thank you. For everything.'

'Yes,' said Sarah, in a small, polite voice. 'Thank you so much for a wonderful time.'

Lily stayed seated. She couldn't bear to feel his cheek against hers in a brotherly kiss. 'Goodbye. I hope you have a good flight.'

Sarah tugged his hand with the tiniest of movements and they set off up the steps. Nobody spoke until they reached the top, when they turned round for a last view of the bay and waved to the jetty.

They all waved back.

'I don't know,' grumbled Vicky. 'It's almost as if she's about to throw a bouquet over her shoulder.'

Cameron drew her to him. 'And who's going to catch it? Dora?'

'You never know,' cackled Dora. 'I'm not dead yet.'

'I don't think Chris will come back,' said Tom. 'Sarah will make sure of that.'

'She's certainly not saying anything like: "Don't look upon it as losing a brother, think of it as gaining a sister."' Cameron laughed.

'They are going to get married, aren't they?' queried Vicky. 'I mean, we're not imagining it, are we?'

'No,' sighed Tom. 'We're not. Chris and I talked about it last night.'

'And?' asked Lily, almost unable to bear the pain.

Tom shrugged. 'I don't know why he's doing it, to be frank.'

'That's because you don't like her,' said Dora. 'Be fair.'

'I don't dislike her. I don't particularly care for her,

but she's no worse than some of the birds Chris has had. But she is tougher, and she is going to take him away from us.'

'Perhaps she has to,' said Lily, standing up.

Tom put his arm round her and Lily, in spite of herself, leant into it. She was so lonely. And she didn't have to be. The thought warmed her.

'You're tired,' he said. 'Bed.'

It was as it had always been.

Lily and Tom. Cameron and Vicky. And now, too, speeding on their way to the airport, Sarah and Chris.

She nodded. A sense of peace stole over her.

She and Tom walked, hand in hand, upstairs to their room, feeling Cameron, Dora and Vicky gazing into their backs.

She should undress, she supposed, in front of him. Not turn away and be discreet. Would that be it? Would they get back together again? Could it be as easy and simple as that?

It all seemed so irrelevant when she was only a tiny speck between the vast vaulted sky and the rushing waves. When she looked up at night, there was nothing between her and the stars, and she was aware that she was more insignificant than even the tiniest of those stellar pinpricks. What did it matter what a pinprick did?

She thought about Bertie and Maud 'losing each other for a while'. She had loved Tom when she married him. Perhaps, in another age, in another society, with a different set of expectations weighting them down, they would have regained the love they'd had. Did all marriages have a hole in their middle, a tough time? Perhaps it was cowardice to leave at that point.

She pulled her T-shirt off, and saw her body in the old silvered mirror, outlined against the distant sea. The weight of the heat against her skin eased by a fraction.

'It's so hot,' she said, refusing to meet his eyes. She didn't want to read a judgement in them, a confirmation of slackening skin or dimpling flesh.

'Yes,' he agreed, unbuttoning his shirt.

She unhooked her bra and felt the weight of her breasts drop against her chest. Her linen trousers dropped past her haunches and she walked over to the chair to fold them. It would be worse, she thought, to be modest. It would be more coquettish.

But it was still hard to slip off her pants and walk casually back to the bed.

Tom had got into bed while her back was turned and was sitting back against the pillows watching her. She forced herself to walk slowly and easily, stepping towards the bed, then pulling the sheet over her body as if it were the natural thing to do.

'Did Cameron change his mind because he believes your father committed suicide and he thinks it's been hanging over the family for too long?'

'Something like that, I expect.' Tom picked up his book and began to read.

'It still doesn't quite make sense to me. You wanted to keep this place so much.'

'Look, I'd really rather not go over it again. I don't think it helps anything.'

She scrabbled around for a magazine, and opened it up. 'OK.' This wasn't turning into the romantic reunion she'd dreaded. Just settling back into the old routine.

'It's too hot,' she said, again, unable to concentrate. 'Far too hot. Unbearable, really.'

His eyes met hers in a kind of tenderness. 'Much too hot.' He took her hand. 'Suffocating. Like a Chinese laundry.'

'Yes,' she agreed, relieved that he'd understood. And that he felt the same. 'Stifling. It would be impossible to . . .'

His hand squeezed hers. 'Shall I turn out the light?'

She nodded. 'It's so late.'

'Very late.' He kissed her fingers before turning away. 'We'll talk in the morning.'

36

Lily opened her eyes and saw the time on her watch – six-thirty – but the heat was still heavy on the air. She slid out of bed, careful not to wake Tom. It was too early. He would be tired.

This was the first day of the rest of her life. A new start. She let the clichés run through her head, as meaningless as blank pieces of paper, and walked down the sand, stopping by the nearest rocks to take off her cotton robe and fold it neatly. She carried on walking, her perspiring naked body seeking the relief of a breeze, and into the silken waters of the sea.

I could go on for ever, she thought. Just keep swimming. Perhaps that's what Bertie had done. Perhaps he hadn't slipped and fallen, but had set out to swim. It would have been easier, physically, without the climb up the hillside. If it had been suicide, after all.

After twenty minutes, she began to tire. That is what Bertie would have done, she thought. After a while, you want to turn round. Your body drives you back. It would have been hard, in the cold and the choppy waves, to keep on going until you drowned. But Bertie was a sick man and had a reason to want to die.

Yet, everything she had ever heard about Bertie

indicated a man who loved life, who would want to drink it down to the very last dregs, however bitter they were. And, in a sudden insight, as clearly as if he had been swimming beside her, his panama hat still on his head to protect himself from the sun, she understood that he was a man without a faith, and who feared death above all. Bertie, she thought, would have turned round.

She sensed the man in the panama hat pause in his swimming and float to look back at the house, and she stopped with him. The Boathouse, a long way away, was small and white, secure and cosy. Go back, Lily. Go back. You haven't finished. You have a job to do. You're needed. The feeling was as strong as a powerful undertow in a dangerous tide, pulling her back to shore instead of sweeping her out.

She turned, and, after another twenty minutes' swimming, walked out of the waves, pulled the cotton robe over her wet body and padded back up the beach. The water had cooled her. She could think straight now. The black, fathomless despair caused by heat and tiredness had been washed away.

She stopped at the jetty and looked back at the beach. Chris had said there was no sense of Bertie here, but he was·wrong. He was an unquiet ghost, seeking redemption.

Thank you, Bertie, she said, wanting a ritual to reach him. To light a candle, or lay some flowers.

But Bertie was gone.

*

Tom emerged, unshaven and smelly, at nine o'clock when she'd cleared up the debris of the night before. He stretched. 'God, I slept well. How about you?'

'Fine. Breakfast?'

'Mm. Brill. Vicky and Cam still in bed?'

'Cam came out to get two cups of tea. They're going as soon as Vicky gets up. With Harley for a few days.'

She waited for him to ask if that was all right with her. It had not, after all, been what they'd originally agreed, and it meant she wouldn't be able to get away. Although, provided Vicky was out of the way, she wasn't sure she cared any more.

Tom stretched and looked at her. 'So we're on our own here for the day?'

'Yes.' She wished she felt less tired and beaten down.

He reached out and took her hand, and, in a moment of tenderness, she drew him to her. He was strong and comforting.

And hot. She drew away, but the contact had soothed them both, she knew.

'There isn't even a breeze.' Lily twisted her hair on to her head in an attempt to cool down. She was drained again.

She cooked Tom bacon and eggs, always a sign of affection between them. Vicky emerged.

'Tom, you're making Lily work so hard. I hope you're going to do lunch. Men,' she said to Lily. 'They

447

don't think, do they?' She departed with Cameron and Harley, leaving breadcrumbs and dirty coffee cups in their bedroom, just before the tide cut them off, and Lily heaved a sigh of relief.

'Will you sail with us, Daddy?' Billy caught Tom as soon as he ventured out on to the jetty, in his boxers.

'No wind.' Tom belched and scanned the horizon. 'And not likely to be much. But we can . . . build sandcastles?'

Billy, who always rejected this as babyish when Lily suggested it, acquiesced.

'Give me five minutes to have some breakfast,' said Tom. 'And I want to talk to your mother.'

A car came bumping along the sand, from round the headland.

'Natasha!' Lily shaded her eyes with her hands. 'Have you left something behind?'

'Probably,' laughed Natasha. 'But Diana and I think you've been working too hard. I have come to invite you all to a barbecue at lunchtime.'

Lily was touched. 'Are you sure you can manage us all? Tom?'

He hesitated. 'I have to leave at about five to get back to town in time this evening.'

'You could always leave straight from Diana's,' suggested Lily.

He thought for a second, then nodded. 'Fine.'

'Coffee, Tash?' Lily indicated the cups.

Natasha looked regretfully at the pot and the

wicker chairs. 'I think the car will float away if I stay even five minutes.'

Tom played with Billy and Daisy. Occasionally shouts of rage drifted up from the beach, but Tom seemed to be making a real effort not to be bad-tempered, and the children would put up with anything just to have him back.

Lily lay in the shade of the Boathouse, praying for rain, or a drop in temperature. The skies were uniformly blue and clear.

By the time they arrived at Diana's, they were moulded back into the shape of a normal family again. The anxiety in Billy's face had cleared, and Daisy pottered amongst the chickens and wild flowers without needing to return to Lily every few minutes. Lily sighed.

'I'll be off then,' said Tom, looking at his watch once lunch had stretched lazily on into the afternoon. It read half-past five.

'Yes,' she agreed.

They all followed him to the car.

'Shall I come back next weekend?'

'It's a long journey,' said Lily. 'For just two days here.'

'I can manage.' He picked Daisy up and kissed her, and ruffled Billy's hair after a brief hug.

'Come back next weekend,' said Billy.

'Yes.' Lily looked at the happiness on her children's faces and her own heart lifted. 'Come back next weekend.'

She was rewarded by a smile that touched the corners of his eyes.

'Are you all right?' asked Dora, as Tom's car pulled away from the battered farm gate.

Lily pulled the band out of her hair, then twisted it up again, to feel air on the back of her neck. 'Fine. Just hot. And tired. I wish I could crawl into a deep freeze and sleep for a week.'

Dora laughed.

But once Tom had gone, the week fractured into sharp, dissonant pieces.

Harley returned on Tuesday, subdued but amenable. 'We've talked,' said Cameron.

'Good.' Dora put her arm round the boy, and miraculously, he stayed, leaning into her. Vicky put on her sunglasses, perhaps, thought Lily, to hide her easy tears.

But without Roger, Billy lost his confidence in sailing. He refused to go anywhere near a new sailing school.

'You're always getting at me,' he shouted when Lily suggested it. 'Go away! Just leave me alone!' And he'd run off into the woods. Lily had to hope that he would be safe, because she didn't have the strength to drag him back.

'He does need a man around,' murmured Dora.

Fury boiled up inside Lily. 'I'm perfectly capable.'

'I'm sorry, my dear,' said Dora. 'That wasn't a criticism of you.'

'You're right, though,' said Lily, gripped with worry for him and feeling the day drain the energy from her.

'You're very brave.' Dora cleared away the breakfast from the table on the jetty, and a few gulls swooped hopefully in looping circles above them. 'If I had to live my life again, courage is the quality I'd have asked for more of. So many things would have turned out fine in the end, if only I'd been brave enough to do them.'

'You mean Cameron . . . ?'

'Oh, I think Cameron has had a better life as Maud and Bertie's son than he would have done as one of the first illegitimate children around, but yes, only a few years later, everyone was having babies without being married. And there was a man once, whom I could have loved, if I had dared risk it.'

Lily watched a pair of cormorants working the water together, never far away from each other, each intent on their own catch. Even at the height of the day, the water was busy, always on the lookout for an opportunity, always organized, always meticulous yet wild.

Brave. Would it be braver to wrench the children away from their home in London and set up on her own, or was it moral courage she needed, some of Maud's steely self-sacrifice and generosity, to go back to Tom and create a family structure for them, living the life of a happy wife?

37

For three days, Dora turned a piece of paper over and over in her pocket, like a lucky talisman. Diana had written it out for her, in her swooping, curlicued hand.

She'd asked Diana if she knew where Roger kept the holiday cottage records.

'Oh, that's my department,' Diana had said. She had returned a few hours later with a scribbled note. Simon and Jill Fairfax. Their address and telephone number.

'It may not be up-to-date. I think they stayed at a b & b this year,' said Diana. 'At least, they didn't come here, and I thought I saw him in town around Eastertime.'

Should she ring, or should she write?

What would she say? 'Hello, it's Dora Savage here.' There would be blank incomprehension at the other end of the phone, followed by a rather forced conversation and promises to meet up whenever they were in London or west again. They wouldn't quite know how to end the conversation.

So a letter would be better. But what could she write? Come and see me if you're in Chiswick sometime? Do you remember Maud and Bertie? They're both dead now, but their sons are . . .

Their sons are what? Splintered apart? Cameron, suddenly, had become his own man, no longer the troublesome younger brother, and Vicky's outburst had drawn a line between them and Lily. That meant that the cousins would spend less time together, and whether Tom got back together with Lily, or whether he found someone else, there would never be that easy, automatic closeness again.

And Sarah would be a polite, chilly, organized wife, as far as the family was concerned, and she would keep them at a distance, as she had done over the business of getting married. Sarah was clever enough – and nice enough – not to have made a fuss about last weekend, but it was clear that she had no time for sentimentality or secrets. She would want Chris to herself and would, carefully, methodically and discreetly, cut the family ties until they had no more power over him. Dora had seen it before.

And now they weren't even keeping the Boathouse on, she could see them all slowly slipping into courtesy visits at Christmas, and phone calls once or twice a year. If they'd kept it, they'd have had to run it together, and there'd still be some reason to function as a family.

Would that have been a good thing?

Dora reminded herself that she was composing a letter to Simon and Jilly, not organizing the Devereaux boys, but she kept coming up against the fact that Simon would have understood all the nuances of the family situation, even forty years later, while Jilly had had virtually no dealings with any of them.

Tell them your news, Dora.

That'd be great. I had a baby by Bertie Devereaux, and he was brought up as Maud's son, but now . . . Er, no. Not for a catching-up letter to a woman she hardly knew and a man she'd known all too well.

She decided to walk to the phone box in the village. It would take over half an hour, and she could rehearse what she was going to say then.

As she dialled, she reflected that they would probably be out. Or away. It was the middle of August, after all, and very few people would be at home. She replaced the receiver. She'd get in touch when everyone got back again.

You have to take risks some time, Dora. She remembered Simon saying that, when he'd proposed. At least, he hadn't exactly proposed, had he? He'd suggested they share a mortgage. He'd suggested that they take a financial, not an emotional risk together. But lurking in the back of her brain ever since was the knowledge that she had refused him out of cowardice.

She punched in the numbers again, and it rang.

'Hello?' His voice reminded her of fruitcake and shortbread: rich, old-fashioned and comfortable, but underneath it, she could still hear the traces of the arrogant young Simon.

'It's Dora. Dora Savage.'

There was a silence. She knew this would be

awkward. Oh, why hadn't she just written a card at Christmas?

'Dora Savage.' He rolled her name round his tongue. 'What a long time it is since I heard your voice.'

'I'm down at the Boathouse. The publican said you and Jilly remembered me.'

'Of course I remember you.' There was laughter in his voice. 'How are you?'

'Fine.' It was absurd to try to wrap up forty years in a few sentences. 'How are you? And Jilly?'

He cleared his throat. 'She . . . passed on, I suppose you say. No, I have to be more honest than that. She died. It happened six months ago, but it still seems extraordinary to say it. Jilly's dead.'

'I'm so sorry.' Dora wished that there wasn't a telephone between them. The grief in his voice reminded her of her sharp sense of loss for Maud, and the more rounded, solid sadness that had settled slowly in her heart since Bertie died. 'That must be very hard for you.' There were no words to ease loss, she'd discovered that, and the triviality of trying always made her feel foolish.

'Yes. We were happy together. I didn't think we would be, but we were.'

Dora wasn't sure what to make of that. 'Do you have children?'

'Three. Richard's something in the City, very successful, but divorcing for the second time. Emma's a teacher and has been having an affair with a married man for years, shows no sign of settling down, and Jon is, well, Jon. I don't know what he's going to do with himself.' He chuckled, self-deprecating and affectionate.

'So cool, then?' said Dora. 'No bourgeois values.'

He laughed. 'Dora. Don't tease. But still, we were going to leave a better world, weren't we? Did we get it wrong?'

Dora thought of her pallid, rigid upbringing. 'No, I don't think we did. It's just harder for them now. They have so much, and they don't really believe in anything. Except a few little moral gew-gaws like fidelity.'

Simon roared with laughter. 'You didn't think fidelity was a little moral gew-gaw when we were together. I was terrified of looking at another woman.'

'Nonsense.' Dora was robust with him. 'You ogled constantly. Bedded, too, by the look of it. And I wouldn't have dared object.'

'Oh, you didn't say anything, I'll give you that.' He laughed again. 'But I knew absolutely. There wouldn't be any second chances.'

Dora sighed. 'Do we ever get second chances?'

'Oh, come on. Where's the old, positive Dora I used to know?'

'She's just old now.' But Dora couldn't help matching his lightness of tone.

'I went past your parents' house in Stockwell the other day,' he said. 'You wouldn't believe it. The front garden is a parking space for a four-by-four and a

Jag. The door was open, and I could see limestone floors. A chandelier. And I caught glimpses of just about the most modern kitchen you could imagine in that pokey old basement. It looks like something out of *House & Garden* magazine.'

Dora laughed, trying to imagine her parents' brown paint and shabby furniture replaced by stone, steel and glass. 'Well, I'd heard the area was back up again.'

'So what about you?'

'It's a long story—'

'Look,' he broke in. 'I'd like to see you. Do you remember the Markham Arms? On the King's Road?'

'Of course.' She and Simon had often met there.

'What about having a drink there when you get back to London?'

Dora had forgotten how impulsive Simon was. 'Well . . .' He would see her, and they would both be old and unattractive, and there would be terrible silences, and all her memories would be . . .

She took a deep breath. Second chances. 'I'd love to. I'll be back in September.'

'That's settled then. What about the second Tuesday of September?'

'The second Tuesday it is. At seven o'clock.'

'I'll see you there. And, Dora? Thanks for getting in touch.'

'Not at all,' she said demurely, before putting the phone down with a smile. He was obviously still the same old Simon.

And was she the same old Dora? She walked back

to the Boathouse, planning what she was going to wear, then stopping in front of the bathroom mirror. It occurred to her that if you were never beautiful to start with, then beauty was not a currency that could easily be debased. She was still, she thought, Dora: tall, thin, horse-faced and eccentric-looking. He'd liked that once. And the old connection was still there: the forty years had fallen away between them after the first few awkward sentences. On the other hand, she might be a fool for thinking anyone would be interested in a woman of seventy-plus.

'But at least you'll have the guts to try this time,' she told her reflection. 'And at the end, you'll know that you've lived.'

38

A flight of geese flew, in formation, overhead, purposeful and determined. Lily wondered if they were going home. Everybody goes back at the end of summer.

The weather had eased to a pallid warmth, but the hillside was still parched and straggly from the fierce temperatures of the preceding weeks. Lily felt the trees closing in on her, pressing against her on either side and choking the freshness out of the air.

She set out to walk along the beach, past the old Edwardian gardens, scrambling up to where the farmland almost touched the cliffs. There was a walkers' path, skirting fields and over stiles, twisting up and down steep, green hills, following the headland for a few hundred yards and then withdrawing back into the woods and fields. The land had been tended in farms and gardens for hundreds of years. Herbs and flowers had escaped from the carefully nurtured plots, sprouting in profusion, almost obscuring the path.

Lily sat down on the side of the hill to watch the summer morning intensify as it reached midday. In the hedges the first gold and yellow signs of autumn were emerging from the green. She remembered Maud's perfume, blowing in on the sea wind on the day of her funeral, but there was no breeze today. Just the heavy stillness of late August and the heat pressing down on the back of her neck. If only you were here, Maud, she thought. What would you do in my place?

It was probably only the new-mown hay from a distant field mingling with the petrol fumes of an unseen, faraway car and the wild mint that fringed the path, but Lily had, once again, the sense of Jicky on the air, a movement so slight and subtle that you could hardly call it a scent.

Maud, of course, would want to do what was right.

Lily made up her mind and got up, brushing the grass off her jeans.

She drove out of Salt Creek, inland towards the Henrys' farm, bumping down a series of narrow, rough-hewn tracks until she seemed to have reached the middle of the earth. It was green and cool. The dogs flopped under the shade of the spreading elder tree in the courtyard, and could hardly be bothered to raise their heads when she arrived, although Boozer let out a snuffling bark before putting his head back on his paws.

Lily opened the door of the barn to see if Diana or Natasha were working there. It was empty, however, echoing with silence and smelling of new wood. Several boxes stood unopened in the middle of it, and canvasses were turned to the wall. Lily turned and rang the farmhouse bell.

'Oh, hello.' Diana looked more relaxed than Lily had ever seen her, with a pair of reading glasses perched on the edge of her nose. Cool air blew across the hall flagstones towards Lily, beckoning her into the welcoming chill of the old, deep farmhouse. 'How lovely to see you. We're just brewing a pot of nettle tea. It's very invigorating. Would you like some?'

'Have you got PG Tips?'

'Lily!' Natasha looked up from a pile of books she was sorting on the kitchen table. 'How are you?'

'Fine. Fine.'

'Just pricing the latest lot of books for the shop. We're always so behind.'

'That's what I've come about,' said Lily. 'I think I know how you could do it all more efficiently, and have more time for the side of it that really matters to you. And I'd like to expand the part you don't have time for: the local crafts in the gallery. I could run courses . . . There are lots of possibilities.'

Diana took her glasses off. 'Tell me more.'

Before she told anyone else, though, she had to talk to Tom.

'Hello.' His voice was warm and friendly.

Until she told him she wasn't coming back.

'But we talked,' he said. 'We agreed.'

'No.' She felt sad. 'We never talked. I think we ran out of things to say to each other a long time ago.'

He was silent.

'But we'll have to co-operate on getting help for

Billy, though. And we'll have to divide the children's time between us. They need you.'

His voice softened. 'You know I would always put the children first.'

'I know.' She swallowed tears. 'You're a good man, Tom. But it was dead between us. We tried to revive it. We both tried very hard.'

'You see, I don't like change,' he said.

And she pressed the button to disconnect the phone, and drove back to Salt Creek cold and scared deep down inside.

When she parked the car under the trees, she knew she couldn't face Dora and the children quite yet. She would climb up to the Moonlight Bench and gather her courage for the task ahead.

Stones and sand slithered under her feet as she scrambled up, loosened by weeks of drought and the death of the grasses that had held them in place. She had to concentrate on where she placed each footstep, irritatingly and unsuitably shod in bright yellow plastic flip-flops with a huge daisy on each toe. She was so engrossed in keeping her foothold that she failed to see that there was already some-one sitting on the bench.

She stopped. Occasionally a determined walker found his way in, but he usually left when she explained that it was private property. But she found it frightening.

'Hello,' she said, when her heart had stopped its drum-roll of alarm.

'Hello,' replied Chris. 'I was going to knock on the door, but I wanted to come up here first.'

She nodded. 'You're not in St Bart's.'

'No.' He looked out over the bay, as if searching for something on the glittering horizon. 'It wasn't the right thing to do. I'm only sorry that I realized it so late.'

Lily looked down. Compared with the creamy cups of sea campion growing around the bench, the absurd plastic flower on each foot marked her out as false and temporary. A breeze flickered across her skin, carrying the evanescent scent of Chris – soap and wood and lavender – like the lightest of kisses. And then it was gone, leaving only the bitter saltiness of the sea on her breath.

'I'm going away,' he said. 'With Natasha and Gem, at first, to see that they start off safely. It's a bit late for me to be a father, but perhaps I can be a friend to her. And I want to make sure this relationship with Gem is going to withstand travelling round the world. I don't want Tash to be left in some dive on her own.'

'Good. She'll love that.' Lily thought of the wistfulness that often crossed Natasha's face when she saw Daisy on Tom's knee.

'So I came to say goodbye. And to explain properly this time.'

'It sounds serious.'

'Yes,' he said. 'It's about as bad as it could possibly be.'

The words echoed in the silence between them. She turned her face to his. 'I don't believe that. I think you should tell me. Then you'll realize that whatever it was may be sad, and perhaps tragic, but not bad. Not in the real sense of the word.'

He studied her. 'Very well.'

He didn't wholly trust her, she thought. But nearly.

'I killed my father,' he said.

'After that summer with Diana, I did my O levels, and left home as soon as possible afterwards, managing to avoid family holidays down here. I used to meet Tom in a pub, or in the park – anything to avoid going back and facing my father. I made excuses. Travelled. Got jobs in bars. Learnt a lot more than I would have done staying at home. I spent three months in Ireland, once, working on a building site, and promised myself that the next development I worked on would be my own. And it was. I started with a run-down terraced house in Fulham, did it up with my own bare hands and sold it at a profit to buy a new one. Mind you, that's not as clever as it sounds, those houses then really were going for nothing.

'Mum called me every week, and occasionally I went home to please her. The little raffish lane off the King's Road was beginning to "come up", as the wealthy bought all the artists' and writers' homes and painted them a respectable gleaming white. Ours was still in a bit of terrace painted like Neapolitan ice-cream. I always counted them as I walked past: pistachio, mint, cream, then, fourth along, ours with its blue Georgian front door.

'My father was always surrounded by friends like a circus ringmaster. I was angry with him then, but now I see that he always had a different, sharper, alternative view on everything and a focused wit. If he'd lived longer, I think that would have meant more to me.

'Every year he'd ask me back to the Boathouse, and every year I'd decline, and he'd look at me as if to say, "Your loss, mate."

'And I knew, in a way, that it was. After that summer, I told him about my successes, but never confided my failures. He knew nothing about failure. He would have despised it.

'It must have been early nineteen seventy-four when my mother phoned me. "We thought it would be nice to have a family reunion this weekend. Just us and Dora."

'Oh, hello, I thought. Dora and Mum have been talking and want a grand reconciliation. I'm ashamed to say that I decided that they could want all they liked.

'It was raining when I let myself into the little house, and saw my father sitting in an armchair. He was usually in his study.

'"Chris." His voice was hoarse and low.

'I stood over him. "Have you got a cold?"

'I thought, for a moment, that he might be drunk,

but then I realized he was just irritated. He hated any sign of weakness. "Nonsense. Just a frog in my throat."

'"Oh. That's a shame." Everything I said to him came out sounding like sarcasm.

'"Darling!" Mum came upstairs from the basement kitchen. "How lovely." She hugged me, and her bones felt frail under her clothes. It was the first time I realized that my parents would get old. "No electricity today, so it's dinner by candlelight. Such fun!" It was the Three-Day Week, when you were allocated days for electricity, and Mum was determined to treat it like a party game. Mainly, however, it was just very cold and dark.

'Behind her, in the shadows, stood Dora, looking shapeless and grey. Throughout my childhood, she and my mother had both been unchangingly glamorous, but they had both aged by decades rather than the months it had been since I'd last seen them. Dora's brightness had faded, and Mum's distinct, curvaceous slimness was blurred with layers of dull clothes.

'"Isn't it marvellous," cried my mother, as I kissed Dora. "Dora's come to live with us."

'I looked at her to find out what was going on. Dora turned away. "Your father's given up his column, so he's very kindly offered me his study as a bedroom. He's writing a book, of course, but he'll do that in the sitting room."

'I knew, then, that something had happened. Fa's been sacked by the paper, I thought. They don't want the voice of the sixties in the seventies. Old hat. New editors. I wasn't, to be honest, very sympathetic. Everyone has their day.

'Cameron burst through the door, still young enough to hug me. I felt the sturdiness of his body in my arms. Six is such a vibrant, hopeful, careless age.

'"I'm in a match this afternoon. My first ever. Please, please come and watch." Whatever was going on had clearly been kept from him. So no change there, then.

'"We'll all watch," said my father. "You know I wouldn't miss it."

'He'd never come to see our matches. When he sent Tom and me to boarding school, he never visited us all term. But he listened to Cameron hungrily as he chattered on, and placed an arm on his shoulders as if just touching him could lighten the darkness of the room. Tom and I had always been irritating distractions to the real business of Dad's life, but now, it seemed, Cameron was his life.

'Tom came downstairs, with Judith, his girlfriend that year. They spent most of their time in bed, listening to Van Morrison and allegedly revising for their A levels. She was an intelligent nonentity. He had broadened out, physically and emotionally, and was less of an elongated schoolboy. We touched each other on the arm, and went out to the pub, leaving Judith with Ma and Dora in the kitchen. It was always easy between me and Tom.

'"So what's up?" I sipped a beer.

'He shook his head. "Nothing, as far as I know."

'"Come off it, Tom. Nobody's talking round here. And where's the party? I've never known home without one."

'He told me I was imagining things. "It's the political situation," he said. "Everybody's depressed. It's so dark all the time."

'That evening, Dad still dominated the dinner table, but he hardly spoke, and he took a long time to eat his food, leaving most of it. Maud was pale, and Dora nervous, jumping up and down to empty pans, wash up and clear away like she always did, but frenzied. Judith tried to start an earnest discussion about whether the IRA hunger striker was achieving anything with his sacrifice and never noticed that no one else was interested.

'Dad tapped a glass with his knife. He loved toasts. He could go on for hours, raising his glass to the cook, to absent friends, and making witticisms based on the news of the day. I filled my glass in expectation.

'"I have to tell you all something," he said. "I have motor neurone disease."

'We didn't know what it was. My mother's eyes filled with tears, and Dora took the plates into the kitchen, again, to conceal what she felt.

'"Modern medicine is marvellous these days," said Judith. "The doctors can work miracles. I'm sure you'll find it much easier to cope with than you think."

'I saw a flash of the old Dad. "Modern medicine can do nothing for this disease," he said, sharply. "I shall be in a wheelchair, and then in a bed. Eventually . . ." My mother put a hand on his arm to stop him and they looked at each other as if there was no one else in the world. I used to wonder if I'd ever look at anyone like that.

'"Will you come and see my matches in a wheel-chair?" asked Cameron.

'"Of course,' he said. "Of course. Whenever I can."

'"No!" shouted Cameron. "I don't want you to."

'We all looked at him.

'Cameron coloured under his smooth, golden skin. "It would be embarrassing," he said, as if it was obvious. And he went on eating.

'Not even Judith could think of a trite remark to cover that up.'

'Cameron was only six,' said Lily. 'If we were all blamed for things we said and did when we were six we'd never move for shame.'

'I don't blame him,' said Chris. 'Truly. But sometimes I still saw the same careless, selfish Cameron. Until now. Until he worked out why we had to sell the Boathouse.'

'Fa said he wanted to talk to me after lunch. The others went out for a walk. For a moment, I thought this terrible disease might bring us together. That he finally needed me, and wanted to apologize.

'"Sit down." He seemed annoyed, more than anything, to have to deal with me in this way, and for this reason.

'"I'm sorry to hear about . . ."

'He waved my sympathy away, like an irritating mosquito.

'"What I'm about to say is for your ears only. Understood?"

'He was giving orders, like a general to a private. "Yes, but . . ."

'"It isn't easy for me to talk . . ." He spoke slowly and softly, slurring his words as if he was mildly intoxicated. ". . . so please don't interrupt or ask unnecessary questions."

'Fate really knows how to get you, I thought. He wouldn't have minded losing a leg. Both legs, even. He'd have managed somehow, if something had happened to his arms or hands, by dictating to Mum or Dora. Even losing his sight couldn't have been as devastating as not being able to speak properly. Communication was as important to him as breathing, and without it he would suffocate. The witty, urbane Bertie Devereaux had never been lost for words.

'"Do you know?" His voice sounded hollow and indistinct. "Ten minutes after I was diagnosed a nurse came in to measure me. I asked her what she was doing, and she said, 'Oh, for your wheelchair, of course.' That's how I found out what sort of an illness it was.

'"It can begin anywhere," he continued, "but in cases like mine, it starts by wasting your tongue and throat. And then the weakness gets progressive, attacking your hands, and then your legs. Or not, I should say, necessarily in that order." He tried to laugh. "It's not an orderly disease." His hand trembled in a palsy on his lap. "Eventually you can't move. But you're completely conscious. There's no slowing down of the intellect at all. I will become, Chris, a brain caged in an utterly immobile body, possibly for years. And I will remain like that, unable even to ask for a glass of water or my choice of radio programme, until the paralysis affects my breathing, when I will gradually choke to death. That could take days, or even weeks. Perhaps months."

'"But the doctors, surely . . ."

'He flapped his hand weakly. "Spare me, please. It may make you feel better, but such platitudes do nothing for me. There's no comfortable injection to let you slip away." He closed his eyes, and we were silent.

'"I won't do it, Chris. I won't tolerate it."

'There was nothing I could say.

'"You must help me." It was another order. He had no intention of giving me a choice. "You must help me kill myself before it goes too far."'

'Do you know how difficult it is to kill yourself?' He took Lily's hand absent-mindedly. 'Especially once you become disabled enough to want to die? Dad was already too uncoordinated to get out of a high window unaided, or clamber over a bridge and throw himself into the Thames. And who's to say that someone wouldn't have rescued and revived him? He couldn't stockpile pills, because Mum bought everything and issued it to him. He had no hiding places. He couldn't go into a shop on his own. Overnight he'd been deprived of the right to drive a car, or the ability to get himself to Beachy Head and throw himself off. He already needed round-the-clock care, and that meant he was watched all the time by kindly people who loved him and wanted to keep him alive. Before he'd realized it, he'd lost the privacy he needed to commit suicide.

'I was afraid he was going to ask me to shoot him or buy rat poison from the chemists. I couldn't have done that.'

'"We'll go to the Boathouse," he said. "You and me. When the time comes."

'I rang my mother regularly after that, and went home, with a sense of dread, every Sunday. Dad withdrew, mentally and physically, as the illness progressed more swiftly than the doctors had predicted. He stopped his regular lunches at *Punch* magazine, cancelled his gambling cronies, failed to return calls and made excuses to avoid the oldest and closest of friends.

'Cameron seemed much quieter. He stopped looking Dad in the eye when his head flopped, and ignored the thin stream of dribble that Maud or Dora constantly wiped away. He often stayed away from the house "with friends", and my mother's face tightened and sharpened each week as she was tugged apart between the conflicting needs of an invalid and a young boy. Dora's slide into middle age was precipitate. She grew thin to the point of transparency, as grief turned Maud dumpy and colourless, but she and Mum clearly gained strength from each other.

'But Fa never mentioned suicide again. I thought he might be accepting his fate. I should have known better. That razor-sharp brain had nothing to do other than to plan his own death.

'One afternoon I drove him to watch Cameron playing football, parking the car at the side of the field, so that he could watch the match without having to get out. There were a few dozen other parents there, following the game by moving from one end of the pitch to the other after the ball and shouting in ragged cheers that drifted patchily with the wind. They gave us some strange looks, bringing the car so close, but my father sat there, mask-like and remote, appearing to watch the game without emotion. He had got to the stage when people thought he couldn't hear, or think, so they addressed their remarks to Dora or my mother. Or they avoided us altogether.

'I got out to stand and cheer Cam on. He was playing extremely well, and, in the last moments of the game, scored the clinching goal. The parents and other boys roared so loudly I didn't hear the hoarse cheer from inside the car, or the sound of the car door opening. Fa tried to get out, to applaud Cameron, but he couldn't make it. I turned to see the car door open, and there he was, lying face down in the dirt.

'All the parents went silent, and even the boys, who were shaking each other's hands for the end of the game, stopped and stared. A few people nudged each other, looking disgusted, obviously assuming he was drunk, but as I tried to pick him up, a woman broke away from a knot of spectators. She was a nurse, and she helped me get him back into his seat.

'"Cameron played well," mumbled my father. "Bloody well." Not even the nurse understood him. She kept saying, "Now, don't worry. We'll get you home soon." Her voice had determined cheeriness, pitched just a couple of degrees too loud. Even she was treating him as if he were half-witted. His eyes were fixed on Cameron, in pride and love, waiting for a wave, or a smile, or some kind of acknowledgement.

'When she returned to her group, they glanced at us with pity. He couldn't turn his head easily, but he saw those looks.

'Cameron pretended Dad wasn't there. At the end of the match he went off with a friend, while we waited outside the school to take him home. As I drove Dad home, I saw his eyes fill with tears. One slowly trickled down his cheek, but his throat and face had wasted so much that he couldn't even cry.

I didn't dare wipe them away. I knew he wanted me to pretend not to notice.

'That was the day he told me that it was time for us both to go back to the Boathouse.'

'Poor Cameron,' said Lily, wondering why she had chosen to speak his name first. 'Poor you. Poor Bertie. Each of you in your own private hells.'

'Yes,' replied Chris. 'It was like being trapped in a thick, glass bottle. I could see the world outside, but I couldn't feel it or make anyone hear.'

'It took six and a half hours to drive down here in those days, and he was a very sick man. But he wouldn't let us stop, except for petrol and for me to stretch my legs. I tried to talk to him, lumbering painfully through each of his favourite topics in turn.

'Did he think the chemical explosion at Flixborough had been sabotage? Would this year's Booker winner match *The Siege of Krishnapur*? Did he fancy Lester Piggott for the Derby on Arthurian? I offered my own pathetic opinions into the silence. "The bookies favour Giacometti," I'd say, like a small child expecting praise for doing his homework.

'A few months earlier he would have had passionate, contrary opinions about each of them, demolishing my arguments and shooting down my suggestions. Now all he offered was a twitch of irritation or a long, slow grunt of frustration. I realized that talking had turned automatically into bragging.

I could do it, without thinking, and he couldn't. I would have liked to apologize, but even that, in itself, would have been condescension from the able-bodied to a sick, proud man.

'You'd think that this would be the time that we really listened to each other. That we'd say all those things that needed to be said between us. The way they do on television programmes.

'But that's not the way life works. You are what you are to the very end. Reconciliation is a dream. An ideal. It doesn't work. Not with people like me and Fa. The gulf between us was as great as ever. He had an old Austin Seven, which had never been fitted with a radio, so we continued our jerky journey through the twisted, shabby streets of seemingly deserted towns and villages in silence.

'Most of all, though, I still didn't really believe that I was driving him down to the Boathouse to kill him. It seemed like a terrible dream.

'We had to wait for the tide, of course, to drive him over. We sat in the pub, by the window overlooking the water, and I had a double Scotch to keep my courage up. There weren't any breathalysers, and even if there had been, it's very unlikely that the Devon constabulary would have popped out from behind a rock asking me to: "Blow into this, sir." But it didn't make me feel any better. I thought the alcohol would dull my feelings but it only seemed to sharpen my awareness. I could, I should, call Fa's doctor. I should not be doing what I was doing now.

'But I knew how proud he was, and that he couldn't bear people's pity. What he was going through was already living hell for someone who hated weakness. Even Joe, who ran the pub in those days, watched him with compassion as I helped him across the room.

'"He oughta be in a wheelchair," he murmured as I ordered another Scotch for us both. "It's a shame, isn't it?"

'"Sometimes he's not as bad," I lied, thinking of the police and the questions afterwards.

'When we finally got into the Boathouse, I lit the fire and cooked scrambled eggs. He couldn't get the food into his mouth, and was furious when I helped him, wiping away the egg that dribbled down his chin with the spoon, like Dora did. The silence between us grew more profound.

'"So what now?" I asked him.

'He made a tiny, dismissive motion with his hand. "Wait," he croaked.

'I played Patience, and stoked up the fire. Poured myself and him another Scotch. At last it was beginning to take effect, numbing the horror of it all.

'"The jetty," he whispered. "Last time on the jetty."

'I set up the chair out there, and he waved me away. I tried to wrap a blanket round him. "You'll get cold."

'"Don't . . . be . . . a . . . fool," was his ghostly reply.

'I wondered if he was planning to die of cold. But he told me to come back in an hour.

477

'He spent the hour watching the tide come in and the sun go down. The air was so full of water that it felt like a damp towel against my skin. That was one of the limp, dank summers we had before the heatwaves of the following years. An hour later, I went out to check he was all right.

'"Now." I could hardly understand the words. "Up the steps. Take me."

'I had to half pull, half carry him up to the Moonlight Bench, and occasionally he slipped out of my grasp or a hand or leg trailed behind, catching on the edge of a stone. He'd let out a grunt of pain, and I'd stop, only to see the fury in his eyes.

'Eventually we got up to the bench and rail, the place where Tom as a toddler had slipped over. Fa made me drag him to the other side of the railings, to the very edge of the cliff. Forty feet below us, I could only see the foam the waves made as the water surged against the rocks, but even at this height, the occasional wave was violent enough to send spray into our faces. It looked like the cauldron of hell to me.

'"Good," he said. "Now go."

'I could hardly hear him. The wind and the sea were roaring in my ears by now. "Say I must have . . . gone . . . for a walk. And slipped."

'"I can't leave you. I can't do this."

'"Don't be so goddam . . . selfish."

'"It's not right. It's just not right."

'"You always were a fucking coward," he replied, almost clearly. And he closed his eyes, as if he were dead already.

'He was asking me to commit a crime that could send me to gaol for fifteen years. He was asking me to kill someone I loved. Because I did love him, I realized then, just as I realized that he had never loved me back. He couldn't have asked it of me if he had. And he had called me a coward.

'I was so angry that I turned around and went down the steps. I would show him.

'Of course, you can't show a dead man anything, but I didn't truly understand that until, halfway down, I heard a noise, like the scuffling of a fox, and looked back to see a shadow, like a great bird, toppling over the cliff. I looked over, to see, but I could make out nothing but the occasional flash of glossy rock and the swirling foam. I should have tried to rescue him.

'But, as Fa said, I'm a coward.'

'You aren't,' said Lily fiercely. 'Not many people could have been that brave.'

Chris laughed. 'Exactly. Not many people. He picked the right son, didn't he? Cameron, for all his faults, would have stayed up all night talking him out of it and holding his hand, and even weeping – if he'd been old enough. And Tom would never have broken the law. No, Dad knew me well.'

'Were the police suspicious?'

'Yes. Or, at least, they certainly covered the ground.'

'I spent the rest of the night looking out of the windows into the black seething water, and listening to the gale howling through the trees and round the headland. I drank the rest of the bottle, but never felt drunk. I should not have helped him. I should have tried to get him out of the water. Should. Should not. The pendulum swung back and forth.

'As soon as the wind died down and the first streaks of light spread across the horizon I went to the phone box and rang the police. I told them that I had woken up to find that he had gone missing in the night.

'There was a helicopter, and boats in the bay. I watched. How does an innocent person behave? Wringing their hands on the jetty? Hovering by the phone box? I just didn't know what I should do.

'A few hours later, they told me that they had found his body, severely battered by the rocks, and would I not go anywhere for a while.

'It was soon clear that he hadn't simply fallen off the jetty, but had fallen from quite a height. They peered at the ground up to the Moonlight Bench, but it was so sodden that our footsteps were muddy grooves in the mountain.

'Trying to pretend that I had no idea what could have happened was the hardest thing I've ever done, and occasionally I said something that made one of them look at me sharply, as if he could see into my soul.

"'I helped him out on to the jetty," I said, "and settled him there."

"'I see. So he needed help to get as far as the jetty."

"'Well, he could *manage* alone, obviously, but I was trying to make it easier for him."

"'But you didn't *help* him to get back."

"'I went out several times to ask him if he wanted to come in, but he told me he wanted to be on his own and that he'd come in when he was ready. The last time I went out there, he was gone, so I assumed he was in bed."

"'You assumed."

"'Yes."

"'You didn't think to check."

'I nearly lost my temper, which would have been dangerous. "I saw no need to."

"'But there was a need to, as it turned out."

"'Yes. I regret not checking."

"'You had a good night's sleep?" I knew I looked a thousand kinds of hell, so he knew perfectly well that I hadn't.

"'Not particularly, no."

"'But you didn't check again?"

"'I'm afraid not."

"'Was your father a wealthy man, Mr Devereaux?"

"'No, not at all. I don't think so, anyway." And it went on, and on. They found some snagged wool from his jacket or something that proved he'd been up by the bench and decided he'd fallen from there. I said it was his favourite spot and that I had been up there several times looking for him.'

'Did they find anything that could have come from your clothes?' asked Lily. 'Today, with DNA . . .'

'I don't know,' replied Chris. 'I don't like to ask whether they keep these cases open. Although, of course, my clothes are long gone.'

'They might have hairs, or anything.'

'Anything,' said Chris. 'Anything. It's what I live with. Joe at the pub, for example, actually told them that he thought Dad could have climbed up to the bench without too much trouble. When he'd seen quite clearly that he couldn't. I've often wondered if he was out on his boat on the bay that evening, and maybe took his own view of it.'

'Did they question Dora or Maud?'

'They seemed too shaken to make much sense. Dora said that he had good days and bad days.'

'"Although," the detective in charge of the case said, "most doctors consider this to be a degenerative disease, without remissions."

'I shrugged. "I don't think even doctors understand it very well."'

'Dora knows, in that case,' said Lily.

'She guessed.' Chris sighed. 'I saw that, that night on the jetty. I think she guessed a long time ago, and didn't want to talk to me about it because . . .'

'Because how could she?' Lily completed his thought. 'How could she ask those sorts of questions? What about your mother?'

'She was too numb with grief to respond to anything much. Tom told me all this on the phone.'

'"I don't understand where Dad could have gone. Or how. He couldn't even get up our little stairs hanging on to the banisters. I can't imagine how he got up the steps. Perhaps he fell off the jetty after all, and got battered against the rocks."

'"Perhaps," I said.

'I'd hoped it was instant, that he had crashed against the rocks and known nothing more, and that he wouldn't have had to struggle helplessly in the water. It's ironic, isn't it? Suffocating – drowning – was the death he'd feared. I can't help wondering how long it took, and whether he wanted his life back when he saw it going. However bleak it would have been.

'Then there was the funeral. Everybody came. Important people spoke importantly. The obituaries called him a man of the age. Friends, embarrassed to have seen so little of him in the past few months, said they would miss him. A few people at the funeral actually told me that it was a blessing "in the circumstances". I didn't reply.

'This was a man who had known everybody. Powerful, clever, influential friends who could cover up anything. He had a wife and a helper who both adored him and would do whatever he told them to. He knew people in the Home Office and the best doctors in the country. He could have turned to anyone. He turned to me because I was worth less to him than any of them. He would have done anything, even choke slowly to death, to avoid Mum facing a prison sentence, but if something went wrong and I was prosecuted, well, I was disposable.

'I've thought about it, and thought about it, and, in the end, I can only conclude that he chose me because he knew I was ruthless enough to do it. That's what he thought of me. And he was very perceptive about people, so he was probably right.

'But I still shouldn't have left him to die alone.'

Lily wanted to hold him tightly, and keep him safe, but she knew now why she, and all the other women, had lost him. He hated himself too much to love anyone else.

'That's not true.' She was daunted, but determined. 'You did it because you were trying to save him suffering. He asked you to. You risked everything for him.'

'Not quite everything,' Chris pointed out. 'In the end, I walked away. In anger. Not compassion or love. Plain, ugly, anger. Please, Lily, don't try to turn me into a martyr over this. I did what he asked me to do, yes. But a very small part of me thinks that I was also getting my revenge. And I think he knew that, too. That's what I really despise about myself.'

'And Cameron worked it all out when he talked to Billy on the Moonlight Bench?'

'Yes. I don't know why no one else ever did. Except Dora, of course.'

'I think they did. That's obviously why your mother prevented you all from coming here. And Tom, well, Tom hates facing up to anything unpleasant.' She remembered him saying to Vicky: 'We're not saying anything . . . And no one will. Ever.'

Vicky was the problem, Lily could see. Not just Vicky herself, but the Vickys of this world, who wouldn't, or couldn't, keep quiet. That was why the Boathouse had been closed for so long: because a careless word or a malicious observation could risk someone believing they ought to report something to the police. Or would they? Most people would probably recognize that helping a very sick man to die wasn't a crime. But could you rely on 'most people' for your freedom? How long was it before you were safe, in the eyes of the law? Never, Lily thought. Although, in the present climate, the police would probably be reluctant to pursue something that had happened so long ago, and which was so inconclusive. But you could never be sure. No wonder Chris found it so hard to trust anybody.

'I thought I couldn't face people knowing. But it makes it better somehow. That they don't judge me.'

'Nobody could possibly judge you, Chris.' She remembered her swim. 'Bertie could never have done

485

it alone, he was frightened to. And he knew you'd never do it if you had a grand reconciliation, so he had to go on being vile to you. But he chose you because he thought you were the strongest. And the best. He never thought about what sort of a legacy he was leaving you as a result. It's haunting him now.'

Chris laughed. 'He's dead, Lily.'

'But before he died, he wanted to say sorry. To say that he loved you.'

He rubbed her hand and looked out to sea. 'Don't be silly. How could you possibly know that?'

'I just do.' She had a thought. 'Tell me. Did he ever swim with his panama hat on?'

Chris smiled. 'Yes, he did. He used to do a rather stately breaststroke out to the rocks, round, and back again. It was his only concession to exercise. He hated sport. How did you know?'

'Well . . . I must have seen a photograph some-where.'

He looked surprised. 'Well, if you find it again, let us know. There are very few photos of him, and I thought they were all in Mum's album.'

'Well,' she persisted. 'He loved you. He just wasn't very good at showing it.'

He looked at her out of the corner of his eye, and cracked a small smile. 'I'll think about it.'

'And think about me,' she said, amazed at her own temerity.

'I'll always think about you. But there's still Tom.'

'And Billy and Daisy,' said Lily. 'I'm leaving Tom. Properly this time. But it's going to be very hard on them, and I need all the goodwill between me and Tom that I can get.'

He nodded.

'Chris.' She traced lines on the bench with her finger, the wood rough against her skin. 'With Sarah. When you left me. Did you . . . ?' She stopped. 'Actually, I'm not going to ask that. Because it doesn't matter. It really doesn't matter. Maud was right.'

'It was too hot,' said Chris. 'And you and Tom . . . ?'

'Much too hot.'

'Good.'

She let herself look at him, properly this time, and everything else seemed very unimportant, as if they were suspended in time together. 'And things change, don't they?' she said.

'Everything changes. In the end.' His voice was tender.

'Perhaps one day . . .' She let the words slip away from her. One day was a long way away.

He got up and looked down at her. She was glad he didn't say goodbye. Or reach out a hand. She couldn't have borne it.

He walked away, scrambling down the dusty hillside, and stopped halfway down, turning back to her. 'Lily,' he shouted, with the exhilaration of the wind and the waves. 'One day.'

*

She turned her head out to sea and began to scramble down towards the beach. She didn't want to see him go. Tomorrow would be different. There would be lists and phone calls, houses to rent and schools to find. Meetings with Diana to pick a coherent strategy out of her muddle of wild flowers and old legends, and conversations with bank managers and estate agents. She had about a week to move them all to somewhere near, somewhere around Totnes or Dartmouth, where there would be friends and fields and places to play. There would be no time for tears.

Just for the moment though, she wanted to watch the sun moving slowly across the horizon, and feel the slate-green water lick gently over the sand.

In the distance, at the edge of the beach, she could see an elderly couple walking arm in arm along the line of the tide, towards Salt Creek. Maud and Bertie, she thought, together again at last. The fancy was so strong that she had the sudden urge to follow them, and look at the faces under their hats, but they were too far away.

Maud and Bertie, she thought again. Or Chris and Lily. One day.

Acknowledgements

Thank you to:

I was lucky enough to have not one, but two, brilliant editors on this book: Harriet Evans at the start, then Clare Ledingham who took over in a seamless transition; as well as Richenda Todd who picked up the inconsistencies and corrected my dodgy arithmetic.

The Boathouse itself was inspired by the glorious Devon coastline, and by two places in particular: Anita and Matthew Robinson's cottage in Dittisham and Merida Drysdale's 'Hut' in Stoke Fleming, which I found through Helena Drysdale and Richard Pomeroy. Both cottages are shared family holiday homes which have seen several generations of children grow up, but, of course, the Devereauxs are quite a different family altogether and I would be surprised if even the most tenuous links and likenesses are to be found between them and any real people. If there are any, these are a complete coincidence: the characters and events in *Remember This* were fully planned before I found the Boathouse, down to the Dartmouth 'Spot' teacups which I created in my head before finding them, exactly as imagined, in the Drysdales' cupboards. Brett and

Peter Moore deserve a thank you in this context, too, for background, along with Mark and Anne Pollard, for local information and making long, dark journeys through the twisty Devon lanes. Sarah Stacey's arm also deserves a mention for its part in the story of writing this book, and Rosalind Miles and Robert Chave passed on research and offered insights into sibling rivalry.

Looking up the meaning of 'support' I found: prop up, sustain, shore up, buoy up, brace, reinforce, buttress; and under 'encouragement' I found: hearten, stimulate, cheer, reassure, console, urge, exhort, rally, comfort, promote, boost and strengthen; so I'd particularly like to thank Anthony Goff for all his support and encouragement.

My family, especially David and my mother, Margaret, do the same at home, particularly in a year which has seen us 'move out'; and, finally, I'd like to add a thank you to all our old friends in Stockwell for a heart-warming goodbye and all our new friends in Faversham for a very welcoming hello.